From
MURPHY
To MILEY

A Carolina Family's Journey of Faith

Courier Publishing
100 Manly Street
Greenville, South Carolina 29601
CourierPublishing.com

PUBLISHED IN THE UNITED STATES OF AMERICA

FROM
MURPHY
TO MILEY

A Carolina Family's Journey of Faith

JANE JUMPER FARMER

DEDICATION

With love and appreciation
for the memory of my Miley grandparents:

Carrie Tate Jumper 1890-1972
Vandy Saylor Jumper 1885-1960

PREFACE

This fictitious family saga was born in childhood talks with my paternal grandmother, Carrie Tate Jumper of Miley, South Carolina, who was an important spiritual mentor in my life. She spoke fondly of her growing-up years as the oldest child in a Methodist pastor's large family in North Carolina. Her many experiences in assisting her father with his pastoral duties instilled in her a strong desire to follow in his footsteps. The time in which she was born denied her that wish. As I review her life, I see that she was a pastor to many, in many ways — including to me.

♦　♦　♦　♦　♦

We laugh at an incident in our own lives after I was married to a Baptist pastor. Grandmother came to see us in our first Baptist pastorium. As we showed her about the house, she said, "I had always hoped one of my daughters would marry a preacher, so that I could live out my last years in a parsonage."

"Grandmother, we have plenty of room here," we said.

Her response was instantaneous. "Oh, but I meant a *Methodist* parsonage!"

♦　♦　♦　♦　♦

My ties to Miley are twofold. Through my father, Ralph Dennis Jumper Sr., I am the oldest granddaughter of Carrie and Saylor. Through my mother, Lois Rivers Jumper Shipes, I am a descendant of the Miley family for whom the town was named. The feisty, petite Miley postmistress, Viola Miley, and her sister, Izora Miley, were my great-great aunts.

Visiting my Jumper grandparents in Miley was a highlight of my growing-up years. Since early adulthood, I have nurtured a wish to write about the vibrant little town and the grandparents who so impressed my heart and my life.

Research for this project actually began years ago, following the passing of both Saylor and Carrie. At the time, I was blessed to be able to interview all ten Jumper children, including my father, Ralph, who was the source of much information regarding the St. Matthews years, in what turned out to be the last year of his life. Each of my aunts and uncles made a unique contribution to the story. Although most are now with Carrie and Saylor in a better place, I hope that they would recognize themselves and the stories they told.

♦　♦　♦　♦　♦

The old doctor's office in Miley is now its post office. A few houses remain here and there, but most evidence of the lumber mill town has been removed.

For readers who have long-ago ties to the area, may your memories be replenished and enlivened through this story. For others, welcome to Miley.

TABLE OF CONTENTS

FROM
MURPHY
TO MILEY

A Carolina Family's Journey of Faith

THE VIOLET
By Jane Taylor

Down in a green and shady bed,
A modest violet grew,
Its stalk was bent, it hung its head,
As if to hide from view.

And yet it was a lovely flower;
Its colours bright and fair;
It might have graced a rosy bower,
Instead of hiding there,

Yet there it was content to bloom,
In modest tints arrayed;
And there diffused its sweet perfume,
Within the silent shade.

Then let me to the valley go,
This pretty flower to see;
That I may also learn to grow
In sweet humility.

CHAPTER 1

LOOK TO MAMA — 1903

The mountains of Western North Carolina faded behind the curtain of dusk as the great iron horse thundered and puffed its way steadily around curves and up slopes.

Inside, Carrie Tate gathered her long, maroon skirt and made her way slowly down the narrow aisle toward the rear of the coach. Mama could use her help with the younger children, and Papa was now asleep near the front of the coach where Carrie had left him. She smiled as she thought how he looked like a preacher even in his sleep. Slouched in the seat as he was, in his usual black tailored suit, there was a patriarchal bearing about her father that commanded respect.

"For all your spunk, your thoughts run deep these days, Carrie." His recent words echoed in her mind. "You'll soon be thirteen, maturing into a real young lady," he added with a hint of pride.

"I have a lot to think about, Papa," she had said, "with this move and all."

"You used to love moving, daughter. Remember how you and the other children would storm me when I returned from Conference? You always hoped we'd be moved to another church. Don't you still find the changes exciting?"

Carrie continued down the aisle, her mind swirling. As the oldest child in a minister's growing family, life had been good, experience-packed and exciting, yet, she knew, sheltered. As long as Carrie could remember, Mama had been burdened with childcare, her artist's hands laying aside paints and brushes for a later time.

Carrie had taken her place naturally as Papa's companion, traveling with him to meetings and revivals, places Mama couldn't go, sometimes even overnight. Papa had often warned Carrie, with a twinkle in his eye, that she was listed in the church record as his "official" replacement, should some catastrophe befall him.

"Since you've already done everything except preach, that would complete your training, and you'd be ready for full appointment by the Conference!"

Carrie had laughed easily. "Just don't call on me to perform any weddings, Papa!"

He chuckled at the joke between them. "Wouldn't think of it, my dear. You'd never remember your lines!"

They were both remembering. How long had it been? Six months? A year?

Carrie and her brother Howard had been riding through town with Papa in their buggy, making visitation calls. As usual, Mama was at home with the children. Howard, younger than Carrie by two years, had been distracted by a neighborhood boy into something more interesting. He had left the buggy, asking Papa to pick him up on the return trip.

"That boy will never make a preacher," Papa sighed. "Can't sit still long enough to make a visit, much less for a church service."

"I hope you won't be too disappointed, Papa. I just don't believe my brother Howard is preacher material."

Papa laughed, fingering his long, dark beard. "Carrie, you should have been a boy. You'd be following right in your Pa's footsteps."

"Why can't women be preachers, Papa? What's the difference?" Her voice held regret.

"It just isn't done, daughter. Women have their place, but it's not in the pulpit. The Lord has a plan for you, and a work for you to do. He'll show it to you in His own time and in His own way. We are not to question the plans of the Almighty. He made you a woman, and that means He doesn't plan for you to be a preacher."

"I guess I'll be a missionary, then," Carrie said resignedly. "At least they take women."

"Well, don't sign up just yet. Mama needs you at home, as do I!"

"Reverend Tate, Reverend Tate! Whoa there! Stop!"

Their conversation was interrupted by the loud shout from behind, nearly masked by the horse's hooves and the creaking of the buggy. Carrie and Papa turned to see a familiar young man in a late-fashioned suit running up behind them, red-faced, breathless.

"What's wrong, son?" Papa asked in his deep, ministerial tone.

"You're an answer to prayer, Reverend. You're just an answer to prayer!"

"Well, we like to be that. But what is your prayer for?"

"Me and my girl, well, we're gettin' married today. Right now, and the Baptist preacher took sick sudden, and ... will you please marry us, Reverend Tate?"

"Son, I'd be happy to perform your marriage. But I don't have my ritual with me."

"But, but ..." the young man's misery deepened.

"Papa," Carrie interrupted, "you can do it. You've read those words many times. You know them!"

"Well, daughter, I appreciate your confidence in me, but suppose I forget them?"

"Don't worry, Papa. What you don't know, I do!"

And so, standing tall and sure beside her father, Carrie had assisted at the wedding.

Now, moving carefully between the seats of the train, Carrie's thoughts shifted again to the move. She had always accepted moving eagerly, always ready for new adventure. But this time, she was reluctant. *I loved Salisbury,* she mused. *And this town, Murphy, is so far away. Why, it's practically in the middle of nowhere. Almost to Tennessee! Close, even, to Georgia!* To Carrie Tate, North Carolina was the center of the world, all she had ever known. *To the ends of the earth. Wasn't that what Jesus had said? Well, You really meant it, didn't You, Lord, because that's exactly where we're headed.*

The train jolted slightly just as Carrie reached her mother, seated on the prickly plush cushions. Baby Mildred was squirming on Mama's lap, while six- year-old Wilbur lay sprawled on a seat across the aisle.

"Little Mildred's restless," Mama said softly. "She senses things are different."

"Let me hold her for a while, Mama. You go and sit beside Papa."

Looking at her mother's calm, but travel-weary expression, Carrie wondered for the first time what being a minister's wife was like for her. *Funny that I never gave it much thought before,* she mused, as Mama gently transferred the stirring child into her arms.

"Thank you, Carrie," Mama was saying, "but Papa looks like he's sleeping, so I'll not disturb him."

"Mama, how do you like all this moving every few years? Is it hard for you?"

Mama glanced at her with slight surprise, then smiled.

"Each one is just a little more difficult than the last," she reflected wistfully. "The family grows, and the move is more complicated. Then too, I guess I'm just a little older each time."

Carrie appraised her mother silently. She *was* older than the last time Carrie had noticed. Her soft brown hair, caught in a neat bun at the neck, held a few wasps of gray. Her skin had lost a little luster.

Mama continued, brighter. "I remember that as a young bride I was so excited about the future. To be a minister's wife, especially Papa's, was a thrilling prospect. And it has been good, in spite of ..." She paused. Carrie caught her breath. This was something Mama had rarely mentioned. "... losing the first child."

"You mean Coke." Carrie didn't know what to say, but Mama relieved her. "Yes, Coke. We were at Ocracoke Island when he was born. That was Papa's first charge."

Carrie had heard all about the beautiful, remote island of Ocracoke, where Papa had taken Mama — Samantha Medora Doggett — as a bride. Sometimes, when Papa was in a relaxed mood, he would launch into stories about the mysterious pirate, Blackbeard, said to have made his home at Ocracoke. Now, Mama was continuing.

"At that time, North Carolina Methodists were all in one big Conference, and Papa was sent to pastor the church at Ocracoke. We lived there with the Howard family who kept the lighthouse. We loved that old lighthouse that looks out over Silver Lake Harbor. It was a very happy time until we lost the baby. He was just nineteen months old. It all happened so fast. Meningitis."

"I'm very sorry, Mama."

Carrie felt a lump in her throat. Even though she hadn't known Coke, she felt close to him. Clearly, in her mind's eye, she could see the little tombstone in the family cemetery at Forest City. Whenever Carrie thought of her brother, Coke, she thought of a little lamb, because of the lamb on his stone. Mama had such a tender spot for lambs. And he was her first. Carrie had often wondered what her life would have been like if Coke had lived. To have an older brother ... not to be the oldest herself. If he had lived, would she have been so close to Papa? Would she have had to stay at home with Mama and the babies?

Mama was still talking, casually. "It's all right. We've accepted it. And besides, you arrived soon afterwards and made our lives full and happy again. You're the apple of your papa's eye, Carrie, and a big help to both of us."

Carrie had always admired her mother's quiet acceptance of all that life brought. What Papa lacked in patience and self-control, Mama made up for. *To some,* Carrie thought, *Mama may seem a little weak and retiring. But I know she's not. She's the strength of our family.*

With a sudden, metallic jolt, shrieking brakes, and screaming children, Carrie, her thoughts, and baby Mildred were cast mercilessly to the hard cold floor of the coach.

Before Carrie could realize what was happening, Mama was up and at her side, at once comforting the baby, lifting Carrie from the floor, calling to her husband.

"D.P.! Wilbur's wedged between the seats! Where are Helen and Warren?"

"They're up here, Medora. They're all right."

The gas lamps flickered threateningly.

"Carrie, take the baby and go to Helen and Warren. I need Papa back here." Even as she spoke, Mama was brushing Carrie off and soothing Wilbur, who still screamed piteously.

Carrie and Papa passed in the aisle. "What happened, Papa?" Carrie asked breathlessly.

"We'll know soon, Carrie." He was brushing the grime of the coach from his once-crisp black suit.

Ten-year-old Helen was rubbing her own forehead. "I was asleep. I think I'm okay."

Papa and Mama had by now rescued Wilbur, whose whimpering had subsided to soft, choking sobs.

Papa's voice rose in alarm. "Howard! Where's Howard?"

"Oh, dear," Mama whispered. "I don't know!"

Before their fears could take hold, the question was answered. Howard and the conductor arrived to see to the welfare of the passengers.

"Mama! Papa! It was a landslide! Rocks and dirt all over the tracks!" His ten-year-old green eyes danced with excitement. "If Mr. Pentley hadn't stopped when he did …"

"We can be grateful to our alert engineer," the conductor added, smoothing his thin hair deftly. "Try to settle down now and get comfortable. We should be able to clear the tracks, but it'll take some time."

"Thank you, Mr. Blake," Papa was taking command. "Yes, we are grateful to Mr. Pentley. And we are grateful to God. Gather around and join me in praising Him."

"Praise God from whom all blessings flow," Papa raised his reassuring voice. Shaky voices joined Papa's strong one, as tears became smiles of relief.

Mama quietly collected her brood and began organizing them for the wait. Carrie felt the warm pressure of Papa's big hand on her shoulder. "Look to your mama, Carrie," he said quietly.

"I'll help her all I can, Papa," she replied, tucking in her own white shirt waist.

"Look to your mama, Carrie, as the kind of woman you should strive to be. She's a cheerful laborer in God's vineyard. She's an uplifter of spirits. A woman of sweetness and courage …"

"… with words of wisdom for every occasion." Carrie finished softly. She knew his "Mama" speech by heart. She also knew its truth.

"That's a big order, Papa."

"Look to your mama, Carrie."

CHAPTER 2

THE ENDS OF THE EARTH

Carrie was wide awake as the train neared Murphy.

"Haven't you slept at all, Carrie?" Mama asked, as she began to rouse the other sleepy children. "It's one o'clock in the morning."

"Mama, you know I was born in the middle of the night, and I've been a night person ever since."

"You were born into it, all right. We never were sure whether your birthday was July 31 or August 1."

"So I chose August. That way, I don't have to wait all month for my birthday." She paused. "Mama, do you suppose we'll have to scrub this parsonage, too?" She held up her young fingers, still raw from cleaning the house they had left.

"I'm sure everything will be clean and nice."

"Well, I'm not. I've done double duty too many times. Scrub the one you leave, then scrub the next one."

"It's not fair!" Helen was awake now. "Scrubbing two houses isn't fair." Helen had been old enough to help this time.

Papa approached, holding the sleeping Mildred. "Warren and Wilbur don't want to be roused, Mama. You and Carrie come and see to them. Helen, hold Mildred; Howard, come help me gather the grips. We're almost there." Papa's voice rose with excitement and anticipation. He would soon have his first glimpse of his new pastorate.

"I'm starved!" Howard appeared to be suffering most from the hours-long delay on the train. "Do they know we're coming? When will we get something to eat?" Mama's cold fried chicken had long since disappeared.

"I'm certain that we'll be given a fitting welcome, even at this hour." Mama's genteel, southern voice was assuring.

"Well, I'm not so certain," Carrie said. "Even if they had a meal for us, it's been cold for hours." She paused, then continued. "We're so far from everything," she groaned, glancing out into the darkness. "And we can't even see what this place looks like."

Years later, Carrie would remember this moment, as she groped toward yet another distant and strange place. "Oh well." She shrugged her shoulders, sighing. "Tomorrow should be interesting."

The train lurched and screeched and came to a jerking stop. The family peered out, nervous.

"There they are!" cried Mama. "I knew we'd be given a proper welcome!"

Papa was the first off, tightly grasping for the first time the hands of the welcoming committee. A half-dozen men and women, smiling, laughing, inquiring, enfolded the family and led them to waiting buggies. Carrie's resistance began to melt much sooner than she had intended.

"We'll take you straight to the parsonage. Supper is waiting," cooed Mrs. Martin, a plain, middle-aged lady with a motherly air.

Carrie tried valiantly to soak in her new surroundings as they drove through the cold, dimly lit streets of Murphy. It was just a little mountain town, nothing unusual. Suddenly, four years loomed large ahead, and she had a startling thought. *This is it! I'll be a grown woman when Papa leaves here. This is the last pastorate I'll share with him.* Where she might be as a grown woman of seventeen, Carrie didn't know. Yet she knew in her heart that she wouldn't be at home. It was a desperate thought for a girl whose ties to family were so strong, who had shared her preacher-father's ministry in a unique way. Still, it was a tantalizing thought. *Where will I be? What will I be doing? Is Murphy the right place to spend the last years of my growing up? It might as well be, because we're here.*

The buggies stopped in front of a large, white, well-lit house.

"It's quite a big house," commented Mama, a little shyly.

"We're proud of our parsonage, Mrs. Tate," replied the driver of the buggy, John Able. He was the youngish, dark-bearded member of the committee. "It has ten rooms, six of them with fireplaces," he added. "I think you'll find it quite comfortable, and we're so happy to have a large family moving in."

Approaching the house, Carrie was taken by the tall, free-standing columns resting on brick pillars beyond the porch, and the crisscross lattice construction of the balustrade. *This is the fanciest house yet,* Carrie thought. *Maybe it'll be clean too.*

It was clean. Clean, warm, and welcoming. Waiting in the large parlor was another delegation of men, women, and a few children.

"Children up at this hour?" Papa was astounded.

"Reverend Tate, I'm Salley McInnis." A tall salt-and-pepper haired lady with a wide smile held out her hand. "This is a special occasion. We allowed some of the children to take a nap and then be roused to be a part of this welcome. The hour is not important. We're so happy you're here to be among us."

Once again the family was engulfed with hugs, handshakes, greetings, introductions. A parsonage family makes friends easily. Warren and Wilbur took up quickly with a little boy who had a toy truck. There was a girl Helen's age.

Carrie was the only older child present. John Able caught her glance. "You'll have many friends," he said assuringly. Carrie hesitated only a moment. "I believe you," she said.

"Supper is waiting," announced Mrs. McInnis. They followed her down a hallway and across a cold porch. Papa, in the rear, was already talking about church matters with some of the men. Mama and Carrie, as usual, were organizing children.

In the dining room they were again accosted by warmth and their stomachs tantalized by the smell of good food. A fresh, white linen cloth was laden with bowls of steaming field peas, rice, corn muffins, ham, sweet potatoes, Carolina beans, eggplant, and sausage balls.

The aroma and taste of those sausage balls! Never had anything been so good. Carrie and Howard exchanged meaningful glances as they asked for more sausage balls, practically ignoring the other dishes. So much warmth on a cold night, and hot sausage balls!

CHAPTER 3

THE FIRST SUNDAY

Every night Carrie dreamed they were back in Salisbury. She had always heard that if you pinched yourself, you'd know whether or not you were dreaming. So, one night while dreaming, she pinched herself. Sure enough, she was back in Salisbury. But now, as she tried to open her eyes against the light, Carrie realized that the pinch had been a dream, too. They were still in Murphy. And this was their first Sunday with the new congregation. It would be an exciting, but tension-filled day.

Carrie reached for her old life-sized rag doll, Polly, a relic of her childhood. Polly had fallen to the floor. "Well, old girl, we'd better dress you in your Sunday best." Polly seemed to smile back through her painted-on face. Polly was really the family doll, though Mama had made her years ago for Carrie. When Mama sewed for the family, she sewed for Polly, too.

Carrie's feet reluctantly hit the cold floor. Quickly she slipped into a shirt waist and skirt and within minutes was busy with Mama in the kitchen. Soon the family was assembled around the cloth-covered table. It was a family rule that everyone would be present at the table for every meal, fully dressed. If one were not at the table, he was sick in bed. Family prayers always followed breakfast. There would be prayers again at bedtime, with everyone on their knees. No excuses. Papa would read the scripture and pray. Now, as he closed the morning prayer by asking a blessing on the meal, Carrie marveled again that he never used the same blessing twice.

"... and receive us to Thyself at last. Amen."

The morning passed, and as the congregation gathered for their first

service of worship with their new pastor and family, there was a heavy
sense of anticipation and curiosity. Carrie thoroughly enjoyed the getting
acquainted games the family and the congregation played with each other.
She felt proud, like a mother hen, as she sat in the fourth pew from the
front with Howard and several of the other children, waiting for Papa and
Mama to enter together, formally, as was their custom. Particularly on the
first day. Others took care of the youngest children. For this hour, Mama
was the pastor's wife, the first lady of the congregation. All her attention
would be on that. And the congregation's attention would be on her. And
Papa. And the new pastor's family. It was size-each-other-up time. And it
was exhilarating.

The pump organ was creakily playing some old favorites as Carrie
settled back. She remembered other Sundays, in other churches. Carrie
had made her profession of faith when she was six years old. Too young,
some said. But she knew even now that it was not. She recalled vividly
the joy and the glow she felt as she walked down the aisle and confidently
took her papa's hand. He knew, too, that it was time. They understood each
other well, Papa and Carrie, and he knew that she was ready. Since that day
Carrie had never doubted that she was one of the Lord's own, just as surely
as she was her beloved Papa's own.

The organ swelled, and Carrie sensed a rustling as heads turned
discreetly toward the center aisle. Men on the left, women on the right,
everyone's attention was centered on the new pastor and his wife as they
regally entered the church. Papa, in his usual black, wore a long-tailed frock
coat. He was a handsome man, tall, well-groomed, bearded. And that frock
coat. Mama, on his arm, a striking contrast in her white Sunday voile, was
a gentle woman. Carrie thought she would burst with pride as they passed.
Mama took her seat in front of Carrie, and Papa strode with dignity and
bearing to his place behind the pulpit. The service had begun.

During the welcoming remarks by church officials and the response by
Papa, Carrie was absorbed by the proceedings. But as Papa concluded his
opening pastoral prayer and began to launch into his sermon, she glanced
to the side to see with horror that Howard was trying out one of his old

tricks on the new congregation. Sitting in front of Howard was an old lady in a tired black silk hat. She suffered from the palsy. Her head shook uncontrollably. Howard was imitating her every movement. Carrie froze, trying to decide what to do, humiliated, yet amused. But it was too late to intervene. Papa had seen him. He had seen Papa's look. There would be no peace this afternoon.

◆   ◆   ◆   ◆   ◆

At home, seated around the table for the formal Sunday dinner, Papa was quiet. Mama was quiet. The children dared not speak. Howard's face was drained of color. As usual, Papa had helped Mama set the table with all the pretty things. He and Mama were very particular about meals, and Carrie had grown up knowing how to meet the door as the minister's daughter. But today, as they ate, Papa's silence was unusual for a first Sunday in a new parsonage, when there was usually a great deal of talk.

After the somber meal Papa invited Howard into his study. The family soon heard the results of that encounter. Papa came out, looking satisfied.

"He's just a normal, mischievous boy, D.P.," Mama said quietly.

Papa smiled. "You're right, Mama. But the boy must learn respect for the Lord's house. From now on, Howard is forbidden to sit anywhere near the elder Mrs. Armstrong, or *ever* to look in her direction."

"Howard's a bird, Papa," Carrie said. "He's always been a bird, and he will probably always be a bird."

Chapter 4

Getting Comfortable

Carrie and Papa were in his study, unpacking his large library. It was a special privilege to be here. Papa was very strict. You didn't go into his study without permission or special invitation. As she lovingly fingered his precious books, Carrie came across a small testament.

"Oh!" she exclaimed. "Oh! Now I know why I couldn't read!"

When Carrie started to school, everyone had said she was a smart girl, and she had become a good reader. She used to look into Papa's study longingly. How great it would be to read one of the books on his bookshelf! Once, when no one was looking, she had slipped in and chosen a small book. This would probably be more suitable for her age. But when she sat down and opened the little book, she was mortified. She couldn't read a single word. Papa must be so intelligent, so far above her, that she would never read his book. Carrie had put the small volume back on the shelf and retreated, feeling like a very insignificant girl indeed. Now, at last, her humiliation was resolved. She had chosen a Hebrew testament.

Later in the afternoon, Carrie was put off by herself in the parlor to practice her music for one hour. It was a long hour. She couldn't leave. She was required to sit and practice. If she didn't, Papa or Mama would promptly be at the door.

She had studied music for a good many years, and, although she loved music, Carrie didn't enjoy sitting down and playing the piano. How much nicer to be helping Mama with the babies, or visiting with Papa, or even studying Latin with Howard! *When I'm grown,* she decided, *I'll let my*

children learn piano if they wish. But I'll never put them off by themselves to
practice one hour.

Walking to school became a highlight of Carrie's life in Murphy.
John Able had been right; she had plenty of friends. The trek to school
was always interesting. There was a lot of political talk, children repeating
what their parents had said. Politics was unmentionable in the parsonage.
You strictly stayed out of that. So Carrie enjoyed hearing what was being
thought and said. There was a family of Republicans in town, who were
scorned. The crowd walking to school passed their house. Remarks were
made among the schoolchildren a good deal, as the mountaineers would
say. Carrie didn't make those remarks, but she was there, listening.

Papa considered it his duty to accept invitations for the family to eat
in the homes of the mountaineers. Here in the edge of Appalachia, things
were sometimes quite different than what they had known in some of the
more genteel areas of North Carolina. But Papa thought he should accept
any invitation, and he really wanted to. Sometimes Carrie most certainly
didn't want to go, or once there, would have liked to leave. Some of the
homes had no screens in the windows. In summer, flies and mosquitoes
had an open invitation. There were no ice boxes, and the food didn't always
have the best odor. Papa would never allow them to make a face or use any
ill manners in the presence of company. So Carrie would close her eyes, put
the food in her mouth, and swallow. It never hurt her. She considered it her
duty, and it was one she would enjoy telling about in later years.

Evenings were filled with studies before the fire, Carrie and Howard
hunched together over their Latin or helping Helen and Warren with their
lessons. Then came bathing and dressing for the night. Family prayers
were said, and all went to bed. After the fires were out, it was cold in some
rooms, even into early summer in the mountains. When they were tucked
into bed, it never failed. Warren always wanted some water. It was up to
Carrie and Howard to see that he got it. This provoked them, since they
had to go into the cold kitchen. One night they decided to cure Warren
of this irksome habit. They prepared a glass of Epsom salts. Warren took
one swallow and screamed for Papa. Papa was never patient with nightly

interruptions, especially of this nature. Carrie and Howard were made to drink the balance.

And so the days of their lives in Murphy went, much as they had in other places. Schoolwork and chores kept them from laziness. There were friends and family for fun, strict discipline to keep them out of trouble and teach them right from wrong. Plenty of love kept the children secure, while Papa and the church kept them close to God, whether they chose to be or not.

CHAPTER 5

REFLECTIONS

The food never hurt Carrie, but the water did. She passed their second winter in Murphy in an upstairs bedroom, recovering from typhoid fever. The crisis of fever and delirium had left her physically spent. During her recuperation, separation from family and friends was emotionally draining. Mama's new baby, little Julia, had to be protected from Carrie's illness. The baby wouldn't know her when she was finally allowed back downstairs. Carrie spent a lot of time thinking about her life, where she had been, and where she might be going. From her window she sometimes saw funeral carriages passing by. She knew some were carrying bodies of those who had died of this same illness. Carrie and Howard had agreed that neither was afraid of death, so sure were they of what lay behind the veil. Both admitted terror of the process of dying. But Carrie was still alive and looked longingly down on the children playing in the yard without her. She yearned to be with them, yet knew that she was no longer one of them. This year in Murphy and this winter of her illness had separated her from her childhood. At fourteen, Carrie was on the threshold of womanhood. She ached to be again the child she had been. At the same time, she welcomed with open arms the excitement, the mystery of young womanhood.

The arrival of mail was the highlight of Carrie's day. Cousin Clara wrote regularly. Wonderful Clara. Carrie's throat constricted with longing for her twin cousin. How they loved each other! So much that, when together, they would often exchange clothes, each trying to be the other. What glorious times they had together at Grandpa Doggett's, the one or two times a year they got together at the farm near Forest City. Once, when Carrie and Clara were left in the care of Grandpa Doggett, they slipped giddily down to the creek to play on the "slick rock." Whoever could jump across the creek without slipping on the "slick rock," he was "the fella." Naturally, they slipped in and wet their bottoms. Grandpa didn't know where to find clothes for them or what to do. So he had them pull their dresses up and lean over a big stump in the yard, while the sun dried their bloomers in short order. As the young cousins were drying their backsides, Clara called out to Grandpa, "Grandpa, tell us about coming home from the war."

Grandpa chuckled. They had heard it many times. He had told it many times. He would tell it again.

"Well," he began, "it was a long, hard war. I was gone a long, hard time. When the war was over, it was a long, hard walk home from Virginia. I could hardly wait to get back to my sweetheart and my own home. But when I finally got here, your grandma wouldn't hug me or let me inside the house until I had gone behind the barn and scrubbed myself with lye soap!"

Carrie also heard from her Green cousins on the Tate side of the family, whose father owned and operated a funeral home in Thomasville. The Greens, with their six children, came to visit every two years, always staying at least a week. What a grand occasion! Carrie and Howard were the oldest of the Tates, while Grady and Paul were the oldest of the Greens, all close in age. When those four could get together, they had all the fun in the world. At night, the older folks would send all the children upstairs. The "big four," in order to dispose of the little ones, would do something to cause them to cry, one by one. The upset child would flee downstairs to the parents, who would keep him. This continued until they had disposed of all. Only the big four were left, to have all the fun they wanted. They planned this every time. While it didn't always work out, they could usually find a way to get rid of the smallest ones.

Now that the danger of spreading Carrie's illness was past, Howard bounded in each afternoon with instructions from her teacher. He brought news of the townspeople, his own latest antics, and books — books, books, books. Carrie was an insatiable reader. Literature — *all* literature — was her great love. She couldn't get enough of the wonderful English poets. She knew and loved them all. During this period, Carrie stored in her memory poems for every occasion that would serve her all of her life.

Sometimes Mama would come and sit on her bed. Together they would recite "The Violet," which Carrie had learned in third grade.

"It's beautiful in itself, Carrie," Mama would say. "And it's a good philosophy of life." It was Mama's philosophy, and it would become Carrie's. But right now, Carrie had no philosophy — just thoughts and wonderings and vague yearnings for something that seemed to lie just beyond her grasp.

Reading to the children helped. As she grew stronger, they would pile onto her bed in the evenings, and she would read to them — *Rebecca of Sunnybrook Farm, Little Lord Fauntleroy,* and the new favorite, *Heidi.* As her great love for books and words, thoughts and ideas grew, Carrie began to have some idea where womanhood might take her.

CHAPTER 6

DAVENPORT COLLEGE
Fall 1905 to Spring 1908

Dearest Papa,

You can rest easy about me here, as I seem to be settling in nicely. I am especially enjoying the lovely mountain views. From the dormitory, one has good sight of Grandfather Mountain. The dining hall looks out on the local Lenoir mountain called Hibriten. This scenery soothes my inclination to homesickness.

It's such good news to know that baby Louise has arrived safely. You and Mama have one out of the nest now, and here comes another to fill my place! I do wish I could hold her and get acquainted, but that will come in due time. Give Mama my love and the baby sweet kisses.

Papa, I do feel so blessed to be here at Davenport. How fortunate that we have a *Methodist* college for *women* in North Carolina — and situated right here in these beloved mountains! Thank you for your sacrifice of the two hundred dollars. That much for the year, even with my forty dollar ministerial discount, seems a lot. I pray that I may be worthy of it.

Your loving daughter,

Carrie

◆　◆　◆　◆　◆

Dearest Mama,

Your letter was most delightfully received. I was surprised to hear from you so soon after Louise's arrival, knowing you must gather strength once again. It is happy news that the baby is thriving, and that Helen is such a help to you, as I was sure she would be.

As you predicted, I am gathering many new acquaintances. One of my roommates and I are fast becoming the closest of friends. Her name is Zelda Cline. Zelda, like me, has a penchant for literature and mischief. But don't worry. We won't be up to too much. As you and Papa have taught us so well, lessons come first, then fun later.

Mama, you would have taken delight in the annual fall outing to Hibriten Mountain that took place last Saturday. This will surely be one of my favorite things to do here. A good group of us got up very early in the morning. We set out on a three-mile hike to the top of Hibriten. There wasn't a lot to see along the way. But once we arrived at the peak, the view opened up to a scenic panorama of Lenoir and the surrounding foothills. Fall is progressing quickly, and the colors are beginning to vibrate. Of course, after such a climb on empty stomachs, all were famished! We had brought along side meat and eggs to cook on the mountain. The sun was rising as we ate, and sweet devotional thoughts were shared by Miss Parker. The return walk grew rather long, but a good afternoon nap brought refreshment.

Study hour is almost ended. Miss Parker will soon be checking to see that all are in, and the lights are out. Oh, Mama, these electric lights are such a fine invention. No lamps to fill, trim, clean, or carry. This is the coming thing! I do hope that one day before so long, every home will have electric lights!

Your loving daughter,

Carrie

♦   ♦   ♦   ♦   ♦

Dearest Papa,

Two surprises awaited me this morning. Rather early, I encountered Dr. Charles Weaver on the walkway in front of Tuttle Hall. Such a handsome man, as befits our college president. He is a little taciturn of face, but full of kindness when he speaks. He inquired after you and Mama and made several positive comments about your alma mater, Wofford College.

The second surprise occurred as I entered Mr. Franklin's English class. As I passed him in the doorway, he announced, so that all could hear, "Miss Carrie Tate is the best-read student that I have seen entering college." I was embarrassed, as I don't like attention called to myself. And now I may be challenged to live up to this assessment. I share this only because I know it will please you and Mama and reward you for your faithful encouragement, as well as for making good books available to your children.

To my pleasure, Mr. Franklin is already delving into the great English poets. We are studying Oliver Goldsmith's *The Village Preacher*. Naturally, I think of you the whole time, Papa. When I am home, I hope we can read this together. Give my love to Mama and the children.

Your loving daughter,
Carrie

♦   ♦   ♦   ♦   ♦

Dearest Howard,

I've been thinking about your question as to what we do for fun here. Of course, study is always first priority. But the college is quite good about providing numerous interesting activities and outings. There are receptions (which you doubtless wouldn't consider "fun"), sporting events, and many clubs and organizations. And then, too, we make our own fun where we can find it.

There is a girl here — I'll call her "Fanny" — who lives close enough to go home every weekend. She always returns with a suitcase filled with edibles, which she stashes in her bottom drawer. It is packed full of chipped beef, Vienna sausage, Uneeda biscuit, lady fingers, peanuts, etc. One night when she was out of her room, I went in with a friend, and we removed all of her food. We hid ourselves behind the dresser. When Fanny returned, she immediately opened her food drawer. Finding it empty, she went into a major panic, running down the hall shouting, "Thief! Thief!" My unnamed friend got so tickled that she wet her pants. That was a bit of homemade fun.

This weekend there will be a reception for the boys from the Weaver School nearby. This is a preparatory school for boys. I really wish it were possible for you to enroll at the Weaver School, Howard. It would prepare you for college, and perhaps whet your interest in higher education.

I must bring this to a close, as it is almost time for Glee Club. Always something interesting to do.

Your loving sister,

Carrie

♦ ♦ ♦ ♦ ♦

Dearest Sister Helen,

Now that the perplexities of the first year are behind, I am settling in for my sophomore year with somewhat more confidence. Our class this year includes twenty-three bright students. I am really enjoying my college years, and I hope that in due time you may experience the same.

This year I've added the Henry Timrod Literary Society to my activities, which will hardly surprise you. Keep up your good reading, Helen. It will serve you well. In literature class we are reading Lord Byron's "She Walks in Beauty." You would enjoy this poem. Read Lord Byron and be ahead in your studies.

You would like to have been here last Saturday. There was the annual reception for the boys of the Weaver School. Upon arrival, each boy chose a ribbon of a certain color. The girl who held a matching ribbon was the boy's "date" for the evening. As you would expect, there was a good deal of fixing going on!

It's hard to realize how baby Tuts is growing. She's keeping everyone on our toes. I do miss her antics, as well as the whole family. Give my love to all.

Your loving sister,

Carrie

♦   ♦   ♦   ♦   ♦

Dearest Mama,

Your letter arrived and the bill that popped out. I know that you squeezed this out of your own allowance. Thank you. Be assured that I will use it prudently. The pretty reception dress arrived yesterday. It fits perfectly, as I expected it would. It will be a nice change from my brown skirt and silk waist. When I wear it, I will think of my sweet Mama sitting up late with the sewing machine after the family is at rest. I will take good care, hoping that Sister Helen might also enjoy it in a few years.

Mama, I could have used your tender ministrations last Saturday. There was a little accident. Don't worry, no one is hurt. The college received a new Stieff piano last week, which was delivered in a sturdy wooden box. With the recent snowfall, Zoe and Scott and some others had the idea of using the piano box for sledding. We dragged it to the top of the hill, and a bunch of us piled in. We were well on the way downhill when we realized we couldn't see where we were going, and we had no way to steer. Pretty soon we landed at the bottom of the hill, hitting a tree, and spilling out all over each other. No one was really hurt. But I did bump my nose, and the red blood spurted out all over the white snow. That was a sight! But I'm fine now, just with a slightly sore nose.

Your loving daughter,

Carrie

◆　◆　◆　◆　◆

Dearest Sister Helen,

I'm glad you're enjoying your studies. It would be a good thing I think for you to follow me here at Davenport. I have really enjoyed college life, and I believe there can be no better place for a minister's daughter than here.

We held our second meeting of the Daughters of Divinity recently. We have a good group of more than a dozen daughters of Methodist ministers who have chosen to participate. Hopefully we will be able to have several service projects throughout the year. It is a good feeling to know that when I leave Davenport, I will leave behind this worthy group. If you should follow me here, then you can help carry the organization into the future.

By the way, we had such a fun time dressing up as our preacher-fathers for our picture. We made good use of one of the "social graces" seminars they sometimes provide for us in the evenings. One of them was on table manners, which you and I could have taught, thanks to Mama and Papa. Another, believe it or not, was on how to iron a man's white shirt! I wouldn't have thought of that subject for "social graces," but it has proved useful. Of course, we've ironed Papa's white shirts from time to time, but since Mama often sends them out, we've missed out on some of the finer points, which the other daughters and I were able to employ as we dressed up for our "preachers" picture!

I am also enjoying my role this year as Missionary to Tuttle Hall. It consists of ministering to spiritual needs of our resident girls, bringing devotionals on some evenings, and generally trying to be a worthy example of Christian living.

Helen, I must confess that at times I relapse into less than a stellar example. The desire for a little mischief overcomes me. Recently, several of us were late getting to breakfast, and we appeared in various stages of incomplete dress. We were reprimanded by Miss

Parker and sent back to our rooms with instructions to return dressed in skirt and blouse. We did so. Little did Miss Parker know that I was dressed *only* in skirt and blouse! And then there is the little matter of stuffing biscuits into our bosoms to be passed around in class. Just a little fun suggestion for you to implement someday. Papa has been so strict with us, that I am determined my children, if I ever have children, are going to have some fun!

One of the more unpleasant aspects of life here is trying to play tennis in these long dresses. I do so enjoy the activity, but feel quite hampered in trying to maneuver inside all the clothes. I hope that by the time you might come here, that the dress regulations will be more relaxed.

Thanks for being such a help to Mama with the younger girls. I know you are a jewel to her. Give hugs to all.

Your loving sister,

Carrie

♦   ♦   ♦   ♦   ♦

Dearest Howard,

My friends were amazed that you actually sent me a letter *in Latin!* It caused quite a stir. I think some of the girls were wishing to meet you. Since I am a bit rusty on my Latin, and they were so enthused, I gave the letter to Zoe and Scott to translate. They had a big time of it. I am enclosing their translation for you to enjoy.

Girls here often ask me about boyfriends back home and dating. When I tell them I didn't need boyfriends because my brother accompanied me everywhere, they are most surprised, finding it hard to believe that my younger brother was, and is, my best friend.

It's getting time for you to consider furthering your studies. What are your inclinations? You really should prepare for your future by getting the best education that you can. Knowing Mama and Papa, I'm sure they are encouraging you to move forward with some plans. Have you considered following Papa at Wofford College in Spartanburg?

You've not mentioned it, but I'd love to hear your thoughts.

Well, it is about time for my piano lesson. Did I tell you that my piano teacher's name is Carrie? I'm sorry for her, as I've just never cared for my name. It seems that Papa and Mama could have done a bit better, although they meant well in naming me for Grandmother Caroline Tate. Happily for me, my friends here call me "Tate." Of course, my teachers call me "Miss Tate." That sounds a little softer to me than Carrie. But the piano teacher doesn't seem to mind her name, so I'll not spoil it for her.

As I was writing the above, our newest yearbook arrived at my door. I'm excited to delve in, but will have to wait until after piano. It's called *The Galax*, for our abundant mountain evergreen herb with the heart-shaped leaves that turn bronze in their second year. I was amazed to learn recently that North Carolina supplies about three-fourths of the world's demand for this plant! It is so abundant here, especially along the roadsides, I would never have thought of it as being in demand!

I must be gone …

Your loving sister and best friend,

Carrie

P.S. I did take a quick peek at my Galax. Especially the picture of our Daughters of Divinity dressed up like our fathers. I can't wait for the family to see this! Then, too, there was a listing of girls' ambitions, and for Carrie Tate it is: "To have a meeting of her committee." I can't deny it.

♦   ♦   ♦   ♦   ♦

Dearest Mama,

It was such a pleasure for me to be at home this summer, and to help you and Papa get settled in your new Madison pastorate. I know you miss Murphy, as we all do, but you and Papa have so much to offer a church that I am happy that you are spread around, so to speak.

One of the first happenings for me upon my return was a note from President Weaver's wife, expressing the hope that I will again consent to sitting with their little girls from time to time. Of course, I sent a note in the affirmative. Their children are about the ages of Julia and Tuts, so they help with my missing of our own little ones. The happiest times I spent last summer were giving baths in the afternoons, getting the girls all dressed up, and taking them for walks. I'm sure that event is Sister's pleasure in my absence.

Oh, Mama. I can hardly believe that my "twin cousin" Clara is getting married! While I am happy for her, if she is happy, I can't help feeling very sorry that she will be living in far-off Montana! Will I ever see her again? I can remember when Clara and I imagined that one day we'd have "twin" wedding dresses. But this "twin" isn't even thinking about wedding dresses. I'm happy for all our fun times growing up, and hope that we will never lose touch.

My courses for the year are all lined up, books in order, and assignments on hand. A good challenge lies ahead, but an interesting one. Thank you, Mama, for your constant love and prayers.

Your loving daughter,

Carrie

◆   ◆   ◆   ◆   ◆

Dearest Mama and Papa,

This year has flown by! It's hard to believe this will be my last letter home from college. And so it should be a special letter. Thank you both with all my heart for the sacrifices you have made to give me the opportunity to follow my dream of college. You have given me advantages I would never have had otherwise, experiences and learning that nothing can take away. What the future holds I know not, but God does. And wherever He leads me, I will take these things along. I take joy in knowing that Howard and Sister Helen will soon be following their own dreams. We are more than blessed to have had parents who have not only valued God and spiritual learning, but have also seen the importance of learning from books and teachers. I hope someday I can pass these values down to my own children, should God give me children.

I do so look forward to being with you and the family in Madison this summer, and to think about what God may have in mind for me beyond summer. Still, I confess to a touch of sentimentality in leaving this place and people who have become dear. In the words of our college song:

> *Banded today in love we are;*
>   *Sadly at last we'll part.*
> *Love, with a kind and holy hand*
>   *Locks memories in each heart.*

Your loving daughter,
Carrie

Carrie Lewis Tate, 1908
Davenport College, Lenoir, North Carolina

CHAPTER 7

GOING BACK HOME

Fall was in the air in Madison. Usually Carrie was enthralled by the season, but something was off this year. She missed the brilliance of autumn in the heart of the mountains. She missed her best friend and brother, Howard, and her good sister, Helen. And she missed the stimulation and challenge of a new school year. Carrie had thought that by now she would be teaching school — or something. She was disappointed that nothing had opened up around Madison, and Papa was adamant that she remain at home.

"You've been away long enough, Carrie. With both Howard and Helen gone, Mama can use some help."

Carrie didn't mind helping Mama. The house was still full with Warren, Wilbur, Mildred, Julia, and Louise, but they were all getting older. Mildred was big enough to help now. For the first time in Carrie's memory, there was no baby in the household. She was secretly thankful; Mama needed a rest, and with Carrie at home, Mama could go out with Papa more.

Still, Carrie was restless, reaching for something, but what? She prayed. *Lord, I know You have a plan for my life. Won't You please show me at least the next step? I trust You, and I'll try to be a little bit patient.* Then she took a deep breath and heaved a sigh.

Carrie's sigh was interrupted by a heavy knock on the door. Like the well-trained minister's daughter that she was, she collected herself and met the door. A middle-aged gentleman removed his hat.

"Good afternoon, Ma'am. I'm Byron Johnston from the Mineral Springs community. Is Reverend Tate at home?"

"I'm sorry, Mr. Johnston. He isn't." Carrie briefly introduced herself, invited Mr. Johnston into the parlor, and offered to get her mother.

"That would be fine, Miss Tate," he replied, taking the chair nearest the door.

When Carrie returned with Mama and introductions had been made, Mr. Johnston stated his mission.

"I represent the Mineral Springs School," he began. "It's a rural, one-room school with less than a dozen pupils. The teacher we had lined up for this year has backed out suddenly. School starts in less than a week, and we have no teacher. I thought Reverend Tate might recommend someone who would qualify."

Carrie was thunderstruck. From somewhere, she heard her own voice saying, "Why, Mr. Johnston, I expect I might be able to teach your school."

"Wonderful! You would board with Mrs. Johnston and me. We are close enough to town that your father could send for you on the weekends. You would be away only during the week. It would be perfect!"

"Mr. Johnston, you can't hire me without knowing anything about me!"

"I know who you come from," he replied. "Reverend Tate held a revival at our church earlier this year. He is already well known in the area. Since you are his daughter, I know it will work out fine. If you'll accept, I'll handle all the details."

And just like that, Carrie Tate became a schoolteacher.

◆ ◆ ◆ ◆ ◆

Dearest Clara,

Can you believe that your twin cousin is now a school marm? Probably no more than I can believe that you are an old married lady!

Teaching school has proved to be an agreeable undertaking. I do like the children and am quite interested in their progress. I don't have discipline problems because I am pleasant, yet firm. One of my mischievous boys declared, "Miss Tate, you must have been a rounder in your day. We've tried every trick we have, and you know about them all!" I also employ Papa's "look." I can't describe it on paper, but he gets a certain threatening look in his eyes and on his face that makes you straighten up. Come to think of it, you've probably seen that "look" at some time.

It is good to know that you are also in pleasant circumstances. You are surely a good wife, and I am happy for your marriage. What I still can't be happy for is that you are so far away. When will we see each other again? I can't imagine when that will be. Whether we are near or far, let's agree to always keep in touch. You are the only person to whom I can confide certain things.

Papa's health is concerning. He's not sick, but I see small changes in him that bother me sometimes. I can't quite put my finger on them. He seems to be less vital, with less energy for his ministry. He is in his study, or sitting in his favorite chair in the kitchen, rather than out among his flock, as he used to be all the time. I tell myself that it is just a natural decrease in energy that comes with age, although he is certainly not yet old. Keep him in your prayers, please.

Papa wants me to stay near home, while I really want to get out into the world and make my own way. Finances are tight in such a large family, and it would please me to be able to make enough money to support myself and to help at home. I've learned that teacher pay is better in South Carolina, so I have decided to take that teacher's exam and apply for jobs there. I am thinking that Gaffney would be a favorable place. Our cousin, Lawrence Tate, and his family live there, and they seem to like it. Also, Limestone College is there. Since I left Davenport after only three years, I could possibly finish my degree, as well as teach. I think I would do well in the atmosphere of a college town, remembering how much I enjoyed Lenoir when I was at Davenport.

I will keep you posted on this plan. Keep your letters coming. They always brighten my way.

Devotedly yours,

Carrie

CHAPTER 8

LEAVING HOME AGAIN

There was sweet sorrow at the train station. The whole family had gathered to see Carrie off. She had always cried easily, and her tears were ready for this parting. Papa blinked back his, while Mama kept a brave smile. Carrie pulled away from the last hug and boarded the coach, finding a window seat so she could wave until they were out of sight.

Carrie had put her plan into action. She was headed to teach in South Carolina, having passed the teacher's exam last spring. Now she was on her way to a small town in the Sand Hills mid-section of the state called St. Matthews, disappointed that she wasn't going to Gaffney, her first choice. Gaffney had been slow to respond, while St. Matthews had responded immediately. Carrie had let them wait an indecent length of time before answering. Finally, giving up on Gaffney, she had accepted the St. Matthews job. Within days there came an offer from Gaffney. Carrie considered it too late. She had given her word to St. Matthews, and she wouldn't back out. She sighed. *Gaffney was my plan. But St. Matthews apparently is God's plan. Heavenly Father, please help me to not look back, and to do my best.* While Carrie knew that God always hears and answers prayer, she couldn't know that, before the end of this day, her destiny would be set.

◆　◆　◆　◆　◆

The first thing Carrie noticed about St. Matthews was that the deep railroad divided the town into two parts, and that three overpass bridges

53

knit it back together. As soon as she had stepped onto the depot platform, she heard her name called and saw two red-haired men coming toward her.

The older man offered his hand. "Miss Tate, I'm Franklin Arden, chairman of the school board. This is my son, Andrew. We are here to welcome you to St. Matthews and to transport you to the Hilton home. The Hilton family is anxious to receive you. They have a daughter, Rosa, who is about your age."

Loading Carrie's bags into his buggy, he continued. "On the way, we'll pass by Belleville School. It's our largest rural school, having eight grades and four classrooms. If you like, we'll stop and let you see where you'll be teaching."

"Why, I'd like that very much," Carrie responded. Mr. Arden assisted her into the buggy. Andrew had taken a seat behind her. It occurred then to Carrie that Andrew had not spoken a word.

◆   ◆   ◆   ◆   ◆

The Hilton family welcomed Carrie with warmth and graciousness. Mr. and Mrs. Hilton were determined that Carrie should feel comfortable in their rambling farmhouse. Their daughter, Rosa, was equally welcoming. A pretty girl, as tall as Carrie, Rosa had a calm personality and straight-forward manner of speaking. Carrie thought instantly that she and Rosa would be friends. The pair spent the hour before dinner in Carrie's room, adjacent to Rosa's, unpacking Carrie's clothes and other belongings and getting acquainted.

"Mother and Daddy raised me as an only child in this big house," Rosa said, "and it was awfully lonesome here during my childhood. They decided to open our home to boarding schoolteachers, and this has proved to be a wonderful way to get to know people. There is always interesting talk at dinner."

"What do you do during the day, Rosa?" Carrie asked.

"I'm the librarian at the high school in St. Matthews."

"So we are fellow school board employees. That will give us even more to talk about."

The girls were helping Mrs. Hilton clear the dishes away after a hearty meal of roast beef, stewed potatoes, and apple pie, when there was a knock at the door.

"You young ladies may answer that," Mrs. Hilton said, carrying the last of the dishes to the kitchen. "I have almost finished here."

Carrie had never met a stranger and was quite comfortable following Rosa into the front hall. Rosa seemed not the least surprised to see two young men standing on the porch.

"Come in," she said. "Carrie Tate, please meet Saylor Jumper and Pierce Furtick. Won't you all have a seat?" she offered, leading the group into the formal parlor.

The tall, thin, dark-haired one called Saylor took the initiative. "Pierce and I were in the neighborhood. We had heard about the arrival of your new boarder and thought we would stop to say hello."

By the time they were seated, Pierce had taken over the conversation. He and Saylor were cousins. They lived close to each other; their mothers were sisters. Saylors. That's where Saylor got his name. Saylor's parents had a nice farm. Pierce and Saylor had gone to school together all their lives, Pierce being a little younger. Wherever Saylor went to school, Pierce followed him. They had gone to a military school in Orangeburg and then to business school there.

"That's as far as I made it," Pierce said. "Saylor went on to Carolina, but I had to get out and get a job."

"We won't stay," Saylor finally interjected. "Miss Tate is probably tired, so we'll be on our way."

"Sure, Bub," Pierce agreed.

"Bub?" Carrie said as the cousins were going down the granite slab steps.

"Bub is Saylor's nickname. His family, as well as some others, call him that. I suppose it's short for 'Brother'. He is the only son among four daughters."

"It was nice of them to stop by," Carrie said when the men were out of sight. "And nice of them to keep the visit brief. Saylor's right. It was a long day, and I look forward to settling in. Thanks to all of you for such a lovely welcome."

"We're happy that you're here," Rosa answered, heading for the stairs.

♦ ♦ ♦ ♦ ♦

It had been a big day. As Carrie drifted into sleep in a comfortable four poster, she was much too tired to realize just *how* big a day it had been.

CHAPTER 9

COURTIN' CAPERS

The weeks passed quickly as Carrie settled into teaching and acquainting herself with her surroundings. She was enjoying her room and its rose and blue damask wallpaper. She was also impressed with the pink floral pitcher and bowl with a matching chamber pot. That matching pot was something to write Mama about!

Carrie's budding friendship with Rosa grew as the days passed. They caught up during the late afternoons in one room or the other, or on the porch swing.

Carrie had noticed that on Tuesdays Rosa would mention that Saylor Jumper would be stopping by for a parlor date. Rosa didn't say a lot about her friendship with Saylor, and Carrie wasn't inclined to pry. When Saylor arrived, she would visit a few minutes and take her leave. She learned that Saylor had been enrolled at the University of South Carolina and was an accomplished pitcher on the baseball team. He had become sick late in his second year — something about drinking river water — and had been forced to drop out. He decided not to return to Carolina, but to enroll in an extension course in accounting through LaSalle University. Carrie also learned that he was musical — playing the piano and singing. That was about the extent of her acquaintance with Saylor.

On a Thursday evening, Franklin Arden and Andrew came calling. The senior Arden carried the conversation, explaining that they were interested in how things were going with Carrie. Was she satisfied with her school and classroom? Was there anything they could do to make her feel more at home in St. Matthews?

While the younger Arden did make a few comments, he appeared to Carrie to be unusually reserved. She learned nothing about him. At the conclusion of the visit, his father extended an invitation from Mrs. Arden for Carrie to have dinner in their home the following Saturday. She accepted, thanked them for the visit, and accompanied them to the door.

Saturday afternoon was brisk and sunny, a perfect autumn day. Andrew Arden arrived for Carrie, not in a buggy this time, but in the family carriage. She dreaded the drive into town, knowing it would be up to her to keep conversation going. However, once she had Andrew talking about himself, he relaxed and told her that his father was the owner of St. Matthews Hardware. Andrew had earned a business degree from the University of South Carolina and was now working at the store.

"Is that what you enjoy?" Carrie asked.

"Enjoy? I guess I hadn't thought about whether or not I enjoy it, but I really do. It's all I have ever known. Growing up in that store, I know every screw, nut, and bolt. If I can't find it, it's not in the store. I was practically born there, and I'll probably die there, too."

As they approached St. Matthews, Andrew moved easily into the history of the town, imparting information that Carrie already knew, but it was easiest to let him talk.

"Actually, Calhoun County is brand new. A year or so ago, this was still Orangeburg County. Calhoun was carved out of Orangeburg, and St. Matthews was made the county seat. So we've been a county seat town for just a short while. This is plantation country, and several beautiful homes survived the War Between the States, including Midway and Belleville. I'd like to show you both of them at another time. Well, here we are."

The horses turned into a lovely Bridge Street Victorian house, complete with slate roof, wrap-around porch, and stained glass windows. Andrew secured the horses and assisted Carrie from the carriage. His father appeared on the porch and hurried down the steps.

"Welcome to our home, Miss Tate! We've all been anticipating your visit. Mother has a wonderful meal ready to serve."

For the first time, it occurred to Carrie that this invitation was more than just a warm welcome for the new teacher.

♦ ♦ ♦ ♦ ♦

Passing by Rosa's open door after returning to the Hiltons, Carrie stopped.

"Come in," Rosa said. "How was your dinner?"

"It was nice. How well do you know the Ardens?"

"Quite well, actually. All my life, I suppose. Good people. Well thought of."

"Andrew?"

"Andrew's a nice boy. Not really a boy anymore. He's socially very shy. It takes a long time for him to warm up, but once he's comfortable with you, he's full of personality. How do you like him?"

"I really can't say. It seemed to me that this was more of a date that his father had set up."

"That could very well be. But you know what, Carrie? You could do a lot worse than Andrew Arden."

"Really? What about you, Rosa? Could you do worse than Saylor Jumper?"

Rosa seemed unsure how to respond. After a long pause, she said, "I could certainly do worse!"

"Are you serious about him?"

"To be honest, I could be. However, I don't think I can say the same for him. Saylor and I have known each other a very long time. We're friends. We have these parlor dates, but he hasn't taken me out anywhere in public. I get the feeling he just comes by here to talk — like he's biding his time for something. Pierce told me there had been a girl at the university. I don't know whether there still is." She paused again, then continued. "Saylor's a fine person. I could get serious if he wanted to, but I'm not sure I could handle his mother." She sighed.

"What's the problem with his mother?"

"She's a difficult person. Ask anyone. It's community opinion. She's a very negative, sharp-tongued, task-master kind of person. She will do anything for anyone, but she won't be a good mother-in-law. Someone wanted to marry Saylor's older sister, Dora, and Sallie would have none of it."

"Why on earth not?"

"Dora had polio when she was eighteen years old. She's something of an invalid. She can get around the house, and do many things, but not like most of us. Her suitor was willing to take care of her, but Sallie refused."

"What about Saylor's father?"

"Uncle Frank, which everyone calls him, is a wonderful, kind man — a Christian — easy-going. The opposite of Aunt Sallie. I don't know why a nice man like Uncle Frank Jumper would wind up with a woman like Sallie Saylor. It's a shame!"

"How does he handle her?"

"Sometimes she rakes him over. He just shrugs and says, 'I don't know what gets into Sallie sometimes.' He will have a great reward in heaven."

Carrie laughed and said, "I hope he will. Well, I guess it's about time for bed. Thanks for the conversation."

Pouring water into the ironstone bowl as she readied for bed, Carrie thought about that conversation. *So Rosa likes Saylor, but has no claim on him.* Carrie liked Saylor, too. But she would not do anything about that.

She didn't have to. On Tuesday, as Carrie was sitting on the steps of the square, white clapboard Belleville school, waiting for her transportation to the Hiltons, Saylor Jumper came up in one of his father's farm wagons. Carrie was surprised, but gave no evidence.

"Good afternoon, Miss Tate. May I call you Carrie?"

"Certainly."

He disembarked and joined her on the steps. After an awkward silence, he said, "Carrie, I would like to ask you for a parlor date."

"That would be agreeable to me," she replied. "But it would have to be Rosa's parlor."

"It would be. Rosa is just a friend. I don't think she would mind."

"And if she does?"

"Well ... if she does, she does. I'm a free man. Are you a free woman?"

"Yes, I am. I will accept your date. When will you come?"

"The day after tomorrow, Thursday evening?"

"All right."

◆   ◆   ◆   ◆   ◆

On Tuesday evening, Carrie noticed that Saylor didn't call on Rosa. Rosa said nothing. Carrie said nothing. Carrie did worry a bit about just how to handle this. In the end, she didn't handle it at all.

Thursday evening came. Carrie was tense. The knock came on the door. Rosa answered. She was surprised to see Saylor. "Come in, Saylor," she said.

Saylor followed Rosa into the parlor. Carrie followed Saylor. They sat down; they made small talk. Rosa apparently thought she had a date. But Carrie didn't take her leave. They sat there. Carrie had to do something to break the awkwardness.

"Saylor, why don't you play for us?"

"Well, I suppose I could do that." He went to the pump organ.

"Any requests?"

"How about 'Dixie'?"

He launched into the melody. After "Dixie," he modulated into "Swanee River."

"I could use some harmonizing," he said. Carrie got up and stood behind him. She motioned for Rosa to come.

But Rosa was sitting, frozen, tears in her eyes. Suddenly, she rose from her chair, ran from the room, and up the stairs. Carrie froze, too. Saylor stopped playing.

"I believe she's upset," he said.

"I think so. I'm sorry, Saylor, but I need to go to her."

"Then go. I'll let myself out."

Carrie rushed to the stairs, wondering what in the world she would say to Rosa. Rosa's door had been slammed shut, but Carrie entered. Rosa was face down on her bed, sobbing. Carrie sat on the bed.

"Rosa, I'm sorry. I don't know what to say to you. This is my fault. I should have told you that Saylor had asked to see me. I just couldn't find the words. Please forgive me for that."

Rosa's sobs continued. It was a while before she spoke.

"I'm so … so humiliated! How will I ever look Saylor in the face again? I'm so embarrassed!"

"I'm the one to be embarrassed, Rosa. There must have been a better way to handle this, and I didn't find it. Yes, I am embarrassed. And I expect Saylor is embarrassed, too. He didn't think you would mind."

"With all those sisters, you'd think he'd know something about women! I should be angry with both of you. I don't know whether I am or not. I'm just so … humiliated!"

"Forgive me, Rosa. Forgive us both. I'll go to my room now and let you have a good cry if you need, but you don't have to."

"That would be best. We'll talk about this tomorrow." So ended the parlor date.

At breakfast, Rosa was silent and puffy-faced. The Hiltons tried to maintain strained conversation. Carrie supposed that Rosa had confided in her parents. Could they have hopes for her relationship with Saylor? If so, the new schoolteacher had interfered. *Still,* Carrie thought, *Saylor and I should be able to get acquainted if we wish. I don't know him. But I have a right to get to know him. O Lord, please help us all to deal with this sensibly.*

In the late afternoon, Rosa came to Carrie's room. "I'm ready to talk now," she said.

"Please sit down." Carrie let Rosa take the initiative.

"I had no right to behave as I did," Rosa said. "I was embarrassed. And now I'm ashamed of being embarrassed. I wish I could have reacted in a more poised way. It's too late now. I thought about it all night. You and Saylor have every right to date. I have no claim on him. The truth is, I'm not really sure whether I care for him, or whether I just want to find a husband, and he is here. I have always wanted to get married and have a houseful of children. After all the loneliness and silence of my childhood, I want the noise and even confusion of a large family. I want to remain friends with you. Saylor knows everything about me — but you are new, mysterious, and more interesting, more of a challenge. I understand that and can't blame him. If you continue to see each other, I don't want you to feel uncomfortable around me. I want us all to remain friends."

"That's very big of you, Rosa. Thank you. I do want to keep your friendship. And I would like to get acquainted with Saylor, too. Let's forget all the discomfort, put our best feet forward, and move on."

That is what they all did.

Vandy Saylor Jumper

CHAPTER 10

GETTING TO KNOW YOU

The deep blue autumn sky sparkled with dotted-swiss clouds as Carrie marveled over the crowd at the State Fair in Columbia. Saylor laughed. "It was probably worse the day before yesterday," he said, "with the Thursday Carolina/Clemson College football game going on. It's too bad that Carolina lost."

It was Saturday, November 6, 1909, and this was Carrie and Saylor's first real date. The sights and sounds of the midway were exhilarating. Aromas of peanuts, popcorn, and corn dogs mingled with shouts of vendors hawking their deep-fried wares. Underneath it all was the cacophony of live music and lights of flashy midway rides. There was a new fair fad, a pink, frothy, sugary concoction called fairy floss, which they sampled. For real sustenance they took refuge in a dining hall operated by a church, where they enjoyed ham loaf and waffle sundaes.

Saylor urged Carrie onto the Ferris wheel, a gigantic yellow orb with colorful, swaying seats, which she pronounced as too rickety. Instead, they enjoyed the grand carousel with its carnival organ music.

After the hectic pace of the midway, it was a relief to get out to livestock expositions and produce displays. Carrie enjoyed the quilting and canning booths, thinking of Mama all the while. Saylor was engrossed in the showing of fine racehorses from up north, overwintering on the fairgrounds. Horses had been a big part of Saylor's life from boyhood. He knew a lot about good stock horses and was attracted to the sleek, pampered thoroughbreds. Saylor also found the automobile shows intriguing. Those contraptions were surely the coming thing. He wondered if he would own one of them one day.

In the mid-afternoon, Saylor reluctantly mentioned that their return train would soon leave. Carrie should be home before dark. Before they left the fairgrounds, they had a souvenir photo made of themselves in an automobile, Saylor sporting a dapper straw boater. Carrie showed off a stylish Edwardian garden hat adorned with ostrich plumes.

The date was not over. There was still the train ride back to St. Matthews, where they continued the conversation of the morning commute. Carrie had been amused that morning to notice that Saylor was clearly out to make an impression, while she was quite willing to be impressed. He talked about his passion for baseball and his pitching career, begun while in school in Orangeburg and continued at the University of South Carolina. The illness that had caused him to leave the university was one of the big disappointments of his life. Still, he pitched whenever there was opportunity.

Saylor was a big hunter. He liked quail hunting and was good at it. If there were two quail flying in opposite directions, he could get both. Sometimes he enjoyed fishing, but not as much as hunting. Once, while out in a boat, he rescued a friend who had fallen overboard and was caught in a whirlpool. Saylor jumped in and, with great effort, pulled his companion to safe water.

They talked about their family backgrounds. Saylor's grandparents on both sides had been well off before the Civil War. They had all been wiped out by the war during Sherman's march. Almost all of their belongings and all of their food had been stolen by the soldiers of the Northern Army. Saylor's mother, Sallie Saylor, had been born during the chaos. Their horses had been hidden in the woods by trusted servants, bribed by the soldiers. The horses were then discovered and taken away.

Saylor's stories reminded Carrie of her own grandparents and the effects of the war on their lives. Her paternal grandfather, Hiram Gilead Tate, who had died last year, had deserted during the war. He wanted to be at home when his wife, Caroline, gave birth to their first child, Carrie's father. Carrie had been named for Caroline. She confessed she had never liked her name. Saylor thought to himself that he liked her name quite well.

Saylor's parents had little benefit of education, having grown up in the aftermath of the conflict, when everyone was poor, and there were no public schools. His father, however, was determined that Saylor and his sisters should have every opportunity to learn. His firstborn, Dora, had been enrolled in a school in Orangeburg, until polio devastated her life. One by one, Franklin Jumper was sending his children to the best schools he could afford. Like Carrie, Saylor was grateful to his parents for the things they had sacrificed for their children. This was one of many shared thoughts the two discovered before the train stopped in St. Matthews.

Later, alone in her room, Carrie knelt beside her bed to pray. *Heavenly Father, are You leading me to this man, Saylor Jumper, and him to me? If not, please show me now. If so, bless us and guide us and show us Your will for our lives. In Jesus' name I pray. Amen.*

Carrie climbed into bed, arranged the covers, and laid her head on her pillow with a deep sense of peace, and something more — a *knowing*. Did Saylor have a knowing, too? Was this their beginning?

♦ ♦ ♦ ♦ ♦

Over the following weeks, the courtship of Carrie and Saylor was real and open, yet quiet and discreet. Saylor created opportunities to see her, and there were casual dates — Saturday buggy trips into Swansea or St. Matthews — and occasional brief conversations after school. Saylor began showing up at Bethel Methodist Church, where Carrie was worshiping on Sundays, rather than going with his family to Calvary Church.

Carrie found herself thinking of Saylor often and wanting to learn more about him. She liked it when he talked about himself and especially wanted to hear about his family, particularly his parents. He obliged her one afternoon on the steps of the school.

"There's a verse in Colossians that, I think, describes my father."

"What is the passage?" she asked, curious.

"Colossians 3:12 and following."

"What does it say?"

"I don't have a Bible right now, and I can't quote it. You could look it up when you get home. It's about Christian virtues. That's my father."

That evening, Carrie located the passage and read: "Put on therefore, as the elect of God, holy and beloved, bowels of mercies, kindness, humbleness of mind, meekness, longsuffering; Forbearing one another, and forgiving one another ... put on charity, which is the bond of perfectness ... And let the peace of God rule in your hearts ... Let the word of Christ dwell in you richly in all wisdom ... singing with grace in your hearts to the Lord."

Carrie put the Bible down. She would like to meet this man. Then she had another thought: *I wonder what his mother 'puts on'?* Saylor didn't say. Carrie knew only what Rosa had said. *Hmm ...*

♦   ♦   ♦   ♦   ♦

While Carrie and Rosa kept their word and maintained their friendship, it was not the same as before the parlor fiasco. Rosa was aware that Carrie was seeing Saylor, but when his name came up, Carrie gave it a casual touch, not wanting to rub salt into Rosa's wound. She preferred to talk about her pupils and teaching experiences.

There had been no more parlor dates with Saylor. However, Andrew Arden had called on Carrie at the Hilton home on several evenings. Carrie tolerated these visits, but did not enjoy them, and had graciously declined another invitation to his home. Still, Andrew's attentions did provide a convenient camouflage to Carrie's and Saylor's blossoming courtship. Carrie was not a secretive person, but she was not ready to discuss Saylor. Yet, when a letter arrived from her sister, Helen, inquiring about gentlemen friends, Carrie realized it was time at least to drop his name to the family in Madison.

♦   ♦   ♦   ♦   ♦

Dearest Helen,

Your long, newsy letter was like a visit home. And I do miss home. I'm happy you've met a young man you can be excited about. Just don't let Charles interfere with your studies. Get all the education you can, while you can.

I'll try to answer your question about my social life and gentlemen friends. While teaching at Belleville School keeps me busy, I do have some social times, especially church and school events. And I do have a couple of gentlemen callers. One is Andrew Arden, whose father is on the school board. And there is a farmer's son, Saylor Jumper, who is studying accounting. Saylor invited me to the State Fair, which was a lot of fun. His parents have extended an invitation to me to join their family for Thanksgiving. It's nice of them to reach out to the new schoolteacher, who will probably be a bit homesick on that day.

I am saving my pennies for train fare home for Christmas, which is coming up rapidly. I am excited to see my dear family and have some time to catch up. Maybe I will get to meet your new beau, Charles.

Give hugs and kisses to all.

Your loving sister,

Carrie

Saylor and Carrie on their first date at the South Carolina State Fair, 1909

CHAPTER 11

THANKSGIVING AT THE FARM

Thanksgiving Day dawned crisp and cold, with the promise of a mild afternoon. Saylor seemed to be holding the horse back through the dappled morning light. There would be little time for personal conversation once they arrived at the Jumper home. Carrie took the opportunity to ask Saylor a question on her mind.

"You've told me things about your father, but not too much about your mother," she said. "What should I expect?"

"Ma's okay," he replied. "She's a bit high strung at times, and she's determined to be in charge. A harder worker you'll never know, and she has a very good heart. She does tend to say what she thinks. Still, if you let her know that you like her, she'll like you back."

"I have no doubt that I'll like her," Carrie replied. She planned to do just that.

"Oh, and she's a wonderful cook! She bakes the best bread you'll ever taste!"

Saylor's home came into view, a sturdy, one-story farmhouse, unpainted. A porch with turned balusters and a bit of gingerbread trim angled around a front ell. Saylor's younger sisters were waiting in the porch swing. Six-year-old Claudine jumped up and ran down the steps shouting greetings, her long blond hair flying. After Saylor hitched the horse, helped Carrie from the buggy, and closed the fence gate, he scooped Claudine into his arms.

"Well, Miss Claudine, may I present to you Miss Carrie?" he said, as the three of them went up the front steps. He lowered Claudine onto the floor in front of Berlie and Minnie.

"Hello, Miss Carrie," they said in unison. Berlie appeared to be around twelve years old; Minnie a few years older. Both were dark-haired and green-eyed like Saylor.

The front door opened, and a tall, slender, graying gentleman appeared. He strode toward Carrie with his hands outstretched to grasp both of hers. So this was Saylor's father.

"Miss Tate, welcome to our home," he declared.

Before Carrie could respond, Sallie Jumper appeared behind him, a thin woman in an apron, her own graying hair pulled back severely.

"Welcome you are, Miss Tate."

"Thank you. Please call me Carrie."

"Well, Carrie, then. Bub, you and Papa take Miss, uh Carrie, into the parlor. Minnie and Berlie, you two git to the kitchen."

"I'd love to help out in the kitchen myself," Carrie offered.

"Not today. You are comp'ny."

The door opened again, and Saylor's older sister, Dora, stepped out, holding on to the door. Tall and thin, a softer version of Saylor, a sweet smile lit up her face.

"We're ... so happy ... to have ... you," she said to Carrie.

"Thank you, Dora. I'm very glad to meet you."

The Jumper parlor was a one-room ell on the front of the house, the porch wrapping around two sides. The moment Carrie entered, she felt at ease. The space was comfortable and practical, yet not showy, cleverly positioned to allow for breezes from three sides in the summer. A fireplace graced the inner wall beside a door opening into a bedroom; low-burning embers knocked the late November chill off the room. As Carrie seated herself, she noticed the piano beside the east window. Maybe Saylor would play after dinner.

Conversation moved easily, fueled by Saylor's father's interest in Carrie, and hers in him. By the time dinner was announced, Carrie knew that she and "Uncle Frank" would be friends.

Minnie led the way into the dining room, where a large, cloth-covered, oval table was heavy with the fruits of Sallie Saylor's labors. Aromas of turkey and stuffing, roast venison, sweet potatoes, fresh-baked bread, and much more, filled the air.

"This looks and smells wonderful," Carrie said, as Saylor held a chair for her.

"It's just humble fare," replied Sallie.

Papa Jumper sat at the head of the table, with Saylor's mother at the end nearest the kitchen. Carrie was between Saylor and Dora, facing Minnie, Berlie, and Claudine.

Papa cleared his throat. "May we pray," he said. "Most gracious Father, we come before Thee thanking Thee for the bounty of this table, and for the hands that prepared it with love. We thank Thee for hearth and home, for family, and for friends. Most especially, we thank Thee for the eternal gift of Thy Son, our Savior, Jesus Christ, in whose name we make this prayer. Amen."

"Amen," came a chorus of voices.

Sumptuous dishes were passed, and plates were loaded. There was a period of quiet enjoyment of the meal before conversation picked up. Saylor's sisters seemed charmed by Carrie. She was used to children, loved them, and knew how to draw them out. Yet she soon realized that Sallie Saylor would be less easy to impress favorably.

"Saylor has told me what a wonderful cook you are, Mrs. Jumper. I can see that he spoke the truth."

"Bub brags on my cooking because he wants me to keep on doing it," she quipped, and the corners of her eyes crinkled.

"Well, Ma," Saylor said. "It seems to be working!"

Carrie made a mental note: *Sallie Jumper has a sense of humor. She's not all business.*

As the meal progressed, Carrie was tempted by seconds, but restrained herself. She was glad she had when an array of tantalizing pies appeared — pecan, apple, mince, and more. It was a difficult decision, but Carrie chose the mince, while Saylor, she noticed, went for the pecan.

"I can't tell you how much I have enjoyed this meal," Carrie said. "It has made Thanksgiving away from my family so much nicer. I do thank you for it."

"It has been our pleasure to have you with us, Carrie," Saylor's father replied.

"Thank you. And now please allow me to help clear the table," Carrie offered.

"You may help in the dining room," his mother said. "But you are too dressed up for the kitchen. Besides, I think Bub may want to give you a tour of the farm, now that the day has warmed up."

"I would like that," Carrie answered.

◆ ◆ ◆ ◆ ◆

Saylor was waiting for Carrie on the side steps. They crossed the yard, the chickens scattering before them, passed the covered well on the left, and went through a fence gate. As Saylor was closing the gate behind them, a big, black hound loped toward them and enthusiastically lunged for Carrie. She backed away.

"Whoa, Bob!" Saylor ordered, pulling the dog away. "He means well," he said. "Just trying to make you welcome. You're not a dog person, are you?"

"Not really. I can tolerate them, but we didn't have dogs, and I never really learned to love them. I'm not afraid, though."

"That's good, because there are several others around the farm. The hunting dogs are in a pen behind the barns."

At that moment Carrie became aware of two huge barns only yards from where they stood. "Oh!" she exclaimed. "I was so preoccupied with the dog that I didn't notice these magnificent barns."

"They are nice," Saylor said. "It's unusual to find two barns facing each other like this. Papa had the idea when he was young, but he built only one of them in the beginning. He added the other some years later. The long tin roof connecting the two is very useful for storing wagons, buggies, and farm paraphernalia."

They moved closer. Carrie was glad she had worn the comfortable half boots that had served her so well at the fair. Saylor was still describing the two huge barns. Carrie saw that there were stables built onto the sides of the barns to house the plowing mules and stock horses for the buggies and wagons.

"Papa is very particular about his horses," Saylor was saying. "The only harsh words he's ever said to me had to do with the horses. I got mad with a horse and hit it across the back with a four-ply whip. Even then, Papa didn't raise his voice. He just said, 'Don't you *ever* hit a horse that way again.' Coming from Papa, it made a big impression, and I have never done that again."

"I really do like your papa, Saylor. He seems to be all that you said." Then she added, "Now that I've seen his wonderful farm, I wonder if he's disappointed that his only son has chosen to study accounting."

"He may be," Saylor replied. "But he has never said so. I think Papa realizes that I'm not really farming material. I don't mind vegetable gardening, and I'll milk a cow because it needs milking, but I don't have a love for it like Papa does. What I have a love for is numbers. Numbers are exact, while farming is anything but exact."

As they meandered back toward the house, Carrie made a suggestion. "It would be nice if you would play for us, Saylor. It's been a good day, and that would just top it off."

"That's a good idea," he replied. "We'd better do it now, as we'll probably have more company dropping in. I'm sure Pierce will show up, as well as Ma's sister, Missy Furtick, who lives next door, and who has a large family."

"How nice for your mother that she has a sister nearby."

"They make the most of it, too. They meet at the fence in the mornings to talk, and Ma always comes back shaking her head and saying, 'I don't know where the morning went!'"

♦ ♦ ♦ ♦ ♦

The parlor was empty when Carrie and Saylor entered, which suited them both. Saylor pulled up a chair for Carrie, and he sat on the swivel stool.

"What shall we play?" he asked.

"Well, I think some Thanksgiving hymns would be good."

"Great idea," Saylor said and began with an introduction to "Come, Ye Thankful People, Come." At first, they sang in unison, and then Carrie gave Saylor the melody and sang the alto part. Their voices blended so beautifully that they continued through all three verses. Saylor continued with "Now Thank We All Our God." Carrie joined with the alto, again through three verses of the hymn. As caught up in their music as they were, they barely realized that family members were gradually filling the room. Pierce had arrived, as had Saylor's Aunt Missy Furtick with her husband, Wade, and several of their children.

"Everyone join in," Saylor said, beginning the introduction to that great old Thanksgiving hymn, "We Gather Together." Papa Jumper's bass could be heard, as well as Berlie's clear soprano. The impromptu choir finished with the long cherished "Doxology," long favored by Carrie's own family.

♦ ♦ ♦ ♦ ♦

In the afterglow of the joyful song fest, Carrie and Saylor made their way back toward the Hiltons. Saylor held the reins with one hand and put his arm around Carrie's shoulder to shield her from the chill of the late afternoon. His favorite horse, Old Prince, led the way, while Bob the black hound trailed behind, finally giving up and sitting disconsolately in the middle of the road as the pair disappeared.

For a while they rode in quietness, satisfied, until Carrie broke the reverie. "I did so enjoy meeting your family, Saylor," she said. "I am especially impressed with Dora. Would you tell me more about her? I know that she had polio when she was about eighteen. But I don't know much more than that."

"Oh, my," Saylor replied, heaving a great sigh. The floodgates broke, and he began talking, and talking. Carrie listened.

"Dora is brave," he began. "Polio is a curse, although we didn't know for a long while exactly what was wrong. It robbed her of the ability to walk and to speak, and she has never fully regained either. The things she is able to do now are the result of years of struggle and disappointment. She still cannot walk unassisted or without holding on to furniture, or whatever is near her. And, of course, you heard her speaking with difficulty. But at least she can move around, and she can make herself understood. For a long time she could do neither. Watching Dora suffering has meant suffering for our whole family. Still, it has drawn us closer. It has made me more aware of how blessed I am, and how life holds so many more opportunities for me than for her. It doesn't seem fair. But you won't hear her complain. She inherited our papa's disposition, which has helped us all. I hold Dora in high esteem."

"Is it true that she has had opportunities to marry, or am I meddling in asking? It's something that Rosa mentioned to me."

"No, you're not meddling. Obviously, it's common knowledge. Dora wanted to get married when she was sixteen. My parents insisted that she was too young and that it was important for her to get more education. So they sent her to school in Orangeburg. In her second year there, she got sick, and that seemed to be the end of any hopes for her to marry. But it wasn't. Dora is beautiful and sweet-spirited, and there was another gentleman who wanted to marry her. My mother pitched a fit and would have none of it. They finally gave up and accepted the finality of it. That suitor has never married, but there is little way for them to see each other, and they don't."

"That's very sad, Saylor."

"Yes, it is. At the same time, you don't know how such a marriage would have worked out. It's possible that Ma's solution is for the best. It's just hard to say."

"Thank you for sharing this. I, too, will hold Dora in high esteem." Old Prince turned in to the Hilton home.

"It was a very special day, Saylor. Thank you."

"Thank you, Carrie. It meant a lot to me. Especially the music. Our voices blend nicely. I think we sing well together."

"Yes, we do," she said.

David Franklin and Sallie Saylor Jumper

CHAPTER 12

CHANGES

On a rainy afternoon in late November, Carrie arrived home after school to find a letter from Mama on the hall table. She picked it up and hurried to her room. Dropping her coat and other belongings on the bed, she sat in the white wicker rocker. With a lot of anticipation, she began to read the letter by the overcast afternoon sun coming through the window.

◆　◆　◆　◆　◆

Dearest Carrie,

Your papa and I debated which of us should write this letter. We decided that I would write on behalf of us both. We have some news which you may find surprising.

Papa has resigned his pastorate here in Madison, and we will soon be moving the family to Danville, Virginia. In Danville, he will go into the real estate business under the tutelage of my sister Nannie's husband, Walter. Once we are moved and settled, he hopes to find appointment to a small church, which will leave him time to pursue business interests. Papa is still a pastor and will always have a pastor's heart. However, our large family with growing educational needs makes it necessary that he find a more lucrative profession. I feel certain that your Uncle Walter will give him appropriate help and guidance. We have been praying for some time about this decision, and we both are confident that it is the right one for this time in our lives.

We are all familiar with the city of Danville from our visits to Nannie and her family. You have had many fun times there with Cousin Clara. You will miss Clara, now in Montana, but I'm sure that you will find other enjoyable pursuits.

We are glad that you are coming home for Christmas and will be able to help us to get settled in Danville. You have always been a big help in such matters. Christmas will be a bit disrupted by the move, but we'll all pull together and make the best of it. Let us know when you can arrive in Danville.

Your loving Mama and Papa

♦ ♦ ♦ ♦ ♦

Carrie was thankful that Saylor stopped by her school the next afternoon. In her thoughts, she was already relating to him the unsettling news from her family.

"How do you feel about this?" he asked.

"I am disturbed," she confessed. "It has never occurred to me that Papa would *ever* leave the ministry."

"I believe you said he plans to find another appointment."

"Yes, that's what the letter said. Maybe what is really bothering me is that I can't picture Papa as a businessman. He has no training in business."

"Are you afraid that this may not be the best decision?"

"How can a man who was trained for ministry, and who has been a servant of God and of people all of his life suddenly become a businessman?"

Saylor was silent for a moment, realizing that her question was rhetorical, and not one she expected him to answer. "Life's a puzzle sometimes," he observed. "When we grow up, we might make choices that our parents question. At the same time, they may begin to make decisions that we, in turn, question."

"That's true. Even though I'm an adult now, my parents are still my parents, and I should respect their decisions about their own lives."

He took her hand and gave a little laugh. "I think that's what I was trying to say." They were quiet for a while, and then Saylor added, "Thanksgiving is past, and Christmas is coming. How about a little shopping trip into town on Saturday?"

She smiled. "That would be really nice," she said, "weather permitting."

◆ ◆ ◆ ◆ ◆

The weather permitted their excursion on Saturday. Carrie was still in a pensive mood, while Saylor seemed light-hearted, wanting to cheer her up.

"What's your favorite Christmas song?" he asked.

"The truth is, I like them all," she answered.

"Okay, here we go. Deck the halls with boughs of holly ..."

She joined right in. "... Fa, la, la, la, la, la, la, la, la ..."

Old Prince trotted in time as they sang "Jingle Bells" and "O Christmas Tree." Saylor dropped the reigns to concentrate on Carrie and their music, knowing that his good horse would get them to town. Soon they moved into traditional carols, their blended voices ringing out with "Joy to the World," "O Come, All Ye Faithful," and "Silent Night."

"Let's not forget the best one," Saylor said.

"Which one is that?" she asked.

"Star of the East," he said. "It's my favorite."

"Star of the East," they sang together, "O Bethlehem's star, guiding us on to heaven a-far ..."

"Whoa! What's this?" Saylor exclaimed. Old Prince had turned into someone's yard and stopped.

"Whose house is this?" Carrie asked. "Why are we stopping here?"

"I don't know why Old Prince turned in here," Saylor answered. "An old classmate of mine lives here."

"What is your classmate's name," Carrie asked.

"Um, her name is Sarah Hill."

"Sarah Hill? The horse must be used to stopping here."

"No, he's not."

"This must be an old girlfriend's house," Carrie said. Saylor was relieved that she was laughing. "You need to re-train your horse, Saylor Jumper."

"No, really. This isn't an old girlfriend's house. I have no idea why the horse stopped here. Maybe he's tired and wants to take a break."

As they continued on their way, Carrie knew she would never let Saylor forget this.

◆   ◆   ◆   ◆   ◆

A week before Christmas, they stood on the platform at the depot in St. Matthews. Carrie was about to board the train for her Christmas trip home. They were both a little uncertain about how to say their goodbyes. While there was little spoken understanding between them, there was a great deal that was unspoken.

"Well," Saylor said, "I wish you a safe trip and a merry Christmas with your family. May I have the pleasure of meeting your return train in January?"

"Thank you. I would like that," she answered. "I will send you word when to expect me." She paused, then added, "I wish you a merry Christmas, too."

And then she was gone.

◆   ◆   ◆   ◆   ◆

"You have some mail," Sallie said as Saylor came into the kitchen, throwing his hat onto the table. "And don't put your hat on my clean table."

"Who from?" he asked, retrieving the hat.

"That girl," she said.

"*That* girl?" he replied. "Now just which girl is *that*?"

"That Carrie girl."

"Oh! *That* girl! Wonderful!"

"Now, don't get serious."

"Why not, Ma? Do you think I'm too young at twenty-five?"

"You're not too young. You're just not settled. Not through with your schooling. Don't have a job."

"You're right about all of that, Ma. I'm working on it. Get used to that Carrie girl, because I'm hoping she'll be coming here again."

She handed him the postcard.

> Danville, Va.
> I'll be coming back on January 3.
> *Carrie Tate*

Standing again on the depot platform on January 3, in the new year of 1910, Saylor was in a buoyant mood. Carrie had returned, and he was watching her train arrive. Saylor couldn't wait to see her. Although she had been gone only two weeks, it seemed more like two months. His eyes caught a flash of scarlet as she stepped from the coach, wrapped in a bright red shawl against the cold. As he greeted her and admired the shawl, she explained. "Helen knitted this for me for Christmas," she said. "Red is not my color, but I didn't want to hurt her feelings."

"I like it," he said. "It brightens a January day."

Saylor picked up her bag, took her arm, and said playfully, "I'm glad that you signed your last name on your postcard. Otherwise, I would never have known *which* Carrie was coming!"

She laughed. "Since the message was public, I thought I should be more formal."

"You met your objective, Miss Tate."

♦ ♦ ♦ ♦ ♦

Saylor returned Carrie to the Hiltons and was making his way home, feeling deflated. Some of the joy had gone out of his day, and he didn't want to believe what she had told him. Carrie was not going to renew her teaching contract in the spring. When she left for Danville in June, she wouldn't be returning in the fall. Over the holidays, her parents had pressured her to come home. They didn't like having her so far away, they missed her and wanted her with them. Randolph-Macon Institute for Women was not far from Danville. They had lured her with the prospect of continuing her education there. Carrie had given in and agreed.

Is that what she really wants? Where does this leave me? He wondered. He thought that she liked him — quite a lot. If she cared for him, why did she yield to her parents so easily? *Maybe it wasn't easy,* he told himself. *Maybe the pressure was so great, she couldn't resist.*

Saylor was aware that Carrie had a very close relationship with her father. *Did she mention me to her family? Are they afraid of losing her to a stranger in South Carolina? Is Papa Tate trying to reel her back in?* While she was gone, Saylor had realized the intensity of his feelings for her. He had been looking forward to their springtime together. Now, it would be a time of parting. For how long?

By the time Saylor neared home, he had made a plan. He began to speak his thoughts aloud to Old Prince. "It's too soon to marry. Ma is right that I'm not prepared to take on a wife, but that can change. I will finish my correspondence course in May, and then I can get a job. I'll save every dime I can for marriage, except what it takes to woo Carrie all the way to Danville."

Since the ending of his baseball days, Saylor had lacked a strong sense of direction in his life. Suddenly, that had changed. In the space of one afternoon, he was aimed, straight as an arrow, in one direction. *Step aside, Papa Tate, Andrew Arden, and whoever else might wish to stand in the way. If she'll just have me, Miss Carrie Tate will be mine.*

◆   ◆   ◆   ◆   ◆

On a balmy, late spring morning, Carrie and Saylor went again to Columbia. The day was bittersweet. They were celebrating Saylor's accounting certification and his new job in the bank at Swansea. It was also their last date before Carrie returned to Danville. Both tried to ignore the cloud of separation hovering over them.

A trolley tour of the city highlighted the contrast between old and new, since much of Columbia had been rebuilt. The new areas gave a modern, up-to-date atmosphere. However, the neighborhoods that had escaped Sherman's torch reminded Carrie and Saylor of all that had been lost.

Carrie enjoyed their stroll down Main Street, with its wide walkways and newly paved avenue. She and Saylor felt the air of pride over the recent coming of electricity to Columbia. A string of electric lanterns was hung across the street in celebration.

"I really wish we could stay into the evening to enjoy the lights of the city," Saylor said, with a laugh. "Mr. Hilton would surely disapprove if I returned you after dark."

At the south end of Main, there was an imposing view of the South Carolina State House. Saylor took Carrie's arm as they crossed Gervais Street to get a closer look. Meandering the grounds of the impressive Greek Revival structure, they encountered a statue of General George Washington, and they paused to read a plaque beneath: "During the occupation of Columbia by Sherman's Army, February 17-19, 1865, soldiers brickbatted this statue, and broke off the lower part of the walking cane." General Washington still had only half of a walking cane.

Continuing, they passed a large, bronze equestrian statue of General Wade Hampton and a monument to the old State House, which was burned by Sherman's troops on February 17, 1865. The new State House, already under construction at the time, was damaged by artillery shells. Its exterior had been completed just a few years ago.

Saylor hired a driver to take them to the next part of their excursion. He was excited to show Carrie what he called his "old stomping grounds," the campus of the University of South Carolina. He explained what he could about the various buildings in the Horseshoe area — that part of the campus originally designated by a solid brick wall more than six feet high. "That wall served to protect the campus from being destroyed by fire during the war," he said. It was impressive.

Soon he took her to his favorite place — the Gamecock baseball field.

Hand in hand, they wandered toward the dugout and found a place to sit nearby. They were quiet. Carrie could feel the memories reverberating through Saylor's mind. He was back out there on the pitcher's mound, hearing the noise of the crowd. After a while, he broke the silence, as if suddenly becoming aware again of her presence.

"Carrie, I brought you here for a reason," he said. "Like most young athletes, all my thoughts and dreams for a long time centered around baseball. I ate, slept, and dreamed baseball. Since my illness ended those hopes, I've actually had few dreams. I've just been drifting along, waiting to see what comes next. Now, you have come along, and I've begun to dream again. Before you leave me, I need to know whether you share my dreams." He looked at her, quizzically.

She was quiet for a moment, meeting his direct gaze. "Saylor," she said finally, "I can't quite answer that question. I need something more specific about your dreams before I can know whether I share them."

"Of course, you do," he said with a nervous laugh. "Okay." He took a deep breath. "Specifically, I mean … now that you're leaving me … I need to know …" He took another breath. "Miss Carrie Tate … when the time is right … would you be willing to change your name to mine?"

"Thank you, Saylor. That helps a lot. Now I can answer your question." It was Carrie's turn to take a breath. "Yes … yes, I do share your dreams."

Saylor grinned. A weight had been lifted. He put his arm around her and pulled her to him, her head resting against his shoulder. They sat there quietly … sharing the dream.

Saylor reached into the pocket of his jacket and brought out a small package wrapped in blue velvet fabric and tied with white ribbon. "I knew you probably wouldn't want an official public engagement, at least not right now. Each of us needs to warm our families up to this gradually. But I want you to have something in celebration of our 'understanding,' and a token of my deepest affection."

Carrie took the package, gently untying the string and unwrapping the blue velvet. She lifted the lid of a little white box to reveal a delicate cameo pin, its white sculpted figure carved into pink shell and set in a white gold frame. "It's beautiful, Saylor. So beautiful. I'll treasure it for all of my life."

"I'll treasure you, my love."

◆ ◆ ◆ ◆ ◆

Saylor didn't care who was watching as he pulled Carrie close in front of the train depot. He hated this. How many more goodbyes would they say?

"Do you know when I knew you were the girl for me?"

"Tell me."

"That night in Rosa's parlor. We had gotten ourselves in an uncomfortable situation. You seemed to know what to do ... asking me to play ... inviting Rosa to harmonize ... then leaving me to go straight to her. I saw a woman of resourcefulness and compassion. When I left that night, I said to myself, 'Saylor, this is the girl for you. Don't let her get away.' And I don't intend to. You are going away from me. But you're not *getting* away. The next time you come here, I pray that I'll be with you, bringing you home as Mrs. Saylor Jumper."

Carrie was unable to respond through her tears, and didn't. She pulled herself away, turned, boarded the train and, once more, was gone.

CHAPTER 13

WAITING

Danville, Va.
June 24, 1910

Dear Saylor,

This is the first time I have ever written to you at home. There is nobody here but me and the little children. It is so dark that I gave them the Flinch cards, lighted the gas, and put them on a big rug in Mama's room to play, while I came to the upstairs porch, where I could have natural light to write to you.

It is raining for the first time in quite a while, and it seems like night on account of the cloud.

What would I give to see you? There are lots of things I want to say to you if I could only see you.

I see Mama coming down the street. It always amuses me to see her in the rain. She has a very dignified walk, and when she is in the rain she tries to hurry, but can't get off her dignity.

When I got that far, it began to rain so hard that I got up and went into the house. It is now Saturday — you see I had to stop overnight. I have been at home all day. Sister is away, and some of the children have gone to a picnic, so I am helping to keep house today.

Well, I am back again. I had to go downstairs just then to help the bakery man put the bread in the pantry. I never had such a time trying to write one poor little letter, or "scroll," as you dared to call one of my letters.

I am in a very meditative mood, so I think I had better stop. I just now woke up to the realization that I hadn't written a word for fifteen minutes.

Sincerely,

Carrie

♦   ♦   ♦   ♦   ♦

Carrie and Saylor found their separation to be more difficult than they had anticipated. Maintaining their closeness through letters wasn't easy. Saylor complained that Carrie's correspondence was too infrequent. Still, when he received her letters, he jokingly referred to them as "scrolls." Saylor's writings were flowery and flowing, sometimes containing eloquent descriptions. Carrie's tended to be accounts of human doings, laced with practical advice and encouragement. She noticed that, while it was she who had a love for great literature, Saylor was the better writer.

Saylor was boarding in Swansea during the week and returning home on weekends. He lived frugally, saving all he could toward their marriage. Every three or four months, he managed to scrape together train fare to Danville. Those visits nourished the couple's love and replenished their hopes for the future. Carrie's family received Saylor warmly, especially her brother, Howard, and her younger sisters, who already saw Saylor as another older brother. Papa Tate remained aloof, observing that Saylor was difficult to know. Saylor felt that he was being evaluated and judged.

"It's not you," Carrie would say. "Papa just doesn't want me to get married, period. Your being so far away doesn't help anything."

"Well, if he doesn't want to be far from you after we're married, there is something he can do about that."

"What is it?" she asked, curious.

"He can relocate."

"I would not have thought of that," she answered. Carrie loved it when Saylor gave her new ways of looking at things.

After these visits, Carrie never failed to ask Papa what he thought of Saylor. The answer was always the same. "He's all right. Just don't get serious." After the third repetition of the conversation, Carrie spoke up to her father.

"Papa, you might as well make up your mind to it. I've made up mine."

Papa Tate saw the determined set of her jaw. She saw the twinkle in his eyes.

"Daughter," he said, "Saylor is a sandlapper; you are a tar heel. Don't you know that sand and tar don't mix?" He sat back with a pleased air.

Carrie met him on his playing field. "Maybe not, ordinarily. But when they do, the bond is everlasting."

◆   ◆   ◆   ◆   ◆

When Saylor was in Danville, the couple often shared concerns for their families. Carrie was worried about her papa's seeming lack of success in business. True to his word, he was pastoring a small flock in Danville. The church, however, paid little, often offering up farm produce in place of cash. Papa didn't talk about it, but Carrie saw signs of financial strain. She was working in a dress shop, selling ladies wear, to pay for her courses in literature and dramatics at Randolph-Macon.

Saylor reported the unwelcome marriage of his sister, Minnie, at the age of sixteen, to Clarence Rucker. Papa Jumper and Ma were adamantly opposed and tried valiantly to stop the elopement. When it was obvious that all was lost, Sallie threw up her hands and said, "Well, she's made her bed, and she'll have to lie in it. And so will we."

Saylor had some pleasant, surprising news for Carrie. Rosa Hilton had married John McLocklin, who had begun to court her shortly before Carrie left for Danville. Carrie knew of the marriage from Rosa's letters. Just this week John had been hired at the bank in Swansea. He and Saylor would be coworkers, and John and Rosa would be moving to Swansea. Carrie was overjoyed by the news.

"It's just amazing how God works things out," she said to Saylor. "Rosa and I used to fantasize that someday when we both were married, we might live in the same town. I doubt that either of us expected that little dream to come true."

◆   ◆   ◆   ◆   ◆

By the fall of 1911, Saylor had begun to press Carrie for a wedding date. "I'm doing as you suggested," he wrote in a letter. "I'm telling people that we plan to shorten the distance between us soon."

She put him off until after Thanksgiving, and then until after Christmas. He ended one of his letters with a postscript that said, "You didn't answer my question."

At last the date was set: Thursday, February 15, 1912. It would be a simple morning ceremony at her parents' home, with Papa officiating.

> Swansea, S.C.
> February 7, 1912
>
> My dear girl,
> Your letter came somewhat unexpectedly today, but I was glad it did and have just finished reading it the second time. It was grand, and made me feel grand. It was just like you, as sweet as could be.
> Yes, the time of our marriage is drawing near, only a week from tomorrow — and then I will have the dearest wife in all the world.
> So, you haven't announced it. That is all right with me, just however suits you, and I'll be satisfied.
> I saw Pierce last Saturday, and he talked like probably he would come with me. I am going to write him and add your invitation. Pierce is one of my best friends and I would be glad for him to come with me.
> Sweetheart, this is short, but it is nearly train time, so I'll have to stop and do better next time. Will write again tomorrow or tomorrow night, and after this week I'll come for you, dear, to be my own sweetheart at home.
> Lovingly yours,
> *Saylor*

♦   ♦   ♦   ♦   ♦

As Saylor signed his name to the letter, he was a happy man. His life seemed to be coming together, and his plans for their marriage were complete. He had rented an upstairs apartment from the Craft family in Swansea, and their furniture was on order. After the wedding, Saylor and Carrie would accompany Pierce by train far as Charlotte, where the newlyweds would disembark for a brief honeymoon. Saylor couldn't wait to begin.

♦   ♦   ♦   ♦   ♦

Mama Tate prepared a wedding supper for the family on Wednesday evening. Afterwards, Pierce gave Saylor and Carrie a few moments alone in the parlor. Saylor was learning to read her moods. He had noticed that she seemed happy, yet subdued.

"Are you still concerned about your parents?" he asked.

"Yes, I am," she admitted. "I feel almost guilty in my own happiness, knowing that they are struggling."

"There's something I've been thinking about," he said. He paused briefly. "I … I mean we … have been so blessed over the last two years. Do you think your father would be willing to accept a gift from me, or rather from us? A thank you for my sweet bride, and the beginning of our life together?"

Tears sprang to her eyes. She waited before answering. "I've had no doubt that you are God's husband for me," she said. "This just confirms it … again."

Chapter 14

The Wedding

Fat, fluffy flakes of snow piled on the ground and nestled against the window panes as Carrie awoke on her wedding day. Inside, the household was already in a flurry of preparation. Carrie stretched and closed her eyes again, breathing a prayer for her marriage. She had prayed and longed for this day, and now she willed herself to remain calm, savoring every moment.

When all was ready, the family gathered in the parlor, Papa and Mama wearing their usual quiet dignity. Carrie's brothers, Howard, Warren, and Wilbur were looking good, but uncomfortable in their church clothes. Warren was disconsolate. "Why did we have to get all dressed up just to walk down the stairs to our own parlor, with our own family?"

"Marriage is a sacred estate, created and ordained by God," Papa explained patiently. "We must honor Him and your sister's marriage with our best."

The younger girls — Mildred, Julia, and Louise — bounced happily down the stairs, feeling festive in the bows and sashes of their Sunday best. Behind them came Helen, pretty and flushed from being in charge of the children, secretly dreaming of her own marriage to Charles.

Quiet descended on the family, and the old grandfather clock in the hall ticked louder as the appointed hour approached, arrived, and passed, but Saylor was not there. Mama, usually the calm in every storm, was filled with anxiety. In a nervous, high-pitched voice she said to Carrie, "What would you do if he didn't come?"

Carrie smiled serenely, certain that the weather was hindering Saylor.

"Mama," she quipped, "I don't think I'd be as upset as you would be."

Immediately they heard the pounding of feet on the front porch, snow being shaken from boots. Mama, now filled with relief, hurried to the door to welcome the groom and his cousin.

Saylor and Pierce came inside, removing their overcoats to reveal dark dress suits. For his wedding, Saylor was handsome in a white, ribbed corduroy vest. Carrie rose to meet him, radiant in a long navy suit with decorative brass buttons down the front. Cuffs, collar, and jacket were trimmed in dark blue velvet, laced with gold threads. Her long, dark hair was pulled into a soft bun at the nape of her neck, fastened with brass hairpins. Saylor gazed at his bride, and their eyes shone with joy. It was time. Their sacred hour had come.

Papa joined their hands as they turned and looked deeply at one another.

"Dearly beloved," Papa began, "we are gathered together ..." Instantly Carrie was twelve years old again, standing proudly beside Papa to assist in another, long-ago marriage. Now, she realized that she could still quote the entire ritual.

◆　◆　◆　◆　◆

"I now pronounce you husband and wife. What God hath joined together, let no man put asunder."

Papa embraced his daughter and extended his hand to Saylor.

"Congratulations, Saylor," he said. "You've become my favorite sandlapper." Looking toward the family, he added, gesturing with upraised hands, "Let us all stand in honor of the marriage of Carrie and Saylor."

As the group stood, Pierce stepped forward and shook Saylor's hand. "My congratulations and best wishes to you both," he said. "And, Carrie, welcome to the family."

"Thank you, Pierce," she said. Then Carrie turned to put her arms around Mama, who was wiping away tears with a daintily embroidered handkerchief. The children lined up to give and receive their departing sister's kisses and hugs. Tears appeared in their green Tate eyes, as each in turn realized the deep significance of this day, this holy hour. When she came to Warren, she laughed and said, "Thank you for getting all dressed up for my special day." He grinned sheepishly as she tousled his hair.

As Carrie reluctantly let go of little Tuts — not so little now — she turned for a final embrace of Mama and Papa, unashamedly weeping now. Saylor took her arm. As she turned to go, the sweetness of her childhood followed.

Their carriage was waiting, bags already aboard. Howard was ready to drive them to the train. As the horse pulled away from the house into a winter wonderland, cries of goodbye and good wishes followed, while the snow swirled around them.

Saylor slipped closer to his bride and whispered, "Have I told you that this is my favorite kind of weather?"

"Then it's a good beginning," said his wife.

CHAPTER 15

EARLY MARRIAGE

Carrie smoothed the perky, daisy-patterned oilcloth, smiling as she thought of Saylor's cleverness. When the kitchen table they ordered failed to arrive, he had found a solid pine door, rested one end on the windowsill and the other on a sawhorse. Carrie added the flowered oilcloth. Presto! A makeshift arrangement became a useful and welcoming table where the newlyweds could share their first meals as a married couple.

Saylor came to the table as Carrie was pouring his morning mint tea. She returned the kettle to the wood-burning stove, sitting across from her new husband for their breakfast blessing, bumping knees under the narrow table. As Saylor sipped his tea, she arose and poured her own scalding hot coffee.

"Our first problem," Saylor quipped, eyeing the steaming drink.

"Not problem — *difference*. And if this is the biggest difference we have, won't we be lucky?"

"Coffee for you, tea for me," he mused.

"Everyday, it will be," she answered.

"Why, my dear, you are a poet! I should have known."

"Hush. Don't tell anyone. It's for you only."

"My lips are sealed."

◆　◆　◆　◆　◆

Weeks later, cuddled on their sofa before the evening fire, Saylor put down the book they had been sharing.

"Papa came into town today."

"And he didn't come to see me?"

"He was in a hurry. Ma was needing her supplies right away. He usually goes into St. Matthews, but he came this way today."

"Well, I'm certainly disappointed."

"Carrie, sometimes I think I'm a little jealous of you and my papa. What is it between you?"

"It's simple. We both love the Lord."

"Well, so do I. But I think you two have achieved something I haven't."

"It's not a matter of achieving anything, dear. It's just an awareness of God's presence moment by moment. While we're speaking of Papa Jumper, do you think he'd mind if I call him 'Dad,' rather than 'Papa,' to distinguish between my own papa and him?"

"He'll be charmed by whatever you call him, Carrie."

"Well … *Dad's* visit must have been important, for you to wait so long to mention it."

"I guess it was important — to him, and to Ma." He seemed hesitant.

"Go ahead, Saylor."

"Carrie, do you remember the old house I showed you in the woods behind Papa's — the old Seible place on Gibson Hill?"

"The one with the bloodstains on the floor and the sunken graves nearby? How could I forget?"

"I'm a little sorry I told you about those things."

"Why?"

"Papa — and Ma — want to help us fix up the place."

"You mean to *live* there?"

"I didn't give him an answer, sweetheart. I just told him we'd discuss it."

"Do you want to live there, Saylor?"

"In a way. But your happiness is the most important thing."

"You think I couldn't be happy at the Seible house, Saylor? You'd be right there with me. That's all I need to be happy. And … I'd love being so near Papa, uh, Dad. Seeing him every day."

"And Ma. And the girls."

"I think your mother could use my help, especially since Claudine's health doesn't seem too good."

"Carrie, you've managed beautifully with my mother so far. I know that she drives hard, but she'd do anything for a person."

"I've seen that, Saylor. I'm counting on that side of her. I can handle your mother."

He looked tenderly at her, his arms around her shoulders. "Yes, Carrie Tate Jumper can handle Sallie Saylor Jumper, and anything or anyone else she's a mind to."

"Then we'll go?"

"I don't know. We won't decide yet. Carrie, it would be very different for you."

"I can handle difference, too, Mr. Jumper. I've been in many a different situation. Besides, if things were always the same, we wouldn't change and grow."

His arms were around her, completely now. "I don't want to change and grow," he murmured. "I want things with us to always be just as they are at this moment."

They were silent for a while, each one thinking. Suddenly Carrie sat straight up. "Saylor! What about your job at the bank? You can't work there if we're living all the way out at Sandy Run!"

"Well, that would be part of the change. I'd be farming with Papa."

"Saylor, you've said yourself you're not a farmer. You're an accountant."

"That's true, but I don't hate farming. I just don't love it. But I've done it all my life, and I know a lot about it. And Papa does need me. He's lost his right-hand man."

"I guess I just hadn't figured out that part of all this. When do you think we'd have to go?"

"There's work to be done on the house. That will take several months."

"Well, it's good that it won't be right away. Rosa's baby is due soon, and I have assured her I'll be around to help when her mother goes home, since I have so much experience with babies. I'd hate to let her down."

"You won't have to, dear."

When Carrie rested her head on her pillow that night, it seemed to her that their decision had already been made.

♦ ♦ ♦ ♦ ♦

Carrie held John and Rosa's newborn, called Elizabeth for Rosa's mother, close to her breast, rocking, humming, and praying. The past week of many sorrows replayed itself in her shaken mind.

First had come the impersonal, yet heartbreaking, news of the sinking of the Titanic. Shock had given way to grief for the many lives lost, as well as for survivors. That tragedy, although far away, had filled Carrie's thoughts.

The next day, Mama's letter had come.

♦ ♦ ♦ ♦ ♦

Dearest Carrie,

It pains me to have to tell you this, but Papa has experienced a breakdown of sorts. He has resigned his pastorate, saying that he will never pastor a church again. I wish I could give you reasons for this, but I can't say I fully understand them. Since we are living in a church parsonage, it will be necessary that we vacate this house in a matter of weeks. At this point, I have no indication what will come next for the family.

I have considered not injecting distressing news into your happiness. But I know that would not be acceptable to you. I also know that you will be in prayer for all of us, and we are in need of prayer.

We pray for you and Saylor, speaking of you daily, missing you, always asking our Heavenly Father to bless and keep you both. I will let you know of any changes in our situation.

Your loving Mama

♦ ♦ ♦ ♦ ♦

As Carrie was trying to absorb this unsettling news, Saylor had arrived home with more. Claudine, now about ten years old, had experienced a seizure. Dr. Fairey was attending her. The episode had passed, but there was little understanding of its cause at this point. The family would have to wait and hope there would be no recurrence.

But this, right now, was the most unkind blow. Carrie cuddled baby Elizabeth in her grandmother's rocker in the front parlor of the familiar Hilton home. She had volunteered to care for the infant while the broken family buried Rosa in the Zion churchyard. Rosa had not survived the birth of the child she longed for — the child who was supposed to be the beginning of a large, wanted family. Saylor would have stayed with Carrie, but she had waved him on. He would be a comfort to John and the Hiltons.

The overcast afternoon ebbed into near darkness in the silent house. Carrie continued to rock, sing, and sometimes weep. *What will become of this precious baby? What will John do? Will another little girl grow up alone in this big house? God, I know You're in control. I know You have a plan. I just can't know what that is. Help us to trust You with all these sorrows.*

Carrie heard footsteps on the porch. Soon Saylor was calling her name.

"Hush, Saylor," she whispered. "Elizabeth is still sleeping."

"Sweetheart, what are you doing in the dark?" he asked, moving toward a lamp on the table.

"I didn't want to wake the baby by getting up," she answered.

"Are you all right?" Now he could see her tear-streaked face.

"I'm fine, Saylor. I'm just sitting here remembering."

"What are you remembering?"

"I'm thinking about something Mama has said to me all my life: 'Never forget in the dark what God has told you in the day.' So, I'm remembering what He has told me in the day."

"What is that?"

"He has said that He will never leave me or forsake me. He has said that His ways are greater than mine, and His thoughts higher than mine. And He has said that He works all things together for good to those who love Him. We can't understand, but we can know that He has a plan for this child, a plan for John, and for the Hiltons. He also has a plan for Papa and Mama, and for Claudine. We must all rest in that."

"Amen," said Saylor.

CHAPTER 16

THE OLD HOUSE

Beneath the flaming reds and oranges of a brilliant autumn sunrise, Carrie and Saylor loaded their simple belongings onto Papa Jumper's farm wagon for their move to the "old house," as it would henceforth be known.

The morning was clear, but cold. They sat close on the seat, behind two horses eager to return home to Sandy Run. On the same day, Papa and Mama Tate were moving their family into a house on Blossom Street in Columbia.

"You're a prophet," Carrie said to Saylor, thinking of the two moves. "You prophesied that Papa would relocate."

"I'm no prophet, Carrie," Saylor answered, amused. "It's just a logical solution to a problem."

"I'm excited that they're going to be so much closer. Maybe our two sets of parents will actually meet."

"Probably so," Saylor said. "Especially since Dr. Fairey is sending Claudine to a doctor in Columbia."

Claudine. Saylor's youngest sister's name had been on their tongues and in their hearts so much lately. Pretty, blond-haired Claudine — called "Sugar" by the family — had early shown signs of brilliance, but seemed now to be regressing into childhood.

◆　◆　◆　◆　◆

Carrie's experience with setting up new households served her well as she readied her own kitchen at the old house. Rather than a door for a table, they now had the simple, sturdy pine table that Saylor had built over the summer. Already Carrie found herself planning the meal she would serve her parents when they came to visit, which they surely would do. Maybe deep-dish tomato pie, depending on the season, chicken and dumplings for Mama, and Papa's favorite, peach cobbler.

Life here would have some challenges, she knew. Their water had to be carried from a downhill spring several hundred feet from the house. But they were young, and the work of carrying water would make them strong. Saylor had promised a well house, to be built next summer, where they could keep things cool. Laundry could be done at the spring, and clothes hung to dry on nearby shrubs.

As she cleaned and trimmed lamps, Carrie thought, too, of Mama, now settling into their house in Columbia, which most surely was equipped with electricity. Mama would like that, and she deserved it.

Evenings at the old house were idyllic in the early months. Saylor was nearly always home by dark, and evenings stretched long ahead. When weather permitted, they sat outside to watch the sunset. Later, usually before a fire, they read together. Once, by lamplight, they worked through an old algebra book Saylor had come across. Numbers were his love, not hers. But she enjoyed having him teach her what she had forgotten. They longed for a piano. One day they would have one. But for now, they lifted their voices in harmony, unaccompanied.

Pierce was a regular weekend visitor. The newly elected auditor of Calhoun County no longer lived with his parents, but had taken rooms in St. Matthews. Yet he rarely missed a Sunday dinner with his feet under his parents' table. Afterwards, he often stopped by to see Carrie and Saylor. On one of his visits, he carried a small, lidded basket.

"I've brought a little housewarming gift," he announced.

"Oh!" Carrie exclaimed with anticipation. "Has your mother sent us some of her wonderful rolls?"

Pierce set the basket on her kitchen table. It tilted and spilled out, not rolls, but two tiny, confused tabby kittens. "Oh!" Carrie exclaimed again, scooping the little creatures up, handing one of them to Saylor. "How cute!"

"Pierce!" It was Saylor's turn to react. "What do you mean bringing cats here? We don't need cats. We need a good ole hound dog!"

"Don't worry, Bub," Pierce consoled. "They're both toms. The last of Mama's litter. She thought, since you don't yet have children, they would liven things up."

"They're perfect," Carrie said, admiring both. "I know exactly what to call them. I miss the antics of my two youngest brothers. The kittens will be Warren and Wilbur."

"Good grief," said Saylor. Still, for all his protests, Saylor enjoyed the playfulness of the kittens during the winter evenings as much as Carrie did. Warren and Wilbur filled the void of no children in the house.

◆   ◆   ◆   ◆   ◆

Even with the kittens, life was lonelier here, especially on days when Carrie stayed at home all day, although there were a few neighbors who sometimes stopped by. Papa Jumper — "Dad," as she now called him — was a fine replacement for her own papa. But Ma — well, Ma was the direct opposite of Carrie's sweet mama. Sallie had shown herself to be a domineering taskmaster, complaining and criticizing at every turn. She seemed ambivalent toward Carrie, both proud of Bub's choice of a wife, but also jealous — jealous of Carrie's education, refinement, and resourcefulness. She would ask Carrie's advice on a matter and adamantly reject it. Then she would turn around and follow it. Ma was happy only when she was working and everyone around her was also working. If she caught a member of the family sitting, relaxing, or playing a game, she would say, "You jist as well git your blanket and go to bed."

Thankfully there was Saylor, patient and loving with both women, sometimes exasperated with Ma, but unfailingly supportive of Carrie.

"She does like to joke and carry on, as long as it's not about her. I try to appeal to that," Saylor said one day, as the couple retreated to the calming solace of their own home.

Sometimes Saylor would apologize for his mother's contrariness. Carrie's answer was always the same. "She challenges me, Saylor. And she certainly enriches my prayers. Her life hasn't been easy, with Dora. And now Claudine."

"She was like this before Dora got sick, Carrie. It's her nature. She's a workhorse and a slave driver."

"Dad is a saint, Saylor."

"He certainly is that."

◆　◆　◆　◆　◆

Carrie's daytime loneliness was relieved when she became the postmistress of Sandy Run. Sallie thought it was a bad idea. "They'll be traipsing dirt into your house every day," she said. Carrie just smiled and did what she wanted.

Saylor put up shelves against the wall of the back room. Carrie collected shoeboxes for sorting. Six days a week, white-bearded Uncle Jerry Wise, their nearest neighbor, came with the mail from Swansea and picked up outgoing items. He also brought his own tall tales, many from his civil war years. Most neighborhood residents called for their mail every day or two in good weather. When it was warm, Carrie opened the window of the back room, placed a bell on the windowsill, and handed out mail from there. Within a few months, Carrie Jumper had discarded her status as a newcomer and become the most in-the-know resident of Sandy Run.

◆　◆　◆　◆　◆

On a cold and blustery late winter Sunday, the entire Jumper family was gathered around Ma's inviting dinner table. Even Minnie and Clarence Rucker had come, having bundled up their two very young sons, the first grandchildren. Over dessert, Papa Jumper stood, clinked his glass, and cleared his throat.

"As some of you may be aware," he began, "God has impressed on my heart for some time that there should be a church in our Sandy Run community. Now we have several fine institutions in the area, but none convenient to the neighborhood. Thus, church attendance is sometimes more lax than ought to be. Of late, the Holy Spirit has indicated to me and others that now is the time for such a church to begin. I have talked with neighbors and kin folk and have communicated with the bishop. He has advised me that the way to start would be with a Sunday School. So, that is what I am proposing."

Berlie was eager with a question. "Papa, where would the Sunday School meet?"

"Right here, Berlie. In a few weeks, when the weather begins to warm, we'll start a Sunday School on our own front porch." He paused and looked around at his family, then continued. "We have workers for the Sunday School right here around our table." He glanced at Minnie and Clarence. "If there are very young children present, Ma will provide nursery services. Berlie, you could teach the young children. Carrie could handle the older girls and women. I will take the older boys and men. Dora and Claudine can help out where needed. Bub, you'd be our song master and musician. We'll gather in the parlor around the piano for that. When the weather isn't good, we'll all find places inside the house. Carrie, you could also spread the word as you hand out the mail."

The group sat silently, looking at Papa. He smiled a great smile and said, "Everyone on board? All who are willing to be a part, please indicate by saying 'aye.'"

"Aye," they all said.

And so it was that God's Holy Spirit, through his servant, David Franklin Jumper, sowed the seeds of what was to become Oak Grove Methodist Church.

CHAPTER 17

CHILDREN

On an early November morning in 1913, Byron Kelston Jumper opened his eyes to the world at Grandmama and Grandpapa Tate's house in Columbia. Kelly was a robust boy, with a good set of lungs announcing his wants to all. Carrie was exhausted, but the light in Saylor's eyes as he gazed on his firstborn son was her reward. Just as the Lord Jesus had promised, she forgot the pain, for joy that a man was born into the world.

Nestled again in the home of her parents, Carrie relived the sheltering peace of her childhood. Peace. That's what she wanted to cultivate in her home, with her own children. She wanted to be like Mama and Papa, except that she most certainly would not be so strict as Papa. She was sure that Saylor wouldn't, either. They would allow a little uproarious fun in their household.

All too soon the young family was back at the old house, where Granmah Sallie presided for several days. Carrie bit her tongue, determined to stay on good terms with Saylor's mother, who complained about Carrie's housekeeping and rearranged things to suit herself. At last it was over, and the new parents were alone with their infant. Carrie slipped easily into motherhood, as Saylor returned their household to normal.

The months of Kelly's infancy passed quickly. Carrie continued her postmistress duties, and Papa Jumper's front porch Sunday School grew in attendance. Saylor had fallen back into farming with apparent satisfaction, and, as long as one didn't dwell on the worldwide and national news, life was good.

Mama and Papa Tate made another move. Papa had bought a tract of land at Edmund, just over in Lexington County. They would live in a house on the property while he sold off the land. So, for a while at least, they were closer than ever. Their younger children were growing up quickly. Carrie's sisters were no longer little girls, but maturing into charming young women. Helen had married her Charles, and the older boys were finding their way into schooling and jobs. Life seemed good for them, too.

♦   ♦   ♦   ♦   ♦

On a day in December of 1914, life seemed less than good. Flu was rampant, and Carrie, in her second pregnancy, succumbed. Shaking with fever, chills, and nausea, she put Kelly into his crib with toys, praying he would be happy. But he whined, sensing that something was wrong with his mama. After what seemed eons, Saylor came home. One look at his ashen face told Carrie that he, too, was sick.

"What will we do?" she asked.

"It'll be all right. I stopped by Ma's. She knows we're sick. She'll surely come."

Before dark, she came, on foot, carrying a pot of chicken soup.

"Ma, why are you walking, for heaven's sake?" Saylor wanted to know.

"I couldn't find a jar lid, and I didn't want the soup to spill. It was simpler just to trot it over."

Ma took over, barking instructions, taking care of everything. By the time she had tended Kelly and gotten Carrie and Saylor settled in their bed, it was dark. Without a word, she went downstairs with Kelly and out the door into the night. Many years later, Kelly still talked about the time when Granmah made her way home on a moonless night through the woods, past the old sunken graves, and across the unplowed field behind her house. She held Kelly over her shoulder with one arm and carried a lantern with the other. It was an omen.

♦   ♦   ♦   ♦   ♦

In mid-March of 1915, Carrie prepared to go to Mama's house at Edmund for the birth of their second child. Sallie insisted that Kelly should stay with her, but Carrie held firm. "Kelly goes with me. My family doesn't get to see much of him, and there is plenty of help. He's their first grandchild. He'll have a good time."

Ralph Dennis Jumper made his appearance near the end of the month. Again, Carrie was exhausted. This time the euphoria she had experienced at Kelly's birth was missing. Ralph was a thin, sickly baby. A week of tender care seemed to rouse him, so that Carrie and Saylor felt they could safely take him home. But the child languished. Carrie was devastated, her confidence shaken. Even Granmah didn't know what to do. It seemed Ralph wasn't going to thrive, and maybe not even survive.

After a sleepless night of keeping vigil over the listless, whimpering babe, Carrie had made a decision by the time morning came.

"Wake up," she said to Saylor, rousing him before daybreak. "We'll leave Kelly with Sallie and take Ralph back to Mama. If anyone can bring him through, it's Mama." Even as she spoke, she remembered Coke, her brother, whom Mama had not been able to save. "If this baby doesn't make it," she added, "that's where I want to be." She wrapped the infant warmly, placed him on a pillow, and prayed he would survive the ride to Edmund.

For a week, Mama Tate cared for Ralph intensely, treating him with a mixture of egg whites. By the end of the week, the child had begun to rally, his limbs filling out, a little color showing in his skin. For another week, Carrie cared for him under the tutelage of her mother, trying to restore her own self confidence. At last, once more, they felt they could return to their own house.

During the first night at home, Ralph slept evenly through the night, waking only for his feedings. That morning, as she rocked her second little son to sleep, Carrie wept. Ralph was going to live.

Kelly and Ralph

CHAPTER 18

WAR AND FIRE

Carrie was in her third pregnancy, the winds of war were blowing across the world, and the United States Constitution had been amended to allow its government to tax the income of its citizens. Carrie and Saylor didn't worry too much about the taxes, but the possibility of the United States entering World War I was another matter.

Taking care of Kelly and Ralph kept Carrie's hands busy and her worries partly at bay during the day. She knew she was blessed. Saylor had proven to be an involved father, rough housing with his boys, reading and telling little stories, singing to them. His favorite pastime was rolling balls to his sons and dreaming of the days when they could really play ball!

♦   ♦   ♦   ♦   ♦

Winslow Saylor Jumper made his appearance at Edmund in February 1917. His lusty, demanding cries allayed Carrie's fears, harbored in the back of her mind since Ralph's birth. They had another healthy son.

When Granmah Sallie arrived to help for a few days after their return home, Carrie noticed what she had been brushing aside. Sallie had staked her claim on Kelly, doting on him, treating Ralph as an afterthought. How would this affect Ralph? As he grew older, he would surely notice. The Tates had already noticed and lavished Ralph with love and attention. Unfortunately, it was Granmah who was far more often around. *Dear Lord,* Carrie prayed, *please take this situation and work it for good in our boys' lives.*

◆   ◆   ◆   ◆   ◆

In April, war became reality as President Woodrow Wilson asked Congress for a declaration of war against Germany. By June, Saylor, along with millions of other men, had registered for the draft. Since he was married with children, he didn't yet have to go. But they knew that could change. By July, Carrie's brother, Howard, had been mustered into the "Old Hickory" Division of the Thirtieth United States Infantry at Camp Sevier, near Greenville.

As Carrie was telling Howard goodbye, he had said, "Someone has to do it, Carrie. Maybe, like Queen Esther of the Bible, I was put here for this time. If I die, I die. But I know whose I am. It'll be okay." But it wasn't okay with Carrie.

One afternoon during the summer, Carrie finished hanging Winslow's diapers out to dry. As she came back inside, she heard the baby waking from his nap, hungry. She changed him, picked him up, and made her way to the porch. Ralph and Kelly were busy digging in the dirt in the yard as Carrie sat wearily into a rocker on the porch, threw a clean diaper over her shoulder, and began to nurse Winslow. Just then, Saylor arrived home, dismounted, and hitched Old Prince.

"What have you been doing?" he asked his wife, noticing that she looked tired.

She sighed a great sigh, looked directly at her husband, and said, "I'm doing the same thing I'll be doing at this time next year." Carrie was pregnant again.

Saylor was quiet for a moment, considering. Then he said, carefully, "Well, it's another chance for a little girl."

She brightened. "Surely it will be," she said. They each managed a weak smile.

◆   ◆   ◆   ◆   ◆

The war was heating up, and Howard, with the Old Hickory Division, had been transferred to Europe. At night, the war worries rolled over

Carrie. She thought of Howard and Pierce's brother, Carlisle Furtick, and so many others. *Where were they? What dangers were they in? Would they make it back?* She felt the anxious thoughts of Mama and Papa Tate and so many other Mamas and Papas the world over, whose grown sons were out there, fighting each other. What about their own boys? Were she and Saylor raising these children to go off to war? What kind of world were they inheriting? Well, she couldn't do anything about the world situation, but she would try to give them peace in their own home, for as long as she could. She tried to remember what God had told her in the day and knew she should turn her worries into prayers.

♦   ♦   ♦   ♦   ♦

For the fourth birth, Mama Tate came from Edmund to the old house. Carrie and Saylor's daughter, Analda Lewis Jumper, arrived in early April 1918. Like Kelly and Winslow, Analda came with a healthy set of lungs. The whole household was alerted to her presence. The family would be hearing from Analda. Besides blessing them with a girl, Analda's arrival assured that Saylor could stay at home from the war. Carrie felt guilty for feeling relieved. Then she reminded herself that it was only natural for a mother to want the father of their children to be at home, and breathed a prayer of thanksgiving.

Papa Tate came to fetch Mama and to greet his first granddaughter. Kelly and Ralph went back to Edmund with them, leaving Carrie with Winslow, Analda, and Granmah. By this time, Sallie and Carrie had arrived at a place of understanding, and some boundaries had been set. For the most part, peace reigned as a routine was established for the new baby. Carrie tried hard to put her fears about the war in God's hands and to enjoy the days with her first daughter. Until another, unthinkable crisis intruded.

Telephones were coming to Sandy Run, and Uncle Jerry Wise had installed one of the newfangled inventions. He got the call. He took the message, wrote it down and went out to find Saylor on the farm. Saylor would need to deliver the news to Carrie.

Saylor came through the door with his father. "This is a surprise," Carrie said when she saw the pair.

Saylor's voice wavered. "Carrie," he said shakily, "you need to sit down." She did so.

"Just tell me what it is, Saylor. Is it Howard? What has happened?"

"No, it's not Howard. Everyone is all right. No one has been hurt. But Mama and Papa Tate's home has burned."

Carrie paled. "Our boys …"

"They're all right, Carrie. Everyone was able to get out."

"Did they lose everything?"

"Yes, pretty much everything."

"Papa's library?"

"Papa's library."

"Mama's paintings?"

"Mama's paintings."

"How are they? What will they do? Where are Kelly and Ralph?"

"We can't answer all the questions right now. Just rest in knowing everyone is okay. Papa Tate told Uncle Jerry he would call back tonight. We'll know more then."

Tears were spilling down Carrie's face. "Oh! Poor Papa! Poor Mama! If I could just get to them, put my arms around them and the girls. Put my arms around Ralph and Kelly. Thank God that we still have them all."

Papa Jumper's firm hands were on Carrie's shoulders. "That's my girl, Carrie," he said. "Let's keep our eyes on our blessings. The loss of material things hurts, but those things can be replaced."

"Not Mama's paintings," Carrie said. "She asked me a few weeks ago to choose one of them, but I didn't. I thought there was plenty of time."

"God never wastes anything, Carrie. Not even this."

She shed more tears, then took a deep breath. "It will be interesting to see how God provides," she said.

◆   ◆   ◆   ◆   ◆

Saylor kissed Carrie goodbye and looked in on the babies in their morning naps. "Pierce and I should have the boys home by late afternoon tomorrow. Berlie will be here to spend the night, so enjoy her visit, and don't worry about things."

"I just wish I could go with you. I wish I could see my family. But don't worry about me. I'll be fine."

Saylor mounted Old Prince and headed for Papa's barn, where he patted his horse's rump. "You get a little vacation here at home," he said. He then hitched one of Papa's work horses to a wagon, made a stop by the smokehouse, and pulled up in front of Papa's house.

♦ ♦ ♦ ♦ ♦

Granmah Sallie had been a whirlwind of activity since early morning, sifting through her household for items that could be passed on to the Tates. Carrie's family had taken shelter after the fire in a vacant tenant house on their Edmund property, until Papa Tate could decide what they should do next. Sallie had been through her kitchen and was now focused on the bedroom. For all her simple practicality, she did have a sense of style in clothing. It was a good thing that Medora Tate and Sallie were about the same size. Sallie went through her Sunday dress clothes, choosing outfits for Medora, including accessories and intimate apparel. Meanwhile, Dora, Berlie, and Claudine had been in their rooms, searching their trunks and chifforobes for things to send for Mildred, Julia, and Louise.

Sallie saw Saylor coming in the front door. "Did you get the things from the smokehouse?" He nodded. "The food goods and utensils I'm sending are on the kitchen table. Some personal things for the ladies are in the satchel on the porch."

"Thanks, Ma," Saylor said. "It's good of you."

As Saylor and Pierce made the eighteen-mile wagon haul to Edmund, Carrie tried to keep her promise that she'd be fine. Still, her thoughts were constantly on Mama and Papa and the children. *How will they manage such a large family in the cramped quarters of a tenant house? Do they have the things they need? What will they do now? How grief-stricken are they over the loss of their home? Papa must be devastated. Has this thrown him even deeper into depression? They've always been the givers, tending to the needs of others. How will they handle being the ones in need? Lord, where are You, and what are You doing? I need to know. I need to see my boys, my family. But for Your grace, we could have lost them all.*

◆   ◆   ◆   ◆   ◆

When Kelly and Ralph saw their father, they climbed all over him. They were about too big for him to hold both at once. Saylor wasn't surprised to see Mama Tate already building a new nest for her brood. The humble house had been cleaned and swept, the kitchen set up with offerings from the community, and cozy areas established for everyone. "What really matters is that we're all together," she said. "God is providing, and all will be well." Yet Saylor could see the strain on her face.

◆   ◆   ◆   ◆   ◆

Berlie's visit proved a good distraction for Carrie. It was hard to believe that Berlie was already a grown woman, into her early twenties, graduated from college and in her first year of teaching at Sandy Run School. Both Carrie and Berlie were night owls. Once the babies were settled, they talked into early morning. Berlie was excited about life.

"Carrie, I don't think I've ever told you that you were my inspiration for becoming a teacher. When you came to teach at Belleville School, I thought you were the most educated and sophisticated young lady I'd ever known. I wanted to be just like you. Papa and Ma have always believed in educating their children. Especially Papa. But it was you who really made me want to push forward. I'm so glad I did."

"I'm glad you did, too. And it's good you're back in the community, and back with Papa and Granmah. They have their hands full."

"I'm sad about my sisters, Carrie. It doesn't seem fair that my parents should have two disabled daughters. Sugar's epilepsy sent her into a backward spiral physically and mentally. She's like a little child now. But strangely, it seems almost a gift to Dora. I'm sure you've noticed that Dora has become Sugar's caregiver. It's like it gives Dora a purpose in life, and it relieves Ma."

"God works in unexpected ways sometimes, Berlie."

Berlie was also excited about Oak Grove Methodist Church, newly moved into a lovely Gothic sanctuary in a peaceful, piney wood. Berlie was its first choir director. "I'm so happy Papa lived to see his dream fulfilled," she said.

"Why, Berlie, don't talk as if Dad might not have lived," Carrie said. She couldn't bear to think of him not being around.

"Oh, it's not that. I'm just glad he got to see it become reality."

"We all are, Berlie. That little church will be a place of peace and hope for many years to come."

◆　◆　◆　◆　◆

After what seemed like a week, Kelly and Ralph were in Carrie's arms again. They were filled with excitement about their adventure of escaping from their grandparents' burning home.

"When Grandpapa yelled, 'Get out!' I got up and ran right out of there, with Kelly behind me." Ralph was proud of being the first one out.

"We watched it burn, Mother," added Kelly. "We saw the roof fall in! Fire and smoke were everywhere! Grandmama and Mildred and Julia and Louise were all crying. Grandpapa wasn't crying, and I didn't cry."

"Neither did I," said Ralph. "Our clothes burned up."

"Our toy cars, too," said Kelly.

Saylor couldn't relay details of the visit quickly enough for Carrie. Especially about her Papa. "How is he, Saylor? Tell me the truth."

"Let him tell you himself, Carrie. Here, he has sent you a letter."

My dear daughter,
Saylor has told me of your great concern that the loss of our

home may have been too distressing for your old papa. I want to assure you that is not at all the case. If anything, it is the exact opposite. It is as though the fire has purified and refined my own longtime faith.

It's a great shame about Mama's paintings. I wish she had distributed them about, which we always talked about doing. As for my books, well, that's the key. In taking my books, our Lord has released me once and for all from the call to the pastoral ministry. The books were holding me there, and I couldn't quite turn my face in a new direction. Now, he has given me a brand-new start, permission to focus on my own family. He's impressed me with a clear view of what's important right now. Carrie, I know that while you were growing up, I often put the church and others ahead of you, your mother, and the rest of the family. I made demands on you that were of myself, not of God. I can't make that up to you now, but I can make it up to Medora and the younger children. Will you forgive me?

Your loving Papa

"Oh, Papa!" Carrie cried, putting down the letter. "What is there to forgive? I loved my childhood. Sometimes I still long for it. You and Mama gave me more than I needed."

"Carrie," Saylor said, "I wish you could have seen your papa's face. There was a look of, almost, triumph."

"It's the work of God," she said. "Beauty from ashes."

◆ ◆ ◆ ◆ ◆

Excitement and flag-waving patriotism were in the air, fueled by the stirring march music of military bands.

Saylor hoisted Kelly onto his shoulders, as Warren supported Ralph. Looking over the heads of the jostling crowds lining Main Street in Columbia, the youngsters were mesmerized by the brown-clad soldiers on parade.

"Boys," Saylor said, "these men are the heroes of the war, the fighting ones who broke the back of the Germans." It was April 5, 1919, and the Thirtieth Infantry Division was marching in Columbia prior to being demobilized at Camp Jackson.

"Look, Mother!" Ralph turned to tell his mother something, but interrupted himself when he saw Carrie wiping tears with the corner of her shawl. "Mama! Why are you crying?"

"I'm crying because I'm so happy that the war is over, and that Uncle Howard is home. And I'm crying because I'm sad that there were so many casualties."

"What's a 'cashty,' Mother?"

"Casualties are the soldiers who got killed and will never be coming home."

"Ralph and Kelly, look," Saylor said. "See the gaps in the lines of soldiers — the empty spaces? Those are the places where the ones who died would have been marching if they had lived."

"Daddy!" said Kelly. "Some lines have lots of gaps. And some lines have almost no soldiers left!"

"That's right, boys," said a voice behind them. It was Grandpapa Tate. With Grandmama, he was standing behind Carrie. "Don't ever forget that your life in this country and your freedom have been paid for by brave men who fought for you. And don't forget that your life in heaven has been paid for by the Lord Jesus Christ." Carrie smiled silently. Papa might no longer be a pastor, but he was still a preacher.

"Yes, sir," Ralph and Kelly said in unison.

"Will we get to see Uncle Howard marching by?" Kelly asked.

"Yes," Saylor answered. "His 119th Regiment is about to pass by."

"How will we know which one is Uncle Howard?" Kelly continued. "They all look alike, and we don't remember Uncle Howard very well. He has been gone away a long time."

Saylor had the answer. "Just keep out a sharp eye," he said. "If one of the soldiers cuts his eyes toward you and grins, that would be Uncle Howard."

Ralph and Kelly watched and watched. It was dizzying trying to look at the faces of the soldiers passing by so quickly. But sure enough, a man marching in one of the rows of many casualties winked and grinned at the boys.

"There he is, Daddy!" shouted Kelly. "Is that Uncle Howard?"

"That's surely Uncle Howard," Saylor said, grinning himself. "That must be him."

"Daddy, will we see Cousin Carlisle?"

"No, boys. Remember, Cousin Carlisle lost his leg and can't march. But we're thankful he didn't get killed, aren't we?"

"Yes, sir."

As the soldiers passed by, people in the crowd reached out, anxious to touch their returning loved ones, now safely home after the grave danger of months thankfully gone by.

"Daddy, will Mother get to hug Uncle Howard? I know she wants to."

"And so do Grandpapa and Grandmama, and all the rest of us," Saylor said.

Carrie answered the question. "As soon as the parade is over, Howard will be mustered out of the army. Then we can see him and get our hugs."

"Will Uncle Howard have mustard on his face, Mother?" Ralph asked, as he was transferred from Warren's shoulders to Wilbur's.

The whole group laughed, but this time it was Grandmama Tate who answered. "No, Noofy," she said, using the Tate family nickname for Ralph, "but he might want some mustard on the wonderful ham we're all going to share this afternoon."

Papa Tate had moved his family into an imposing, roomy granite home on Lincoln Street in Columbia, its small yard defined by a low stone wall, just blocks from where they stood. Analda was there now in the care of Mildred, while Julia and Louise entertained Winslow. This afternoon the entire family, including Helen and Charles, would gather for the first time in a long while. In the midst of joy and sorrow, in the Tate household, rejoicing would reign.

CHAPTER 19

ST. MATTHEWS

"There ain't no sense in none of it," Granmah Sallie exclaimed as the two-horse wagon, weighed down with furniture, belongings, Carrie, Saylor, and their children, pulled creakily away from the old house.

Papa Jumper, standing beside her in his old farm coat, pulled a handkerchief from his pocket and wiped away a tear. With the other hand, he responded to the goodbye waves and calls of the grandchildren.

"It'll be all right, Sallie. You know it's the right thing, the only thing. Blame it on the old boll weevil. It wiped us out. There's been no living to be had on the farm this year. Bub's had to borrow money to live. He has mouths to feed, and another on the way. Moving to town's the only reasonable answer. Let's just be grateful to God that the City Market needs a bookkeeper. Carrie and Saylor have promised that Kelly can come on weekends. Pierce is usually coming this way, as well as others. And the children will have good schools."

"If that uppity Carrie wasn't so picky about schools and books and such! There's a perfectly good school in Sandy Run, especially with Berlie a teacher there. And now Dora's got to take over the post office, and all that dirt will be traipsed into my house every day. It just don't make no sense, Frank."

"Ah, Sallie," he said with a sigh, putting his arm around her shoulder. "You're a good one, sometimes in spite of yourself. God's working things out. He knows what He's doing."

"If He'd jist listen to me, I could tell 'im a thing or two."

"He does listen to you, Sallie. He listens every day," he said as they turned sadly toward home.

♦   ♦   ♦   ♦   ♦

"Ooo … ooo … oooh … whoo … whOO … WHOO … !

Ralph clung closer to the dirt and grass under the bridge, bracing himself for the noise and vibrations of the giant locomotive as it puffed closer and closer to St. Matthews, then gradually slowed to a stop at the depot. The clanging of metal reverberating into his bones was the thrill of living in this town. He felt like an ant beside the huge train. He could see the tops of the cars from his perch above the big ditch that held the tracks. Buggies, wagons, and cars passed overhead on three bridges without having to stop. Ralph missed Papa Jumper's farm, the dogs, and the horses. But trains were bigger, faster, more powerful, and more exciting than horses! This little shelter under the north bridge was where he came whenever he could, hoping to see a train coming into town on its way to or from Columbia. It was more fun when Kelly was here with him, and they could watch the trains together. But often, as today, Kelly was at the farm, where he went every weekend. Winslow was afraid of trains, and Analda, much too young to come. While he wished for Kelly to be here, he was the oldest when Kelly was gone, and he kinda liked that.

Over the top of the train and across the big ditch, Ralph could see the City Market, the grocery store on Main Street where his daddy worked. He could imagine Daddy bent over his desk in the platform office. Sometimes, when they visited the store, Daddy would let them climb up into his perch, where they could look around above the store and feel very big and important.

Ralph stood under the bridge and waved to the engineer as the train gathered steam and speed, continuing on its journey north. He stayed until the caboose passed by, the brakemen responding to his waves and smiles. He sighed. It was probably time to go home. He scrambled out from under the bridge and up the bank to the road from Columbia which ran alongside the big ditch, brushing off his above-the-knee pants. This was the street he lived on, and he was just a couple of blocks from his house. He crossed the road and kicked an old bottle along, glad that it was late May, and he was now allowed to go barefoot. As he came to his neighborhood, he thought how he liked living between the Gressetts and the Pricketts, with only three houses on the block, and plenty of yard space between and behind. Daddy complained that Mother and Mrs. Prickett spent too much time on one porch or the other, talking. He said that they wasted as much time as Granmah and Aunt Missy. But Mother really enjoyed having Mrs. Prickett next door.

As his house came into view, Ralph remembered that Grandmama Tate was here. It seemed to him that she was sweeter when they went to her house in Columbia. Two weeks ago, when she had arrived, she had taken charge of things, and she didn't mind using the switch when it was called for. Still, he decided, he liked her being here.

Now he could see Lucy, the cook, on the back porch, probably using the water pump there. They still didn't have electricity, but Mother really loved that water pump, which meant no more hauling water uphill from a spring. Ralph had heard Daddy say that he was paying Mr. Gressett one dollar a month for the water, which came from the Gressetts' well next door. Ralph liked Lucy. She was young, and she liked the children. Mother had taught her to bake really good biscuits. Lucy didn't get mad when he and Kelly and Winslow threw biscuits at her. Mother didn't like it, but she didn't get really mad. Grandpapa Tate had been so strict on her growing up, that she wanted her children to have some fun. But it was supposed to be *good* fun. Mother could get puffed up like a bullfrog when she was really mad, and Daddy could give a rant that the neighbors could hear. And then there was that razor strop hanging by the back door. It was threatened more than it was used, but Ralph didn't like it one bit. It had been used on Kelly and Ralph once after they had sneaked off to the peanut brittle factory, hoping to get a taste. After Daddy had applied the strop, he said, "You boys don't want to eat that candy anyway. It's a family business, and I've heard they let their boys mix the candy with their feet."

Lucy spied Ralph coming and ran out to meet him. "Ralph! Ralph! We got a big s'prise fo' you!"

"Did you bake a pound cake, Lucy?"

"Nossuh. Dis s'prise way better than a poun' cake!"

"What is it, then?"

"You better come inside." She led the way. Ralph followed her down the hall to his parents' bedroom, which was closed. She knocked on the door. "Ralph, he be here," she said. Grandmama Tate opened the door.

"Come in, Ralph," she said. "Come and take a peek at your new little sister."

"Little sister?"

"That's right. You have a new baby sister. Her name is Dora Lellan."

"Come on in, Ralph." His mother's voice sounded weary. "Lellan is right here in the cradle beside my bed." Sure enough, there was a tiny baby in the cradle.

"Isn't she sweet?" Mother said.

"I guess," Ralph said. "But why do we need another sister? And where did she come from?"

Now Ralph heard his daddy's voice behind him. "The stork brought her," Saylor said.

"The stork?"

"That's right. A stork is a big bird who delivers babies."

"I didn't see him," offered Ralph, puzzled.

"That's because he comes when no one is watching," his father answered.

"I was watching," Ralph said. "And I didn't see him."

CHAPTER 20

CHRISTMAS IN COLUMBIA

The comforting aroma of sweet potatoes baking in the oven of the wood-burning stove wafted its way toward Carrie, sitting at her New Home sewing machine, pedaling away. These days, with a growing family, it seemed she spent more and more time right here. As she had commented to Agnes Prickett just yesterday, "I consider a day to be lost if I don't make at least one garment."

Today Carrie was finishing up Christmas clothes for the children. Hopefully by bedtime, these would be carefully folded and packed into valises waiting on Carrie's bed, all ready for Christmas at Mama and Papa Tate's in Columbia. She heard the back door slam and glanced at the clock. That would be Winslow, up from his Lucy-imposed nap, running out to meet Kelly and Ralph on their way home from school.

"Hush!" she heard Lucy saying as the boys bounded inside, wanting their sweet potato snacks. "You'll wake my baby Lellan. I jus' got her down." As Lucy spoke, Analda's wails could be heard as the toddler bounced inside the big-baby crib, demanding to be part of the activity. Not yet three, Analda loved to be in the center of everything.

"We'd better get her under control while she's young," Saylor had said. "She'll be a party girl for certain."

"Maybe we'll turn her over to my papa," Carrie had quipped, not knowing that she was prophesying.

"I'll take care of Analda," Carrie called to Lucy. "You tend to the boys."

As Carrie came into the kitchen with Analda in tow, she said to the children, "Lucy is heating your bath water by the fire in my room. As soon as you finish your snacks, let's get started."

"Baths?" Ralph wailed. "It's not bath day! We just bathed on Saturday!" Ralph hated baths worse than the others. Last Saturday, Saylor had to fetch him out from under the Gressetts' bed next door, where he was hiding to escape the weekly ordeal.

"We can't arrive at Grandmama Tate's house dirty," Carrie said. "Ralph, you bathe first. If you don't want to bathe, you can stay at home with Lucy, while the rest of us have Christmas in Columbia."

"Ha ha!" taunted Kelly. "You have to bathe first!"

"That's enough, Kelly, or you'll be the one to bathe first."

♦   ♦   ♦   ♦   ♦

Excitement about the Christmas trip was building as the children submitted to their cleaning rituals. "Mother, please let us take the street car from Union Station to Grandmama's," Kelly pleaded.

"Please, please, Mother," Ralph chimed in.

"Pu-*leeze!*" echoed Winslow.

"We've had this discussion already. We have too many bags and babies to take the streetcar. For ten cents, a jitney bus will take our whole crowd right to Grandmama's door."

"Pl-*eee-ze!*"

"We took the streetcar last summer, and we'll do it again next spring. Uncle Charles will be at Grandmama's, and I'm sure he'll take you downtown to ride the streetcars and to see the electric Christmas lights."

"You can bathe now, Kelly," said Lucy, holding a towel out for Ralph. "Mr. Charles be a nice man."

"You like Uncle Charles because he always throws you a quarter for a biscuit," said Ralph, wrapping himself in the warm towel.

"The water's too cold," complained Kelly, easing one foot into the tub.

"There be more hot on the stove," Lucy said. "I'll get it."

"Granmah loves Uncle Charles, too," Kelly said, easing the other foot in and waiting for the hot water. "When he goes hunting partridges with Daddy and Cousin Pierce, they come home arguing about who shot which bird, and Granmah serves them her scuppernong wine and cake. Uncle Charles brags on her wine. 'Aunt Sallie,' he says, 'You have the *very finest* wine.' And Granmah always says, 'Have some more, Charles.' She thinks he's a mighty fine man. But Aunt Helen doesn't think he's fine, because he won't go home when she's ready. 'Aw, shaddup, Helen,' he says. 'I can't leave until I get my birds.' They have a big fuss every time."

"But they always make up," said Carrie. "They never hold grudges." She paused. "And remember, you have a new uncle. Aunt Mildred has married a Columbia businessman named Hugh Smith. So now you also have Uncle Hugh."

"I'll bet I won't like him like Uncle Charles," said Ralph, struggling with his union suit.

"You must give Uncle Hugh a chance," said their mother.

♦　♦　♦　♦　♦

Saylor stood on the depot platform saying goodbye to Carrie and their five children. "Kelly," he said, tousling the hair of his firstborn, "You're the big guy now. Help your mother with the other children."

"Yes, sir," Kelly replied, standing as tall as he could.

As the train pulled into the station, Winslow began to cry. Saylor lifted him, comforting him as the giant cars came to a stop. The doors opened, passengers disembarked, and then came the "All a-bo-ard!" Kelly proudly led the way into the coach, followed by Ralph holding Analda's hand and Carrie carrying baby Lellan. Saylor came aboard with Winslow to get the family settled. "Here, Winslow, you can sit between your two big brothers. Analda, you sit back here with Mother and Lellan."

Winslow was not comforted, still whimpering and clinging for dear life to Saylor. Soon the conductor saved the day, passing through the coach with a basket, calling, "Magazines! Candy bars! Anyone?"

"Right here," Saylor answered, digging into his pockets. "Four candy bars, please."

"Saylor," Carrie protested.

"It'll be okay," Saylor said. "There's never been a boy who could eat a Hershey bar and cry at the same time." Bending over to kiss Carrie and the girls, he added, "I'll join you all in a few days."

♦   ♦   ♦   ♦   ♦

Candy was the cure. By the time the huge, castle-like Union Station came into view on the lower end of Main in Columbia, Winslow had fallen in love with trains. Instead of being fearful, he was now charmed by the world rushing by, the swaying of the cars, the lonesome warning whistles, and even the hissing puffs of steam. It was a new day for Winslow.

Kelly proudly raised his arm to hail a jitney bus as the family disembarked and gathered around their baggage. Soon a jitney operator began picking up their grips and piling them onto the back of the partially loaded vehicle.

Kelly took charge of helping the youngsters aboard, the family filling the bus to capacity, with Kelly and Ralph seated up front beside the driver. A cold, windy ride energized the children, as well as Carrie, and put them in a holiday mood as they passed through the streets of Columbia, enjoying the festive decorations adorning homes and businesses. Ten minutes later they had reached their destination of 2315 Lincoln Street, its doorway beckoning with boughs of pine, holly, fruits, and red bows.

♦   ♦   ♦   ♦   ♦

Grandpapa Tate's roomy house was filled to capacity and beyond with everyone gathered for the holiday. Christmas Eve was all about fireworks, a spectacle of light and noise directed by Saylor, Charles, Warren, and Wilbur. Of the children, only Kelly and Ralph were allowed near the firecrackers, but even little Analda was helped by her daddy to enjoy the swirling steel wool sparklers. After the show, the big family gathered in front of a roaring fire beside the heavily decorated Christmas tree, ornamented with colorful strands of delicate electric bulbs, garlands of popcorn, and paper snowflakes crafted by the children. Suddenly, the living room window opened, and a red-garbed, white-bearded fellow stuck one booted leg through, then another, landing awkwardly and amazingly on Grandmama's white brocade sofa, which had suddenly been vacated by Julia and Louise. Everyone gasped. Santa Claus! Winslow screamed, and Saylor scooped him up. "Ho, ho, ho!" boomed Santa, heading straight for Winslow, who increased his frantic protests. "Ho, ho, ho, little Winslow. I have something special for you right here," he said, holding out a bag to the child. Curiosity slowed Winslow's screams. Saylor took the bag, opening it. "Look, Winslow. Look. Santa has brought you your very own bag of peppermints."

"I want peppermints, too!" insisted Analda, already being accommodated by Santa. When the children all had their candy, Santa began to reach under the tree, handing out gaily wrapped presents. When all were delivered, he announced, "Children, you must go to bed soon. When you awake, you'll find gifts in your stockings. Merry Christmas to all, and to all a good night!" With that, he turned, climbed onto the sofa, and exited out the window. Kelly and Ralph looked at each other and then at Grandmama Tate, marveling that she had said nothing about Santa standing on her sofa. Each of them noticed that Santa had sounded a lot like Uncle Charles, who was mysteriously absent from the group.

Grandpapa Tate cleared his throat from the wing-backed chair in the corner, picked up his Bible, and began reading the age-old Christmas story: "And there were in the same country shepherds abiding in their fields, keeping watch over their flocks by night …"

"… And the shepherds returned, glorifying and praising God for all the things that they had heard and seen … "

Most of the children were now asleep.

◆   ◆   ◆   ◆   ◆

Christmas breakfast was a huge meal of Grandmama's Christmas pancakes, butter, and molasses. Only after long family prayers did

Grandpapa Tate give permission for the children to rush to the living room to check their Christmas stockings. The long socks were stuffed to the brim with apples, oranges, raisins, and nuts, topped off with peppermint candy canes. Below the stockings was a gift for each child, including a doll for Analda, a cap gun for Winslow, and matching Daisy air rifles for Kelly and Ralph. Cries of joy gave way to demands to be let outside to play with their toys. Winslow was allowed onto the porch to try out his cap gun, but Kelly and Ralph were put off.

"It's still cold out, and we need to teach you how to use them," Saylor said. "We'll do it after dinner. Enjoy your Christmas stockings until then."

After what seemed to the boys to be a week, Christmas dinner was finally ready, and the family gathered for another special meal, for which the children had little appetite. Roast chicken, vegetables, molded jello salads, and deviled eggs were enthusiastically savored by the adults, while the children pushed the food around on their plates, holding out for mince meat pies, cookies, and fruitcake. At last the meal was finished.

"Can we go out and shoot our guns now?" Kelly and Ralph begged, almost in unison.

"After a little nap," said Saylor, feeling stuffed and sleepy. It was a long, long nap.

◆　◆　◆　◆　◆

Finally, it was time. The boys picked up their guns and headed outside. Saylor and Uncle Charles found a piece of cardboard and fashioned a target, which they fastened to a pine tree in the backyard.

"You can't just start out shooting," said Saylor. "We have to show you how to do this. First, you have to understand the gun. It works by the force of a piston compressing the air in front of it to power a pellet."

Uncle Charles added to the explanation. "A powerful spring or charge of compressed gas drives the piston when the gun is fired," he said.

"Uh-huh," said Kelly.

"I see," added Ralph.

"You need to practice to train your muscles, improve your hand-eye coordination, and perfect your trigger squeeze," said Saylor, lifting a gun, aiming, and firing. "Perfect! A bull's-eye!! Here goes another."

"My turn, Saylor," said Uncle Charles, holding the other gun. "I can do as well. Ready, aim, fire! Aha! Told you!!"

And so it went. By the time Saylor and Charles seemed to be slowing down, Wilbur and Warren took their places. Kelly and Ralph sat glumly on the back steps, despairing of ever getting to shoot their guns. "It seems to me," observed Kelly, "that the grown-ups got themselves air rifles for Christmas."

"Yes, they did," said Ralph. "But just remember one thing," he added with a laugh.

"What's that?"

"They will all have to go back to work tomorrow."

♦　♦　♦　♦　♦

'Twas the evening of Christmas Day, and all through the house, no one was stirring, except for a mouse. Grandpapa and Grandmama Tate, Lellan, Analda, and even Winslow were snug in their beds, exhausted from the exciting day. Julia and Louise were at a party. Where the other adults were, no one seemed to know. Kelly and Ralph were down on their pallets beside the now darkened Christmas tree, trying to go to sleep, as they had been instructed.

Suddenly Kelly sat straight up, shook Ralph, and said, "Wake up! But be quiet about it. Follow me." Ralph followed. Two stealthy figures in red union suits crawled quietly out the living room door, into the hallway, and up the stairs.

"Where are we going?" asked Ralph.

"Shh! I'll show you."

At the top of the stairs, the pair saw a beam of light coming from beneath a bedroom door. Muffled voices could be heard from inside. "Who is in there?" asked Ralph.

"Shh! It's Mother and Daddy and Aunt Helen and Uncle Charles."

"What are they doing?"

"They're sinning!"

"Sinning?"

"Yes, sinning."

"What kind of sinning?"

"They're playing with cards — *gamblin'* cards. Grandpapa Tate says that's it's a sin to even *touch* a gamblin' card. I heard Mother tell Daddy so."

"Where'd they get 'em?"

"I saw 'em tucked inside Mother's Christmas present from Aunt Helen."

"What will happen if Grandpapa finds out?"

"I don't know, but I expect he can raise a pretty good ruckus when he's riled."

The boys lay quietly on the floor, still unable to understand the voices, until their mother raised hers.

"Saylor, this isn't working. You and Charles aren't playing fair. If this is to continue, we'll have to play couples." Grumbling and murmuring followed.

Kelly and Ralph were almost asleep on the floor when suddenly Uncle Charles yelled, "Confound it, Helen!"

Kelly's eyes widened and Ralph's jaw dropped.

"I'm through with this! I'm out of here!"

The door swung open, and light flooded the hallway. Charles strode through, not seeing the boys huddled against the darkened wall. Taking the steps two at a time, he strode purposefully down the stairs. The bedroom door remained slightly ajar. "Don't worry about him," Aunt Helen was saying. "He'll get over it. He always does."

"Well, it's probably time we should check on the children anyway," said Carrie.

Kelly and Ralph were instantly on their feet, taking the stairs so quickly they were hardly aware of them. In the nick of time, they plunged onto their pallets and began to feign sleep.

"They're sound asleep," they heard their mother say. "Worn out from all the excitement. It was a good Christmas, Saylor. I think the boys really like their air rifles."

"Um … yes, I think they do. Merry Christmas, Carrie."

CHAPTER 21

AUTOMOBILES

Papa Jumper broke down and bought himself a Tin Lizzie, a Ford Model T. "I looked around the community," he told Uncle Jerry Wise, "and saw that I'm about the only one left travelin' in a horse 'n buggy. So, I figured it was time."

"Well, it's your Model T, not mine," said Sallie, when he brought it home. "I don't set no store by newfangled gadgets. Like that washing machine Medora Tate has bought. Don't tell me that thing can wash clothes. I wouldn't want that plunder roun' me!"

Learning to drive the newfangled thing was no easy task, with its three pedals in the floor, and the accelerator on the steering wheel. But Papa practiced and finally was on the road, blissfully unaware of his own ignorance about the automobile. He knew only that you put gasoline in the tank, worked the pedals and accelerator, and went on your way.

On a weekend in late winter, Kelly and Ralph were with the family as they headed out to Oak Grove Church on ungraded clay ruts. About halfway there, the Ford quit running. Papa got out and looked around. He went under the hood, looking, then put the hood down. He stood there, perplexed.

"Papa," Dora said, "why don't you look under the hood again?"

"Well, Dora," he answered, "why don't you git out and look under the hood. Maybe you can see somethin' I can't."

"I told you we don't need this contraption," said Granmah Sallie. "Give me my horse 'n buggy. I know they'll git me where I'm going."

There they sat, until Uncle Jerry came up behind in his own Tin Lizzie.

"What seems to be the trouble, Uncle Frank?"

Papa scratched his head. "I don't rightly know," he said. "It just stopped running."

"Well, first thing you need to ask is, does it have gas?"

"I think so, but I'll check. He went to the gas tank, took the lid off, and looked inside.

"Yes, it has gas," he said.

"Well, here's the next thing," Uncle Jerry said, returning to his own car and coming back with a pair of pliers and a roll of haywire.

"This is all you need to git 'er going again!" he declared.

A bit late, the Franklin Jumper family pulled into the yard of Oak Grove Methodist Church in their brand-new automobile.

◆   ◆   ◆   ◆   ◆

A warm spring Saturday afternoon was the perfect time for Saylor to gather his boys in the back lot for some ball tossing and lessons. Kelly, Ralph, and even Winslow were getting big enough to begin learning the basics of the game, and Saylor was more than ready to teach them. He was excited about the brand-new New York Yankee Stadium. *Who knows,* he thought, *whether one of my sons might one day take up where I left off.*

For Carrie, with the boys out back and the girls still napping, it was the perfect time for a little peace and quiet on the front porch. Hopefully, the worst of the pollen season was over. She and Lucy had given the porch its spring cleaning this morning, and the rocking chairs were all wiped down. It was now officially porch season, and Agnes Prickett would probably pop over before too long. Carrie took a deep breath and closed her eyes. *Sometimes,* she thought, *it's good to just sit and let a little time pass …*

Cousin Pierce had been looking for a chance to talk privately with Carrie. Even though he had been living with the family for the past six months, his own apartment having become unavailable, he rarely had time alone with her. This was his opportunity, and he joined her on the porch.

"Excuse me, Carrie," he said, sitting in the rocker nearest her. "I hope

I'm not disturbing your quiet."

"Of course not, Pierce. I'm happy to have you join me."

"The boys are having a big time," he said. "And Bub seems relaxed. I take it he's enjoying his new job at the bank."

"He is. He likes being assistant cashier and having more contact with people. He is enrolling in another extension course in order to upgrade his skills in case of another opportunity or promotion. I don't think it's likely he'll try to go back to farming, in light of the last experience."

"I'm sure Uncle Frank misses him."

"Yes, but Dad has always managed well, whether he has Saylor or not. He will continue to do so."

"I want to thank you again for putting up with me these months. I know it has crowded you to let me have a room, but it certainly has been helpful to me."

"It's been a pleasure having you here, Pierce. You're so neat and quiet, we've hardly known you were around."

"I beg your forgiveness for the times I've brought unannounced company for supper."

"You're forgiven. We've enjoyed getting to know Izzie. After you're married, you'll have a better understanding of such domestic issues. We'll miss you when you're gone. Have you set a date?"

Pierce cleared his throat. "That's something I've been wanting to talk about," he said, uncertainly. "The date, I mean. Actually, there may not be a date. Right now, I just don't know whether I'm going to marry Izzie."

"What on earth do you mean, Pierce? You and Izzie are so well suited."

"We seem to be suited in every way but one."

"What's that?"

"We can't agree on church. I'm a staunch Methodist. Izzie is a dyed-in-the-wool Baptist. She wants me to go to the Baptist church with her. I believe it is her place to go to the Methodist church with me. We can't solve it. I am absolutely not going to join any Baptist church, so I think we may just call the whole thing off!"

"Pierce," Carrie said, "it's silly, to have a falling out over something like that. There's nothing to solve. You just go to your church and Izzie can go to hers."

Pierce was silent, thinking. Finally, he spoke. "I hadn't thought of doing it that way. Hearing the way you put it, maybe that's what we'll do." And so they did. Pierce was a Methodist and Izzie was a Baptist for the many years of their marriage.

Once Pierce's primary problem had been resolved, he redirected the conversation. "I've been meaning to ask Bub if he's thinking of getting an automobile for the family. It's quite the thing, these days."

"We've talked of it, but made no decision. It would certainly facilitate getting back and forth to Sandy Run, as well as to Columbia. We'll see." She paused, laughed, and continued. "It may surprise you to know that I've been thinking I might like to learn to drive an automobile myself."

Pierce found the idea amusing. "I can just see you and Izzie cruising down Main Street in your Tin Lizzie," he said, slapping one of his short legs, pleased with his humor. "Izzie in her Tin Lizzie! Ha ha!"

"With Saylor and Pierce in the second seat," Carrie laughed.

"Ha!" Pierce declared. "That day will never come!"

Conversation was interrupted by the tin beeping of a horn as a car slowly pulled up to the front of the house. Saylor and the boys were already running to see what was going on. A brash young salesman hopped out of the red touring car.

"Hello there, Mr. Jumper," he said, extending his hand, which Saylor accepted. "This here two-cylinder Maxwell Touring car is just what's needed for your nice fam'ly. It'll get you out to your Ma's in short order, and to Columbia as well."

"I see you've done your homework, young man," Saylor observed.

"Yessir," the ambitious youth replied. "This here automobile is just the thing, an enormous success. Ever'body wants one. You cain't go wrong with this baby. It's got advanced twin-cylinder design with water cooling, mechanical inlet valves, two-speed planetary transmission, shaft drive ..."

"I see," said Saylor, shooing the boys away from their efforts to crawl all over the car.

"It's okay, they're curious. Let 'em look, Mr. Jumper. Picture your wonderful fam'ly aboard this beautiful vehicle. In fact, why don't you all climb in, and we'll take 'er for a spin."

Before he finished his spiel the children filled the car, and Saylor climbed into the front beside the salesman. Carrie and Pierce observed silently from the porch.

"Here's all you do … just crank 'er up."

Nothing happened. The motor did not turn over. All was silence and stillness. "Oops! Just a moment here," he said, trying again. Nothing. The salesman sat there, trying repeatedly to start the obstinate engine, perplexed, red-faced. "Never had this happen before," he said.

"Would you like to use my horse to pull 'er off?" asked Saylor.

♦ ♦ ♦ ♦ ♦

Buying an automobile was inevitable. Saylor finally decided on a brand new five-passenger Dort Sport Touring car, gray, known for its steel rimmed tires. With a sixth child on the way, Saylor realized what he really needed was a bus, but the Dort would have to do for now. The children were ecstatic about the four-door vehicle with its celluloid windows and snap-on curtains, but they were none too impressed with Saylor's driving. Somewhat accustomed to driving Papa Jumper's Model T with its three pedals in the floor, he had difficulty adjusting to the gearshift, which was not easy to change. Saylor was constantly scraping the gears, the windshield wiper was hand-operated, there was no heater, and the roads were corduroy rough. If a trip was made without having to stop to change a tire or having to find a mule to pull the vehicle out, it was a blessing.

A Saturday winter-time trip to Granmah's was an ordeal. An hour or so was required to make the thirteen-mile ride. Before it was time to leave to return home, bricks would be warmed in the fireplace and wrapped in rags to keep feet warm. The family would wrap themselves in blankets and lap robes and pile into the Dort, Carrie in back with the youngest children. Saylor and Papa Jumper would then stand and talk at the car for a half hour or more, while the children got colder and colder, and Carrie got mad. "You've had all day to talk, Saylor," she would say. "Let's go. It's cold!"

"Going right now," he would answer, and they would talk some more. Saylor could have his family home before midnight without a flat tire, and if they didn't get stuck. He learned to travel with tube patches, a hand pump, and a lug wrench, while Carrie kept at least one blanket in the car for the rest of her life. When a tire had to be changed, she would get out the blanket, find a place away from the car to spread it, gather the children onto the blanket, and rummage in her bag for treats or small toys that she kept stowed away for their enjoyment and entertainment.

Saylor and Pierce made a memorable weekend trip to the home place with just Ralph and Kelly along. As they arrived at Sandy Run, and Saylor pulled the car up to the porch, a man with a slight limp was going in the front door.

"Who is that?" asked Kelly.

"That's my brother, Carlisle Furtick," said Pierce. "I guess you haven't seen him in a while. Come to visit Uncle Frank and Aunt Sallie, I'm sure."

The men went into the house to socialize, but the boys held back, distracted by this and that. "Do you realize who that is?" asked Kelly, in a soft voice.

"Cousin Pierce said it was Carlisle Furtick."

"That's right," said Kelly. "Carlisle Furtick is the man with the wooden leg!"

"Wow! I've never seen a man with a wooden leg."

"Well, we're seein' 'im now."

"I sure would like to feel that leg,"

"Well, come on. Maybe we can."

The two curious boys went into the front room where the adults were gathered by a fire. They sat at first on the floor near their daddy, but gradually wriggled themselves across Granmah's beige and rose-colored Aubusson rug, closer to the man with the wooden leg. At last they were both able to crawl beneath his chair. "You feel it first," Ralph whispered to Kelly. Kelly reached out his hand, took hold of one leg, and squeezed.

"You boys have got the wrong leg," said Carlisle Furtick. "Get the other one. I won't feel that one."

In a flash, both boys backed out from under the chair and fled the room, their father behind them, roaring threats. They never did get to feel the wooden leg.

◆　◆　◆　◆　◆

That evening, on the way back to St. Matthews, the Dort had a flat tire.

"Get out, boys," Saylor said to Kelly and Ralph. "You might as well learn how to do this, since it's something you'll have to know how to do. Kelly, you get the jack. Ralph, you can hand me the patch kit."

Saylor took the jack from Kelly and positioned it underneath the rear axle of the car. He then lifted the car until the tire was two or three inches off the ground. "Now you have to loosen the lugs," he said, as Pierce handed him the lug wrench. "See, you place the wrench over the lugs and twist, like this, until they loosen and you can remove them. But don't lose them in the grass or the dirt. Here, Kelly, you see if you can take the tube out of the tire."

"Okay," Saylor said, as the lesson continued. "We have to search for the leak, find the place where the air is coming out." He held the tube up to his ear and turned it, listening and feeling for a spurt of air, looking closely at the tube. The leak was soon located.

"Now we have to patch the tube."

Ralph took a patch from the kit and handed it to his father. Saylor applied the patch. "Let's put the tube back into the tire, boys." Kelly and Ralph both helped with the procedure. "Good. Pierce, hand me the pump and let's fill 'er up."

"Let me do it, Daddy," Kelly said.

"Me, too," said Ralph.

"You can take turns pumping," he said.

The tube wouldn't hold the pressure, which meant the patch hadn't secured the leak. They took the tube out of the tire and tried again. Failure. After the third fruitless try, Pierce had had enough. "Drat it, Bub," he said.

"I'll just spit on it." He spat on the patch and stuck it back on the tube. They inserted the tube back into the tire and pumped it until it was fully pressurized. The patch held.

Saylor repositioned the tire and called for the lug wrench. "Let me do it," said Kelly.

"And me," echoed Ralph.

"You'd better let me finish this, boys. We want this tire to stay on the car!" With that, he tightened the lugs, let the jack down, stored the jack, wrench, pump, and patch kit, and proceeded to St. Matthews.

◆   ◆   ◆   ◆   ◆

Carrie hadn't given up on her wish to be able to drive a car. It would be convenient for running errands around town, and she wouldn't have to wait for Saylor to take her where she needed to go. Besides, no one seemed crazy about Saylor's driving. He continued to scrape the gears every time. However, her driving lessons weren't going well. They had been out several times, but Saylor wasn't the best teacher. He'd get mad and yell. She'd get nervous. Every lesson had ended in failure.

One beautiful afternoon they decided to give it one more try. They got out on the highway north of St. Matthews, where the traffic was light. Things were going fairly well this time. Saylor curbed his impatience. Carrie tried to keep herself calm. Suddenly, an old dog loped across in front of the car. Carrie threw up her hands in panic.

"My soul, Carrie," Saylor yelled as he grabbed the wheel. "That's the time you're supposed to hold the car. Don't turn it loose. You'll run into something!"

"I'm just going to quit," she said. "You don't know how to teach, and nobody else cares to teach me. I'm never going to drive again."

And she never did.

CHAPTER 22

SUGAR 'N SALT

"*My wild Irish Rose ...*"

Carrie heard the melody floating through the house and picked up on the lyrics: "*The sweetest flow'r that grows ...*"

Saylor was having his midday fest on the piano before returning to work for the afternoon. Sacrificing to buy the piano had blessed them, and now their home was regularly filled with his music. In the evenings, he sang and played hymns while Carrie was preparing the children for bed. Then he began reading them the stories of Daniel Boone. Carrie played, too, but she still didn't enjoy just sitting and playing, as Saylor did. Both hoped that their children would catch the music bug and begin to learn and enjoy making melody. She was already teaching Kelly and Ralph some of the fundamentals of music. Ralph, particularly, showed some interest in the piano. In the meantime, it was good for them to hear Saylor when he was immersed in the "velvet touch."

Carrie's mind went back to the time when Saylor's playing was confined to the piano in his parents' home. In those days, he complained about his style. "Your playing is soft and sweet," he had said to her. "In comparison, my music seems more mechanical. What can I do?"

"Well," she had answered, pondering. "You might try having the music come more from your heart than your hands. Let the *feelings* you're trying to convey flow through your fingers into the notes, and maybe you'll be happier." Saylor had taken her words to heart and worked at it when he could. At last they agreed that he had achieved what they came to call the "velvet touch." Sometimes Carrie would pull up a chair and sit beside Saylor as he played, singing along as she worked on tatting or other needlework.

Today, there was no time for sitting and singing. The baby was due soon, and Mama was here. It was August, and it was hot. Carrie needed to wash her long, long hair so that it would be clean for the big event. This afternoon, she would sit out in the sun to let it dry.

Saylor kissed Carrie goodbye and left for the bank, saying as he went down the back steps, "Mm … tonight's roast smells good already." The house was quiet. Lucy was cleaning the kitchen and starting supper. The boys were all next door playing with the Gressett children. Analda had reluctantly succumbed to a nap, and Mama was rocking Lellan on the porch.

With her hair squeaky clean, Carrie toweled it, wrapped the towel around her shoulders, brushed the still wet hair down her back, and went to join Mama.

"It looks like Lellan has given in to a nap, too," she observed.

"Your two girls are certainly different," commented Mama. "Analda is such a ball of fire that Lellan's calm personality is surprising."

"They are different, Mama. Look at your children. I'd say we're all different, too, wouldn't you?"

"Of course. God makes each one unique. And we'll soon see who our next little person is. How are you feeling?"

"Just fine. Relieved now that my hair is clean. I'll put a chair out in the sun so that it can … oh! OH!"

"What is it?"

"Oh, Mama, I think the baby is starting to come!"

"Are you sure?"

"I'm sure. Oh, Mama, my hair! What will I do? It's still wet!"

"Wrap it in the towel. I'll send for the doctor."

Mama Tate was on her feet, rushing into the house with the sleeping toddler still in her arms. Gently, she laid Lellan on the first bed she came to, and then ran for Lucy.

"Lucy! Stop what you're doing! Quick! Run downtown and get Dr.

Fairey! Then go to the bank and alert Mr. Jumper! Mrs. Jumper's baby is coming!"

Carolyn Elizabeth Jumper was born before Carrie's hair could dry. Wrapped in a towel in the August heat as she gave birth, her hair had soured, and there was nothing she could do about that. Her boys arrived home expecting supper and found, in addition, a new baby sister.

"That stork sure is sneaky," said Ralph. "I didn't see him — again."

◆　◆　◆　◆　◆

Grandmama Tate had taken the train back to Columbia on a Saturday afternoon, when Papa Jumper and Granmah Sallie pulled up in the Ford Model T, come to meet their newest granddaughter. With Minnie's two boys and three girls, this made a total of eleven grandchildren. Before they could get out of the car, the boys came running toward them, filled with excitement, but not about the new baby.

"Papa, Granmah," Winslow called out. "Kelly and Ralph took me to the 'skawkta'!"

"He means the chautauqua," corrected Kelly.

"Really?" Papa answered, getting out of the car and swinging Winslow into the air. "Oh my, you're getting too big for this. What did you see at the chautauqua?"

"A big tent with a magician, a clown, and animals."

"Winslow was afraid of the clowns," said Ralph.

"Was not!" Winslow protested.

"Was too! He's so funny!"

"Don't pick on the boy, Ralph," said Papa.

Granmah Sallie had gotten out of the car and come around to hug Saylor's boys. "What did the magicians do?" she asked.

"They pulled all kinds of things, like rabbits, out of a stovepipe hat. Cats, dogs, puppies, and everything!"

"We don't know how they got 'em all stuffed down in that hat," offered Kelly. "But they would git 'em out. And I got a prize!"

"What was the prize for?" asked Granmah.

"It was for saying a rhyme after the clown," said Kelly:

Sticky sticky stambo
sticky sticky stambo
arry barry besky
   eepengnon.

"I got a prize for repeating the rhyme three times."

"Aren't you the smart one," said Granmah. "Now, where is your new baby sister, Carolyn?"

Saylor and Carrie, with the babe in her arms, were coming out the front door as they spoke. "Here's our new baby," said Granmah, going onto the porch and sitting down in a rocking chair. Carrie dutifully placed Carolyn in her waiting arms. "How sweet she is," said Granmah. "Look at that fine blond hair. It's just like Claudine's."

"Congratulations, Bub!" said Papa, placing his arm around Saylor's shoulders. "Three boys and three girls! Now that's just a perfect family!"

"Perfect," said Saylor. "Complete!"

The adults settled themselves on the porch as the children went about their various interests. Papa picked up on the conversation. "Now that you have your sixth," he observed, "you've by-passed Minnie."

That was the opening Sallie had wanted. "I'm just so upset about Minnie I don't know what to do," she began, fretfully. The others braced themselves. They had heard this before. "I don't know what's to become of her and the children. That Clarence Rucker is a worthless rascal, and that's all there is to it!"

"Now, Sallie," Papa tried to interrupt, but she was on a roll.

"We saw in the beginning there wasn't no good to him, but Minnie was so blind. His father left him three fine farms, and now he's about to lose the last one. I just don't know what will happen. I try to take them some food along to help out, but it pains me to no end that Clarence gits to eat my good cookin', too!"

"Sallie," Papa tried again. "You can't solve Minnie's problems. You need to step back and let her handle them."

"How can she handle anything when he keeps her barefoot and with child, as they say, while he's out drinkin' and wastin' money?"

"You have to leave it to God, Sallie. He understands the situation far better than we do."

"If He understands it, why is He so slow about doin' somethin'?" she asked.

◆   ◆   ◆   ◆   ◆

On Sunday morning, Saylor got the younger children a breakfast of biscuits and eggs and turned them out to play on the front porch. Kelly and Ralph had gone home with Papa and Granmah. "I won't try to get them to Sunday School," he said to Carrie, "even though I'm the superintendent. In fact, I guess I won't make it myself today," he added.

"You really should go to church," Carrie said. "They need you in the choir. Agnes said yesterday that we were welcome to send Winslow and Analda over to her this morning. That will leave only Lellan and baby Carolyn. I'll keep both here in the bedroom, and all will be well."

"If you're sure," he said.

"I'm sure."

Before Saylor left for the church, just blocks away, he instructed Winslow and Analda. "Go out the back door and over to Mrs. Prickett's to play. Be sure to obey her, and use your manners," he said, going out the front.

Winslow and Analda went out the back door. On the back porch was a table that was a catch-all place for household supplies. As they passed by, Analda noticed two big sacks that had recently been placed on the table. "What's in those big bags?" she asked, always curious.

"One has salt in it, and the other has sugar," Winslow said. He pointed to a number on the bottom of each bag. "I know my numbers," he said. "That's a ten."

"Let's open them," suggested Analda.

◆   ◆   ◆   ◆   ◆

Carrie could hear Saylor roaring before he set foot in the house. She was in the kitchen, trying to clean the white granular stuff off of Analda and Winslow, shaking it out of their clothes, trying to keep them from tracking it any further. "You two go to the front porch and play with Lellan," she said. "And try to stay out of trouble." Cautiously, she stepped out onto the back porch, observing that Saylor's face was drained of its color.

"They had a big time," she said. It was not the right thing to say.

"A mighty expensive time," bellowed Saylor, his color going from white to red. "Don't they know how much sugar and salt cost? What are we going to do with this mess?"

"It is a mess," she agreed. Her big wooden biscuit bowl lay in the center of the table, filled to overflowing with the white particles, which were scattered like sand over the remainder of the table and the floor, and tracked through the back door. Two wooden spoons remained atop the mixture, and two empty cloth bags lay under the table.

"First," Carrie began, "let's sweep up what's on the floor. Then we'll scoop the remainder back into the bags. Maybe we'll find some use for it."

They never did.

◆   ◆   ◆   ◆   ◆

The still-green grass sparkled as the sun bounced off the early morning dew. It was the beginning of a fresh, glowing September day. But Ralph was in a foul humor as he got ready for school. He didn't like school to begin with, and today he was angry about having to go. Once again, Kelly had failed to show up on Monday morning after his weekend at the farm. That meant that Kelly didn't have to go to school. It wasn't fair. This had happened before. Ralph usually compensated himself for the injustice by taking his own day off. His perch below the bridge was always beckoning, and when Kelly was absent, he would give himself a day of train-watching. He'd found it wasn't hard to alter his attendance record when reports came to his parents. But today there was a complication. Winslow. Winslow had started to school this year, and it was Ralph's job to accompany him. How could he play hooky with Winslow along? His brain was buzzing with solutions.

By the time they set out for school, Ralph was putting a plan into play. "Kelly doesn't have to go to school today," he complained to Winslow. "It's not fair."

"It's not fair!" echoed Winslow.

"I don't want to go to school," Ralph continued. "Do you want to go?"

"I don't want to go," answered Winslow.

"Well, then. If you don't want to go, we won't go."

"Okay. But where will we go?"

"Under the bridge over the railroad. Remember, you aren't afraid of trains anymore. You love trains now."

"I do love trains," Winslow said.

As the pair approached what was to be their hideout for the day, they saw Mr. Wallace Jones, the chief of police, entering the clay path from his own street, on his way to work. Ralph was afraid of Wallace Jones. He had it in for boys — especially for Kelly and Ralph Jumper. They had sicced their dog, Jack, on little Sally Jones, sending her running and screaming in terror toward home. Chief Jones had talked to Saylor about his boys. Saylor had warned them. "You'd better watch yourselves," he had said. "If Chief Jones gets the least little chance, he's going to lock you up in the jail." Ralph grabbed Winslow's arm. "Keep on walking," he said. "We'll turn back after Mr. Jones is out of sight." They slowed their pace, continuing past the bridge. When it was safe, Ralph said, "Okay, we can turn around now."

Ralph and Winslow settled themselves into their safe little nook. No one could see them under the bridge, but they had a view of much of the town. "This is nice," said Ralph.

"This *is* nice," said Winslow, settling comfortably against the bank, sheltered from the sun and from prying eyes.

It was nice, that is, until the first train came roaring in, belching smoke and puffing steam. Winslow forgot that he loved trains and began to bellow.

As the smothering, steaming smoke settled under the bridge and around their heads, they held their hands over their eyes and mouth, coughing. Winslow wanted out. "Take me home!" he yelled.

"We can't go home," coughed Ralph.

"Then take me to school!"

"Can't *(cough)* go to school!"

"Take me to the *(cough)* bank!"

"Can't go to the bank." In desperation, Ralph had an idea. "Follow me," he said. They crawled out from under the bridge, up the bank, and slipped across the road. Making themselves as small as possible, crouching when there was grass tall enough to hide two boys, they finally came, unseen, to what they called the back lot — the field behind their daddy's garden, grown up waist high in brown sage. There they lay, catching their breath. Winslow was now satisfied. He calmed down. But then he wanted to play.

"Be still, and be quiet," Ralph ordered.

"Okay." Winslow could be quiet, but he couldn't be still, holding his hand in the air and waving it about."

"Put your hands down and be quiet," said Ralph, wasting his breath. What he feared came to pass. Lucy saw from the kitchen window. Lucy told. They heard their mother's voice calling them to the house. Ralph caught the fussing from Carrie. When Saylor came home, he got the razor strop. Ralph was cured of playing hooky, at least for now.

CHAPTER 23

STORM CLOUDS

Carrie sat at her sewing machine, pedaling rhythmically. This was where she did some of her best thinking. She had just come from a meeting of the Missionary Society of her church. The meeting was still on her mind. Meetings and committees appealed to something in Carrie's nature. There was satisfaction in a community of people coming together to share ideas and work toward a common goal. In this case, that goal was to support the spreading of the Gospel of Jesus Christ. Carrie had never forgotten the strong calling she had felt as a young woman to be a minister of the Gospel. The fulfillment of that calling had been denied her, not by Christ himself, but by the time and society in which he had placed her.

Yet she had never lost that sense of a call on her life. To minister and serve in one's own family and circumstances was the task of every believer. She was doing this, she thought. Still, she sensed that there was something out there, an assignment that God had for her, that she had not yet fulfilled. Could it be something that she could do through the vehicle of this family that she and Saylor were raising? *Father, give me a mission. One that will challenge me, to which I can give my all, and which I will recognize when it comes. Amen.*

"Mother, the ice man is here!" Analda was always excited to see the ice man come around, which he did every day. "May I go outside and pet his horse and get a chunk of ice to chew?"

"Yes. Tell him I'll take the usual twenty-five pounds."

The ice man came in a horse-drawn covered wagon carrying ice in two hundred pound blocks. He gave Analda a chunk while she petted his horse. He cut off the block the family wanted, lifted it with his giant tongs, and brought it right into the hall, where he placed it in the ice box refrigerator. A box on top held the ice, and underneath a compartment kept things cold. A hole in the floor below served as a drain for the water as it melted.

"Hello, Miss Tate," he called out to Carrie.

"Hello, Hammie. I hope you're doing well. It's good to see you."

"Fine, thank you, ma'am. I'll see you tomorrow."

"Mother, why does the ice man call you 'Miss Tate'?"

"Because I used to teach him before I was married."

"Doesn't he know that you got married?"

"With all these children around, I certainly hope so."

"Mother, when can we make some ice cream again?"

"I don't know. Ice cream is a very special treat that we haven't had in a while. We'll talk to Daddy about it."

"Here comes Daddy home right now ... Daddy, Daddy, can we make ice cream?" She held out her arms, expecting her daddy to catch her up, as usual.

"We'll talk about it," he said. "Where are your brothers?"

"Outside."

"Run and play with them. I need to talk with Mother," he said. Carrie knew something was wrong.

"What is it, Saylor?"

"I got a phone call at the bank." He paused. "Ma's fears for Minnie have been realized. She has had a breakdown and has been taken to the State Hospital in Columbia."

"Oh, no! Where are the children?"

"Bubba and Mac are with Clarence. They're old enough to fend for themselves. Ma has the three girls." He hesitated again. "Carrie, you know Ma can't take care of them. She and Papa have their hands full with Claudine and Dora."

"That's true." She paused, but only for a moment. "Do what you have to do, Saylor. Go and get them. I'll get things ready here."

♦   ♦   ♦   ♦   ♦

Ralph's yell was a piercing scream that cut through the Sunday morning calm. "They've got my paper! They've got my paper! It's *my* job to bring in the Sunday paper! I want to read Slim Jim! They won't let me have it!"

"What's all the fuss about?" Saylor asked, looking up from the game of checkers he was playing with himself.

"Those Rucker girls have the paper! They won't let me see Slim Jim!"

"Okay, Ralph. Calm down. I'll see what I can do."

Saylor tapped on the girls' door and stepped into the room, where all three were spread out with the Sunday funnies. "Myrtle," he said, "It's Ralph's job to bring the papers off the porch. So, let's give him the funnies for now, and you can see them when he's finished. This is a big family, and we have to share." The girls handed over the papers — but as soon as the door was closed, their wails and protests could be heard.

"I'll take it from here," Carrie said to Saylor, entering the room. Myrtle was angry. "Uncle Saylor hurt my feelings," she said. "Why does Ralph get the paper first?"

"Saylor didn't mean to hurt your feelings, Myrtle. Bringing in the papers is a big thing to Ralph, especially on Sundays. Let's not take that away from him. It won't take him long to read Slim Jim and one or two others to Winslow and Analda. It's their Sunday morning ritual. It's okay. You didn't know that, Myrtle. Please help Jewell and Dorothy to get ready for Sunday School. By then, you'll have the paper all to yourselves, with plenty of time to read it."

Myrtle had burst into tears. Carrie wrapped her arms around the shaking girl. "I don't know what's going to happen," she cried. "What's going to happen to Mama? What's going to happen to us?"

"Everything will be all right, Myrtle. Your mama is getting the rest and help she needs. She'll get better. Before you know it, you'll be going back home."

"We don't want to go back home to our daddy. He's mean."

"Your daddy is trying hard to turn over a new leaf, Myrtle. He wants all of his girls back home. And when you do go back, you'll have two families — yours and ours. For now, you're part of our family, and after this, you always will be. Dry your tears and make your mama proud of how you're taking care of your sisters. All will be well. And remember, we're going to make a churn of ice cream this afternoon."

"What flavor? What flavor?" asked little Dorothy, jumping up and down.

"Strawberry, silly," said Jewell. "Don't you remember that we picked them yesterday?"

"I helped pick," said Dorothy.

"Yes, but you ate more than you picked."

♦   ♦   ♦   ♦   ♦

The whole family was excited about making ice cream. Kelly, at the farm, was missing out. Ralph and Winslow didn't complain about having to watch Lellan and Carolyn on the porch. Saylor sat down with his checkers, while Carrie supervised a crowd in the kitchen.

Myrtle broke the yellow-yolked eggs into an earthen crock, whipping them into a froth with a metal whisk. Jewell stirred together sugar, milk, and cream, adding just a pinch of salt. In a third bowl, Analda and Dorothy crushed the bright red-ripe berries, already washed, sliced, and sugared. "No tasting," advised Carrie. When the custard ingredients were combined, Myrtle ladled the mouth-watering concoction into the long, narrow container that would fit into the churn.

"Is this enough custard?" she asked. "It's not full."

"It's full enough," Carrie replied. "As the custard freezes, it expands," she explained. "Too much custard will cause an overflow, which we don't want." She then inserted a wooden dasher, centered it, and added a tight-fitting lid. "All ready."

Saylor put away his checkers. It was time to take over. He placed the cylinder of custard into the wooden churn, situated the churning mechanism over it, and tightened. He took a block of ice from the box in the hall, placed it in a dishpan on the back porch. He set the churn into another dishpan. Ralph and Winslow cracked the ice with a hammer as Saylor chipped it off with a pick. They quickly placed the cold chunks around the cylinder in the churn, forming a layer. Next, coarsely granulated rock salt was added to slow the melting of the ice.

"Not too much salt," Saylor cautioned. "Too much will make the ice cream freeze too hard. But not too little, either, or the ice will melt too quickly."

"Then how much?" asked Ralph.

"You just have to guess," admitted Saylor. "But if it melts too quickly, you can always add more salt, so err on the side of too little." Winslow began turning the crank as the ice and salt layers were built up. "You turn it faster in the beginning, so that more of the cream can come into contact with the ice, then slower as it churns, so that it can begin to harden. As the ice melts, it creates a slurry of salty water for even cooling. Do you see the weep hole near the top of the churn? That's to let the water out as it melts, so that you can add more ice and salt if needed. Let Ralph have a turn, so that your arm can rest."

"How long will it take?" asked Ralph.

"Oh, probably twenty to thirty minutes. We'll know it's getting ready when it becomes harder to turn the crank."

◆　◆　◆　◆　◆

"It's ready. Perfect!" called Saylor, lifting off the lid. "Gather around. Bring on the bowls!"

An assortment of bowls, cups, and spoons had been made ready. "Put some in this little cup for Lellan first. Analda, you help Lellan. You'll have yours soon," Carrie said, as she lifted tow-headed Carolyn into the highchair. "Myrtle, will you give Carolyn her first taste of ice cream?"

Carolyn shuddered at the unexpected cold touch of the wondrous, sweet fluff before the taste registered. Then she grinned and smacked her lips for more. "Look," Myrtle said, "she likes it!"

"Who wouldn't," said Winslow, taking his bowlful to the porch steps.

"Where's mine? I want mine!" Dorothy was jumping up and down.

"Give it to the younger ones first, Saylor. The older ones know how to wait."

"No, we don't!" protested Ralph. "I'm starving!"

"I don't think you will," said Saylor, filling a bowl for Analda. "Don't worry. There's plenty for all."

"Can I lick the dasher?" asked Ralph.

"Yes, but I won't pull it out until everyone has been served," Saylor said, handing Ralph his portion. "Eat your bowlful first. Mother, are you ready for yours?"

"Yes, but Myrtle still doesn't have hers. She's been feeding Carolyn."

"Ice cream coming up for Myrtle," said Saylor, digging into the churn again.

"Get some for yourself, Saylor," Carrie said as he handed her a bowlful. "Then we'll pack some ice around and let it rest a while."

"What about my dasher?" yelled Ralph.

"Get me a pan, and I'll pull it out now," said Saylor, tugging at the dasher. "I'll have to scrape some off. You don't need this much ice cream."

"Yes, I do," said Ralph.

"Please don't pack it up," said Winslow. "I want some more."

"Me too! This ice cream is good!" said Jewell.

"And me!" shouted Dorothy. "It feels good in my tummy."

Saylor and Carrie looked at each other. She nodded.

"Anybody for seconds?" asked Saylor, digging down again.

♦ ♦ ♦ ♦ ♦

Weeks merged into months, and more months, as the Jumper children and the Rucker girls tried to blend themselves into an extended family. The process was like Saylor's driving. Forward progress, some backward, with frequent scraping of the gears. Gradually, each child found a place within the larger group. Then, suddenly, it was over. Minnie was pronounced well,

Clarence was sober, and their girls were going home.

The day when Saylor loaded them and their belongings into the Dort to return them to Sandy Run was bittersweet. The family gathered around the vehicle to say their goodbyes. Carrie hugged each girl, whispering words of love and encouragement. Then she said aloud to the group, "Remember what I told you in the beginning. You're going back home, but now you have two families — yours and ours. We've grown to love you dearly. If you need us, we'll be right here," she added with assurance. As she turned to go back into the house, she wondered how she and Saylor would adjust to having only six children. She needn't have worried. Several months later, they realized that Carrie was carrying their seventh child.

"I thought we had a good number," said Saylor. "But if we're going to start over, this one will be a boy."

♦　♦　♦　♦　♦

Analda had started school, and Winslow had inherited Ralph's job of accompanying her. Kelly and Ralph were now free to walk together without the younger ones tagging along.

"I don't know whether you've figured it out or not," Kelly said one sunny morning in May 1925. "There's going to be another baby in the family."

"I've suspected it," said Ralph. "Grandmama Tate is here. When she comes without Grandpapa, there's always a new baby before she leaves." "And when Dr. Fairey comes, then it won't be long," said Kelly.

"So much for the stork," said Ralph.

"It's not a good time for another baby," Kelly observed, "with Daddy out of work."

"He's not out of work," objected Ralph. "He's just gone back to farming with Papa Jumper. I never did quite understand what happened to his job at the bank."

"Two banks combined," explained Kelly. "There weren't enough jobs for everyone, so Daddy lost out."

"I know it's not a good time for farming, either," said Ralph. "We're in a year of drought, and Daddy and Papa are worried about the crops. Daddy just doesn't seem to have good luck with farming. It was the boll weevil last time, and now this. I heard him telling Mother that this is the second time in their marriage that he's had to borrow money to feed his children. And both times, he was farming."

"I don't think we need to worry. Mother and Daddy have always found a way, and I believe they always will. Especially when it comes to food," he added. "The way Mother cans everything, I can't imagine there would ever be too little food at our house."

"No matter how hot it is, she gits in that kitchen when the garden's coming in," said Ralph. "When she gits barefoot and ties that apron tight around her middle, she can really put 'er out!"

◆   ◆   ◆   ◆   ◆

On the afternoon of May 30, Granmah Sallie and a midwife presided over the birth of Benjamin Rucker at Sandy Run. In St. Matthews, Grandmama Tate and Dr. Fairey assisted Carrie with the arrival of Frank Tate Jumper. No one took the time to note the exact times of the births, so the two cousins always argued over who was the oldest.

"This is the first time I've had to pay the doctor with borrowed money," Saylor said when it was all over. "We'd be in trouble without the kindness of Mr. Prickett."

"It'll be all right, Saylor. You'll soon pay it back."

"If it takes my whole life."

"It won't," she said, smiling. "God always provides."

CHAPTER 24

WHERE IS MILEY?

"Miley? Where on earth is Miley?" Carrie asked, hearing the word for the first time.

"It's a lumber mill town in Hampton County, about twenty-five miles south of Bamberg and ten miles north of Hampton."

"What's the job?" she asked.

"Head bookkeeper of the Lightsey Brothers Lumber Mill."

"So, Miley is a lumber mill town," she said, testing the words on her tongue. "How did you learn of it?"

"Robert Cain, Uncle Jerry's son-in-law, travels for Butler Brothers Dry Goods. He called in Miley and heard about the job. He remembered that I am looking for something and got the contact information. Quite nice of him."

"Yes, it was, but that's a long way from here. You've never really lived anywhere else, Saylor."

"We have no income, Carrie. We are a big family. Something's got to open up."

"Are you going to look into it?"

"I plan to call the phone number tomorrow morning."

♦　♦　♦　♦　♦

At her sewing machine, Carrie found it hard to concentrate on her work — underwear for Saylor and the boys. Miles away, in the little town they called Miley, South Carolina, Saylor and Pierce should soon arrive. After spending the night in the local hotel, Saylor would have an interview with Mr. Fred Lightsey, one of the owners of the mill, tomorrow morning. Carrie was not in favor of this trip, which seemed a waste. What were the chances they would actually move their large family so far? What did they know about this place? Saylor had promised to give a full report, sparing no detail. Carrie would have gone to see for herself, if it weren't just too complicated. Why waste her time, too? She gave up on sewing, sat back, and closed her eyes.

◆   ◆   ◆   ◆   ◆

Saylor and Pierce, in the Dort, were below Ehrhardt, the last village before Miley. An interesting play of light and shadow splashed through the swampy landscape, bouncing off low shrubs in the woods. Spanish moss hung from trees, lending an air of mystery. The roads were dismal, with twelve-inch boards laid in ruts to get automobiles through the Salkehatchie River area, and low, rickety wooden bridges. Periodically, mounds were built up in case of an oncoming car.

"My soul, Bub!" Pierce exclaimed, his heart in his throat. "This is the jumping-off place, for sure."

"Well, with a name like Jumper, maybe this is where I should be," Saylor answered, trying to lighten things up.

"Can you imagine yourself living in this eerie area?"

"No, I can't. But what I can imagine is … being able to feed my family."

"I suppose I should be thankful it's just Izzie and me, two cats, and our camellias," Pierce said.

◆   ◆   ◆   ◆   ◆

Carrie nodded off. Suddenly, she was in the Dort with Saylor, with the Miley crossroads just ahead. There was a store on the right, and on the left, a sign beside a dirt road that said "Miley, 1 Mile." After the turn, there was a little house with moss-draped trees. The road continued straight for a bit, inclined slightly, then curved a little. Carrie noticed a large, unpainted house with a kitchen off the back and a screened-in front porch — a nice home place. There followed a row of shanties, then an open field. More moss-draped trees hugged the road before another slight curve and a straight stretch into Miley. Two good houses appeared on the right, followed by a row of front porch dwellings on the left, all built alike. The mill loomed large on the right. Across from it, a side road turned left, serving more houses. As the hotel appeared, Carrie awoke. She got up, found pencil and paper, and began to draw.

♦   ♦   ♦   ♦   ♦

The Dort pulled up in front of the modern, two-story clapboard Miley Hotel. Guests were enjoying some late afternoon rocking on the long downstairs porch. "Well, here we are," Saylor said to Pierce. "We'll see what happens now."

♦   ♦   ♦   ♦   ♦

"Carrie, it's a better job than most have right now," Saylor said, reporting in to his all-ears wife. "Starting pay is $125 a month, with annual raises."

"Can you do the job?"

"It's a big business with the mill cutting 100,000 feet of lumber a day. There's also a planing mill for molding and flooring. The operation is served by the Hampton-Branchville Railroad, which is owned by the mill. There are well over 200 employees. I couldn't have handled it without this last two-year extension course. It may be providential that I decided to upgrade my skills."

"Do you think it's providential that we should go to Miley?"

"I can only say that I really didn't like the place. But I think, too, that it would be temporary. Surely something else will open up closer to home."

"Tell me more about the town and the people. Don't leave anything out."

"It's a busy, bustling, even noisy town. There are more than 100 houses, the hotel, two stores, the doctor's office, the mill office. It would be a big adjustment for us, Carrie. Here in St. Matthews, the population is fairly homogeneous, since most people have lived here for generations. But in Miley, I get the idea that there are few natives and that almost everyone has come from somewhere else for jobs. They are rough, working-class people, except for some teachers who live in the hotel. There were also more educated people in the office."

"Mr. Lightsey?"

"I am favorably impressed. I also met his older brother, Henry. Decent, Christian people, it seemed to me."

"Did they offer you the job?"

"They did."

"When do you have to answer?"

"Soon. They really need to fill the position." Saylor declined to mention the comment of a lumber buyer in the hotel that the last accountant had thrown the office keys in the road and walked away. No need to worry his wife with what was probably idle gossip.

"Where would we live?"

"They showed me a sturdy house, a bit bigger and different from the mill row houses. It's across from the mill, but facing the side road, with a vacant lot between the house and the main road. I understand it was built for Dr. Sample, who has now moved to Hampton. His afternoon office is just across the road. The house would be available for us to rent. The mill supplies water and electricity. There is a room off the back porch for a bathroom, but no fixtures in it yet. I could buy the fixtures, or pay two dollars extra rent."

Carrie laughed. "You'd better choose the extra rent, since it would be temporary. The only thing that appeals to me is the water and electricity, but I would never decide to move for either. We've got to think about whether this — a lumber mill town — is the place for us, or our children."

"We could stand anything for a short while, Carrie. I've got to have a job. Now."

"I think you have decided, Saylor. All I can say is that I'll pray about it."

"As will I," he said.

She handed him the paper with the drawing from her dream. "Is Miley anything like this?" she asked.

He took the paper, looked at it, and caught his breath. "Very close," he said.

Later, in bed, he added, "One more thing I forgot to mention."

She braced herself. "What's that?"

"The dirt. Miley dirt is black. Someone said it's from the soot in the mill. But it is said to grow good watermelons."

"Oh, no! My girls' white dresses! Carolyn, with her light hair, looks especially beautiful in white."

"Best not to wear whites in Miley," he mumbled sleepily. "Save 'em for when we come back."

♦ ♦ ♦ ♦ ♦

On Sunday morning, amidst the bustle of getting everyone ready for church, Saylor took a moment to pull Carrie aside. "I've got to give an answer to Mr. Lightsey tomorrow, Carrie. I strongly feel I should take this job. Just for now. I don't want to feel as though I'm dragging you along. We need to go forward together."

"I agree with you about that, Saylor. Still, I dreamed about it again last night and can't escape the feeling that Miley just isn't the place for us, or our children. However, I am still praying about it."

"As I am," he said.

♦ ♦ ♦ ♦ ♦

The morning worship service at St. Paul Methodist Church was underway. Carrie filed into the choir loft with the other women on the front row, the men, including Saylor, behind. She immediately glanced up into the balcony to see that their children were present and seated, the older ones taking responsibility for the younger. She and Saylor could see everything they did from this vantage point.

Carrie had come to love this sanctuary, elegant in its simplicity, the catty-cornered nave, with its dark-stained wood, fanning out from the pulpit in the center. It felt like home. *Where would we worship in Miley?* she wondered. Saylor had asked about churches and learned that there was a Methodist church in Hampton, ten miles away. A Baptist church was planned for Miley but was stalled for lack of funds. *Maybe we would have church at home,* she decided.

The pianist was giving an introduction to the first song, "He Leadeth Me, O Blessed Tho't!" The congregation and choir raised their voices in one of William Bradbury's beloved hymns:

He leadeth me! O blessed tho't!
O words with heav'nly comfort fraught!
Whate'er I do, where'er I be,
Still 'tis His hand that leadeth me!

He leadeth me, He leadeth me,
By His own hand He leadeth me:
His faithful foll'wer I would be,
For by His hand He leadeth me.

Sometimes 'mid scenes of deepest gloom,
Sometimes where Eden's bowers bloom,
By waters still, o'er troubled sea,
Still 'til His hand that leadeth me!

Lord, I would clasp Thy hand in mine,
Nor ever murmur nor repine,
Content, whatever lot I see,
Since 'til Thy hand that leadeth me!

And when my task on earth is done,
When, by Thy grace, the vict'ry's won,
E'en death's cold wave I will not flee,
Since God thro' Jordan leadeth me!

Carrie felt Saylor's eyes on her throughout the hymn. Its message was sinking deep into her heart and mind. He surely knew that.

Pastor Robinson began his sermon. "My text for today," he said, "is just one verse — Luke 9:32: 'And he said to them all, if any man will come after me, let him deny himself, and take up his cross daily, and follow me.' " Every word of the message pierced Carrie's turbulent heart. She had walked with her Lord long enough to recognize His voice. She heard, and she was flooded with a sense of peace.

♦   ♦   ♦   ♦   ♦

Saylor couldn't wait to get to Carrie after the service. He looked at her questioningly. She laughed. "When did you write the pastor's sermon?" she asked. Then she took a deep breath. "Miley, here we come," she said.

Map of Miley

CHAPTER 25

MOVING TO MILEY

The family piled haphazardly into the Dort just before Saylor pulled out of Pierce and Izzie's driveway, headed for home. Tomorrow was moving day. "It was gracious of Izzie to have this big gang for a farewell dinner," he said.

From the backseat, with squirming, nap-fighting, six-month-old Frank in her lap, Carrie replied, "Indeed. A challenge it was, too, with Izzie not being accustomed to cooking for a crowd. She certainly rose to the occasion with her nice tablecloth and beautiful tea rose china." She paused, then continued. "I just wish the boys hadn't humiliated me by asking her if she had any 'lasses. Especially after that wonderful dessert."

"Their poor manners are probably our own fault," Saylor observed. "We've fallen into the bad habit of letting them end their meals by sopping syrup or molasses with biscuits. Now they're just not satisfied without them."

"With lots of butter!" chirped Winslow.

"My parents would have been horrified," Carrie said.

"Well, they're not here," said Saylor. "And you've always said you didn't want to be as strict."

"No, I don't," she answered. "But I *do* want to instill good manners. I want them to at least *know* how to do. It's why I like to have a more formal Sunday dinner when I can. From what you've told me about how things are in Miley, it's going to be important."

They dropped the subject, and Carrie's thoughts returned to the monumental chore ahead. Despite all her childhood experiences with moving, she was running behind. She was not ready for tomorrow. With Saylor working in Miley and living at the hotel for months, the challenge of packing up had been hers. She hadn't minded, but she was tired. With all the good-byes, she had been delayed. Saylor had returned just before Christmas, in time for an abbreviated holiday visit with the Tates in Columbia. Both sets of grandparents were saddened by the move. The Tates were disappointed, but quietly supportive, while Granmah Sallie had pitched her usual fit.

"There just ain't no sense in none of it, Bub," she had whined. "How can you go way down there and leave us like this? Look at your papa. I'm telling you he's not well. He mopes around the house instead of tending to the farm. How do you think I can do all of this by myself?"

"Now, Sallie," Papa Jumper began. "There's nothing wrong with me. It's just this cold winter hurts my bones. I'll be good as new come springtime."

"You don't have bones in your stomach," she retorted. "You have a stomachache all the time, and won't go see Dr. Fairey. It cain't be my cookin'. It never hurt you before."

"Your cookin' is fine, Sallie. I'm just a little off my feed, as they say. I'll be all right. And Berlie's new husband, Luther, is good about helpin' when I need a hand. Bub and Carrie'll be back up here in the midlands before you can snap your fingers. You don't need to be upset."

"All right, I won't be upset. But only if Kelly stays right here where he belongs, and where he is needed."

Saylor stood his mother down. "Ma, Kelly is *our* son. He belongs with *us*. He's going with us."

She held her peace. For once. For now.

Saylor interrupted Carrie's thoughts. "There's a car moving up close behind," he said, slowing. "Well, I do believe it's Pierce. Did anyone leave anything?"

"Do you all have your coats and shoes?" Carrie asked, looking around. "Hats?"

Saylor eased the automobile to the side of the road. Pierce pulled his

Model T next to the family. "Y'all missing anything?" he asked, trying to hide a grin.

"Don't think so," Saylor answered.

"Well, are you missing anyone?" Everyone looked around.

"Nope. We're all here," Saylor observed, after quickly counting heads. "So, what's the trouble?"

Before the words were out of his mouth, a cotton-topped, curly-haired toddler popped up and reached out toward her daddy. Carolyn! They had forgotten Carolyn!

"Found this little 'un on the back steps playing with the cats. We'd have kept her, but I figured you all couldn't do without this cutie."

"No way!" exclaimed Saylor, red-faced, lifting the teary toddler into his own vehicle, and depositing her beside Carrie on the floor between the back seats. "I guess you'll never let us live this down," he said to Pierce.

"Never will. Y'all be safe now."

♦   ♦   ♦   ♦   ♦

A green Chevy truck, slat-sided and open at the top, belonging to Lightsey Brothers Lumber Company, was parked outside the house, its driver and his helper leaning back against the seats, each enjoying a cigarette.

Inside, Carrie slowly came awake. Never a morning person in the first place, she was bone-weary, with no desire to get up. From the kitchen, she could hear the familiar noises of Saylor urging the children on with their breakfast of ham biscuits. She could hear Frank crying to be changed and fed. Suddenly, she remembered. *This is the day. What does this day hold?* She knew. *Miley, here … we … come, one … two … three!* Her feet hit the cold morning floor. The thing was on.

Lucy came in early to fry up a chicken dinner for the family to have for supper in Miley and to clean up the St. Matthews house after they were gone. But Lucy was distraught, and all but useless.

"This be the worst day of my life!" she declared, loud enough for the

movers to hear. "What am I gon' do without my babies? What are they gon'
do without me? I'm tellin' you, Miz Jumper, I gon' follow you'uns to Miley.
You go to Miley; I go to Miley!"

"Lucy, I think you'd best talk that over with your parents."

"I be grown. I make my own choice. Nothin' here for Lucy. I go to
Miley."

"Now, Lucy. You don't know that Miley would be the place for you. It
may not be the place for us, and we probably won't be there long. We may
be back sooner than you think."

"If'n you come back, Lucy come back, too. Where Jumper babies be,
Lucy be."

Lucy continued to weep and wail and carry on. Carrie left her to it in
the kitchen. Heavy-hearted, she moved through the house, trying to focus
on managing the move.

"Sis," she called out to Analda, "you and Lellan get bundled up to
entertain Carolyn and Frank on the front porch, but stay out of the way
of the movers. And, if you want to take your cat to Miley, keep her on the
porch. There'll be no scouring the neighborhood for her when it's time to
leave."

"Mother, will I be riding my tricycle on a paved road in Miley?" Analda
asked.

"No, Sis. You'll be riding right down the middle of a dirt road."

Outside at the truck, Kelly and Ralph stood by as Saylor talked with the
movers. Kelly felt torn between his parents and his grandparents. He loved
his family and wanted to go with them. As a thirteen-year-old, he was not
immune to the allure of adventure. Still, he was aware of recent changes in
Papa and worried sometimes. He did wish Granmah wouldn't carry on so
about things, but he was accustomed to her manner. As much as she doted
on Kelly, he was not exempt from her rants. A little distance was a welcome
idea.

Ralph was torn, too, but differently. He had picked up on his daddy's
dislike of Miley, and his mind was made up to be unhappy before he arrived.
Besides, he didn't want to leave his next-door sweetheart, Miss Helen

Gressett. He had plans to marry that pretty, dark-haired girl someday. For now, he hated to say goodbye, even for the short while he knew it would surely be. *Oh well,* he said to his almost twelve-year-old self, *my moving away for a little while will just make her like me even more than I think she does.*

"Boys," Saylor called to them, "no more time for dawdling. Time to load. Let's get those boxes from the house. Find Winslow. He's big enough to help."

◆ ◆ ◆ ◆ ◆

Carrie and Lucy were packing the ham sandwiches into a basket for a picnic, along with slices of Lucy's pound cake. Suddenly a child's bloodcurdling scream cut through the air. Carrie dropped a sandwich and ran for the front door, her heart pounding, Lucy at her heels. Saylor was scooping Lellan into his arms, as the child continued to wail and point toward the wicker sofa teetering atop the other furniture on the truck.

"It's gonna fall off! It's gonna fall off!" the distraught five-year-old cried.

"No, it's not," Saylor said quietly and comfortingly. "Look. It's tied on tight. See the ropes? It's not going to fall off. It just looks like it is. Everything will be okay."

Carrie and Lucy went limp with relief.

◆ ◆ ◆ ◆ ◆

Somehow, somehow ... they got it all together, much later than they had planned. By the grace and help of God, Carrie knew, everything and everyone found a place on the truck or in the car. Lucy, still weeping, detached herself from the children. Ralph managed a weak smile as he waved goodbye to Miss Helen Gressett. Analda had kept a tight rein on her cat and now held the pet firmly in her lap. With Saylor under the wheel and Ralph and Kelly in front with him, the others had distributed themselves into the back of the car. Carrie was on one bucket seat, holding Frank, while

Analda and the cat occupied the other. Carolyn, Winslow and Lellan filled the remaining space on the floor of the car. They pulled out onto the road behind the truck. Somehow, they were on their way, in the cold, to Miley.

◆ ◆ ◆ ◆ ◆

"Eee-agh!"

Somewhere north of Orangeburg, Analda let out a yelp.

"Ooh, noo! The cat peed on me! I'm wet! Daddy! Catch up with the truck, please! I need to change my clothes!" she yelled.

Saylor turned his head slightly. "There'll be no catching up with the truck for that reason!" he bellowed.

Carrie fumbled for the pillowcase she had filled with everything she could think of that they might need on the trip. She found a towel, and handed it to the stricken Analda. "Winslow, hold the cat for a while. Sis, soak it up with this. It will dry."

"Oo-whee," said Winslow, reluctantly taking the cat. "It stinks!"

"Mother, when are we going to stop?" Lellan wanted to know. "I'm tired of this."

"We'll be getting out to stretch before long," Carrie answered. "Everyone just be patient."

◆ ◆ ◆ ◆ ◆

The sun was well into the afternoon sky, and the Dort had been separated from the truck. Saylor found a grassy spot near the Edisto River where they could take a break from the grind of the trip. Carrie spread out her big patchwork quilt and got out the picnic basket. They were all famished and cranky, especially Saylor.

"Let's all be thankful for no rain and no flat tires," Carrie offered, cheerfully.

"But not thankful for these awful roads," lamented Saylor. "Someday, I hope there'll be decent roads through here."

"We won't need them by the time they come," said Ralph. "We'll be back home."

"What's this weird stuff hanging from the trees?" asked Winslow, looking around, perplexed.

"Old Greybeard the pirate's whiskers," said Saylor. "He came down the Edisto River and caught his whiskers in the trees. They've been here ever since."

"Now, Saylor," said Carrie.

"They're parasites," said Ralph.

"Nope," Kelly answered. "We studied them in school. They're actually plants that like to grow on the limbs of trees in swampy areas."

"So, we'll see lots more," Saylor said. "We're going deep into the swamps. In fact, Miley is surrounded by swamps — the Salkehatchie, the Whippy, and on the other side of Hampton, the Coosawhatchie."

"Is Miley in a swamp?" asked Analda.

"No," said her daddy. "It's not in a swamp. It's higher, sandy land, but you'll probably go swimming in a swamp if we're not gone by summer."

"Not me," yelled Lellan. "I don't like swamps!"

"Don't they have alligators?" Winslow wanted to know.

"Sure do," said Saylor. "Great big, long alligators with sharp teeth! And snakes!"

"Saylor, stop scaring the children," Carrie said. "You won't be anywhere near an alligator."

"Why is the water in the Edisto River black?" asked Ralph.

"We studied that, too," said Kelly. "It's because of the tannic acid in the decomposing plants in the area."

"Okay, smarty pants," Ralph said. "So, you know it all."

◆   ◆   ◆   ◆   ◆

As the children were reluctantly getting back into the Dort, Carrie glanced at the late afternoon sun and pulled Saylor aside. "Saylor, we're not going to get to Miley before dark, are we?"

"No way," he answered.

"We're going to have to go through the swamp in the dark?"

"Yes."

"That's what I was afraid of."

"Don't worry. The Dort's got a fine set of headlights."

♦   ♦   ♦   ♦   ♦

By the time they reached the village of Ehrhardt, darkness had begun to fall. The Spanish moss grew thicker, hovering close to the road, which sank lower into the Salkehatchie River swamps. The headlights of the car illuminated the drooping, eerie plants.

"It's so spooky," whined Winslow.

"I'm scared, Mother," cried Carolyn.

"I like it," said Analda. "Let's tell ghost stories."

The idea of ghosts didn't scare Carrie, but rickety board bridges had always made her nervous. These low, widely spaced boards were all that separated the family from the murky, mysterious, threatening waters of the swamps. Carrie was petrified, yet she couldn't let the children guess her fear. Shakily, she began singing, Saylor joined in and, gradually, most of the children. "This Little Light of Mine," "Jesus Loves Me, This I Know," and every Sunday School song they could think of carried them through the creeping shadows into the blackness of the night.

After the last bridge, the car crested the only hill since Orangeburg, and Saylor took a deep breath. "The worst is over," he announced. "It won't be too long now." Carrie was more than thankful.

♦   ♦   ♦   ♦   ♦

"Daddy, would you tell us more about our house in Miley?" Analda asked, as they passed over the last few miles.

"Well, let's see, Sis. You know it has a screened porch across the front. A center hallway goes all the way through the house to a screened back porch. Off the porch to the left is the bathroom. To the right is the kitchen. Going back to the front door, there are two rooms on the left. The front room will be for the boys, the second room for you girls. In the girls' room, there is a window that opens onto the back porch, just outside the bathroom."

"You mean we'll be able to hop through the window and be at the bathroom door?" asked Analda.

"That's right."

"I like that," said Lellan.

"Going back again to the front hallway, there are two rooms on the right. The first room has a fireplace and will be our living room, at least during the winter. The next room is a dining room with a built-in china closet, a fireplace, and a door into the kitchen. We'll not use it as a dining room; instead, it will be mine and Mother's bedroom, and Frank will be in there with us. And that's about it. Not long until we can move right in."

"I do hope the truck has arrived," Carrie said.

The headlights of the Dort illuminated the sign that said "Miley, 1 Mile" as they turned left toward the mill village. The children anxiously peered through the celluloid windows, straining to see anything they could. But there was no moonlight, and darkness reigned. They passed some houses, but saw few lights.

"Has everyone gone to bed already?" Kelly asked. "I know they have electric lights here, but I don't see many."

"The mill whistle blows at five o'clock in the morning," Saylor explained. "So, people go to bed early, especially during the winter."

As the vehicle neared the village, dogs began to announce the family's arrival. "Our grand entrance is going to wake everyone up," Saylor said. "The new family won't be very popular. All right," he said, slowing and turning left. "This is our road, and this is our house, on the left." A streetlight across the road illuminated the shallow yard.

"Oh, no!" Carrie moaned. "The truck's not here! Where could it be?"

"It'll be here directly," Saylor assured her. "We'll go on in, take a look around, and get our supper out. I'm about starved again."

"Me too!" shouted Ralph.

Analda and Winslow were the first out, bounding up the front steps, thankful for the dim glow of the streetlight. The front door was unlocked. They began feeling for a string pull for the light in the hallway. "We need someone taller," said Analda.

"Here I am," said Kelly, groping for the pull. "Here it is," he announced, pulling. Nothing happened. He looked up. "There's no bulb," he said, dismayed. "Look in another room," he said, even as Ralph's voice came from the living room. "None in here, either."

"Daddy," Analda called outside to Saylor, who was helping Carrie and the younger children out of the vehicle. "Someone has stolen the light bulbs!"

"I'll be right in," he said.

Saylor, thinking ahead, had left wood in the fireplace. Soon the cold, dim living room was warming up. Carrie spread her quilt on the floor. "This will be a memorable picnic," she said, unpacking the cold fried chicken. "Everyone sit down. The missing light bulbs should be a reminder to each of us not to be selfish, but to think of the other fellow. I'm sure we'll have plenty of light by tomorrow night."

To the family's great relief, the moving truck rumbled up as they were eating. "Try to find our lamps, beds, and bedding first," Carrie said. "Put everything else against the walls. We'll make the beds up and get right in them. Tomorrow's another day." No one protested about going to bed, not even Analda.

Much later, Carrie and Saylor were finally settled, with Frank, in their own room. "This reminds me of when Papa moved our family to Murphy," she reminisced. "We thought we were going to the ends of the earth. Except that when we arrived in the middle of the night, there was a welcoming committee and a wonderful, hot meal."

"This isn't Murphy, Carrie," Saylor said pointedly, "and this isn't a pastor's family. Welcome to Miley."

CHAPTER 26

SETTLED IN

Analda giddily escaped the prison of the front porch, where she and Lellan had been charged with entertaining Carolyn and Frank, as Mother did her Saturday morning chores. Mercifully, Mother had released her by giving her an errand down the road. "Sis," she had said, "please take this pattern to Mrs. Crosby. I promised her I would send it. And while you're down there, I'd like for you to check on the progress at the church."

"Yes, Mother," Analda had replied, concealing her glee over being set free. She paused a moment in the middle of the road, between her own house and the back of the doctor's office, breathing deeply the smell of new-cut wood, soot, and steam from the mill behind her. Now that spring had come, and she was finally allowed to go barefoot, she savored the cool softness of the Miley sand between her toes. Never mind that her feet would be black when she got home.

Analda liked Miley. Daddy mourned for home in the midlands, and he and Mother still talked of going back. Her older brothers, too, declared they didn't like the lumber mill town, with its rough-hewn, backward people and three-room school. For Analda, the wail of the saw, the high whine of the planer, and the hustle-bustle of the town appealed to her love of activity and excitement. The pleasure of the mill sounds made her think of Mrs. Barfield, who lived on the main road. Mrs. Barfield had said to Mother, "If I don't get my work done while the mill is humming, it won't be done. I can't work without that mill humming."

Analda took the little rutted road diagonally across from her house that would lead her to Mrs. Crosby. At her right, as she walked, was the back of the hotel, the back of the big store, and the platform that led to a warehouse. Then the road curved and went past six or seven houses on the right. On Analda's left, across from the houses, there was an open field where folks planted flowers and vegetables and tossed basketballs.

Analda was glad that Mother was making friends among some of the Miley people. It hadn't been easy, even with Mother being a person who never saw a stranger. When Mother walked with the children for their first day at school, people had peered out of windows and doors and stared. Yet there now appeared to be a growing acceptance of their family, and a certain appreciation. Maybe the Jumpers were growing more accustomed to the Miley people, too. Mrs. Crosby was Mother's first and so-far best friend here. She was a seamstress, and her husband was a machinist in the shop at the mill. Her brother, Mr. Charlie Godley, who ran both the stores for the Lightseys, was also quite friendly with Mother and Daddy.

Beyond the houses, Analda could see the Hampton-Branchville railroad, owned by the Lightseys, which ran as far as Canadys in Colleton County. Since there were no trains on Sundays, Daddy had taken the children on the railroad pump car as far as Moselle and back. The railroad ran straight through the swamps of the Salkehatchie River. It was thrilling to be above the water, but safe from it, one more thing Analda liked about living in Miley.

Mrs. Crosby answered the knock promptly. "I've brought the pattern Mother promised to send," Analda said.

"Thank you, Analda. Sit here on the porch a few minutes and tell me what's going on with your family today."

"A lot," answered Analda, squirming onto a rocker. "Mother and Lucy are unpacking Mother's good dishes and putting up curtains, because Grandmama and Grandpapa Tate are coming to visit soon. Mother never has completely unpacked, but now she says she can't let her mama catch her living like this."

"Well, unpacking is a good sign. Maybe that means you plan to stay in Miley a while longer."

SETTLED IN

181

"I hope so. Daddy has gone to Columbia. Grandpapa Jumper is very sick. He has stomach cancer and had to have an operation. When Daddy comes back, he will bring Grandmama and Grandpapa Tate. And Kelly has gone back to stay. With Grandpapa Jumper being sick, Granmah says she just can't manage things without Kelly."

"That's very hard for your family, being split up like that. And I know you're all sad about your grandfather. Your mother tells me how much everyone loves him."

"Yes, Mother has cried a lot about Grandpapa Jumper. And about Kelly. I heard her saying to Daddy that this is the only disagreement they haven't been able to work out."

"Her tears spring from a loving heart," Mrs. Crosby said. "Tell your mother that you all have our prayers."

"Thank you, ma'am."

As Analda began to skip down the steps, Mrs. Crosby called after her, "And please tell her that I'd love to meet your Tate grandparents while they're here."

"Yes, ma'am."

Analda's hands were now free. A series of cartwheels catapulted her past two more houses. Down here, the noise of the mill was challenged by the clanging and banging of train engines pushing coal cars up to the second level of the coal chute, which was on a spur of the railroad behind these houses.

The road curved left. Catching her breath, Analda strolled past an open area and stood before the site for the new church. There she paused, brushing off her now-black hands and taking note of the red brick pillars being built for the foundation.

Analda was excited about the church. She had made her profession of faith just before the family had left St. Matthews, and she missed church. They sometimes went to the Methodist church in Hampton, but the roads through Whippy Swamp were not good, and it wasn't a reasonable thing to do on a regular basis. Analda hoped that her family would stay in Miley long enough to worship God here. She knew that her mother had quietly helped this church to come to be. In her first conversations with Mr. Henry Lightsey, Carrie had broached the idea of a *community* church, rather than a denominational one. Carrie thought that it would attract more participation and would be a unifying force for the town. Worship services could be held on Sunday nights, so that pastors of different denominations could preach. Mr. Lightsey liked the idea. In fact, he was enthusiastic about the possibilities, and construction had begun. Mr. Humphries, the sales manager for Lightsey Brothers, had already started a Sunday School, which was meeting at the school until the church could be built.

One more cartwheel landed Analda in front of the Miley School. The white clapboard building housed three rooms. Two were classrooms, while the third held cloak rooms and a stage. There were fold-away walls which could convert the stage room into an auditorium. When the Jumpers arrived in Miley, the school was full. The new students had been forced to share seats with the "Miley people," as they called them. Everyone had stared boldly. It was really awkward.

One room of the school held grades one through three, with Analda in second and Winslow in third. School was hard for Analda. It was not the studies, but the sitting and being forced to focus on things that didn't interest her. She was thinking about what she would do when she could get out of there. Miss Green, her teacher, always wore a red tam to school. Once, she left the tam at school. Some of the boys had burned it in the pot-bellied stove. The next day, they all spent time helping Miss Green in a fruitless search for her red tam.

The second classroom was for fourth, fifth, and sixth grades. Ralph was in fifth, Kelly in sixth. Things weren't going well for Ralph. He clashed with Miss Burns, the teacher, and she clearly didn't like Ralph. Mother had already had to intervene, having a talk with Ralph and Miss Burns. Analda wasn't sure things had improved.

Heading for home, she thought about the PTA. The school's Parent Teacher Association had been important in St. Matthews. There was no PTA in Miley. Mother talked about the need. Would a PTA be her next effort? God had certainly given Mother things to do here. *Maybe moving to*

Miley was more than just a necessity. Maybe it was a plan of God. Hmm ...

From the school, the Jumper house was now straight ahead, back toward the mill. Running and skipping, Analda passed houses on the right, waving to people on porches or in yards, but not stopping. Especially, she didn't stop, but ran faster, kicking up the black sand, past a certain scary house. It was said that someone had committed suicide there. Shot herself. In the blue room. The room was now blue because they had painted over the blood on the walls to try to hide what was unthinkable and unmentionable. Everyone tried to pass by that particular house as quickly as possible. Someone lived there now, but Analda didn't really know them and didn't see how they could sleep at night. She moved on.

Two houses from her own, Analda saw Mr. Cy Parker sitting on his porch, all cleaned up for the weekend. She could see his wife, Minnie, planting flowers in the field across from their house. Mr. Cy was a supervisor with the woods crew. Every Monday morning, as the five o'clock whistle blew, the woods crew left on the log train to go into the forests, perhaps as far as Canadys, to harvest timber belonging to the Lightseys. The crew would usually be gone until Friday evening, sending the loaded train, the Old 44, back to Miley each day. It was rough, hard, physical work. You had to be hearty to work on the woods crew. Mr. Cy was certainly qualified. He was tall and well built, with big, thick lumberjack hands and a large appetite for food and enjoyment. Unfortunately, for drink, too. Analda wondered if Cy was getting ready for his weekend binge, and Minnie, perhaps, was trying to stay out of his way.

"Hey there, Miss Analda," he called from the porch behind the white picket fence and broom-swept yard.

"Hello, Mr. Cy," she answered, intending to hurry on. It was almost time for the noon whistle and dinnertime. While the Jumpers didn't do a lot with breakfast, there were always two big meals — at noon and at night.

Cy wouldn't be passed by. "Stop in a minute," he called out.

She opened the gate and stepped inside the yard, pausing for some small talk about the weather and such. As she indicated she would move on, he said, "You know, Miss Analda, my wife Minnie is a little off." Analda said nothing. "You know what I mean — a little tetched in the head, kinda 'witchy.' Still, Puss is a good woman. But I tell you, when Minnie gits sick and I git drunk, it's a helluva time!"

"I must be getting along," said Analda as the noon whistle sounded, making itself heard for miles around.

CHAPTER 27

WALKING TO THE STORE

Ralph and Winslow hurriedly pushed back from the dinner table, as Lucy began clearing away. There was no room in the kitchen for their big table, so they had placed it on the back porch, which was screened in and partially built up from the floor. For the winter, Saylor had tacked oilcloth over the screens, while the wood-burning stove in the kitchen warmed the space. The arrangement was makeshift, but still it was a workable dining room. As the weather warmed, the oilcloth would be removed for the summer.

"Mother, we're headed out to go fishing with the Goodings," Ralph said.

"That's fine, Ralph. Just stay away from the swamp until your daddy gets back. It's still too cool to swim, anyway. That swamp scares me. If you don't want it to be off-limits for the rest of the summer, stay away. Saylor will take you swimming soon enough."

"Yes, ma'am."

"Sis," she said, "Carolyn and Frank and I are going to take our naps. I'll give you and Lellan your Saturday nickels, and you may run to the store for me."

"Yes, Mother."

♦　♦　♦　♦　♦

A walk to the store was always fun. Actually, there were two stores in Miley, the big store and the little store, across the road from each other.

You could get anything you needed from those two stores. That was a good thing, since Miley people didn't get to Hampton often. The little store, on the mill side of the road, sold gasoline, tires, meat, cigarettes, cold drinks, ice, ice cream, and parched peanuts. The big store sold everything else. The children especially loved its amazing candy counter. And then there was the trash box behind the store. Glorious things were thought to be in the trash box. They had plundered it on occasion, finding of value, so far, cigar boxes, which were prized for holding treasures, and a small spool of thread. The thrill of the hunt was the thing when it came to the trash box.

With Lellan tripping along beside Analda, they rounded the corner in front of the doctor's office, where, except for the noise of the mill, all seemed quiet, at least for the moment. There could be a lot stirring at the doctor's office, especially on weekends, when fights and accidents were apt to happen. The doctor had no nurse right now, so Minnie Parker helped, and even Mother had helped him a time or two. Between the doctor's office and the hotel, they passed several small outbuildings facing the road and the side of the hotel.

"What's inside those little buildings?" Lellan wondered aloud.

"Daddy told me there are hoses and fire hydrants. Those buildings are also scattered throughout the mill. If a fire breaks out in Miley, a very shrill fire whistle blows. Everyone drops what they are doing and rushes to fight the fire."

"That would be scary," Lellan responded.

"Fire is always scary," Analda said. "Especially here, with all this wood. I hope I never have to hear the fire whistle blow."

"Me, too!" said Lellan.

The girls were now beneath the sprawling oak tree where, just a short while ago, mill hands had spread out below its canopy to enjoy dinners they had brought from home. They had also sat on the front porch of the doctor's office, as well as under trees in the vacant lot beside the Jumper home. They were now busy at work again.

The girls came next to the big, two-story white clapboard hotel, with its full-length double verandas. On the hotel porch, a couple of guests were leisurely rocking, but not enjoying a quiet afternoon, since Miley was rarely quiet, especially not on Saturdays. There were cars and a number of horse-drawn farm wagons, bringing farming families and farm hands to town to sell goods and get supplies for another week.

Most Miley folks referred to the hotel as the boarding house, which was a more accurate description. While there were actual visitors to Miley, such as businessmen buying lumber, some of the "guests" were residents — school teachers or secretaries. Noon meals were served to certain people in the big dining room, but the hotel was a bit mysterious for ordinary citizens and children. Most were left to wonder what went on inside. Except for Analda.

"Let's go inside," she suggested. "We can speak to Flossie, the cook. I love to see her white cook's hat."

"Oh, no, Sis! We can't do that!" protested Lellan. "Mother has told us that we are never to go inside the hotel, unless someone comes out and invites us in. Besides," she added, still clutching her nickel in her five-year-old hand, "I want to buy candy!"

"Okay," said Analda, with a little laugh.

Between the hotel and the big store was a well-trodden pathway leading toward the school. Children who rode the school bus got off here and walked the rest of the way. There was much coming and going on a daily basis. Trucks also pulled in here to unload goods going to the warehouse behind the store.

The big store was fronted by a long shed porch with a dirt floor. Benches lined the walls on either side of the steps. A wide, wooden walkway led from the street to the steps. Above, on the top of the store, was a big sign: U.S. Post Office, Miley, S.C. Since today was Saturday, most spots on the benches were taken, as weary farmers waited on their wives to finish in the store. Most of them waved a hand in greeting as Analda and Lellan passed.

"I hope Miss Miley is here today," said Lellan. Miss Viola Miley was the well-liked, cheerful postmistress and freight agent for the mill. The post office was a rather large room inside the store, about six feet from the outside wall, where there were tables for sorting mail. As Analda and

Lellan approached, to their right were two windows with counters, one large and one small, separated by a span of post office boxes.

"I wish we had a post office box," said Lellan. "It must be fun to open them and see what's inside."

"Me, too," said Analda. "Daddy says there would just be another key to get lost, so we call for our mail."

The popular, petite Miss Miley reigned over all things having to do with the mail, which was brought in from Hampton every day at 11:00 a.m. sharp. It came by rail on the 200, a one-coach electric train, operated by Mr. Bowers, which carried freight and a dozen or so passengers to and from Hampton. The arrival of the mail usually heralded a morning break for townspeople.

"I see her," said Analda, "but it looks like she's busy, as usual." Several people were in line at Miss Vi's window. "Let's make our purchases, and maybe we can speak to her on our way out."

The girls waited their turn at the glass-fronted candy counter, containing bins of every kind of candy a child can imagine. For a nickel, you could get a wealth of mixed candy, a big candy bar, a cold drink, or a cinnamon roll. Seeing them, Mr. Godley nodded. "Be with you girls shortly," he said, waving a hand. They used their wait time to make their choices.

"It's hard to decide," said Lellan.

"But you have to decide," advised Analda. "Here comes Mr. Godley."

"Okay, girls, what will it be?" he asked, taking two small paper bags from behind the counter.

"We'll each take a nickel's worth of mixed hard candies," said Analda, making the decision for both of them, even as Mr. Godley scooped up the sweets and dropped them onto the scale. Analda smiled as she saw him add an extra piece for each.

"Here you are," he said, handing them the bags. "What else can I get for you?"

"Mother needs fifty cents worth of grits and fifty cents worth of corn meal," said Analda. Mr. Godley reached behind him to a shelf stocked with small packages of pre-weighed staples. "Please put them on my daddy's account," she said, unnecessarily. Part of Saylor's job as paymaster was to deduct from the millhands' pay what they owed at the stores, where nearly everyone in town had accounts. Taking money to pay for purchases at the store wasn't usually necessary.

As they turned to go, Miss Miley, now freed to chat, hailed them. "Hello there, Misses Jumper," she said. "Did your mother not come with you?"

"No, ma'am," said Analda. "She's very busy. Grandmama and Grandpapa Tate are coming." Sometimes, after her nap, but never on a Saturday, Carrie would clean up and walk to the store, where she and Miss Vi often enjoyed a chat, usually laughing a lot.

"Please tell your mother 'hello' for me, and that I'm praying for Grandfather Jumper," she said, as they headed out the door.

"Thank you, Miss Miley," they said.

Normally, after leaving the store, Analda and Lellan would have headed for their daddy's window in the Lightsey Brothers Lumber Mill office, between the big store and the railroad. Saylor's desk was near the window facing the store, from which he paid the mill hands and settled accounts on Saturday evenings after the mill knocked off. Tonight, someone else would be doing that. They felt a little sad, missing their daddy. Saylor always made over the children when they appeared at his window, as did others in the office.

The walk toward home was a little brisker, since the girls had their candy to anticipate. Still, Lellan had to stop under the big oak tree for a whirl around it, maneuvering the rough, exposed roots with her dirty bare feet.

"Come on," urged Analda.

As soon as they were on the edge of their own yard, Analda handed her mother's purchases to Lellan. "Please take these inside to Mother, and tell her that we are back," she said. Immediately she took her little brown paper sack of candy, ran into the side yard and scooted up the chinaberry tree. She climbed until she found her favorite branch and hid herself among the fresh spring leaves of its umbrella-like canopy. There, unseen by the world, she savored the sweet treats all by herself, in delicious privacy.

Miley Post Office and General Store

Chapter 28

BACK TO OCRACOKE

The mill hummed, steadily processing wood from tree to finished lumber products of all kinds. Across from the Jumper house were the dry kilns, ovens for controlling moisture content. There was the smell of fresh cut wood and the high-pitched cry of the trim saw. Mules hauled loads of lumber to the yard, where millions of feet were stored in stacks.

◆ ◆ ◆ ◆ ◆

"Aahh." Grandpapa Tate sighed heavily as he settled back into a rocking chair on the front porch, relishing the breeze that sifted through the screens. "Aahh," he said again, not realizing he was about to introduce a new family saying: "Anything that takes me back to Ocracoke!"

"What takes you back to Ocracoke, Grandpapa?" Ralph asked, passing across the porch on his way somewhere.

"Aahh, it's that smell of new lumber, combined with the pungent aroma of the swamp. There was a big sawmill on Ocracoke. That smell, mingled with the salt air, made for a fresh, soothing scent that I've found nowhere else. This is the closest thing. It takes me right back to Ocracoke. Makes me want to rear back and take another nap."

"Well, why don't you do that, Papa," urged Carrie, who really wanted some one-on-one time with her mama. She smiled, happy to see Papa so relaxed, despite the fact that he still insisted on wearing a black dress suit daily, clearly out of place in Miley.

"Well, Carrie," her mother began, "it's good to see you're getting settled here."

Carrie laughed. "It's taken some time, Mama. Recently, I remembered something I had completely forgotten."

"What was that?"

"About a year ago, in St. Matthews, before we ever heard of Miley, and couldn't have imagined it if we had, I prayed a special prayer. I was sitting at my sewing machine, and I asked God to give me a mission field. I had been having a sense that there was something He had for me to do, that I hadn't yet done. I quickly forgot the prayer. Now that we've been in Miley for months, it has dawned on me that Miley is the answer. There's a lot to do here, and I have realized that I may as well get busy."

Mama Tate laughed softly. "Sometimes, we must be careful what we ask for," she said, with a twinkle in her eyes, "because we just might get it." She paused, then continued. "I understand there are things here that may be displeasing, but there must be some good things, too."

"There certainly are," Carrie answered. "We're learning to appreciate different types of people. Workers here come from varied backgrounds and levels of education. There are professional people, supervisors, mechanics … all the way down to unskilled day laborers. We can't stereotype people in Miley. The children will miss certain advantages by living here, but there are others to make up for it. For one thing, the informal atmosphere is easier for a family with a lot of children. I can be more relaxed about things, not having to put on a front or maintain standards that are difficult to achieve. Soon after we arrived, we realized that we were more dressed up than the Miley folks. It may have made them uncomfortable. Now we're doing more like they do. I can let the children be themselves here, and I think they are having more fun. The school hasn't been easy, but they are adjusting, and I am thinking about organizing a PTA. There isn't a strong sense of community, and I believe that would help, as well as the church."

"Tell me more about the church."

"Oh, Mama! Everyone is excited about the church. The foundation is underway. We are blessed that Mr. Henry Lightsey is enthusiastic and involved with it. And the pews! The pews are being made in the mill. They'll be very nice. Not solid, but strongly constructed out of two-by-fours with rounded edges. I do hope you'll get to see them one day."

"It sounds as if you're thinking you may be here a while."

"I really can't say. We talk of going back, and Saylor is definitely homesick, especially with Dad being so sick. It's hard on him having to go back and forth. He always comes back depressed. Please pray for him."

"Yes, we could see that on the trip here. He's concerned about his papa, and he feels torn. We will continue to pray." They were quiet for a moment. Then she asked, "How is Saylor's job going?"

"I'd say that it's going well, but it is a constant challenge. There are so many aspects of the mill. Miley is a town with a very definite reason for its place on the map. It brings live trees into many uses, from basic building materials to ornamental objects. The mill makes drawer pulls and decorative trim that smaller lumber companies buy to resell. As far as bookkeeping goes, everything comes back to Saylor. Every transaction of the mill comes across his desk, including purchases and sales of the stores. The books are audited periodically by a Mr. Derrick who comes and stays in the hotel for several days. Saylor says that's not stressful for him since he has confidence in his work. It probably stresses me more," she said, laughing.

"There's something else I've been wanting to ask about," Carrie's mother continued. "Obviously, Lucy made good on her promise to follow you to Miley. How is that working out?"

"For us, it's been a blessing. I haven't had to train someone new, and the children like her and her cooking, especially Winslow. Sometimes, when she isn't working, he goes to her house to eat with her. I'm not sure that coming here was the best thing for her, though. She got married soon after she arrived."

"Who did she marry?"

"She married Andy Bostian, who works in the boiler room of the mill, a dangerous job. It's where they feed large boilers with saw dust from a pipe to make steam. Andy seems to be a good man, but she met him at the juke joint in the colored quarters behind the mill. There's a long building there where they dance and socialize, and where Andy plays the piano. I worry about the influence of the place. They're not living in the quarters, but in the colored section on the main road. I've been encouraging her to get involved in the church, since there are two churches for the coloreds here. So far, things seem to be okay. Sometimes, however, Lucy gets a little obstinate, like this morning."

"What happened?"

"She loves to cook chicken. This morning I planned a roast for our dinner tonight. She objected, saying she wanted to cook 'checken,' as she calls it. I insisted on the roast."

"How is the relationship between whites and coloreds in general?" her mother asked.

"I would say that there is a close working relationship, but we don't mix socially. There is mutual understanding and respect. They are our friends. We like them, and they like us. They have it hard, since their men can't work inside the mill, and the women can't work there at all. Still, they seem happy-go-lucky; things don't appear to bother them as much as they do the whites. Many of them hum while they work. Our children have visited in their homes. Ralph, especially, knows the names of many more than I do. Several have come here asking for help in ordering things from catalogs and such. It's been a pleasure to help with that. Which reminds me, Mama. I have you to thank for something."

"What in the world?"

"Not long after we arrived, there was a baby born in the quarters who was sickly. It seemed the child might not live. I remembered what you did for Ralph as an infant. The mixture of egg whites. I went to the quarters every morning for a week and treated the baby in the same way. He survived. Thank you."

♦ ♦ ♦ ♦ ♦

"Well, look who's up from their naps," Carrie's mother said, holding out her arms. "It's Frank Tate and Carolyn." Frank was nearly a year old and officially a toddler, having already taken his first steps. Three-and-a-half-year-old Carolyn stood ready to catch him. Grandmama Tate lifted Frank onto her lap, while Carolyn climbed onto her mother's. The grownup talk was over, for now.

♦　♦　♦　♦　♦

The afternoon on the porch continued, with the children in and out, Grandmama and Grandpapa Tate getting reacquainted. The whole group walked through the neighborhood, where they stopped to see Mrs. Crosby, and others. Then they moved on and viewed the foundation for the church. Below the school and church was an area closer to the swamp, where violets grew in the springtime. Mr. Hersch Padgett had a saw-filing operation there, where he filed cross-cut saws for the mill. He showed his set-up to the adults as Carolyn, Lellan, and Analda gathered violets to take back home, and Frank Tate sat on Grandpapa's shoulders. Carrie would have liked to bottle this day. She missed her parents more than she had realized.

As the group strolled back toward home, past the Parkers' house, they paused to speak to Minnie, who filled them in on Miley doings. Mrs. Parker, from her porch, could see many comings and goings in the town, especially the passing back and forth between the school and the big store. Turning to leave, they suddenly heard squealing of brakes, squawking, and cursing. A car had turned off the main road and hit a Jumper chicken. The annoyed driver, Mr. Mixon, had jumped out of the car. Seeing a whole neighborhood coming toward him, he composed himself and became apologetic. "I'm sorry, Mrs. Jumper, ma'am, but it appears I have killed your chicken."

"It's quite all right," Carrie said. "It was the chicken's fault. Carolyn, would you run and call Lucy to come and get the chicken? It will have to be cooked." Mr. Mixon continued on his way, and the group reassembled themselves on the front porch, the children jostling for places on the benches spanning each end. As they settled in, Carrie said to her mother, "Minnie thinks she has the best view in Miley. However, I expect that we have the choice spot right here. We see everyone who comes and goes on our street, as well as many who pass on the main road, since we are so near the mill." Then she laughed, lowered her voice, and added, "Sometimes Saylor and I sit on the porch at night and observe comings and goings that probably aren't meant for us, since we can't be seen."

Lucy came out of the house to fetch the hapless chicken, placing it in a dishpan. As she crossed the porch to go back through the house, she was heard to say, "I told you we gon' have checken."

Rev. D.P. (Doctor Pinckney) and Medora Doggett Tate

CHAPTER 29

LOW COUNTRY SUMMER

Doodlebug, doodlebug,
Won't you come out?
Doodlebug, doodlebug,
Your house is on fire!

Carrie smiled, sitting on the porch, adding needlework to one of the girls' dresses. In between noises of the mill came childish voices from underneath the house. Lellan and her friend, Gladys Stone from next door, were teaching the doodle bug rhyme to Carolyn. The dry sand under the house was ideal for the inverted cone-shaped dwellings of the doodlebug. Covered in sand, the little critters lay in wait at the bottom for ants to come by as breakfast. With twigs or sticks or tiny fingers, the bugs could be coaxed out of hiding, a source of fascination for the children.

"What a stroke of genius!" Saylor had declared. "Having Ralph and Winslow to clean the growth out from under the house was a real good idea."

"Not genius, Saylor. It's just making the most of what we have. The house is high enough off the ground to provide a shady play place for the younger ones. Even Frank is big enough now to push his wooden cars along roads made by pulling blocks of wood through the sand. They can have tunnels and bridges and all sorts of things under there."

Availability of wood was another blessing of life in Miley. Periodically, dump wagons from the mill brought loads of wood scraps to residents, useful for cooking, heating, and toys for children. At fifty cents a load, they dumped wood into the yard. Carrie had pieces cut into small block sizes, piling some underneath the house and some behind the catty-cornered cook stove in the kitchen.

"What I dread now," she said, "is the reward we promised the boys for a job well done — cleaning out a swimming hole in the swamp."

"It's inevitable, Carrie. Swimming is a rite of childhood."

"It wasn't a rite *or* a right of my childhood," she commented. "Sneaking off to wade in Doggett Creek at Grandpa's was the extent of it."

"That's why you're afraid of water," he said. "The key is to teach them to swim. The older boys and Analda have already learned in the pond at Sandy Run. We'll teach Lellan next, then Carolyn, and Frank won't be able to remember when he didn't swim. Being able to swim and understanding the dangers will keep them safe."

"I hope and pray so," she said, with a sigh. Carrie's trusting relationship with her Heavenly Father usually came easily. But when it came to trusting Him with her children in water, she felt she would always struggle.

"We'll go this afternoon," he said. "I've already scouted out the spot." She sighed again.

Oh, they tell me of a home far beyond the skies
Oh, they tell me of a home far away
Oh, they tell me of a home where no storm clouds rise
Oh, they tell me of an unclouded day

Saylor was having his afternoon fest on the piano. Carrie, hearing the words of the old Josiah Alwood song, stopped what she was doing, pulled an oak chair up to the piano, and joined him on the chorus, her alto blending with his melody. It was a song they had sung together at numerous funerals.

Oh, the land of cloudless day
Oh, the land of an unclouded sky
Oh, they tell me of a home where no storm clouds rise
Oh, they tell me of an unclouded day

Tears came to Carrie's eyes, and she knew they were in Saylor's, too. Both of their hearts were very tender in these days. It was hard to understand why God, in His providence, had separated them from Papa Jumper during his last days, his time of suffering, his time of awaiting his call to meet his Savior. The words of the song ministered to them, giving them comfort, just as they both knew He comforted Saylor's papa.

"Daddy," Ralph called out, coming into the living room followed by Winslow and Analda, "when are we going? You said we'd go this afternoon."

At the end of the chorus, Saylor stopped singing, not scolding Ralph for interrupting. A promise was a promise. "Okay. You and Winslow and Analda put tools in the Dort. We'll need a hoe, maybe a shovel, clippers and a pitchfork. Then put on your bathing suits."

"Hooray!" they yelled, hurrying away.

"All of you stay close to your daddy," Carrie called after them. "Do exactly what he tells you to do. And hurry back. I won't be able to nap while you're gone."

♦　♦　♦　♦　♦

Making their way in the Dort through Miley, waving to folks along the street, they crossed the railroad. Saylor turned left onto a sandy road, parallel to the railroad, leading to the swamp. "If you're ever driving a car on this road," Saylor advised, "be careful. These ruts are deep and the sand can throw a vehicle." Ralph thought to himself that he'd like to try that out some day.

In less than a half mile, they came to the first bridge. Eight runs of the Salkehatchie River formed swampland through the area. Eight flat board bridges had been built. At the seventh bridge, Saylor pulled over to the edge of the road and parked. "This is the spot," he said. "Between here and the railroad. The water is plenty deep for good swimming, and the growth not too thick. Let's get to work."

They unloaded their tools and eased down the sunny embankment and into the foot-deep water at the edge. For a while they all worked together, cutting and pulling away vines and undergrowth, throwing debris onto the bank. For the children, the allure of the water was strong, and all three gradually drifted off for play. The swamp was fresh and cool, its dark water giving off an indescribable, primeval smell, running quickly from the railroad to flow underneath the bridge.

"Come on back here and help," Saylor would call. The children would return, pull out a few more strands of growth, then allow the current to coax them off to play again. Saylor didn't really mind, remembering his own carefree swims in the fishpond at Sandy Run. It was good to see his children enjoying themselves. They'd have grownup worries in due time. As he looked at the three, it hit him suddenly and hard that his eldest wasn't here. Kelly was missing the fun, the whole experience. At the same time, he thought, *Kelly is back home at Sandy Run. And we're here in this strange land. Kelly is with Papa, and we're missing that.* With determination, he shook himself back to reality.

"Daddy," Ralph called. "We need a diving board!"

"Soon enough," Saylor answered. "We'll attach a board to the trestle. I'm sure Horace Roberts from the mill can find us a good thick one."

The promise had been kept.

♦   ♦   ♦   ♦   ♦

Carrie met Dr. Sample on the front porch. "Saylor's very sick," she said, urgently. "Chills, fever, dizziness. He thinks he's going to die. He called each child in to talk, and now the children are afraid."

"I think I know what could be going on. We'll see. Take me to him." While the doctor was in the bedroom examining their daddy, Ralph, Winslow, and Analda were seated in a row on the wicker sofa. Lellan and

Carolyn sat cross-legged on the living room rug, as Frank crawled around, too young to be anxious.

Presently Dr. Sample and Carrie emerged. Dr. Sample sat down in the wicker chair, leaving the rocker for Carrie. Frank climbed onto her lap.

"Well, boys and girls," the doctor began, "I know you've been worried. Mr. Jumper will be all right. He has malaria. I'm sure you've heard about malaria. It's carried by mosquitoes in swampy areas."

"Did Daddy get malaria because we've been going to the swamp?" asked Ralph.

"It could be," the doctor answered. "However, you don't have to go to the swamp to get malaria. Just living in the area makes you susceptible. It's a big problem around here. Anyone can get it, even you children. Once you have it, it stays in you for a long time, and it can come out on you for years. You'll know when it's coming out, because you'll feel dizzy, and it can be hard to move."

"Can malaria kill you?" asked Analda, apprehensively.

"Yes, it can, especially if you're old and weak. And it can certainly make you feel like you're going to die. But most people recover, and so will Mr. Jumper. Fortunately, there's medicine to help." He reached into his black bag and pulled out a big jug of quinine tablets.

"They know about quinine," Carrie said. "We've had some since the government distributed it last month. It's hard to get the children to take it."

"I hate trying to swallow tablets," Winslow complained.

"Me, too!" said Lellan and Carolyn in unison.

"Just look at how sick your daddy has been," the doctor continued. "Do you want to get that sick?"

"No," the children responded.

"Then take the quinine. Put it on the table and take it every day, just like you eat your meals."

"Yes, sir," some said.

"Thank you for coming, Dr. Sample," Carrie said, accompanying him to the door. "I'm sure Saylor will get better, and I'm also sure the children will take the quinine."

"My pleasure, Mrs. Jumper," he said, and was gone to his office across the road.

Carrie returned to the children and sat back down. "We're thankful to God for the medicine and thankful that Daddy will get well. Let's all get down on our knees, like we do at family prayer time, and thank God for our blessings."

The children knelt in a circle, while Carrie prayed. "Heavenly Father, we thank Thee for being with us today. We are thankful for Dr. Sample and for the assurance that Saylor is going to get well. We thank Thee for the medicine, and most of all, we thank Thee for Thy healing power. In Jesus' name, Amen."

Carrie began singing, and the children joined in. "Praise God from whom all blessings flow …"

♦ ♦ ♦ ♦ ♦

Several evenings later, Carrie was getting the children settled for bed when they heard feisty strains of "The Bullfrog Song" coming from the piano.

"Daddy!" The children began to shout and rush into the living room.

"Daddy, you're feeling better!"

"Yes, I am," he declared, reaching out as they jostled for hugs. "I'm definitely feeling better. How about a Daniel Boone story?"

"Yay!" cried the younger ones.

"Nah," said Ralph, shrugging. "Winslow and I are getting too old for Daniel Boone stories."

"Too old? No one is ever too old for Daniel Boone! Not even Daniel Boone himself."

"Well, okay."

Propped up on one of the double beds in the girls' room, children piled around him, he began: 'I can't say as ever I was lost, but I was bewildered once for three days …' "

Halfway into the story, Carolyn burst into tears. "It's too sad! It's just too sad!" she cried.

"Do you want me to stop?" Saylor asked his most temperamental child. She paused. "No," she sniffed. "Go ahead."

Saylor continued to the end. "'All you need for happiness is a good gun, a good horse, and a good wife.'" All had finished well.

♦ ♦ ♦ ♦ ♦

Sleeping with the windows open during the warm weather was a pleasure. You could hear the steam being cut down at night, as well as the sounds of the water pump. The family had long since learned to sleep through the five o'clock morning whistle, which awakened mill hands who had to walk a mile or two or three to work, and to signal the departure of the woods crew on Mondays. But the six forty-five and seven o'clock whistles would often arouse them.

The morning after Saylor's recovery, Analda, Lellan, and Carolyn awakened to the chopping sounds of his hoe in the garden outside their window. They were greatly comforted, knowing Daddy was better and busy in the garden he had made in the vacant lot beside the house.

Normally, breakfast was a hit-and-miss affair. This morning, however, Carrie had prepared a celebratory meal of grits, eggs, and bacon. The smells urged the girls onto their feet and through the window into the dining room.

With the family gathered around the table, Saylor in his usual place at the end near the buffet, Analda broached her subject. "Daddy, since you're feeling better, do you think we could go to the beach? We live close enough now to go and come in a day. Lots of people do it. The Goodings, the Crosbys, the Mixons … "

Saylor sighed and paused before responding. "Analda … you know I'd like nothing better than to take you to the beach. But … with Grandpapa Jumper so sick, that's where we should go. I'm afraid you'll have to be satisfied with the swamp this summer. By this time next year … " he trailed off.

Saylor didn't need to say any more.

CHAPTER 30

A BETTER WORLD

Saturday, October 21, 1926, offered a hint of fall in the air. Autumn was still Carrie's favorite season, arriving a bit later than she liked in the low country. Even here it heralded the approach of Thanksgiving, Christmas, and a new year. *We could certainly use a new year,* she thought. This morning her footsteps were heavy, and her heart more so. Saylor had gone to his father's bedside. Dad's heavenly homegoing was imminent. Carrie yearned to be with him, too, but it just wasn't practical. Someone had to care for the family and prepare for what lay ahead.

The children were scattered about, finishing weekend chores and making plans with friends. Well into a new school year, they were settling nicely into life in Miley. Lellan was now in first grade, leaving only Carolyn and Frank at home on weekday mornings. While Carolyn required more attention than most of the other children, Frank, at only eighteen months, was easygoing and independent, never at a loss to entertain himself.

Washing and ironing were chores that were ordinarily exported to wash women who arrived on Monday mornings to collect the family laundry. Because nothing was normal today, Lucy had set the ironing board up in the kitchen, heating alternating flat irons on the hot cook stove. Shirts, trousers, and dresses were being pressed and hung in the closet beside the fireplace in the living room, ready to be packed into suitcases if necessary. The uncertainty meant that preparations couldn't be left until Monday. It bothered Carrie to be preoccupied with mundane chores when she would rather focus on Dad and this holy time in his life. Still, she realized that these necessities were a blessing from God to keep her pushing on and caring for others, rather than being lost in sorrow.

There came a knock on the front door. Since no one seemed to be bothering to respond, Carrie answered. Maxie Martin, one of the older Martin boys, who helped Cecil Godley in the big store on Saturdays, stood there, a yellow Western Union envelope in his hand. Carrie knew its contents instantly. She thanked Maxie, took the telegram, and returned to the living room to sit down. Her shaking hands opened the message:

> Papa has gone to a better world
> — *Saylor*

All kinds of vehicles were crowded onto the grounds of Oak Grove Methodist Church. Horse-drawn family carriages and buggies, a few wagons, roadsters, Model T's, touring cars of every description, and several bicycles leaning against pine trees signified an event of significance in the community of Sandy Run. From the open windows of the sanctuary, pump organ strains of David Franklin Jumper's favorite hymns — he loved them all — could be heard by mourners scattered across the yard, some sitting on or waiting in their own cars. Others were already gathered in the cemetery behind the church to assure themselves of a satisfactory space. Uncle Frank, as he had been called even by those who were of no relation, had gone to glory.

Inside, the family and extended family more than filled the small nave of the church, with standing room only. As Papa's loved ones processed to fill the pews, the now-widowed Sallie Saylor Jumper, in full mourning garb, clung to Saylor with her left arm and to Kelly with her right, while Carrie followed. Berlie and Luther pushed Dora in a wheelchair. Minnie and Clarence Rucker were there, followed by Claudine, a child now in a beautiful young woman's body. Grandchildren, cousins, nieces, nephews, and all manner of kin overfilled the remaining space.

The opening song was introduced, a hymn by Samuel Stennett, chosen by Uncle Frank himself.

On Jordan's stormy banks I stand,
And cast a wishful eye
To Canaan's fair and happy land,
Where my possessions lie.

I am bound for the promised land,
I am bound for the promised land;
O who will come and go with Me?
I am bound for the promised land.

As the congregation seated themselves, Carrie noted, through early tears, the largest gathering yet of Saylor's extended family and her own. She was grateful for the presence of her parents and most of her siblings. Warren and Wilbur were otherwise occupied, but Howard was here, along with Helen and Charles, Mildred and Hugh, Julia and Louise. It was a bitter-sweet reality that sorrow was often the catalyst for congenial gathering. At the Jumper homestead before the funeral, Saylor's bereft mother had complained that folks were acting more like they were at a family reunion than gathered for a burial. "It's an earthly foretaste of the reunion that Dad is experiencing in heaven, even now," Carrie had commented, knowing the words might not be well received.

Carrie's father, the Reverend D.P. Tate, had been invited to participate in the service, along with several local ministers who had served God in the community alongside the deceased. Papa Tate strode to the platform.

"Let us read these verses from the Old Testament," he began. "From the first Psalm:

"Blessed is the man that walketh not in the counsel of the ungodly, nor standeth in the way of sinners, nor sitteth in the seat of the scornful. But his delight is in the law of the Lord; and in his law doth he meditate day and night. And he shall be like a tree planted by the rivers of water, that bringeth forth his fruit in his season; his leaf also shall not wither; and whatsoever he doeth shall prosper.

"David Franklin Jumper found his treasure in the presence of the Lord, the maker of heaven and earth. His delight was in the precepts of

God. His meditation day and night was upon the Word of God his Savior. How like him to use this final opportunity to invite others to join him in his progress to the promised land. Like that tree, planted by the rivers of water, his roots sank deep into the sandy soil of his forebears. He bore his fruit in his season. That fruit was borne in the lives of many who sit here today.

"Because he was here, because he invested himself in your lives and in the life of this community, you bear witness to him by your presence in this sacred place today. This place itself was fruit of his labors. This place is a leaf of David Franklin Jumper that does not wither. This place prospers because he prospered in the Lord. Sandy Run has lost a servant, an example, a witness, a peacemaker, a spiritual giant. Won't you walk alongside? Won't you take the hand extended to you by God's Son, our Savior Jesus Christ? Won't you accompany His servant, David Franklin Jumper, on the journey to a better world? Let us pray ..."

♦   ♦   ♦   ♦   ♦

The day of farewells and reunion left loved ones emotionally drained and physically exhausted. Carrie was in the dining room feeding the children a supper of leftovers from the cloth-covered remains of the generous noon meal provided by church and community. As they ate, she overheard the conversation in the kitchen between Sallie and Saylor.

"It's time for you to come home, Bub," his mother insisted. "It's past time. There ain't no sense for you to be down in that strange town. That's not your home. It's not where you belong. You belong here. You're needed here."

"I agree that this is home, Ma. This is where I'd like to be. But when I do come back, it won't be to farm. I've seen already that I can't feed my family by farming. When there's a job to be had, I'll come back. Not until then."

"Is that Carrie girl holding you there?" she asked.

"No. Carrie and I make our decisions together. We left here together, and we'll come back together. In the meantime, rent out the fields and sell all the farm equipment you can, including some of the livestock. Kelly and Luther can help you handle the rest. When God opens the door, we'll be back."

♦ ♦ ♦ ♦ ♦

Dad

I entered the home of sorrow
   On the morning after the day
When the loving Heavenly Father
   Had taken dear Dad away.

He spent his full life in the vineyard.
   He worked for the Lord every day,
And tried to teach others to know Him
   In his sweet every day kind of way.

No matter how hard seemed life's pathway,
   No matter how long seemed the day,
He could always lend you some comfort
   As you trudged along life's dusty way.

He bore his long suffering with patience,
   Was never once known to repine,
And answered when asked for the reason,
   "The hand that leads me is divine."

And when at the church they sang,
   "I am bound for the promised land,"
I am sure that I heard Dad singing
   In the midst of the heavenly band.

Gently they lowered the casket
   Beneath the clay and the dust,
But his soul had sped onward and upward
   To the land where he stationed his trust.

And I think when he reached realms immortal,
   And came to the heavenly gate,
That he found it flung wide with a welcome,
   And Dad didn't have to wait.

— Carrie T. Jumper
1926

Oak Grove Methodist Church, Swansea, South Carolina

CHAPTER 31

A SUNDAY SURPRISE

Leroy Humphries sighed and relaxed deeper into his porch rocker, enjoying the spring evening in Miley. Little Louise was playing in the yard, while her mother, big Louise, was preparing supper. It was quiet in the town at last, with the mill noises ceased, mill workers gone home, and smells of supper in the air all around.

Humphries had been in this town long enough to feel ingrained into its fabric and spirit. Had it been only seven years since he had arrived here, fresh out of school, newly hired as a lumber grader? He had worked hard, been promoted to yard foreman, and now, in 1928, was sales manager for the mill. In the process, he had married Louise Luteman, whose mother was managing the boarding house. Louise had a two-year-old child, little Louise, whom he had adopted as his own. He couldn't love a biological child more. Life was mostly good.

The Humphries house sat on the street that ran behind the neighborhood garden spot. He could see his neighbors across the way — Jumpers, Parkers, and others. Adding to the pleasure of the evening, Saylor Jumper had begun a song fest on the piano as he awaited his own call to supper. *All that music must make the Jumper household a happy place. It certainly adds to happiness in Miley. Jumper surely knows he has an audience,* he thought. The glad notes of "Hosannah" wafted through open windows across the vicinity, entertaining and uplifting passersby. Some would step in tune with the music. Yet Humphries had the idea that when Saylor Jumper was making melody, there was no one else in the world. At times Mrs. Jumper would join in, and they would harmonize. Their children would sing, too. By the time they were grown, the Jumper children would surely know every hymn in the Methodist hymnal, as well as many others.

I'm glad that God brought the Jumpers to Miley, his thoughts ambled on. *Carrie and Saylor are intelligent, talented people. They're also humble and have hearts for service.* Saylor's music had enhanced the Sunday School and the church worship services. While Carrie couldn't be regular in Sunday School, she usually got her children there, and helped when she could. Humphries had watched Carrie Jumper organize a PTA, encouraging leadership among the locals, helping to build a growing sense of community in Miley.

Humphries' thoughts were interrupted, not by his awaited call to supper, but by shouts coming from the area between the houses and the railroad, closer to the church. He didn't have to look to know that a gang of neighborhood kids had gathered near the coal chute. It was a rite of passage for youngsters in Miley to get big enough to climb up to the highest level of the chute housing coal for firing steam engines. It was an exciting, unsafe, dirty practice, but one that signaled the beginning of manhood for boys, and sometimes was attempted by girls, too. Again, Humphries didn't have to look to see who the kids were. He could name them with good accuracy: Ralph and Winslow Jumper, Ralph Crosby, some Goodings, Priesters, and Ritters. When those fellows arrived home for supper, they would be filthy. The Jumpers, with all those children, must have huge baskets for laundry hidden under their beds, awaiting pickup on Monday mornings. The Humphries' basket would be quite small by comparison.

Soon he saw Minnie Parker come out onto her porch and sit down in the swing, without Cy, who was working in the logging camps during the week. He wondered if Minnie had gotten over her snit. There was a new manager of the hotel, Mrs. Crawford, who was perking things up at the facility. Under her leadership, the Lightseys had decided to add additional rooms, allowing increased occupancy. The new wing, nearly complete now, had blocked Mrs. Parker's view of people entering and leaving the big store, cutting down on her source of local news, *never* gossip. Minnie would have a long time to pout.

♦   ♦   ♦   ♦   ♦

Things were off to a rough start at the Jumper house. "Ralph! Winslow!" Carrie called out. "Lucy's drunk! Help her out to the porch and I'll get a quilt. She's got to be sobered up."

Lucy resisted, her head pounding and spinning. "Lucy ain't drunk," she insisted. "Lucy be sober. Lucy gon' cook checken."

Analda heard the commotion and came running. Carrie was spreading the quilt on the floor. "Sis, there's still coffee from breakfast. Bring me a cupful. Black. Tell Lellan to bring me a pillow."

Ralph and Winslow snickered, amused by the whole ordeal. Analda felt sorry for Lucy, and for her mother. Mother had gained quite a bit of weight lately, and getting down on that porch floor must have been a struggle.

But, knowing Mother, Lucy would be sobered up and back on her feet whether she wanted to be or not.

"It's probably a good thing for you children to see what drink can do to a person," Carrie said. They laughed. Living in Miley, they had already seen that.

♦   ♦   ♦   ♦   ♦

Analda fled the school yard, hurt and angry, not waiting for Juanita Ritter and Vera Gooding. She stuffed the note Juanita had handed her into her pocket. Where was Ralph when she needed him? Ralph was no longer in the Miley School. From seventh grade on, students boarded the bus in the mornings at the big store to be transported to school in Brunson. The bus had to go ten miles south through Whippy Swamp and Crocketville to the edge of Hampton. It then turned nearly north for six miles to Brunson. It would be a while before Ralph got home.

Going to Brunson when you reached seventh grade was a big deal, another rite of passage for Miley children. Hard Gooding drove the bus, narrow as a razor blade, children sitting across from each other, knees nearly touching. There was camaraderie during the ride, along with cliques, fights, and gossip. No matter what went on in the bus, once in Brunson, the Miley crowd always stood up for each other. Ralph usually came home full of tall tales. Analda couldn't wait until she could be right in the middle of all that. But right now she just wished Ralph were already home.

Analda didn't want to speak to Mother yet, but she might have to. She was hungry, and Lucy's biscuits would be in the kitchen. "Mother, I'm home," she called out, not waiting for an answer. Instead of biscuits today, a pot of lima beans sat simmering on the stove. Analda helped herself, spooning some into a cup and eating as quickly as possible.

As Lellan and Winslow were straggling in from school, Analda finished her beans and headed outside, scampering up into the shelter of the china-berry tree, where she impatiently waited for Ralph. *How could Mother have done this to me?* she thought, nursing her wounds. *How could she?*

At last she saw him, ambling toward home from behind the hotel. She shimmied down the tree and ran to meet him, pulling the offending note from her pocket.

"Ralph," she called quickly, "do you know anything about this?" She unfolded the paper and handed it to him.

"Your mother is going to have another baby," he read.

"Um ... don't know a thing," he said, not convincingly.

"Tell me the truth, Ralph Jumper. If you don't tell me the truth, I'll harass you for the rest of your life!"

"Well, you'll probably do that anyway, Sis. But you should have already figured it out. Haven't you noticed how big Mother has gotten?"

"Well, yes. I noticed it this morning when Lucy was drunk, but I just thought she'd been eating too many of Daddy's vegetables. How could she tell other people before she told me? I'm so embarrassed that my own friends knew before I did."

"She probably didn't tell anyone, Sis. You know grownups don't talk about these things. Mother has had so many babies and gained so much weight over the years that she can hide it for a long time. But she can't hide it anymore. People are figuring it out, that's all. I doubt that she told anyone ahead of you."

Analda sighed with relief. "Oh! Maybe not. Still, I'm not going to let

Juanita and Vera know that I didn't know. I'll figure out something to tell them ..."

"Well ... I gotta go. Winslow and I have practice at the ball field. Daddy is getting off early to practice for the game with Hampton on Saturday."

♦   ♦   ♦   ♦   ♦

The next morning Analda was ready when she encountered Juanita and Vera in the school yard.

"You didn't know, did you?" Juanita challenged.

"Of course, I knew," Analda retorted confidently. "I was surprised that you knew, and I didn't want Mother to think I had told."

"Well," said Vera. "What do you think the baby will be?"

"I have no idea what it will be," said Analda. "But I do know what it won't be."

"What do you mean?"

"It won't be a Gooding or a Ritter!"

♦   ♦   ♦   ♦   ♦

Eight-year-old Lellan had received a coveted invitation to spend the night at the hotel from her classmate, Catherine Crawford, whose mother was the manager. That gave Lellan two friends in the hotel. Henry Whitaker, another classmate, was a newcomer to Miley. His mother, Mrs. Whitaker, had divorced, which raised a few eyebrows around town. She moved into the hotel with Henry, where she operated a beauty parlor on the first floor in the mornings. In the afternoons, she worked as Dr. Sample's nurse. "Whit" — as everyone, including the children, called her — was gregarious and outgoing, a genuine people person, always ready to help. The night was never too dark, rainy, or cold that she wouldn't go — doctor or not. Whit quickly found herself at the heart of goings-on in Miley. She was aware of Mrs. Jumper's condition and was keeping a close eye on the house across the road from the doctor's office.

♦ ♦ ♦ ♦ ♦

Carrie's brother, Wilbur Tate, his lively wife, Donnie, and their six-year-old daughter, Betty, had moved to Yemassee. Wilbur had taken a job with the Atlantic Coastline Railroad there.

"Just think," Carrie exclaimed after hearing the news, "I have a brother living in the same county!"

"Yes," agreed Saylor, "but if he steps across the railroad tracks in the heart of Yemassee, he'll be in Beaufort County."

"True," she admitted, "yet they are living in the Hampton County side."

♦ ♦ ♦ ♦ ♦

On Saturday, June 23, the Wilbur Tates motored to Miley to visit, and to take Lellan and Carolyn back with them for a few days.

Lellan carried their suitcase confidently down the front steps, as Saylor held five-year-old Carolyn.

"I'm a big girl now," Carolyn said proudly. "I can go visiting."

"You certainly can," Saylor answered. "Lellan will be right there with you. You two be sweet, and help Aunt Donnie."

As they pulled away, Carrie commented, "It will seem strange to have only four children in the house."

Saylor laughed. "It won't be for very long," he said.

♦ ♦ ♦ ♦ ♦

On Sunday morning, Saylor was serving breakfast to the children. "Sis," he said, "Mother didn't have a good night, and she is resting. I'll need you to get Frank dressed for Sunday School."

"Daddy, Frank is three years old. He dresses himself now."

"Yes, but you can make sure he looks nice and gets there on time."

"Yes, sir."

♦ ♦ ♦ ♦ ♦

Winslow headed out to Sunday School a little early, as he often did. As he went down the front steps, he noticed Priester Booster sitting under a tree in the vacant lot beside the house. The old man signaled for Winslow to come over. He was chewing a plug of Brown Mule tobacco, a stream of dark down his chin. "Want a chew?" he asked Winslow, spitting into an old tin can, holding out a cut.

"I don't know," said Winslow. "It doesn't smell too good."

"It's juicy and sweet. You're big enough, and you'll like it."

"Well, maybe," Winslow said, accepting a bite of the dark brown stuff. He began to chew and choke.

"Don't swallow the juice," cautioned Priester. "It can upset your stomach."

"Too late," said Winslow. "I already did. I gotta go to Sunday School. Bye." He could see that Ralph and Analda had headed toward the church, with Frank holding their hands, making two steps for each of their one.

Winslow sat on his own front steps, his stomach churning, spitting out the nasty concoction. *What to do?* He might be sick. *Can't go to Sunday School like this,* he thought. *Can't go back inside. They'll make me stay in the yard for the rest of the day. Better try to go to Sunday School.* Slowly and with uncertainty, he made his way down the street, his head spinning. He stopped once on the Parkers' steps, stomach still lurching, then made another effort. When he reached the church, everyone had gone inside. He sat down on the wide steps leading to the double doors at the left side of the pretty white sanctuary. He wished he could throw up, but couldn't. He sat there, waiting for relief. It came unexpectedly in the form of a light breeze that seemed to clear his head. Slowly, his stomach settled.

Mrs. Ed Miley, who lived in a nice country home about a mile beyond Sauls' grocery at the Miley crossroads, was Sunday School teacher for the older children. The roll was to be answered with a Bible verse. Winslow couldn't think. He was late. Ralph would have already taken "Jesus wept."

Maybe he could do "God is love."

Winslow got up and went inside.

◆   ◆   ◆   ◆   ◆

Sunday School was over. Ralph, Winslow, Analda, and Frank headed back toward home with thoughts of Sunday dinner and maybe an afternoon frolic in the swamp if Daddy agreed. Minnie and Cy were sitting on their porch when the group passed by.

"How's Miz Jumper?" Minnie asked.

"She's doing just fine," Analda answered, knowingly.

Analda bounced up the steps of home first and headed into the hall. Saylor heard her and called out, "Sis, come in here." Analda stepped into the living room, a bit startled to see Dr. Sample stretched out on the couch. Saylor was holding a pink bundle.

"Oh!" she cried. "The baby's here! Is it a girl?"

"Looks like a girl to me," Saylor said. By this time the others had gathered.

"Oh!" said Winslow in total surprise. "A baby?"

Dr. Sample had sat up on the couch, enjoying the moment.

"Where's Mother?" asked Analda.

"Mrs. Whitaker is with her," Saylor answered. "You'll see her in a little while. Frank, come and look who we have here. You have a brand-new baby sister!" Frank held back, unsure of how to respond.

Ralph stood by, saying little. It was all old hat to him. Finally, he asked, "What's her name?"

"Zelda. Zelda Cline."

Saylor presented Zelda, green eyes wide and alert, to each child, saying, "Meet your sister, Zelda." Zelda seemed to look intently at Ralph, Winslow, Analda, and Frank."

"She's taking a good look at each of you," Saylor said. "She's trying to see what she's gotten herself into!"

Whit appeared at the door. "You may come and see your mother now," she said, smiling. "Isn't your baby sister beautiful?"

Carrie was propped up in bed, her long hair freshly brushed, the room and covers as neat as a pin.

"Mother," Analda said, receiving Carrie's embrace and kiss. "You named the baby for your college friend, Zelda Cline."

"Yes," she said. "We tried to think of a different middle name, but nothing sounds right with Zelda except Cline. So she's Zelda Cline."

Frank had climbed onto his mother's bed. "We have a new baby!" he said.

"We certainly do!" Carrie held out her arms to him. "You have a brand-new baby sister! Do you like her?"

"Uh-huh. Lellan and Carolyn don't know that we have a baby sister."

"Won't they be surprised!"

CHAPTER 32

HARD TIMES

Hunched over a page of figures at his office desk, Saylor struggled to concentrate. Jake Lee, a colorful preacher, caretaker for the office, the mill, and the stores, was sweeping up.

"Good morning, Jake."

"Good morning, Mr. Jumper."

"How are things at your house?"

"Good, suh. The Lawd has done blessed me wid another head."

"A new baby? You have another new baby?"

"Yes, suh. Another little girl."

"Well, congratulations! Tell me something. Aren't you a little bit old to keep having babies?"

"Well, suh, you see my wife, she in her prime."

"I see."

Saylor's attention turned to a knock on the window. Lellan and Carolyn were waiting there with a jar of refreshment.

"Well, what have we here?" he asked, raising the window and taking the jar of cold blue beverage.

"Blackberry acid, Daddy. We're taking a break on the porch and Mother knew you'd like some, too."

"Thank her for me," he said. "I guess they haven't gotten back with the new car yet."

"Not yet, Daddy."

"They should be here soon. Surely before I come for dinner. You girls run on home now, and I'll see you in a little while."

"Bye, Daddy."

Miss Sweeney, a secretary for Lightsey Brothers, along with Mrs. McDonald, placed a stack of files on Saylor's desk. "Excuse me, Mr. Jumper. Here are the records you requested. I couldn't help overhearing. Are you getting a new car?"

"Yes, we certainly are. The old Dort is done for. The parts that aren't worn out have been destroyed by the children," he said. "Even the cloth top got a split. The boys stuck their heads out and split it more."

She laughed. "Maybe a hard top will fare better. What are you getting?"

"A 1929 Essex Super Six Sedan, four doors, blue. We're all excited. Kelly is here for a visit. He and Ralph have gone to Bamberg to bring it home. I'm hoping they'll be back before dinner, so I can take it for a spin before I come back to work."

"That sounds exciting. By the way, please thank Mrs. Jumper for saving our supper at the boarding house the other night."

"How so?"

"Cook was making a pan of cornbread when the corn meal ran out. The store was closed. She sent little Carolyn Crawford to ask if Mrs. Jumper had some to spare. She did, and we enjoyed our cornbread."

"I'm sure Carrie was happy to do that. She tries to keep the larder well stocked, since we are feeding a crowd, too."

"Well, may the new car be all you hope for."

To Saylor's disappointment, the boys had not come with the car when he arrived home for dinner. "They should be here by now," he said to Carrie. "Bamberg's not that far."

"I'm sure they'll be here soon, Saylor. Enjoy your dinner, and maybe they'll come before you finish eating."

After dinner Saylor's anxiety about the children and the new car was increasing, so he skipped his usual piano session, took a seat in the wicker rocking chair, and began to nod off.

Beep. Beep.

Startled, Saylor leapt to his feet, turned, and looked through the window.

"They're here! They're here!" he called. "And she's a beaut!"

Everyone gathered around the shiny new vehicle. "What took you so long?" Saylor asked. "Bamberg's not that far."

"Well, Daddy," Kelly began to explain, handing the key to his father. "We ran into some complications."

"What complications?"

"Between Bamberg and Ehrhardt we heard a terrible noise. Pretty soon we realized that the front left wheel was coming off. I got the car off the road. We hitched a ride back into Bamberg. The dealer sent a crew out to fix it, and here we are."

Saylor was nearly speechless. "Thank goodness you're okay," he finally managed. "That could have been bad."

"All's well that ends well," said Ralph.

Analda and Winslow were already in the car, anxious to take a ride. Carrie had come out to see, but declined to get inside. "I'll be in it soon enough," she said to Saylor. "Take the children for a ride."

The next morning the car wouldn't crank. Saylor tried. Kelly tried. Ralph and Winslow tried. The motor wouldn't fire. "Let's look under the hood," Saylor said, frustrated.

All four were bent over, looking under the blue hood of their brand-new Essex automobile, when Norris Mixon passed in his own car. "No need to look under the hood," he yelled. "There's nothing there!"

Within a week, the Essex was gone, having been returned to the dealer. In its place sat a 1929 six-cylinder, two-toned green Chevrolet sedan.

◆   ◆   ◆   ◆   ◆

"If I'd known the stock market would crash," Saylor moaned, "I'd never have forked over eight hundred dollars for a new car!"

"I think having the new car is providential," Carrie said. "The Dort was worn out, and we'd have been facing this crisis without reliable transportation. I can see many reasons why God provided this automobile at this time."

"We may be driving it straight to the poorhouse!" Saylor said.

Six-year-old Carolyn, overhearing this exchange, was aghast. *Eight hundred dollars! Where did Daddy get that much money?* After all the poor-mouthing she'd been hearing, she couldn't believe it! The distressed child burst into tears. Unknown to her parents, she had read in a book a graphic description of a destitute family laboriously trudging up a hill to the poorhouse. "I don't want to go to the poorhouse!" she wailed.

Carrie pulled Carolyn onto her lap. "We're not going to the poorhouse, Carolyn," she said comfortingly, stroking blond curls. "God will take care of us. Saylor, I wish you wouldn't say these things in front of the children."

"They might as well hear them," he countered, "because that's how it is!"

"You must admit, it will be interesting to see how God provides," she said.

"Not *that* interesting!"

◆　◆　◆　◆　◆

Saylor continued to worry, with good reason. He saw people being cut off daily. Jobs were scarce and wages low. The mill was running only two or three days a week. He realized he and his family were better off than many. He still had a job, even though he had been cut back to his starting salary.

The Lightseys were good to their workers and did everything they could to ease the pain and to keep things going. The mill paid off in cash only every two weeks. In between, they issued trading coupons that could be used to buy things out of the stores. In the case of an emergency, you might be able to get cash.

The children were fascinated with the "checkbooks," as they called the mill coupons. There were different colors for different amounts. Saylor's signature was on each, as well as the name and number of the person to whom it was issued. A twenty-five cents checkbook had little perforated sections worth five cents each. You could spend it a nickel at a time, tearing off a five cents section. It would be put in the cash register at the store, just like money. Or you could spend the whole thing. The children got a nickel, sometimes in coupons, after their baths each Saturday, even during the Depression. They learned to spend their money very carefully. Occasionally they got into trouble for losing checkbooks. They were small and flat, subject to falling into a crack behind Carrie's bedroom mantel.

"It's the same thing as throwing away money!" Saylor would bellow. "It's just pure-t-carelessness!"

♦　♦　♦　♦　♦

Carrie continued to trust God, to pray, and to put feet to her prayers. There was always a need to fill. She felt that poverty was to be less pitied than ignorance. There were people who knew how to manage and to make the best of things, and people who didn't. Still, even among those who had coping skills, poverty could get the upper hand.

Carrie took on relief work, distributing food and clothing supplies at her own expense, putting many hours into the effort. She worked closely with Mr. Godley at the store to get needed supplies to people on farms. Their car was key. Ralph was driving, and soon thereafter, Winslow. Saylor allowed them to use his car for mercy missions and to assist Carrie in distribution of relief. Much later she learned that she should have been paid for her efforts, but never was.

"It doesn't matter," she said. "In the long run, I was paid, because we were blessed. I'd do it all over again."

The Zach Terry family was one of many who suffered extreme hardship. With the Terrys already on relief, Zach's wife died and left him with six young children. Carrie, Mrs. Crosby, and Mrs. Barfield sewed most of one night to make clothes for the children to wear to their mother's funeral. Miley mourned and rallied around the family until they could get on their feet.

Late one Friday afternoon, there came a knock on the Jumper door. Cy Parker stood there, fresh from the logging train, his coveralls black with pitch. When Carrie invited him to come inside, he declined. "No, thank you ma'am, Miz Jumper. I cain't come in. I am dirty." He then proceeded to describe to Carrie a family he had come upon deep in the woods. They were clearly about to starve to death, the children running around half naked. Carrie would remember his words for the rest of her life. "I ain't got no money to do nuttin' for 'em, but I knowed that if you knowed about 'em, sump'n would be done." And something was done.

The following weekend, Carolyn came in from play bursting with something to tell her mother. "Mother! Mother! Guess what Mr. Parker said about you!"

"There's no telling," Carrie said.

"He said, 'I tell you what ... that Miz Jumper is a (*bad word*) good woman!'"

Carrie suppressed a smile. "Well, I tell you, coming from Cy, that's a compliment!"

◆　◆　◆　◆　◆

On June 2, 1930, Carrie and Saylor experienced their greatest blessing of the early Depression years with the birth of Stella Nell. Nell was their ninth child and fifth daughter, a light in a bleak world.

"I really didn't care if the new baby was a boy or a girl," Carrie said. "Since she's a girl, I'm glad. With just two years between, I believe she and Zelda will be a lot of company for each other."

"Friends for life," said Saylor.

CHAPTER 33

MAKING DO

Carrie stepped out the back door, down the steps, across her own backyard, and past the pen that confined two hogs awaiting cold-weather slaughter. She crossed into the backyard of the Longs, whose white frame house was the first in a row of similar dwellings facing the main road. Carrie was concerned about the Long family, Lucius and Eunice and their growing boys, Bobby, Buck, and Barry. She was pretty sure that on many nights they would have had little for supper if she or Saylor hadn't handed them vegetables from their garden. Especially, she was concerned about Eunice's state of mind. Lucius' hours at the mill had been drastically cut, and he didn't handle down-time well. Winslow had reported to Carrie and Saylor that last Saturday he had seen Lucius, who obviously had a few drinks under his belt, sitting on the bench outside the big store, singing, "Corina, Corina." Carrie wanted to get Eunice out of the house and away from preoccupation with her troubles.

Eunice answered her knock. "Good morning, Eunice. Winslow is going to drive me into Hampton this afternoon for an errand and a little browsing. Come along with us. It'll do you good to get out of the house."

"Thank you, Mrs. Jumper. I'd surely like to go, but I can't. I don't have any stockings." Even during the Depression, a woman didn't leave her house without stockings.

"Yes, you do," Carrie said, reaching into the pocket of her dress. "Here's a pair."

"Oh, no! I can't take those!" Eunice protested.

"Of course, you can," Carrie answered, resorting to her kind, but authoritative schoolteacher voice. "Meet us at our car at 2:30."

♦　♦　♦　♦　♦

Saylor was pitching a baseball to Winslow between the house and the garage after supper. He didn't want to lose his pitching arm, and he still liked to talk to his boys about his erstwhile college career. He'd carefully explain to Winslow just how to hold the mitt, and he'd throw it right in, obviously enjoying the practice. "I'm still pretty good," he said, "but I just don't have the steam I used to have."

"You have steam enough for me," Winslow said.

As they were finishing up, Ralph came around the house. "Winslow," he said, "we've got to go work the swamp garden."

Saylor had expanded his gardening since the crash, planting several more small plots around the yard, and one in the field across from the house. He had also rented an acre behind the church, not far from Hersh Padgett's filing bench and the swamp. The swamp garden was primarily Ralph's domain. Saylor felt it important that his boys should know the basics of gardening, and Ralph had taken to it right well. He had broken up the new garden with just a hand plow, working after school and in the evenings. Winslow was his reluctant assistant, and Frank was big enough to set the thin sticks that could be had from the mill for the running butter beans.

At the garden, Ralph assigned Winslow a row to weed, while he started at the other end. Soon the younger boy was sitting on a stump to rest, his hoe thrown down. "No time for sittin' down now," Ralph shouted. "I'll let you know when it's time for sittin'." A few minutes later, Winslow looked back to see Ralph, leaning on his own hoe, talking to Mr. Padgett. Caught, Ralph grinned. "Well, when I got here, it was time."

♦　♦　♦　♦　♦

Many a butter bean shelling took place on the Jumper front porch, sometimes deep into the night. Hulls were haphazardly thrown onto the floor, creating a morning job for one of the girls. They were then scattered back into the garden.

Bedtime was never a serious matter. The regimentation of Carrie's childhood was thrown out, as she had predicted. In hot weather, she placed a quilt on the floor of the large front porch for sleepyheads to use, until they staggered to their beds or slept the night through right there. In time, a porch cot was added. Years later, grandchildren would spat over who got the cot. If you won, you could lie there, pretending to be asleep while privy to adult conversation that you weren't supposed to hear. That front porch with its swing and its cot was a magical place of refreshment, the best place in the world.

♦　♦　♦　♦　♦

The beans had to be canned, along with corn, tomatoes, okra, and everything else that Saylor raised. What wasn't produced in the gardens, Carrie bought from Crandel Herndon, who brought vegetables on a horse-drawn wagon from Hampton.

Canning was a hot job, done over a wood-burning stove in the heat of summer. The Jumper children would forever have a vision of their mother, bathed in perspiration, carefully filling two-quart jars with everything needed to feed a large family. Peaches were a favorite. With a long fork, Carrie placed as many peaches as a jar would hold as the children looked on appreciatively. Oh, the smell and taste of peach cobblers to come! Even small amounts of food were canned, nothing wasted, while Carrie's girls learned skills to carry through their own lives. A curing room had been added to the back of the garage, lined with shelves awaiting the summer's bounty. All the hard work was rewarded by the sight of those jars lined up like soldiers in dress uniform.

It never really occurred to the Jumper children that they might be hungry, and they never were. Yet they were aware that others might be.

Saylor urged them to appreciate what they had, and to share as they could. Carrie spoke often of the source of their blessings, a Heavenly Father who cared, provided, and guided.

"Every good and perfect gift comes from above," she reminded them in her familiar, lilting voice. "It's why I believe in giving to the church, even in hard times. When you give to God, your personal money stretches farther."

From Carrie's kitchen, many pots of grits, cheese, and butter or vegetable soup and cornbread were ferried by the feet of the Jumper children around the neighborhood in times of illness, want, trouble, or just surplus. Whatever the Jumpers had, they shared, whenever they could. Carrie was thankful for Miss Izora Miley's contribution to the community for these times. The sister of petite Miss Vi, Miss Izora was tall and commanding. In her capacity as home demonstration agent, she taught women to stretch their food budget with casseroles, macaroni and cheese, and creamed chicken on biscuits.

◆ ◆ ◆ ◆ ◆

It was cold enough to butcher hogs, as they say, and so the day was planned. "Sis, bring me my butchering bloomers," Carrie called out. "And make sure everyone is up. It's all hands on deck today." She quickly donned the bloomers, made of thick, brown burlap, lined for warmth under a heavy dress, and worn only for this occasion.

Over a hasty, but hearty breakfast, Carolyn began to wail. "Daddy, do we have to kill the hogs? Please don't kill the hogs. I don't want them to die."

"Carolyn, it's why the hogs are born — to feed people. And I notice that you really enjoy their bacon. It has to be."

Lucy, reporting early, offered the child some comfort. "It'll be okay, Miss Carolyn. Some things just *beez*."

"Well, let's get outside," Saylor urged. "The Long boys are waiting." The Long boys usually helped out with butchering, being paid with meat, usually more than they had earned.

Late in the afternoon, when the worst of the work was nearly over,

Carolyn went inside to the kitchen stove, where she opened the damper to warm her numb-with-cold knees and legs, pulling up her bloomers to access the heat. She soon heard a snapping sound, like an air rifle popping. She looked down at her knee — blood was pouring from a hole in the flesh.

"Mother! Mother! I've been shot! Something shot me!"

Everyone came running, huddling around Carolyn anxiously.

Carrie stanched the blood, which was minimal, with a handkerchief. Saylor examined the wound, scratched his head. "The only thing I can figure is ... one of the shells must have gotten into the fire; some powder remained and exploded, shooting Carolyn."

"It's okay," Carolyn said solemnly. "It's okay for me to be shot, since I'm the only one who cared about the hogs."

♦　♦　♦　♦　♦

While food was adequate for the Jumpers, other things were more scarce, especially cash money, useful for solving problems. Carrie stood in the hall before the bookshelf built for the space by Horace Roberts, the mill foreman, to house their collection of Harvard Classics, Colliers Encyclopedias, and numerous children's books. She was thankful they had purchased most of their library before money became nearly nonexistent. The Jumpers eagerly and generously shared books with Miley residents. "We have everything we need," Carrie said, "except money, and that's the least important. I have Daddy, and we'll work things out together." The children learned to be frugal and resourceful, using things that were available, and then reusing or repurposing.

Carrie's sewing skills were valuable. New garments could be made from old, dresses for the girls from her own. Still, Carrie couldn't sew all the clothing needed by the family, nor had she cash for paying others to sew. Clothes were handed down, mended, worn with imperfections, and done without. Saylor's gardening jackets were his old, worn dress coats. Now he had the perfect excuse to continue wearing what he called his "shakos" — the old, frayed-brim hats that he loved, which Carrie constantly threatened to discard. She joked that she burned one occasionally.

Shoes were another problem, since the long, narrow Jumper feet were hard to fit into the common sizes of footwear. Shoes were no problem for Frank, however, who eschewed them all year long, refusing to wear them even for Sunday School. Carolyn found herself in regular battle with her younger brother over this matter. She was embarrassed for Frank to go without shoes. Carrie took a different approach.

"Far be it from me," she said, "to turn a boy against Sunday School over shoes."

♦   ♦   ♦   ♦   ♦

"Mother," Analda asked, helping Carrie with the canning in the kitchen, "is it wrong to ask God to provide you with something nice to wear, when you know your friends barely have everyday clothes?" Analda's class at Brunson High School was planning a trip to Savannah to hear President Roosevelt speak from his train en route from Warm Springs, Georgia. Analda felt she had no clothes appropriate for the outing.

"It's never wrong to talk with God about your wants or your needs, Sis. He's interested in everything about you. Sometimes He gives us exactly what we ask for; sometimes He answers in a way we don't expect. But He always answers, and sometimes He uses His answers to teach us things He wants us to know. Ask Him, and see what happens."

On Saturday afternoon before the trip on Monday, the family was gathered around the table, talking. Analda had not yet had an answer to her prayers. "I guess I could just wear my old paisley dress, wool sweater, and worn-out flats," she sighed. "There's nothing at the big store that would fit me, much less look good for a trip."

In the midst of her despair, Saylor came in. "Sis, some cash came into the office this afternoon," he announced.

Analda nearly bounced out of her chair. "Really? I can't believe it! Just in time, too! Mother, Tharpe's in Varnville stays open late on Saturdays. Can we go shopping?" Analda came home that evening with a new dress, a new sweater, and her very first high-heeled pumps. On the much-anticipated trip, those high heels nearly killed her.

"Sometimes we must be careful what we pray for," Carrie said with a chuckle.

♦ ♦ ♦ ♦ ♦

"It's check-off night," Saylor said, pushing back from the supper table. "I have to go back to work." As was his custom, he went around the table, his lanky form bent over, gently kissing the foreheads of his children. Then he kissed his wife.

"Daddy," said Ralph, "Ralph Crosby and I have been planning to go to see the Tuten girls in Varnville. We were to go in the Crosby car, but it has a flat tire. May I use the Chevrolet?" Ralph, who had been working on a WPA program, paying fifteen cents a week for his lunches, was ready for some fun.

"That's fine, son. Just be careful, watch the other fella, conserve gas, and don't be out late."

"Yes, sir."

Soon Ralph was in the car, cranking it for the evening outing. Except that it didn't crank. The motor made no attempt to turn over. The battery was dead.

"Well, it looks like the two Ralphs are grounded tonight," Winslow observed wryly from the porch. "I guess you can go with me to the Barfields and listen to the Lone Ranger on the radio."

"Rats!" said Ralph, heading on foot toward the Crosby house to deliver the bad news.

"Wait for me," called Frank, tagging along behind, barefoot as always.

Presently the two Ralphs appeared. Frank pulled a wagon behind them containing a battery. The Crosby battery was inserted into the Jumper car, and off the Ralphs went. The evening was saved.

Saylor returned from the office, and Carrie related the incident. "Determination inspires resourcefulness," she observed.

"Pretty girls do, too," said Saylor.

Saylor at work in the Lightsey Lumber Mill office

CHAPTER 34

MILEY SINGS

"There's something I've been thinking about," she said.

"Mm ... I thought so."

"I believe it's time to do more than just think."

"Uh-oh."

It was evening, first dark. They were almost to the church on one of their occasional walks alone. This was their thinking and talking time. It was good to have older children to supervise younger ones when you needed time together.

"So, what's on your mind?" he asked as they settled onto the sanctuary steps.

"Miley needs to have a singing," she said.

"You mean ... here at the church?"

"No, not at the church. At our house. They'll come better if it's at our house. People who don't come to the church would be more willing to come to a home. Especially people who have never been to our house."

"Hasn't everyone in Miley been to our house?"

"No, not at all, if you'll think about it. Many Miley folks are shy and keep to themselves."

"True. How will we go about it?"

♦   ♦   ♦   ♦   ♦

On the designated day, Carrie sent the children around town spreading the word. "There will be a singing at our house tonight. Please come. You don't have to be a singer. We'll all learn together. Seven o'clock sharp."

Carrie filled the house with flowers Saylor had planted around the edges of his gardens. She gathered chairs into the living room from around the house, squeezing in as many as space allowed. "If we don't have enough," she said, "that would be a good problem to have."

By seven o'clock most chairs were filled. Some who came were expected, while others were a pleasant surprise. The Barfields, the Longs, Mrs. Crosby, Minnie Parker, the Mixons showed up. Friends of the older children came, too. Analda brought Juanita Ritter and Vera Gooding. Ralph brought Charles Boyles, new to Miley. Charles was not holding a grudge after Analda and Juanita had pushed him into a ditch in his white suit, his initiation into Miley. Carolyn Crawford came from the hotel and sat with Lellan. Mr. Roberts and his wife, Queenie, arrived late, as did Mr. Humphries. Some of the younger children gathered on the porch, listening and singing through the raised windows. Cecil Godley, who was now old enough to help his father, Charlie, in the big store, slipped onto the porch with Frank. The store had just closed.

Saylor was at the piano, playing some of his favorites, including "Stepping in the Light," as the group gathered, adding to a mood of anticipation. Carrie, in her element, was busy greeting, organizing, managing, and ministering. She passed out hymnbooks brought from the church, knowing some present couldn't read and write. It didn't matter. She wouldn't make them uncomfortable, as they seemed to know. Everyone was smiling and happy.

"This is a real good idea," several said to Carrie. "Thanks for inviting us."

"I've marked the first hymn," she said. "We'll start with something familiar." She read the words of the first stanza of "Amazing Grace" and talked about the meaning of the words. "Now let's sing," she said, and the room rang with sweet sound. By the last stanza most were warmed up and glad they had come.

For this singing, the first of many to come, Carrie called for favorites, always reading and commenting on the words. She took the time to teach a little music as she went, emphasizing time, tempo, and harmony. The evening of music passed quickly. "We'll finish by singing the Doxology," she said, and voices raised in praise. Everyone agreed that they wanted to do this again, and often.

♦ ♦ ♦ ♦ ♦

Carrie's first cousin, Carlisle Doggett, of Rutherford County, North Carolina, had come to Hampton County as principal of Brunson High School. He remained there quite a number of years and became a regular visitor to the Jumper home in Miley. On one such visit, he commented to Carrie and Saylor as he puffed on his pipe, "You know, there's an interesting thing about Miley. I've noticed that students who come from Miley are quite musical. They seem to be natural-born singers."

Saylor gave Carrie a secret wink.

CHAPTER 35

RETURN TO SANDY RUN

Carrie, Carolyn, and Zelda were in the living room eating oranges, throwing the peelings into a crackling fire, and enjoying the tangy, citrus smell. Saylor came in, slamming the door. "I'm sick of the leaky barn doors in this house," he complained. "I wish I could go back to Sandy Run and build us a tight little house."

Carrie chuckled. "With this big family, a little house would certainly be tight," she said lightly. Inwardly, she sighed. She was concerned about Saylor. The work and worry of these hard years were taking a toll. He had recently returned from a visit home, where, as always, a load of guilt had been dumped on him by his mother. Carrie didn't know what to do. So, she did what she always did. She prayed.

♦   ♦   ♦   ♦   ♦

They were alone in their car, a rare occurrence. The older children were in school, the younger ones in the care of Rosa at home. Lucy had recently left Miley to move with Andy to Brunson. "We want to get out of this sawmill town," they had said.

Nearing the Miley crossroads, Carrie said, "Saylor, turn into this little field road, and let's talk before we get home." They had done this before. Saylor turned right and pulled into the edge of a plowed under cornfield.

"What's up?" he asked.

"Nothing's up. However, I've been thinking."

FROM MURPHY TO MILEY

"You do that a lot."

"Well, so do you."

"There's a lot to think about these days."

"What I'm thinking, mainly, is that we need to make a change of some kind."

"What do you mean?"

"You really want to go back to Sandy Run, don't you?"

"Well, yes. But it's a pipe dream. It's unrealistic."

"I know you worry about Kelly, and Granmah, and Dora, and Claudine."

"Mostly about Kelly, I think. He's growing up, and he needs to have a life of his own. It's not normal for a young man to be strapped with an aging grandmother and two ailing aunts. If we were there, I could relieve him and let him go about his life."

"We could try a summer or two at the old house. Maybe it would work out for us to eventually go back."

"The house is not in good shape. It's certainly not the tight little house I have in mind."

"It wouldn't matter during the summer. You could take the boys up on weekends this spring and get it ready. It would give you some good time with them and something to think about besides this Depression."

"Hmm ..."

♦　♦　♦　♦　♦

Eleven-year-old Lellan was angry. She normally enjoyed being at Granmah's. The others complained that Granmah favored boys and didn't like girls, but Lellan got along with her feisty grandmother. Not today.

"Stop, Granmah. I don't want to hear this. You're not going to turn me against my family like you did Kelly. It's wrong. My mother doesn't talk ugly about you and never will. You should be that good."

For once, Sallie Saylor Jumper was silent. It was a long silence. "I'm sorry, Lellan. I won't do it again." And she never did. Not to Lellan.

Sashaying through the field and the woods to the old house, Lellan couldn't believe she had stood up to Granmah Sallie. Lellan didn't like confrontation. Something had just come over her. Mother managed to stay on good terms with Granmah, at least outwardly. It couldn't be easy. Someone needed to stand up for Mother. Lellan was glad she had.

The summer had been challenging, but fun, too. Living in the old Seible house was hard. Water had to be hauled up from the spring. Still, there were plenty of able bodies to do that, and the spring itself brought enjoyment. Mother kept it pretty. They bathed there, shampooed their hair, washed clothes, and cooled off, along with watermelons, in the pleasant flow.

Lellan found her mother in the kitchen, canning, just as she did at home. Ralph and Kelly had grown a garden, and Saylor brought vegetables from home when he came on the weekends.

"Can you use some help, Mother? Where are the others?"

"Scattered about. Mostly gone to Sandy Run creek for a good swim. They took Zelda, and Nell has gone down for a nap."

Lellan realized that she had her mother for a rare moment alone. "Let me fill the jars," she offered. As they worked, they talked.

"Mother, why can't I be nervy, like Sis? Kelly and Ralph tell her things they won't tell me. They laugh and carry on. I feel left out."

"Lellan, God makes each one of us unique. He has made you to be who you are, and not to be like anyone else. Your daddy and I are thankful for the way He made you. We have to worry more about Sis. She can be reckless, acting before she considers the consequences. You are like your father — level-headed, responsible, faithful. You're a blessing. We don't want you any other way. Now stop comparing yourself to others and be who God plans for you to be."

◆   ◆   ◆   ◆   ◆

The highlight of the summer for Carrie was her sister Helen's two-week visit. Saylor met the Saturday train in St. Matthews. Helen adored Zelda and Nell, her two youngest nieces. She had come to sew dresses, while Carrie did handwork. Carrie liked a personal touch on her children's clothes when possible

— a little embroidery, tatting, or even crochet. They couldn't wait to get started.

At the supper table, everyone was in high spirits, anxious to catch up on news from the Tate side of the family. Near the end of the meal, Zelda asked permission to leave the table. "Mother, I've finished. May I go upstairs to play now?"

"Yes, Zelda, you may go. But come back down soon. We'll be serving up peach cobbler."

Zelda traipsed up the stairs in Frank's hand-me-down khaki pants, her preferred mode of dress. Since it was still daylight, the three-year-old wasn't afraid to go up alone. However, the children found the house to be spooky at night, with its shadowy, unpainted walls. There was a scary closet at the top of the stairs where they would go when they wanted to be brave. At night, you had to go out on the back porch to get water from a bucket. No one wanted to do that alone. And then there were the blood stains on the floor upstairs.

Zelda enjoyed looking out the big bedroom window. From here she could see the top of Granmah's house. As she gazed down into her own yard, she saw a mule tied to a tree in the front. It was Granmah's mule, with a burlap sack flung over its back. The boys must have ridden it when they came home for supper. Zelda looked again. A limb of the tree extended over the slanted roof of the house. "Hmm," she said. Soon she was out of the window on the roof, climbing onto the limb. Making her way carefully down the branch, she found herself poised just above the mule. She lowered herself so that she dangled from her hands. Letting go of the rough bark, she fell onto the back of the mule. The startled animal yanked itself loose from the tree and took off, dumping Zelda and the sack onto the ground.

Zelda's screams brought the family running. "What happened?" Saylor asked, scooping up the traumatized child, checking for injuries. "Did you fall from the house?"

Winslow, close behind, seeing the fleeing mule, knew the answer. "She fell off the mule," he said.

Carrie had arrived and taken Zelda into her arms, comforting the child and asking her what hurt. When Saylor was satisfied there were probably no broken bones, he went after the mule, eventually returning it to its home.

Carrie, carrying Zelda, whose sobs were subsiding, said to a concerned Helen, "As you can see, this is our tomboy."

♦   ♦   ♦   ♦   ♦

Carrie and Helen talked far into the night, each relishing the other's company. When Carrie had finally caught up on the news from home, Helen asked, "How are Dora and Claudine?"

"Doing well. Dora still walks by holding onto things. She does a lot for someone with her limitations. In addition to being the Sandy Run postmistress, she plans the meals, does some food preparation, all of the sewing, and looks after Claudine. Claudine is a sweet-natured girl, but still a girl mentally. Her epilepsy is controlled with medication and diet. She gets along well with most of the children, especially Ralph and Winslow. Which reminds me. The older children have gotten themselves involved in a bit of drama."

"What kind of drama?"

"It concerns Dora and a man named Albert Wise who courted her and wanted to marry her years ago. They have remained friends and have passed notes from time to time."

"Where does he live? Is he married?"

"He never married. He lives up the hill with his brother's family. According to Granmah Sallie, Winslow has been the note carrier this summer. You can imagine how she feels about that."

"From what you've told me about Dora, it sounds to me that she would have been able to manage being in a marriage quite well."

"I think that's probably true. We'll never know. Albert was willing to marry her, knowing the circumstances. Analda and Ralph have been co-conspirators in a couple of visits. That has really made Sallie mad."

"I think it's hilarious. But how do you feel about their being involved in that?"

"It certainly has kept them entertained. And I think Dora deserves a little happiness. She'll miss the children when we leave."

"I feel sad for her," said Helen.

♦   ♦   ♦   ♦   ♦

On the final Sunday of the summer sojourn, Granmah Sallie hosted a family dinner. In addition to the local crowd, Minnie and Clarence Rucker came from their home in Columbia. Their older children, busy with their own lives, were not present. Dorothy was still at home and came with her parents. Ben, born the same day as Frank, was there, as was his younger sister, Caroline, a year older than Zelda. Zelda and Caroline enjoyed each other's company, but Frank and Ben were too different to blend well. Ben was bookish and introverted, while Frank was outdoorsy and personable. Yet, for this one day, differences were insignificant, and the family enjoyed a tranquil gathering. Except for one thing.

In mid-afternoon, Carrie was seated on the front porch swing with Minnie, catching up with the doings of the oldest Rucker children. Ralph pulled up near the front steps in Saylor's Chevrolet. At the same time, as if on cue, Winslow and Analda came out the front door on each side of Dora, helping her to walk. They proceeded across the porch, down the steps, and into the automobile. The Chevrolet pulled away from the house with Dora in the front passenger seat, Winslow and Analda in back, barely in time. The front door slammed, and Granmah Sallie came tearing across the porch in high gear.

"Stop!" she yelled. "Come back right this minute." She was too late. "There ain't no sense in it. There ain't no sense in none of it." She retreated into the house in a huff.

"Well," said Minnie. "What do you make of all that?"

"I think it's just fine," said Carrie.

♦   ♦   ♦   ♦   ♦

Saylor and Carrie sat on their personal log in the edge of the woods, their Sandy Run talking place. "Be careful," she said. "Do you remember what happened the last time we came here?"

"Can't forget," he said. "We got chiggers. Bad. You bathed in lye soap and were fine the next day. I didn't, and was miserable for days."

"We discovered that lye soap doesn't work if you don't use it right away." They laughed, remembering.

"Well," she said. "What do you think?"

"About what?"

"About the summer. Do you think we'll do this again next year?"

He sighed. He paused. He finally answered. "I can't say for sure. The children seemed to enjoy it. You seemed to enjoy it. But I really didn't enjoy it."

"Why not?"

"For one thing, I didn't enjoy all of you being caught up in my family's issues. The biggest thing is ... I was lonely in Miley. I hated coming home to that empty house that echoed silence. I hardly played the piano, because there was no one to hear."

"The Miley folks heard."

"I don't play for the Miley folks. That's another thing. The Miley folks kept telling me how much they missed our family. 'Summer in Miley is no fun without the Jumpers,' they said, and even the swamp was a dud. It was too quiet and too boring. I think they meant it. I didn't realize how big a part of Miley our children are. It surprised me."

"So, you think we'll stay in Miley next summer?"

"I don't know. Besides the things I've mentioned, it wasn't easy from a practical standpoint. All the moving of furniture and household things was an effort and an expense. About all I can say for sure is ... we'll see."

Ruth Dora Jumper

CHAPTER 36

GREAT JEHOVAH

"No church will ever do for me what the Miley church did," Analda would recall years later. "The things we did there nourished my spirit and gave me guidance." Analda loved to sit on the center back, light-stained oak pew of the pretty, well-lit sanctuary with her friends. Sunday School was held in the mornings and preaching in the evenings. Mr. Humphries was ever-present and always arrived early to fuel the pot-bellied, wood-burning stove, not too far from the piano on the right side. Humphries' faithfulness was legendary, as was his reputation for repeating himself as he taught Sunday School. Mr. and Mrs. Roberts were rarely absent. Queenie Roberts had taught herself to play piano and relieved Saylor of that responsibility.

The children, particularly Nell, loved the little alcove at the front of the church reserved for youngsters. Mr. Roberts had built a sandbox, a foot deep, raised, with small chairs fit up to it. Children could move figurines of Bible characters around during stories. On the wall was a hanger for big pictures illustrating the lessons.

Analda could name the parade of area pastors who came to serve up the Word of God and minister to the hearts of the community as they were available. Among them were The Reverends Dugan, Ulmer, and Swindall. Especially Swindall. Analda enjoyed watching him in the simple, yet elegant, mill-crafted pulpit, raised and centering the church. As he preached, he would pound the pulpit, throw back his flying white hair and shout, "Great Jehovah!" Analda thought he had wings.

While there were separate churches for whites and coloreds, during Revival, preachers would stand under the big oak beside the hotel during the dinner break. There, all who wished could gather around for a brief sermon and prayer.

Most of the ministers managed to eat supper at Carrie Jumper's table and remain to sit on the front porch or in the living room for fellowship and conversation. They rarely seemed in a hurry to leave.

Carrie relished setting a pretty, bountiful table laden with two bowls of each dish. Her silver was plated, and she had no fine china, but favored pretty dishes. Occasionally she would buy a set, sometimes collecting them piece by piece. Equally at ease whether entertaining casually or formally, she deemed atmosphere as far more important than mere appearances.

"I miss Lucy's biscuits!" declared Frank one evening. "When is Lucy coming back?"

"Now, Frank," Carrie replied. "Rosa is learning to bake biscuits, and her rolls are delicious." Rosa had been trained up north in an elegant mansion. She knew how to do and loved to use Carrie's formal tablecloths and napkins.

"I don't care about tablecloths and napkins," Frank had said. "I care about biscuits."

"When is Reverend Ulmer coming?" Carolyn always wanted to know. "He's my favorite." Otis Ulmer had grown up in St. Matthews. Carrie and Saylor remembered him as a young coach, and it took some adjustment for them to view him as the full-fledged pastor of Brunson Baptist Church. He held the post for many years and grew to be an esteemed member of the extended Jumper family. For Saylor, he was a touch of home.

Saylor attended church services more regularly than Carrie. While she got everyone else off, she often had to care for an infant or young children. She never worried about not getting there, knowing she had done her part. Yet even from afar, her presence and involvement were always felt.

Early in their Miley sojourn, Carrie had started a Christian Endeavor organization for young people. Christian Endeavor met on Sunday evenings before preaching and became an anchor for social events and courting.

Even those youths who were not regular church goers attended Christian Endeavor. Its motto was faithfully repeated each week:

Life is a mirror of kings and slaves.
It's just what you think and do.
Give to the world the best that you have
And the best will come back to you.

Easter and Christmas were central to the church calendar. The Easter play was at the church, directed by the teachers, including both sacred and secular features. Carrie was often involved in devising costumes. When Zelda was a violet, a purple crepe paper yoke and petals with yellow centers filled the bill. The year she was the wind was more challenging, causing considerable fretting. Finally Carrie found some very pale gray cheesecloth from Frank Rivers' store in Hampton. She pulled together panels around the shoulders which trailed after Zelda. Another year, Zelda and Nell were Mary and Martha and had to say some real nice things to each other, a source of great entertainment for Carolyn.

Carrie usually made new clothes for the children at Easter. It bothered Carolyn that her mother never had a new dress for Easter. It bothered Carrie not at all.

♦   ♦   ♦   ♦   ♦

"Mother, you picked a really bad day to be sick. The Christmas play is tonight. What will we do?"

"Sis, I assure you I didn't choose this." Carrie lay in bed enduring painful cramps and nausea. "It must be something I ate. You girls will have to take charge. You can do it. I'll advise you from here. Give me a few minutes to think things through."

Carrie went over a mental checklist. It could have been worse. The older boys weren't involved, but all the girls had parts in the play. Thankfully, new coats and dresses were completed and hanging in wait, costumes finished.

The children knew their parts. Nell had practiced her solo, a little song about Mary, already this morning. Analda was reciting a quite long poem — "Lady Judith's Vision," by Mrs. E.V. Wilson. They had found the poem in one of Carrie's old college drama books. For weeks Carrie had been in her element directing Analda's expression of the tale of Christ ministering to a woman's grief for her child at Christmas.

As Analda recited, Carrie had coached. "Downward in inflection ... upward ... stronger ... faster ... more contrast ... emphasis ... life and snap ... animation ... pause."

"You're ready," she said now. "We'll go over it once more this afternoon. Maybe I'll be feeling better."

In the afternoon, the electricity went off, leaving little light for bathing, dressing, and meal preparation. Saylor was to bring kerosene for the empty lamp when he came home. With no heat or hot water in the bathroom, baths would be taken in the bedroom before the fire. Carrie was still unable to be on her feet. She called from her bed.

"Sis, Lellan, bring the tin tub and start getting bath water heated. We'll have to begin now. Bathe the younger ones first."

Analda was proud of the progress they were making. The younger children were bathed, given a light supper, and dressed for the program. Frank would accompany them to the church, costumes in hand, while the older girls got ready in peace. At least that was the plan.

Darkness arrived, and Saylor had not come with the kerosene. Surely he would be here soon. The bedroom door opened. It was not Saylor, but Zelda, having forgotten her costume.

"It's in the chair by the window," Carrie said.

In the semi-darkness, Zelda, proudly garbed in new dress and coat, tripped and fell — straight into the bath water. She screamed. Carrie called out for Analda.

"What? This can't be!" Analda yelled, frantically snatching Zelda from the water. Everything was wet. "What will we do now?"

"First, we'll calm down," Carrie said. "Then we'll towel her as dry as we can. Get her clothes off and wrap her in a dry towel."

Zelda wailed loudly as Lellan and Carolyn arrived to add their consternation to the confusion. "Oh no! What on earth will we do?" Their voices were almost in unison.

"We'll calm down," Carrie said again, "and carry on. Lellan, you'll need to iron her dress dry. Carolyn, get her some dry socks. She can wear her old shoes and her old coat."

"Oh, Mother! I feel so bad. I'm so sorry!"

"Come here, Zelda." Carrie welcomed the suffering, shivering child into her arms. "It wasn't your fault, Zee," she said, soothingly. "It was an accident; accidents just happen. Everything will be all right. It's only inconvenience. Dry your tears now, and we'll all do what we must do. Come, get under the covers with me while the girls get your clothes ready."

Lellan went to the kitchen and put the iron on the hot cookstove to heat. She rolled Zelda's wet dress in a towel and set up the ironing board. By candlelight she cautiously ironed the new dress, realizing there would be little time for the older girls to bathe.

By the time Zelda was re-dressed and ready to go, all nerves were shot. Carolyn was ready to escort Zelda back to the church when Saylor arrived with the kerosene. Tempers were flaring. Analda was shouting at Zelda, whose high-pitched wailing resumed. "And don't you dare go out on stage in that old coat!"

Saylor paused, took in the situation, and put his foot down. "All right, nobody's going to the play!"

That suited Analda just fine. "I'm certainly not," she declared.

"Oh, well, you most certainly are!" he boomed out.

So Analda went to the Christmas play, sulking, having lost all desire to put any expression whatsoever into her poem. As she came out on stage, she saw Saylor slipping in and sitting down. He was wearing the funny expression on his face that he always wore when they were performing, as though he were afraid they'd goof up.

Analda made him proud.

CHAPTER 37

MURDER AT THE MILL

Zelda scampered outside beneath an overcast sky with the energy and excitement of a six-year-old. Old Salkehatchie Road, running through the heart of Miley, was being paved. The Works Progress Administration project was giving badly needed jobs to area residents. Zelda had become a sort of mascot of the crew, who had learned to watch for her every day as she came to oversee the undertaking. The paving was coming closer and closer to her own house. Soon she would only have to step outside her door to observe and interact with the workers.

Inside the house, Saylor kissed Carrie and gave her a little hug before he returned to work after dinner. As he turned to leave, Rosa commented to Lellan, "Your mother and daddy such a lovely couple. They lovely when he leave in the morning, they lovely when he come home for dinner, and they lovely again when he get home at night."

"I think she means *loving*," Carrie whispered, smiling, as she and Lellan passed through the hall together. Carrie went into the bedroom to read her Spiritual Life Development devotional and begin her afternoon nap. Lellan continued outside with Carrie's shopping list for the big store in hand.

As she walked around Dr. Sample's office, waving at Zelda and the paving crew, glancing at low-hanging, darkening clouds, she remembered that Miley was in mourning. Louise Humphries had died too soon of cancer, leaving her husband to finish raising little Louise. A small town like this felt each other's woes.

Mrs. Ackerman, who, with her husband, had recently come to manage the Miley hotel, was on the porch of the facility. She called out in greeting to Lellan. "Good afternoon, Lellan. Let me thank you again for coming with Mrs. Jumper to welcome us to Miley. We're fitting right in and enjoying the town already. We're sorry to hear about Mrs. Humphries. We haven't been here long enough to have known her, but we're sad for Miley, and for the family."

"Thank you, Mrs. Ackerman. Miley is sad about Mrs. Humphries, but we're glad to have you and Mr. Ackerman. I'm sure Colleton County misses you both."

"We hope so. But we've brought a little of Colleton County to Miley. Tell Mrs. Jumper that the Gullah workers from Edisto we spoke of have already begun arriving here. These jobs will make their lives much better."

"That's good. We're glad to have them."

"You might also mention to your mother that some of them have wives who will be available for household work, if she has a need. They're a bit difficult to understand, but I'm sure Mrs. Jumper wouldn't mind that."

"Thank you. I'll tell her. Right now we're in pretty good shape. Our former cook, Lucy, has returned with her husband to Miley. She is working on the days Rosa doesn't. Yet I know Mother would like to hire the Gullah ladies when she can."

Entering the store, Lellan looked to see if Miss Vi was busy in the post office. The vivacious postmistress was finishing up with a customer and spoke as Lellan passed her window.

"Hello, Lellan. It's good to see you. How are things at the Jumpers?"

"All is well," Lellan said. "We're just sad about Mrs. Humphries, like everyone else."

"Yes, it's too bad. We should be praying for Leroy. He has a hard road ahead. Such a nice man, too."

Lellan saw Cecil Godley, Charlie's son, filling drawstring bags with Golden Grain tobacco and stamping them. Lellan greeted Cecil and handed him her mother's list. She followed him to the side of the store nearest the mill office, which was reserved for hardware. He took down the light bulbs Carrie had asked for. "Your daddy still playing checkers?" he asked.

"He certainly is."

"I'd like to take 'im on sometime."

"He'd like that. But I warn you, not many can best him. In fact, he has a hard time finding partners. Kelly and Ralph won't play with him anymore. He is very competitive, and they can never win."

"It looks like he'd let 'em win sometimes."

"Not Daddy. Winslow will still play. He says he doesn't mind getting beat."

"I heard Mr. Jumper was in a checkers magazine."

"Yes, he has had some of his problems and solutions published. And he has picked up a checker mate by mail from the magazine."

"From where?"

"Up North, I think. Maybe Michigan."

"Well, I'd like to play 'im anyway. Let 'im beat me a time or two. Maybe I can learn something."

"I'll tell him. I expect he'll take you on. In fact, I'm stepping over to his window right now."

Lellan waved again to Miss Vi on the way out, noticing, as she went down the steps, a number of people gathered over at the meat market across the street in front of the mill. Not thinking too much about the matter, she continued to Saylor's window at the side of the mill office.

◆   ◆   ◆   ◆   ◆

Saylor, seated at his office desk, was in conversation with Jake Lee.

"Well, Jake, it's good to see you back at work."

"Thank you, suh."

"Tell me something. How does a good preacher like you get himself thrown into jail?" Saylor knew that the custodian had been caught selling a stolen cow.

"Well, suh. The Lawd moves in mysterious ways to git the gospel to them pris'ners."

"I hope you did some good," Saylor said.

Suddenly Lucille McDonald burst into Saylor's office. "Something's going on over at the mill," she said, anxiety in her voice. "There's a crowd gathered.

I'm afraid someone's been hurt, or something. Mr. Fred has stepped over."

Lellan appeared at Saylor's window. "Daddy, what's going on at the mill?" she asked.

"I don't know, Lellan. Mr. Lightsey has gone over there. You'd better go home the back way," he said solemnly.

◆ ◆ ◆ ◆ ◆

At the supper table, mourning for Louise Humphries had taken a back seat to excitement about the murder at the mill. There had been an argument inside the mill between Maxie Martin and Jack Parler, who had made a remark about a girl Maxie was dating. Maxie had followed the man outside and pushed him down beside the meat market. His head had hit a post of the market porch.

"It wouldn't have been so bad," Frank related animatedly, "except that Jack was a free bleeder. They couldn't stop the bleeding. By the time Dr. Sample got there, it was too late. Jack is dead, and Maxie is in jail."

Ralph, Winslow, and Analda were upset. They considered both Jack and Maxie, though older, to be among their friends. Lellan, because she had been in close proximity to the unhappy event, felt almost as if she had been involved.

"Mother, what can we do?" she asked, wringing her hands.

"We can pray for both families," Carrie answered.

"And we can remember to be very careful about our actions," added Saylor. "Lives can be destroyed in a careless moment."

◆ ◆ ◆ ◆ ◆

The older children attended Maxie's trial at the courthouse in Hampton. Lellan felt sorry for people with little means and little knowledge. The Lightseys tried to be supportive of Maxie, but couldn't condone his actions. He pled guilty to manslaughter and was given a sentence of several years in prison.

The mood in Miley was somber.

CHAPTER 38

TEN

The mood in the Jumper household on January 2, 1935, was one of elation over the safe arrival of Carrie and Saylor's tenth child.

Carrie eased herself up in bed, still exhausted, as Whit bathed the new arrival. "I don't know what we would have done without you, Whit. Coming in the middle of the night, even before Dr. Sample could get here."

"It's what I do," answered Whit with a wink. "And you know what a weakness I have for babies. Congratulations on ten children! Five girls and now five boys. How did you manage to even it out like that?"

Carrie gave a weary laugh. "You'll have to ask God that question, Whit. He's totally in charge of such matters. We would have been happy with either."

"I'm glad for you. You have all been in a bit of a pickle here, with everyone sick except Lellan and Mr. Jumper. Poor Lellan!"

"She has handled it well, with the help of our good neighbors. We couldn't have managed without all of you."

Whit wrapped the infant boy in the plaid blanket with a raised lamb, her gift for the new baby. She settled him snuggly into Carrie's open arms. "I'll tell the others they can come see the baby now. At least those who are feeling better."

Saylor came into the room with Carolyn. "What a cute little brother," she announced, proudly, gingerly touching the brown fuzz on his pink head. "It was time for another boy. What's his name?"

"Philbert Hoyle," Saylor replied.

"Philbert Hoyle? Did you name him for a funnies character?"

"Well, yes. We just like the name." Saylor was a bit defensive. "We'll call him Phil."

"It really has a nice ring," Carrie said. "I think he'll like his name."

"I hope so," said Carolyn.

♦ ♦ ♦ ♦ ♦

Saylor was a bit downhearted to realize that their firstborn, Kelly, was not at home to celebrate the birth of his newest brother. He sighed a deep sigh. *Well, it can't be helped. He's grown at twenty-one and probably wouldn't have been here anyway. It is what it is.*

Tall, dark-haired Ralph was almost twenty and busy with own life, working as a saw filer in the mill and courting a Hampton belle. Ralph was congratulatory, but distracted.

Winslow, a month shy of eighteen, had graduated from high school and was working alongside Ralph in the Miley mill. With a head full of glossy brown hair, which Zelda and Nell loved to comb and put in rollers, he was pleasant and shy. Winslow was happiest when the family was engaged in a rousing game of horseshoes, boisterously splitting hairs, shouting arguments. Also like Ralph, Winslow accepted the new arrival quietly.

Analda, at sixteen, had boyfriends on the string. She was resigned to having to help care for another younger sibling. She had thought that Frank, then Zelda, then Nell would be the end of it. Still, since her parents were obviously happy, she decided to be happy, too.

Thirteen-year-old Lellan was worn out, but thankful that she had not taken sick with the others. She made up her mind that she didn't want a houseful of children. She would be busy with other things, like maybe teaching school. Not that she didn't want children. Just not quite so many.

Carolyn, eleven years old and the most sensitive, felt herself caught between older siblings and younger, but was happy to be in the family nonetheless. She felt closest to her next-youngest sibling, Frank, who was nine.

Frank was in love with life and in love with baseball. He shared this bond more and more with Saylor, who, at fifty, still pitched for the Miley team. His father saw Frank as the one who might continue the career Saylor had lost. Saylor had taught him all the ways to hold the ball to make a curve, a fast ball, a drop, and all the things that pitchers know.

Saylor had recently been pitching a game against Bamberg, mowing down heavy hitters. Ralph was standing beside the Bamberg manager, who had asked, "Who is that old man pitching? He's striking out all my best hitters."

Frank sometimes got the razor strop for playing ball too late, forgetting his responsibility to carry in the stove wood. Once the strop was applied, he still had to bring in the stove wood. Frank was glad the new baby was a brother. He had felt a bit outnumbered with the other boys being so much older. He had had sisters aplenty.

Zelda and Nell, both recovering from sickness, spent the day of the birth playing with paper dolls cut from Sears and Roebuck catalogs and calling each other "Miss Lady." Six-year-old Zelda was enamored with the idea of having a baby in the house. With only two years between Zelda and Nell, she didn't remember much of Nell's babyhood. Nell was her playmate. Phil was a new interest.

Nell, at four, while entranced with the infant, was confused. She had grown accustomed to being the baby, and her place in the family had been usurped. She quickly saw that real babies are a lot more demanding than her dolls.

♦ ♦ ♦ ♦ ♦

Life with ten children settled into a routine, aided by the spoken and unspoken assumption that older children would help with younger. As Easter appeared on the horizon, Carrie was once again busy sewing for her children. Her sewing partner and best friend in Miley continued to be Mrs. Crosby, who lived on the street behind the field. Myrtle Crosby came to the house for a sewing session. Three-month-old Phil was nestled in his cradle near the seamstresses.

"Honestly, Carrie," Myrtle commented, "I never thought I'd know a family with ten children, every one of them *spoiled*."

"*Spoiled?*" Carrie responded. "How could you call my children *spoiled?* I couldn't possibly spoil ten children at once."

"Maybe that's not the right word," said Myrtle. "Maybe a better word would be *catered to*."

"That's not right, either," said Carrie. "The right word is *loved*, and that's quite a different thing than *spoiled*. Our children are all loved, and each one knows it."

"How have you accomplished that with so many?"

"Well … while it hasn't always been easy, it has been possible. We don't do this perfectly, but Saylor and I try every day, both of us, to make each child feel cared for in some way. A loving word, a secret hug, a simple surprise, or a few minutes of alone time says, 'We are aware of you and how special you are. You are safe with us, and you are safe with God.'"

Saylor and Carrie Jumper family: (front row, l to r) Phil, Saylor, Carrie, Nell; (back row) Frank, Carolyn, Kelly, Lellan, Ralph, Analda, Winslow, Zelda (Columbia, South Carolina, 1942). Photo taken on the day Winslow went off to World War II.

CHAPTER 39

SUMMER OF CRISIS

Carrie scooped Phil into her arms and carried him to the front porch where, with a shawl thrown over her shoulders, she began to nurse her toddler son. Soon she was lost in thought, reviewing in her mind the letter she had just written to her parents.

> Dearest Mama and Papa,
>
> It's hard to believe that another winter has come and gone. Our youngest child is nearly eighteen months old, and our oldest daughter has graduated from high school. Analda sends her thanks for your offer that she come to Columbia and live with you while taking a business course. She says that the offer is "under consideration." I don't know what she will decide. She is tied to a boyfriend here, but we hope that she will look beyond Miley as she prepares herself for the adult world.
>
> Saylor and I have surpassed you in number of children, but will never be your equal as parents. Your guidance and presence in all our lives has been a cherished gift.
>
> Papa, thank you for your winter visit. As always, your being here lifted our spirits through some bleak weather. Zelda and Nell enjoyed getting reacquainted. I especially remember Zelda sitting at your feet and looking up, up, up as if she would never get to the top of you. Mama, we missed you so much. Hopefully, you will be feeling well enough to come the next time.

I should update you on what has been happening here. As you know, Mr. Henry Lightsey passed away, and we do all miss him. Recently a tree was planted, and a plaque was posted in his memory in the churchyard. He had such a heart for people and the community. Mr. Fred does, too, but is more distracted by the day-to-day running of the mill. Since Mr. Henry passed, there has been no buffer between Saylor and Mr. Fred's tendency to be overbearing. Saylor has been worn out with work, with the hard years of this Depression, and with concern for children who are reaching courting age. That's another topic entirely. Then there is the constant of his mother, sisters, and Kelly.

After a season of prayer and deliberation, Saylor wrote out his resignation and left the office. We said little about the matter to the children, just that Saylor and I had decided to move the family back to Sandy Run, even though Saylor has been offered a similar position across the county. After two weeks, Mr. Fred sent an intermediary to Saylor imploring him to return, with concessions that would ease the workload. A little to my surprise, Saylor responded positively and has gone back to his job. He really does like the work, but still wishes it were not so far from Sandy Run. So, we settle back in, hoping that God is working all these things together for good, as He consistently has done. As always, we know we can count on your constant prayers, just as you may count on ours.

Your loving daughter,
Carrie

Carrie's reverie was disrupted as Saylor's chords wafted through the window. He was warming up on the piano with "The Old Spinning Wheel in the Parlor." Carrie began to hum along as Zelda bounced onto the porch, plopped into the swing, one of her favorite places, dragging her bare feet along the cool boards of the floor. A light breeze flitted across the porch.

"Who has seen the wind?
Neither you nor I.
But when the trees bow down their heads,
The wind is passing by."

"Mother, you must know all the poems in the world," said Zelda.

"Hardly, there are so many. It's good to have a poem for every occasion, though. These words are from one written by Christina Rosetti. Can you say it with me?"

While Zelda and Carrie were engrossed in the poem, Carolyn came into the yard from down the street, up the steps and onto the porch.

"Mother," she interrupted, "seeing you here on the porch reminds me of what I heard at school the other day."

"What was that, Carolyn?"

"Jolene Miles told me that her mother said, 'Mrs. Jumper doesn't get a god's thing done. She just sits on the porch all day long.'"

"Carolyn, you know we're too busy to worry about what people say. That's so far wrong that it's funny. Except that I have no idea what she means by 'a god's thing.'"

For the rest of their lives, members of the Jumper family would remember and quote Mrs. Miles.

♦ ♦ ♦ ♦ ♦

A casual glance out the kitchen window was a shock to Carrie's senses. Saylor was sprawled on the ground beside the back steps. In a flash she was across the dining room and down the steps.

"What on earth happened?" she asked as he eased himself into a sitting position, his hand on his left ankle, moaning with pain.

"I don't exactly know. Somehow, I missed the bottom step. I seem to have twisted my ankle."

"I'll send someone for Dr. Sample."

Dr. Sample gently probed and turned the already swelling ankle. "It looks like you'll be hobbling around for a while, Mr. Jumper. It's a sprain and will take some time to heal. I'll wrap it for stability. Elevate it, use a heating pad, crutches, and give it a rest. Absolutely no baseball until it's well."

"This is a rotten development," said Saylor.

♦   ♦   ♦   ♦   ♦

It was very early morning. Saylor hobbled down the hall toward the bathroom, not wanting to awaken the family. *Thank goodness it's summertime and no fires to be built,* he thought. Entering the dining room he turned, trying to protect the swollen, throbbing ankle. He swerved, hitting a small set of shelves containing canned food. A jar fell and broke. Glass bounced from the floor, a jagged edge cutting Saylor's left leg. He yelled, falling to the floor, grasping the cut with both hands, trying to stanch the flow of blood. "Carrie!" he called. "Carrie! Come here. I'm hurt!"

Suddenly Carrie was there, as were the children. She began issuing orders. "Sis, get a towel! Ralph, get up the glass. Lellan, wipe up the spill. Saylor, keep pressing on the wound until we can get it wrapped."

♦   ♦   ♦   ♦   ♦

"Thank goodness for grown sons," Saylor commented, easing himself onto the bed as Carrie prepared to dress the wound. "It'll be all right. It hurts, but it's not that bad a cut."

"We'll get Dr. Sample," Carrie said.

"No," Saylor said. "It's Sunday. Give the man a rest. He's worn out from yesterday, sewing up old George after he got knifed in a fight."

"Yeah," said Frank. "He scooped up George's innards, put them back in, and stitched 'im up."

"I hope he'll live," said Carolyn.

"He will," said Ralph. "They usually do."

◆　◆　◆　◆　◆

"This is worse than you thought, I think, Mr. Jumper," Dr. Sample said on Monday. "You should have sent for me. You know I would have come."

"Just hated to bother you, Doc," said Saylor. "Everybody needs a day off."

"Well, now you have a double reason to stay off those feet. I'll check on you tomorrow."

"Thanks."

Saylor was restless and impatient. He couldn't work or tend his gardens. He couldn't play baseball, checkers, or the piano. He couldn't even get to the bathroom. This was worse than bad.

A week passed, then two. Enforced rest aided the healing of the ankle, but not the cut. Dr. Sample faithfully checked the wound daily, cleansing and changing bandages, giving medication for pain, verbal encouragement.

"It's the weekend again," Saylor said. "You're not coming back over here until Monday. I'll be fine."

"All right, but just be sure you call me if it gets worse."

It got worse. Saylor would not call Dr. Sample. Carrie's anxiety built. The wound was inflamed. Saylor was feverish, tossing, incoherent. She knew he was in serious trouble, but she didn't want to alarm the children. After midnight on Monday morning, Carrie slipped out onto the porch, knelt beside the cot, and, in agony of spirit, she prayed.

Much later, she leapt to her feet, having received marching orders: *Get Saylor to the hospital — NOW!*

Carrie calmly awakened the oldest five of the children, letting the others sleep. "Get up, I'm getting Daddy to the hospital," she whispered to each. "Ralph, pull the car around to the front steps, and get yourself ready to drive us to Columbia. Winslow, we'll need help. Run and get Mr. Humphries and Mr. Roberts. Ask them to come as quickly as they can. Sis, come to the bedroom and help me pack Saylor's things. Lellan, you can pack mine. I'll help you know what to put in the bags. Carolyn, put blankets and pillows in the back seat of the car. Especially pillows. We'll have to keep Daddy's leg elevated as much as we can."

♦ ♦ ♦ ♦ ♦

Saylor and Ralph were in the car, ready. Mr. Humphries and Mr. Roberts had a quick prayer with Carrie on the porch before she turned to speak to her children. "Sis, you are in charge. Especially, take care of Phil."

"Mother, he's not weaned! What will I do?"

"You'll get him on a bottle. You can do it. Whit will help you. Myrtle will help you. Anything you need while we're gone, you can charge to our account at the store, as usual. Older children will all help with the younger ones. Sis and Ralph are the final authority. Sis, you will cook. Lellan will clean the house, Carolyn will wash dishes. Winslow will do whatever is needed. Ralph will deal with anything to do with finances, or with the house and garden. You'll make us proud. We are counting on each of you."

"Mother," Carolyn cried, clinging to Carrie. "Will Daddy be coming home? I'm so scared!"

"Carolyn, I spent a long while in prayer tonight. God has given me assurance that Saylor will be all right. He is desperately sick and he may suffer, but he will get well. We can trust our Heavenly Father in this. He will get each of us through." She kissed faces around the group and then said, "Have someone at the office at ten o'clock tomorrow morning. I will call you." Then she turned and went down the steps and into the front seat of the car beside Ralph, as Leroy Humphries held the door.

The car pulled away, and the children looked into the darkness as the taillights disappeared. Would their father ever return?

"Well," said Analda, taking a deep breath, "it's 2:30 in the morning. We should all go back to bed and try to get some sleep before the younger ones wake up to find Mother and Daddy gone — especially Phil. Lord, please ... help!"

♦ ♦ ♦ ♦ ♦

Analda needed all the help she could get. Phil refused the bottle and cried for his mother, constantly. Analda sent for Whit, who seemed to have a special way with Phil. He continued to scream with hunger, brushing the bottle angrily away. Eventually Whit took him out on the porch and shielded him from the morning coolness with Carrie's nursing shawl. Suddenly, all was quiet. A hurdle had been crossed.

With Phil settled for an exhausted morning nap, Analda sat down on the porch to catch her breath, turning her thoughts to getting the household organized. Frank sauntered onto the porch and sat down beside her. The two watched as Dr. Sample's car pulled up beside his office, and he emerged, walking purposefully toward the Jumper house.

"Good morning," he said, entering the porch.

"Good morning," Analda and Frank said.

The doctor walked into the house and into Carrie and Saylor's bedroom. He returned to the porch. "They're not there," he said.

"They've gone to the hospital," Analda and Frank answered.

"Well … they did the right thing," the doctor said, going down the steps.

◆   ◆   ◆   ◆   ◆

The phone news was not good. Carrie's voice sounded weary, but still confident. The doctors had said that if they had waited until morning to get Saylor to the hospital, it would have been too late. His life was in danger, as was his leg. They were doing all they could to save both, but it would be touch and go for a while.

Analda hung up the phone, sat down in Saylor's office chair, bowed her face into her hands, and wept. Lellan's arms were around her, as Lellan, too, cried. "What will we do? Oh, Sis, what will we do?"

Analda wiped her tears away, stood up, and hugged Lellan. "We'll do exactly what Mother has asked us to do. Let's go home."

◆   ◆   ◆   ◆   ◆

The summer was long and hard. Phil clung to Analda continuously, refusing to give her a moment alone, except when asleep. He slept with her. She kept crackers on the windowsill in the bedroom to appease him when he awoke during the night. Analda lost twelve pounds. Her boyfriend grew impatient over no time alone with her. There was always a child on her lap, or children around.

The news on Saylor improved, slowly. Yes, he was going to live. Yes, they thought they could save his leg. No, he would not be coming home any time soon.

The older children carried out their duties. They were determined to do a good job. Myrtle Crosby said the house looked better than when Carrie was at home. Ralph and Winslow tended the gardens. Every other morning at seven forty-five, Carolyn, Frank, and Zelda went to the swamp garden to cut okra. Analda, Lellan, and Carolyn used what their mother had taught them about canning. She continued to teach and to encourage over the phone.

Nell had her sixth birthday. Analda and Lellan put a big blue bow in her hair and gave her a donut party with her friends. Laughing, they told the little girls that they could not eat the donut holes. Lillie Mae obliged by eating around the hole.

Laughter combined with power struggles and arguments. Lellan would work until the mail came in late morning, but no longer. She had to write to her boyfriends. When Analda complained, she presented her defense. "You get to see your boyfriend all the time. He's right here in Miley. But it's summertime, and mine are in Brunson, Estill, Varnville, and Hampton. I have to write to them. It's only fair."

Carolyn would try to get out of washing dishes by having to practice her piano.

"You may get away with that with Mother," Analda said. "But not with me. I run a tight ship."

"You're also bossy," countered Carolyn.

Lellan refused to help with Phil. "He doesn't like me," she protested. "He likes you."

"I don't blame him for not liking you," Analda retorted. And then, for added effect, "Someday I'll leave here, and you'll all be sorry."

On one difficult day, Analda had had more than she could take. "You've got to help me with Phil," she said to Lellan.

"He doesn't like me."

"Then I'm going to take him to Miss Hattie."

"You can't take that baby to the quarters."

"Then you're going to take care of him."

"He doesn't like me."

Analda put Phil in the wagon with ice and cookies, and off they went to Miss Hattie in the quarters behind the mill. Analda returned home, sat down on the porch, put her feet up, and watched the world go by — for a little while.

Zelda and Nell were ornery, not wanting to obey the older children. Ralph could get exasperated. Nell's earlier nickname of Baby still stuck. "I can do something with Baby, but not with that one there," he complained, referring to Zelda, who stood defiantly, hands on her hips.

Nell was prone to temper tantrums. Once, when she didn't get her way, she trekked her little chairs down the road and set them down in front of Minnie Parker's house, refusing to retrieve them. Ralph, with switch in hand, marched her down to get the chairs. The neighbors were offended. "Look at that big, grown man making that little child carry those chairs."

Word came from Carrie that Saylor was depressed and would cry to see the baby, Phil. When a photographer happened by, Ralph and Analda scraped up enough money to have Phil's picture made sitting on the front steps in his swimsuit.

◆ ◆ ◆ ◆ ◆

The big argument that the family would often recall happened at the supper table. With neither Saylor nor Carrie at home to respond to and guide conversation, it sometimes got out of hand.

When Ralph and Analda disagreed, things could get loud. As verbose as Analda was, Ralph would sometimes argue her into a corner of frustration. On one such occasion, she let him have it with both verbal barrels.

"You big old bull ... you heifer-looking sow!"

Laughter around the table dispelled the animosity, but a new family saying had been birthed: You big old bull ... you heifer-looking sow. When

Carrie heard of it, she said to Analda, "In your heart you were cussing him out, but looking for a way not to say a bad word."

♦   ♦   ♦   ♦   ♦

Summer was waning when Saylor finally came home. The family made it into the grand occasion that it was, although their daddy was not yet well. Carrie and Saylor brought each child a gift, carefully thought out. Lellan remembered hers for the rest of her life — a piece of deep red voile fabric with white dots. Carrie later made it into a dress with a white organdy bow at the top, Lellan's all-time favorite dress.

♦   ♦   ♦   ♦   ♦

The summer held one more crisis. Analda was going to the store, and Phil wanted to go. They were taking the car, which had to be choked. Analda got in to crank the car. Suddenly it lurched backwards, and the back wheel knocked Phil into the sand. Analda heard him scream, jumped out, and grabbed him just in time. The car continued backwards, across the street, and into the garden. Analda ran straight across the street to Dr. Sample's office with the baby. Phil was frightened and crying, his face a little red and scratched from the sand, but otherwise the toddler was unhurt. Carrie was alerted. She ran, hysterical, to the doctor's office. She had endured Saylor's long ordeal with assurance, but this was too much. She collapsed with weeping and had to be taken home. Ralph, helping her up, said to Analda in consternation, "Why did you run over the baby?"

♦   ♦   ♦   ♦   ♦

Later, after everyone had regained composure and thankfulness that Phil was unharmed, the family sat around the living room, reliving the events of the summer. Carrie and Saylor congratulated the children on how well they had managed to keep things together.

"Yes," said Ralph, only partially in jest, "I ran this place singlehandedly."

"You big old bull ... you heifer-looking sow!" said Analda.

CHAPTER 40

FUN

Shading her eyes from the afternoon sun, Carrie went down the back steps, across the yard, and into the edge of the big peanut field behind the house. She had spied Mr. Priester's truck and knew he had come to survey his peanuts. Miley's loose, sandy soil was excellent for growing the goober peas.

"Hello, there, Mrs. Jumper," he called, knowing the purpose of her visit. "How are you today?"

"Very well, thank you," she replied.

"What can I do for you?"

She laughed. "The usual, Mr. Priester. Would you be willing to spare some peanuts for a PTA boiling?"

"Just as usual," he answered with a big smile. "You may have a bushel from these two rows. I know you'll supervise the children so that they won't tear up the field during the picking."

"Of course," she answered. "And we do heartily thank you."

On the afternoon before the boiling, Carrie gathered Miley children to pick the peanuts off the vines as a group, a time of much joking, happy chatter, and anticipation. The next morning, the washing and rinsing of the peanuts began with two big black wash pots stationed between the school and the Mixon house. By afternoon the fire was built, something for the boys to do under Carrie's supervision. Always heavy on seasoning, she carefully oversaw the addition of a box or two of salt for a big pot of peanuts.

The primary seasoning of a peanut boiling was the fellowship and friendship cultivated by the event. No one was left out. If someone didn't have a way to get to the boiling, Carrie sent one of her boys to bring them. Softball and other games were favored by the children as they waited for the goobers to cook. In the competition to see who could eat the most, Pauline Mixon invariably won. For young people, the attraction of the event was peanuts and courting. For all, the smell of boiling peanuts and burning wood combined with the evening air to create an atmosphere of closeness and contentment.

◆   ◆   ◆   ◆   ◆

Carrie's life-long intention that her children should have fun and not just rules bore heavy fruit in Miley. In good times and bad, an underlying sense of fun and adventure was encouraged and cultivated. The fun began around their own table with the boisterous telling of tales and simple enjoyment of each other and spread to the community beyond.

Much of life's pleasure came from simple gifts provided by nature and combined with human creativity. In the summer, family picnics and watermelon slicings were favored. During cold weather, Saylor often took the children for walks in the woods. Sometimes they walked at night with him to the church. "Yoo-hoo! Whoo-ee!" he'd holler into the darkness, listening for the echo. "I'll give someone a quarter to go around the church and come back." There were no takers.

In the spring the girls picked fistfuls of violets blooming behind the church, near Hersh Padgett's filing bench, which Carrie would make into bouquets. When the violets weren't blooming, they doodled for bugs beneath Padgett's shed. There, the dirt was dry and the honeysuckle smelled sweetly. If the boys were present, their nearness to the swamp would call to them to go fishing. Instead, they would be offered a penny a worm to dig for fishing bait.

At home, there was card-playing and cheating and carrying on with horseshoes. Saylor taught his children how to ring a horseshoe really well.

On Sundays, a crowd would gather with loud arguing over a hair, while Saylor measured with a broom straw.

Stilts were built by most of the children with two-by-fours and blocks placed according to skill. The goal was to have the foot part as high as the porch floor.

The mill was scary at night, and while playing around the lumberyard was strictly forbidden, the rules weren't always followed. The children would spread the word about town. "We're going to play out tonight." A bunch of kids would meet over at the doctor's office. Sometimes they followed Mr. Dubose on his rounds. The affable night watchman had a keypunch and relished telling gruesome ghost stories as he punched in at certain stations. There was also high adventure to be found just in sneaking around to spy on the watchman. One, who was big and fat, would spot them and try to chase them down, but could never catch the culprits.

On Sunday afternoons, children played hide and seek around the stacks in the lumberyard, never considering that the stacks might fall. Occasionally they were reported to parents. Saylor was angry, and Carrie lectured on the dangers, exacting promises of not repeating the offense.

Carrie and Saylor were big on holidays and liked to do seasonal extras. Carrie decorated with natural things, favoring pansies in bloom, pointing out the little faces of each. On Easter morning, colored eggs appeared on their plates. With much ado, they tipped each other's eggs to crack the shells. The day before, nests had been made around the house from Spanish moss. Before everyone was awake, Saylor placed eggs in these, then continued to hide them all over the yard. On the hunt, the children always made a run for the pillar that had a missing brick.

◆   ◆   ◆   ◆   ◆

Courting in Miley was facilitated by frequent parties in homes. Since many of the Jumper children were courting at the same time, they initiated gatherings, and some of the siblings were nearly always present. Louise Humphries had a record player that was put to good use. A party could be decided on at six o'clock, and within ten minutes all the young people of the community would be informed. Radios were the thing, and sometimes a group would go over to the Barfields' house to enjoy string music on Saturday nights. Mrs. Barfield liked to cut fool with a step or two. Also on Saturdays, the Lucky Strike Hit Parade featuring the top ten tunes was popular.

The PTA sometimes sponsored square dances at the school. Saylor enjoyed these as he danced and called the sets. At times there were square dances in homes. Analda rarely went to bed early, because, as Carrie pointed out, "You're afraid you'll miss something." Once, she did decide to go to bed at a reasonable hour. Juanita Ritter came in and woke her up. As she was leaving the house, her mother said, "I thought you were going to bed early tonight."

"I was," she said, "but now I'm going to a square dance." Analda enjoyed whatever she was doing. Worry about consequences had to wait. Sis and Juanita would each tell their parents they were studying together at the other's house. In reality, they met their boyfriends and rode around during that time. Sometimes, Analda would get one of the girls to run the clock back. When she returned, she sneaked into her parents' bedroom and moved it forward.

The front porch was the scene of much courting, but offered the least privacy, especially after dates. During the winter, couples sat on the living room sofa. Saylor played for a time before he got up and left, all the while listening to what the young folks were saying. Later, at the table, it would all come out. He'd tell on you before the whole crowd, always finding something to tease.

By the time the children reached courting age, they were interested in how their parents came to be married. Saylor always explained it in the same way. "I just lined up the girls and chose the one I wanted — your mother."

Christian Endeavor meetings contributed to courting intrigue. Billy Barker lived below Miley near the Goodings. Billy faithfully walked the two miles into Miley to lead Christian Endeavor, with its officers, program, singing, and socials. Most of the young people were there with their dates.

Carolyn got a lot of teasing because Billy thought she was so pretty. "Her hair is like an angel's," he said to Carrie.

Corky Barnes was a country boy from the Hickory Grove section. His mother was a friend of Carrie's in the Home Demonstration Club. Corky was naive and was considered to be so country. He came to Miley to sell vegetables and to attend church in a noisy old Model T. He liked Lellan and was faithful in his constantly thwarted efforts to get a date. The other girls would try to protect her by sending him from house to house in a hunt. Once, his car broke down in front of the Jumper house. Winslow was in the front room playing a game. Seeing him, Win said, "Oh no, there's Corky Barnes." He ran, not wanting to get stuck with Corky. Lellan, hearing the noisy approach of the Ford, rushed, crying, to hide in the bathroom. She was sure that he had come looking for her. Carolyn joined her in the hiding place.

Carrie welcomed Corky. "Mrs. Jumper, may I use your bathroom to wash my hands?" he asked politely.

"Of course, Corky," she said, leading him straight to the bathroom.

♦   ♦   ♦   ♦   ♦

A boy old enough to date could have a fairly good time with fifty cents in his pocket. He needed two gallons of gas, a dime for a movie, money for Cokes.

Winslow and Analda were double dating toward Toby's Bluff, out from Varnville, where courters gathered, in Saylor's 1929 Chevrolet. A tire ran off the rut on a sandy road, sending the vehicle off the edge, where it did a nosedive, occupants screaming, into the sand. The hinged front seat reared up, and a watermelon in the back rolled underneath. Analda and her boyfriend were tossed on top of Winslow and his date. It took them some time to unsnarl themselves, as they were unable to dislocate the front seat. Someone finally figured out that the watermelon was the problem. Shaken and afraid of what Saylor would say, they walked four miles to Toby's Bluff, where they hoped some of the others would be. Ralph, found at Toby's

Bluff, returned them all to the scene of the upset. Seeing the car, he said, "Good grief, you really stood 'er on end, didn't you?"

During the winter, after dates in a cold car, the children would slip into their parents' bedroom to warm up beside the fire, where Fanny, the dog, often reigned supreme. If Carrie and Saylor were already in bed, they would leave the door ajar, welcoming the latecomers, who often warmed blankets to take to bed for the comfort of their cold feet.

◆   ◆   ◆   ◆   ◆

And then there was that magnificent swamp, the meeting place for all the young people in the summer. One day a bunch had gathered. Ralph had been working in watermelons that day, loading them from Mr. Boyles' field onto railroad box cars. He brought a big one and tied it to the bridge to cool in the stream. Then he swam upstream. Before he could get back, the crowd burst his watermelon and ate it while he swam frantically, protesting loudly, back downstream.

While Maxie Martin was still in prison for killing Jack Parler, his younger brother, Mikie, often joined the crowd in the swamp. Mikie Martin was a funny boy who would go under the water and make sounds like a frog. A great entertainer who tried hard to overcome the stigma of his older brother's misdeed, he was well-liked and added to the fun of the swamp.

Saylor often took the younger children swimming on Sunday afternoons, after being nagged as he tried to read the Sunday paper. Carrie said, always, "Don't stay long. I won't take an easy breath while you're gone." For the little ones, walking down the trestle to the swamp was scary at first. Saylor would hold their hands tightly as they feared falling between the creosote-soaked cross ties into the river. On Sundays there were no trains, but if a motorcar approached, they just stepped aside.

Saylor taught several of the children to swim after they'd grown comfortable paddling around in a tight inner tube. Zelda wanted to dive, but was afraid to take the plunge. She sat on the end of the diving board trying to get the nerve to fall off on her head. Finally, Saylor said, "I'll catch you, Zee, and give you a nickel, too." She made the tumble. From then on she developed her diving and got to be more skillful than some of the boys, learning every dive they did, and winning her share of diving contests.

A swamp is a swamp, and snakes and alligators live in swamps. The Jumper children had plenty of exposure to both. Snakes occasionally floated, coiled, down the river. The children learned to calmly get out of the way and let them pass. While alligators were a bigger matter, the older children would continue to swim in sight of them. Frank and his buddy, Keith Roberts, loved the critters. Frank shot his first alligator at the age of twelve in the swamp. It measured six feet and six inches. He sold it for one dollar to a man who ate alligator tails.

Except for school and church, Frank was footloose and fancy free about Miley, and usually barefoot. He was everywhere and into everything. His parents tried at times to curtail his wanderlust, with varying degrees of success. During one of those times, Frank was confined to his yard. Saylor, in his office, learned that someone had a big alligator over at the meat market. He was sorry that Frank couldn't see it. He started to go home and get him, when Frank appeared at his window saying, "If you want to see the biggest alligator you've ever seen in your life, come on."

◆ ◆ ◆ ◆ ◆

Zelda and Nell, like their older sisters before them, looked forward to weekly visits to the big store, coins in hand. The girls would usually get sacks of candy, clutching the sweet treats as they sat on the platform between the back of the store and the railroad. In winter, the warm metal of the platform heated their bottoms as they listened for the whistle and rumble of the Old 44 coming in from the logging camps. It creaked and groaned to a stop as the girls counted its cars, usually a half dozen or so. Once in a while, the train-watchers bypassed the usual candy in favor of boiled peanuts they bought from a boy in a horse and buggy.

As Phil grew into boyhood, he found much amusement in harassing

Zelda and Nell. It was fun to let the rooster or the goat loose in the yard to chase the girls, who ran frantically, yelling and losing their shoes.

◆   ◆   ◆   ◆   ◆

Nell swished her gypsy skirts and breathed deeply of the fall air, ambling down the street toward the school for the PTA Halloween carnival.

Early dark had fallen. It was warm enough that windows were still open, and housewives were starting their evening meal. Nell could see smoke coming from chimneys and smell meat frying, identifying what everyone was having for supper. Their own early repast was over, and Lellan rushed past Nell on the way to her fortune-telling assignment. There would be a spook house, bobbing for apples, fishing for prizes, confections for sale, and other booths.

Nell touched her mask, glad for a little while that she could be someone else. Unaware of her own prettiness, Nell saw herself as common and boring, shrinking from attention. To be a real gypsy would be so much more fun than being plain ole Stella Nell living in plain ole Miley. Even as she fantasized, Nell knew she really didn't want to be a gypsy. She just wanted to be common, like she was. And she wished Mother wouldn't stand up in front of the PTA, teary-eyed, saying, "These precious children … how wonderful for them to have the opportunity for education." Nell wanted to crawl into a hole when Mother did things like that.

As Nell entered the school, she could see Lellan already on the job. Dressed as a doll, Lellan sat in a big cardboard box with her arms sticking out, bobbing her head, answering three questions for a dime. On the other side of the room, the cake walk had begun. Analda and Juanita and their boyfriends joined other couples who walked in a circle, music playing. Carolyn was holding out a stick which each couple touched as they passed. The music stopped. Louise Humphries and her date, Charles Boyles, the newest boy in Miley, were touching the stick and got the first cake, choosing the box of shaped tea cakes made by Carrie.

♦ ♦ ♦ ♦ ♦

Someone was gently shaking Zelda. "Zeldee ... Zeldee," Saylor called softly, "It's time to wake up."

Zelda's sleepy eyes popped open. "Daddy, is this the day for the cane grinding at the Terry farm?"

"That it is," he answered. "Now hop out of bed and get dressed quickly. Mother is packing food. We'll eat breakfast in the country."

"Oohh," she said as her startled, once-warm foot hit the winter cold of the floor. No matter. Zelda was excited. There would be lots of good food brought by community women — biscuits, cheese grits, cornbread, sausage, venison, banana pudding, and much more.

Once there, Zelda delayed her breakfast in favor of watching the grinding. Stalks of cane were being fed into a slot between two revolving wheels, pulled around in a circle by a horse. Juice ran down into a container. Already she could smell that good smell. They had a few stalks of the cane at home, raised by Saylor in his garden. He would peel the cane joint by joint for Nell and Zelda on the back steps. He'd cut it into bite-sized chunks. The juice of the cane was sweet, but Zelda liked the chew better. Here, at the grinding, a huge vat was filled with the juice, beneath a covered shed. Below that, an open-ended, bricked pit contained a hot fire. Designated stirrers used great wooden paddles to keep the hot liquid moving until it was cooked into the consistency of syrup. Foam accumulated around the edges to be wiped away and discarded. Zelda had burned many a finger trying to get a little taste of the syrup by slipping her fingers into the foam. Today she remembered the danger and avoided injury. Life was sweet.

CHAPTER 41

STAR OF THE EAST

"It's my catalog! Give it back!"

"Is not!"

"Is too! You just had it!"

"For only five minutes. Carolyn snatched it away before I could look good."

"Give me the catalog," Carrie said, intervening. "We'll draw straws and set a clock. Everyone can have a fair turn."

◆　◆　◆　◆　◆

It was the most exciting time of the year in Miley, in the Jumper household, and around the world. All the fun of the year rose to a crescendo, exploding in fireworks on Christmas Eve. It all began with the arrival of the Sears and Roebuck Christmas catalog. From the moment Miss Vi received the first shipment, Miley was abuzz. Seeing the prized book became a priority of every man, woman, and child. Even its smell was appealing. In a large family like the Jumpers, it was a struggle to get your hands on the thing that would fuel hopes and dreams for weeks to come.

The next sign of the approach of Christmas was the bucket of candy. In early December, Carrie purchased a big tin of sweet treats and stashed it in her closet in the bedroom, snitching strictly forbidden. In the evenings as the family played games, like bingo, winners were allowed to go to the bucket and choose a piece of candy.

When the big night finally arrived, Saylor would have a bundle of fireworks under his arm when he knocked off from work. Kelly would be there, and at first dark there'd be a big time building a fire in the front yard. Sparklers would be ignited and whirled by the youngsters. The older children preferred tossing exploding firecrackers around. Saylor seemed oblivious to dangers and laughed heartily, enjoying the merriment of his children.

Before bedtime, stockings would be hung, usually Saylor's old socks. In the morning, there would be a horn in the top of each. Early risers blew the horns to awaken the others. Santa brought carefully chosen gifts to each child, always a doll for Nell. After a hearty breakfast, presents under the tree were opened as Saylor handed them out. Nell usually felt sorry for her daddy on Christmas morning as he tried hard to get them to appreciate what they had. "You have so much more than we did," he always said. "We only had fruit and nuts at Christmas." Once, he had gotten a little wagon, which he pulled around all day. Nell pictured a poor little underprivileged boy pulling a wagon, all in the world he had. Later, as Saylor opened the simple wrapped gifts from his children, he made a fuss over each one. It was just what he wanted. "I don't deserve all of this," he said.

No Christmas was complete without the Christmas theme song, "Star of the East." The favored song was sung by the family around the piano. It was frequently sung as a duet for special occasions by Saylor, carrying the melody, and Carrie, singing alto. The hopefulness of its message never failed to raise spirits.

On Sunday afternoons, downtown Miley was quiet and deserted, everything shuttered. A group of girls sometimes walked down the middle of the street, arm-in-arm, singing. During the Christmas season, along with traditional carols, they sang "Star of the East":

Star of the East. Oh Bethlehem's star,
Guiding us on to heaven afar!
Sorrow and grief are lull'd by thy light,
Thou hope of each mortal, in death's lonely night!

Fearless and tranquil, we look up to Thee!
Knowing thou beam'st through eternity!
Help us to follow where Thou still dost guide,
Pilgrims of earth so wide.

Oh star that leads to God above!
Whose rays are peace and joy and love!
Watch o'er us still till life hath ceased,
Beam on, bright star, sweet Bethlehem star!

In later years, Zelda was heard to say, "The words of this song were Mother and Daddy."

CHAPTER 42

SWEET TEA

A nalda folded her pajamas and robe and added them to her suitcase. "Sis, are you really going to Columbia to live with Grandmama and Grandpapa Tate?" Lellan asked, watching.

"I've been telling you I'd leave here one day."

"Yes, you've been promising us that for a long time. But I never thought you really would."

"Don't get too happy. I'll be back next weekend."

"Just be sure you come back next summer for the tea sale."

They both groaned. "We shouldn't complain," added Lellan. "It's Mother's way to help us follow our dreams."

◆　◆　◆　◆　◆

Nell sniffled as she wiped away her tears. It was early morning. Nell and Zelda were outside under a tree between the house and garage, washing jars. A table had been set there for the chore, along with pans of hot and cold water. The quart jars were washed in hot soapy water, rinsed in the cold, and turned upside down to drain on newspapers.

Later, Zelda and Frank pulled a wooden wagon across the Miley road to the little store to buy ice. Frank was disgusted. "I don't see why Nell has to have the same tantrum every day. She knows she's going to get a whipping, and that she'll still have to wash the jars."

"She's stubborn," explained Zelda.

A fifty-pound chunk of ice was heaved onto the wagon. "What if she had to chip up the ice, like Lellan and Carolyn," Frank said, pulling the load back across the road, dancing a jig. "Ouch!" he said. "The pavement is already hot. I liked the road better when it was dirt."

"I like it paved," said Zelda, in her summer sandals.

◆   ◆   ◆   ◆   ◆

Inside the house, the hustle was on. The 200 (the mail train) had come at eleven o'clock. Carrie stopped to read mail, glancing at Lellan, who was corresponding with nine different boys, with impatience. By the time the mill whistle sounded at noon, the tea, which Carrie had already made, had to be ready. Lellan should be getting the ice chipped. Carrie wanted twenty-five quarts of the cold drink waiting on the porch before the whistle blew.

Carrie sat on the porch with the tea book in her lap. No one else was allowed to keep the book. She sighed. Her children were all put out by the tea sale, because it entailed responsibilities for them. That was a good thing. It kept them out of devilment, while they wished their mother had never had this big idea. It hadn't actually been her idea, but had been sort of dropped in her lap. God sometimes works in that way. It had all begun with Charlie.

Carrie now had a cook named Clara. In the evenings, as all the cooks before her had done, Clara would take a plate of food home with her, along with some sweet tea. Her husband, Charlie, had the bright idea that he would like to buy a plate of dinner from Carrie's kitchen for his noon meal, along with a quart of tea. The tea was added to the price of his meal for a nickel. Other mill hands began asking to buy tea, and so it began.

"You take charge," Carrie had said to Analda, "and you can keep the profit. It will give you a little spending money." By the time sales had grown to thirty quarts, it was too big for Analda to handle. Her mother had taken over.

Carrie checked the names of her customers off in the notebook as they came to the front porch for their tea. Most of them brought their lunch in round aluminum buckets with lids and handles. They hung the buckets on the steam pipes in the mill to stay warm. At noon, some scattered themselves about on the porch of the doctor's office across from the Jumpers to eat their meal. Others spread out beneath the oak tree in the vacant area beside Saylor's garden. It was a simple matter to step over to the Jumper house to get their tea, as well as to return the empty jars to the front steps for collection.

As the business grew, Saylor arranged with Mr. Lightsey to take the money for the tea out of the salaries of the mill hands. He would then pay Carrie for the tea with twenty-five-cent coupons from the mill — "checkbooks," the children called the little perforated papers. She made enough money to dress her older girls for school.

"Here comes Solly," shouted Phil, helping the girls to hand the tea out the screened porch door. "Here's your special jar, Solly," Phil said. One of Carrie's jars was a little flatter in shape than the others. Solly thought it held more, although it actually didn't, and he had laid claim to that jar. Phil was in charge of seeing that the flat jar went to Solly.

"And here's your biscuit my Mary send you every day," said Solly, giving Phil one of Mary's biscuits, still warm, wrapped in a napkin.

♦ ♦ ♦ ♦ ♦

"Mother, don't you get tired of wearing that same old dress every Sunday?" Zelda asked her mother, mournfully.

Carrie smoothed the sides of her old paisley dress. "Not at all, Zelda. I like my Sunday dress. Every time I wear this dress, it reminds me … Lellan is in college. And Carolyn will be going soon."

CHAPTER 43

RED SKY

"How much do you want?" Frank asked Mr. Horace Roberts. Fueling cars was his favorite part of the job at the little store.

"Give it five gallons," the mill superintendent said. Frank pumped gas to the five-gallon mark on the side of the round glass dome above the tank and into the car.

The teenager was growing up tall and strong. To his sisters' relief, he now wore shoes, sometimes. Frank felt good about living in Miley, enjoying things the area had to offer — hunting, fishing, the swamp, alligators. Best of all, Mr. Loadholdt, his boss at the store, allowed him to work his afternoon and Saturday hours around his passion, baseball.

♦ ♦ ♦ ♦ ♦

At home, Carrie sat at the dining room table to write to her parents. The aroma of Clara's roast drifted into the room. Carrie was thankful that Clara was working out nicely. Saylor laughed that he could never catch her feeling well. When he inquired after her each morning, she always gave a recital of her troubles. Then she went on about her work, fitting in amiably, bonding with the children, and noticing rapid changes in the family. Ralph had left Miley and married Lois, his Hampton belle. Analda, Lellan, and Carolyn were all in Columbia. It seemed strange to have a smaller number around the table, although traffic picked up considerably at the end of the week.

"Miss Lellan's coming home soon," Clara would say happily, or "Miss Carolyn is coming home." Analda managed to find her way back nearly every weekend.

Carrie started writing: *Dearest Mama and Papa …*

The front door opened and Saylor appeared in the hallway. It was still too early for dinner. "What's wrong?" Carrie called out as he approached, expecting his answer.

Saylor stood in the doorway, frowning. "Dora called. Ma's worse," he said.

Carrie stood quickly. "I'll help you get your things together. Clara will fix your plate. You can eat and be on your way."

"No, Carrie. *We'll* get *our* things together. Ma is asking for *you*."

◆   ◆   ◆   ◆   ◆

Zelda strode past the doctor's office and the hotel, between the little store on the right and the big store on the left, and beyond the mill office. Daddy was not in the office. He and Mother had gone to Sandy Run to see Granmah, who was very sick. Zelda hoped Granmah was better and that she wouldn't die. She continued across the railroad, then turned to look back. The family Chevrolet was approaching. Mother was in the passenger seat, but Winslow was driving. They pulled up beside Zelda, the window open.

"Come home, Zelda," Carrie said.

"I'll be home later, Mother. I'm going to see the Harveys."

"No. Come home. Now."

Granmah Sallie had gone to glory.

◆   ◆   ◆   ◆   ◆

Nell was happily ensconced in her not-so-secret play place behind her mother's catty-cornered cook stove in the kitchen, her retreat for solace and privacy. She liked to read to Phil in the cozy nook, but he was getting big enough now that they were crowded. Today, she was absorbed in her dolls.

Nell was relieved to be back home after Granmah's funeral. She felt sorry for Daddy. She had stood beside him in Granmah's parlor as he lifted Phil up to look into the casket. "That's my mama," he had said.

I don't know what I would do if I lost Mother. But Daddy's grown. I don't think grown men need their mamas very much. Nell had never known her grandfather, but she had liked going to Granmah's. The sand wasn't dirty, and there was always plenty of good food, especially yeast bread. Pearlie, who worked for Granmah, was usually jolly and joking, but not this time. Pearlie was sad about Granmah. Nell was too, but she hadn't felt close to her grandmother. Granmah had always hugged them when they got there, but after that, she paid attention to the boys, not the girls.

Nell had been happy to see her Rucker cousins at Granmah's, especially Ben and Caroline. She didn't know the older ones very well. She felt sorry for Aunt Minnie, too. Uncle Clarence Rucker had died, and Aunt Minnie seemed sad, and sick herself.

The mill whistle blew. At first Nell took little notice, accustomed to noises, but it was too early in the afternoon for the five o'clock whistle. And it didn't sound right. It was shrill. It blew again, insistently, then again and again. Something was wrong. Nell dropped her dolls, crawled out from behind the stove, and went to find her mother.

◆   ◆   ◆   ◆   ◆

Frank ran for home. A large plume of smoke rose from the mill behind him, across from the hotel. "Mother! Mother!" he cried. Carrie met him on the porch. "The mill's on fire! The mill's on fire! What should we do? Should I go back and help?"

"Calm down, Frank. I'm sure they've activated the equipment in the mill. Fire trucks will come. Let the grown men fight it. Go to the garage, get the big tin tub, set it on the mill side of the house, and fill it with water. The house is in danger."

"They're already hosing the front of the hotel and taking furniture out," he said, frightened and running toward the garage.

"We'll have to do that, too," she called. Zelda, Nell, and Phil were looking at her, eyes wide with fear. "Get what you'll need overnight. I'm sending you to Mrs. Miley."

Carrie hurried to help Frank, already hosing water into the tub. "Frank, I'll do this. Drive the children to Mrs. Miley's house near the crossroads. They'll be safe there."

People were running toward the blaze to help as Frank carried out his mother's instructions. No fire trucks had come. "What's going to happen?" Nell asked.

"It's a big fire," said Phil. "The mill is going to burn down!"

"No, it's not," said Zelda. "We're all going to pray and ask God to put the fire out."

"And to keep everyone safe," added Nell.

◆　◆　◆　◆　◆

Saylor rushed home from behind the store and the hotel as a ladder truck sped into town, sirens wailing. "It's the dry kilns," he yelled to Carrie. "They're bringing hoses from the fire buildings on this side of the hotel to use on the doctor's office and this house. The wind is blowing embers around. There could be other fires. We have to get our furniture out. People are coming to help."

"Let's get the piano first," she said.

◆　◆　◆　◆　◆

Frank left the children with Mrs. Miley, offering his mother's profuse thanks. Darkness had fallen. The sky above Miley blazed red and black with flame and smoke, visible for miles around. Traffic on Salkehatchie Road was heavy. Onlookers and volunteers flocked into town, mixed with fire fighters. Frank pulled off the road to let a ladder truck from Bamberg go past, horn blasting, siren screaming. He sat there, the gravity of the event hitting him. Questions bombarded his brain. *What will happen to the mill? What will happen to Miley? What will happen to Daddy's job?* For the first time in his eventful, yet sheltered fifteen years, Frank Tate Jumper felt the weight of anxiety. Grandmama Tate's oft-repeated phrase, passed down to him by his mother, surfaced: *Never forget in the dark what God has told you in the day.* Right now, Frank just couldn't remember what that was.

◆   ◆   ◆   ◆   ◆

Inside the mill, Winslow and others pumped water from internal hoses, trying to stop the fire. Heat soon drove them outside. He stood at a distance from the inferno, sweating and disheveled, as trained firefighters worked, hindered by wind-blown ash. Winslow's Hampton friend, Warren Shipes, stood nearby. A gasp arose from the crowd. The cover over the dry kilns was collapsing. A fresh burst of flames and smoke shot into the sky, followed by another gasp and a shout. "Mr. Lightsey is down! Someone get Dr. Sample!"

Winslow was horrified. "Warren, run to my house! Get my daddy!" Warren dashed toward the Jumper home.

◆   ◆   ◆   ◆   ◆

Saylor, Frank, and Cy Parker feverishly hosed water onto the side of the house. Hot tar in the wooden planks sizzled and smoked. Fear hung in the air. A blaze could ignite at any moment.

Carrie stood aside with Myrtle Crosby, Mrs. Barfield, and Minnie Parker, watching, praying. Sweat poured from her face. Her simple dress was soaked with perspiration. Most of their furniture and many personal belongings stood in the field behind the house, eerily illuminated by fire from the mill. She remembered the blaze that had destroyed her parents' home years ago. Thankfully, she and Saylor would not lose so many treasures and, so far, no one had been hurt.

◆   ◆   ◆   ◆   ◆

Near the crossroads, Mrs. Ed Miley fed Carrie's children and readied them for bed. She showed them to a pretty bedroom adjacent to a screened porch, entered through glass doors. "Wow! Look at that red sky!" called Phil, running onto the porch ahead of Mrs. Miley and the girls. "Boy, I wish I could see that fire!"

"Let's be glad we are safe right here," said Mrs. Miley. The group stood in awe and silence for a while. "Okay," their hostess said, "let's go inside now and pray before bed."

♦ ♦ ♦ ♦ ♦

"Mr. Jumper, Mr. Jumper!" Warren shouted, still running to the steaming house. "Winslow wants you to come. Mr. Lightsey is down!"

"Take over, Frank. Stay with the house." Saylor turned and sprinted toward the mill, bypassing the much younger man. The crowd around the mill owner parted to allow Saylor through. Dr. Sample hovered over his fallen friend. Mr. Fred's sons, Norris and Oswald, bent over their father, urging him to respond.

"We've got to get him away from here," the doctor barked. "Are there medical people here? I don't want just anyone moving him."

♦ ♦ ♦ ♦ ♦

A group of men gently laid Fred Lightsey onto a sofa inside the hotel, but Dr. Sample knew it was over. Miley's patriarch had passed away.

♦ ♦ ♦ ♦ ♦

Frank returned the children home the next morning.

"Did everyone sleep outside?" Phil asked, amazed to see the family's belongings still strewn in the field behind the house.

"No one slept," said Frank.

Smoke still rose from the ruins of the dry kilns. The green deck had burned, along with the dry shed, where lumber came out before being taken to the planer mill, which had been destroyed. The sawmill central had been spared, as well as the vast lumberyard. The crowds of people had gone home, while a few firefighters, the sheriff's department, and county emergency officials monitored the scene.

Four people had moved Carrie and Saylor's piano from the endangered house. Now, it took six strong men to return it to the living room.

Miley was grief-stricken and exhausted.

Miley Hotel

CHAPTER 44

ORPHANS AT THE DOOR

"If you and Aunt Carrie won't take Ben and Caroline, an orphanage is the only choice," said Jewell Rucker to Saylor on the phone. "Since Mama died, Myrtle and I have tried our best to care for them, but it isn't working. Neither of us makes much money. Our older brothers can't do it, and Dorothy is too far away in Texas."

"When do you want to send them?"

"Bubba can drive them down tonight."

◆ ◆ ◆ ◆ ◆

"I always wanted twins," Carrie said, helping Ben settle into the boys' room. "And now I have them."

"I'm the oldest," said Ben.

"No, you're not," Frank retorted. "I was born first. I looked up and saw the stork headed for the Ruckers."

In the girls' room, Nell happily laid down blankets for a sleeping pallet, giving her space on the bed to Caroline. "This is great," Nell said. "I'm glad you're here."

"I'll sleep on the pallet tomorrow," Zelda said.

◆ ◆ ◆ ◆ ◆

"Thank you for the dress, Aunt Carrie," Caroline said. "It was sweet of you to make this." She twirled so that the skirt flared around her. "I really like it."

"I'll make you a dress now," Carrie said to Zelda, sensing Zelda's resentment of Caroline's dress. Zelda was in the sixth grade in the Miley School. Caroline should have gone to Brunson for the seventh. Her unstable situation had held her back, so she and Zelda found themselves in the same grade, in constant contact, as were Frank and Ben.

♦   ♦   ♦   ♦   ♦

"Here's another package for Caroline," Frank announced, dropping the mail on the table. Caroline tore into the box, pulling out a brand new, bright yellow and orange bathing suit. "Look at this," she said. "It's so cute. I love it!" Zelda loved it, too.

"I wish I could get packages from sisters," Zelda said.

"Oh, darn! It's too snug. It doesn't fit," wailed Caroline.

"It will fit me perfectly," said Zelda.

♦   ♦   ♦   ♦   ♦

Saylor sliced into a Sunday afternoon watermelon on the back steps. "You look really nice in your new dress," he said, glancing at Zelda. "Don't get watermelon juice on it."

Zelda's dress was the prettiest she had ever had, shirred all across the front, with blue flowers. "I'll be careful," she said.

She was careful. None of the sweet fruit stained her dress. But a ball of seeds shot right out of her mouth, headed straight for Caroline's face.

SPLAT!

"How dare you?" Caroline screamed. "I'll show you a thing or two!" Zelda was no match for the larger, stronger girl. She found herself thrown into prickly shrubbery, her favorite dress hopelessly torn.

♦   ♦   ♦   ♦   ♦

Zelda sat sullenly on the porch bench, hands around her knees. Carrie sat in a rocker.

"It's time for us to talk about this, Zelda," Carrie said kindly, yet firmly. "How would you feel if Daddy died?"

"Bad."

"How would you feel if I died?"

"Terrible, Mother."

"That's what has happened to Caroline. She's lost both her parents. She's been separated from her older brothers and sisters. She's had to leave everything familiar and come to a strange place to live. She needs kindness and friendship, Zelda, not resentment. You have much more than Caroline has ever had. You have no reason to be jealous of Caroline."

Tears filled Zelda's eyes. "I'm sorry, Mother. I didn't realize ... I'll try to do better."

And she did.

♦   ♦   ♦   ♦   ♦

Caroline left Miley after a year or two to live with her older sister, Dorothy, in Dallas. Ben remained for four years and graduated from Brunson High School.

Chapter 45

RUMBLINGS

Grandpapa Tate looked out the kitchen window as Analda sashayed up the sidewalk in her smart, padded-shoulder suit, her short, light brown hair stylishly curled. "She's the wildest thing I've ever seen," he murmured.

"After three years, you should be used to it," Grandmama Tate replied, with a soft laugh. "She certainly keeps things interesting."

"That she does," he said, hearing Analda coming in the front door.

In a moment she was in the kitchen, her clutch bag tossed onto the table, hugging her grandparents. "I might as well go ahead and tell you," she announced, green eyes sparkling. "I have news. I'm getting married."

"Oh," said Grandpapa. There followed a great pause. "May I ask … to whom?"

"Grandpapa! You know it's Lewie," she answered.

"Lewie? Why, just a couple of weeks ago, it was that Miley fellow you were going to marry."

"I know, Grandpapa. But things change. I'm going to marry Lewie."

Grandmama finally spoke. "When will the event take place?"

"We'll go to Miley this weekend to tell Mother and Daddy. The wedding will be at home the next weekend."

"I think we should all sit down," said Grandpapa, pulling out kitchen chairs for both ladies. "Why such short notice?"

"Well, with all that's going on in Europe, and the military building up, Lewie thinks there'll be war, and he'll probably be going into the Navy. We want to be married before all that happens."

"This country needs to stay out of what's going on in Europe," said Grandpapa. "I am praying that we will. The last war was enough for our lifetime."

"Well, whether there's war or not, Lewie and I will be married."

♦ ♦ ♦ ♦ ♦

The big announcement turned the Miley household upside down, while Saylor blew his stack. "This is a disaster," he declared privately to Carrie. "She's had such a hard time making up her mind. After they're married, it will be too late for changing minds."

"Now, Saylor, we've been praying about this very thing for some time. Lewie seems to be a nice boy. Let's just trust that Analda has made the right choice."

"The whole world's gone love-crazy," he said, ignoring her soothing words. "Ralph and Lois eloped. Now it's Analda and Lewie. Carolyn is seeing that Gooding boy. And they're telling me that Lellan has met some fellow from the wrong side of the swamp called Rabbit, of all things."

"It's a nickname for Reginald."

"Surely we're not going to have a Rabbit in the family one fine day."

"I hardly think so. They've just met. Right now we should be concerned, not with rabbits, but with a wedding ceremony. If you'll call the Methodist pastor in Hampton from your office, I'll go to the hotel and call my sister, Julia. It's summer. She's not teaching school and she loves weddings. I'm sure she'll come and help. We can improvise a *prie-dieu*, Zelda and Nell can wear their matching dotted-swiss Easter dresses to light the candles, and ..."

"Whatever you do about the wedding will be fine with me. I won't be there; I'll be down in the Salkehatchie swamp, fishing."

"Now, Saylor ..."

♦ ♦ ♦ ♦ ♦

Ralph and Lois held the ceremony up, calling the hotel from Hampton to send a message that they were running late and would arrive in fifteen minutes. While Jumpers and Harrells crowded the living room, Saylor spent the delay with Analda in her room. The tears he'd been fighting all day had their way.

Analda and Lewie's nuptials, which took place at 5:10, rather than at 5:00, were simple and sweet. Julia and Clara served up a worthy wedding supper, the jubilant newlyweds took their leave, and it was over.

Late that night, in bed, Carrie said, "I think it was a very nice little wedding."

"I don't remember much about it," Saylor said.

♦   ♦   ♦   ♦   ♦

Carrie sat bundled in her winter coat on the front porch, impatiently waiting for Saylor to finish the checkers game he was playing against himself. They were overdue for a visit with Leroy Humphries and his brand-new wife, Florine. The Lightsey Brothers sales manager, always the judicious one, had refrained from remarrying until after Louise was grown.

The year of 1940 was almost gone. Some very good things had come with the year, mingled with anxieties about the build-up of tensions and fighting in Europe. Ralph and Lois had given them their first grandchild, Dennis, born in the middle of a hurricane, and Analda and Lewie would soon add a second. Carrie was warmed as she remembered the Christmas just past. She had placed the baby in Nell's doll cradle. It was like having a real live baby Jesus, they all agreed. Carrie quietly worried about the world of their grandchildren. The Germans had relentlessly bombed England throughout the summer. Thankfully, Britain had prevailed so far. Could that country continue to hold out against the evil Axis powers?

Carrie's irritation with Saylor was growing as she noticed Phil cruising homeward on the new bicycle, coming to a skidding stop at the steps, Miley sand flying. Nell rushed past Carrie, zipping down the steps. "Phil, you selfish thing, it's my turn for the bicycle. You said you'd be back in fifteen minutes and it's been thirty. Now I'm late!" She grabbed the handlebars as Phil grudgingly released them.

"I don't know what you two used to fight over before the bicycle," Carrie observed. "Maybe we should return it to Analda and Lewie."

"No, no … don't do that, Mother," Nell called as she pedaled down the street.

"It's the best Christmas gift," said Phil. "I'm glad Analda married Lewie. They give great presents. And Lewie likes kids."

"Phil, go inside and ask your daddy if he can finish that game later. I'm getting cold out here."

"Yes, Mother."

◆　◆　◆　◆　◆

"I'm sorry, Carrie," Saylor said, pulling on his coat. "I know my checkers and music can be annoying. Thank goodness there are things to distract me from war worries. We have too many children who are of fighting age."

CHAPTER 46

WORLD WAR II

1941

News of the bombing of Pearl Harbor by the Japanese had failed to distract Frank from the chief delight of his life, baseball. He sat slumped in study hall the next day, idly doodling, dreaming. Somehow this edgy winter would end ... spring would strut forth — and with it, baseball. Frank would be pitching the season opener against Brunson's archrival, Hampton. He could see himself now ... confidently warming up for the kill.

"Let's all file into the auditorium," his teacher instructed. Professor Doggett, the esteemed principal of Brunson High School, who happened to be his mother's cousin, wanted the students to hear an important address by President Roosevelt on the radio. Frank knew what the President would probably say.

"Yesterday, December 7, 1941 ... a date which will live in infamy," the President began. And so, the war with Japan was official. Frank knew that his parents and nearly everyone he knew had heard the address. The sixteen year-old could not imagine how this would play out in the lives of his older brothers, as well as himself. *A day at a time is how I'll take it. Maybe it'll be over before I have to go. In the meantime ... I'll play ball.*

1942

"I'm sorry it's taken so long," Horace Roberts apologized, lifting himself from his knees and returning his hammer to his tool belt. "It's almost done, and you have a much bigger room."

"It's a blessing," Carrie said, "with Christmas coming and the family growing every year. Taking the wall down between the hall and the living room was a good idea."

"Maybe I can finish the new back porch in the spring."

"Thank you for working so hard to get these improvements made. I know it's not easy for you to find the time, with your big job at the mill. And with the war going on," she added, the conflict never straying far from her thoughts.

"Remind me of where your children are," he said.

"Ralph and his family are in Columbia. His second child, Jane, our first granddaughter, was born in August. Because of the children, he has not had to go into the service. Kelly is excused because of eyesight problems. But Winslow was drafted into the Navy in September. He has already been assigned to the USS Boston, but has not yet deployed overseas. Analda's husband, Lewie, volunteered for the Navy and is stationed in Hawaii for now. Lewie King Jr. is a year old, and Analda is running a rooming house in Columbia. Lellan's beau, Rabbit, is in the Army and is in officer's school at Fort Benning."

"Are they serious?"

"It's hard to say. They've been off and on."

"I feel for you, trying to keep up with all that."

"Saylor's in charge of keeping up. I'm in charge of praying. I worry about him, though. He keeps his ear to the radio every possible moment, gleaning all the news he can. We have no one in actual fighting right now, but that can change. I don't know how we'll cope then."

"You're a woman of faith, Mrs. Jumper. That will carry you through. I know it's how you manage to remain cheerful, with many concerns."

"A merry heart doeth good like a medicine; but a broken spirit drieth up the bones," she said, quoting from Proverbs. "I try to be cheerful for the sake of our younger children. They live in the present moment. I hate for the war to be a blight on their childhood, so I try to save my own broken-spirit moments for the night. I do my crying in the dark."

"You're a wise woman."

♦ ♦ ♦ ♦ ♦

"Mother! Mother!" Phil flew through the front door and down the hall. "Mrs. Ackerman says that Mikie Martin has been killed in the fighting in Africa." Miley had experienced its first death of the war. The stark truth spoke. Carrie could no longer insulate her children. Phil was scared. The blackouts had made a strong impression on her youngest son ... and now this.

♦ ♦ ♦ ♦ ♦

"Thank you for coming to see me," Mildred Martin said as Carrie took her leave from the sympathy call. "It means more to me than I can say. Since the trouble we had with Maxie, people have avoided us. You are the only woman in Miley who has called on me."

"I'm sure there will be others," Carrie said. "Everyone has great compassion for you. Mikie's death hurts us all. He'll be greatly missed in Miley. He left a legacy of laughter and patriotism." Stepping onto the simple porch, Carrie noticed the service flag hanging by the door, announcing a family member serving the country. The star in the center was now gold. No one wanted a gold star.

♦ ♦ ♦ ♦ ♦

Winslow's face was black with the soot of gun powder; the grimy, smelly stuff filled his nostrils. The *USS Boston* was in the now-placid, dark blue waters of the Caribbean, practicing for war in the South Pacific. His assignment with anti-aircraft directors, exciting at first, was already wearing thin, and this wasn't even the real thing. *At least the seasickness is gone. But not the homesickness. If Mother and Daddy could see me now ...*

♦ ♦ ♦ ♦ ♦

"Winslow says his ship will return to Boston, where he'll have two weeks liberty before they leave for the South Pacific," Saylor said to Lucille McDonald in the office. "It'll be a somber Christmas."

1943

Saylor, feeling much older than his years, came into the house with his arm around Frank, who held a letter in his hand. "You tell her," Saylor said.

"Mother," Frank hesitated. Everything would be different now. "I've … I've been drafted."

"Sit down, Carrie," Saylor said, seeing the color drain from his wife's face. "We've known this was coming. It's not a surprise. Oswald Lightsey says he thinks he can keep Frank out for six months."

"I don't want that," said Frank. "It's my duty to go."

"Yes, it is your duty," Carrie sniffed through tears. "As hard as it is, and as much as we hate it, it's your duty. We'll all have to bear up."

Like Winslow, Frank was inducted at Fort Jackson in Columbia. As he walked into the recruiting office, he recognized an officer — Captain Jack Miley, one of two sons of Mr. and Mrs. Ed Miley.

"Do you want Army, Navy, or Coast Guard?" the captain asked. "I remember that Winslow chose the Navy."

"Put me in the Army," said Frank.

Zelda, now fifteen, wearing blue jeans rolled up to just below her knees and Girl Scout brown oxfords, came from mail call at the store with a batch of letters. Zelda was going about her life; her parents saw that she was not deprived of playing basketball for Brunson High or other enjoyable activities. Still, the war was haunting her teen years. It was a heavy, frightening time. There were blackouts, with shades drawn at night and the top half of headlights painted black because of the threat of German bombers. Zelda had heard of German submarines all along the east coast. It was thought that the mill in Miley would be a good target because of the lumber it produced for defense. Planes were constantly flying over. Who knew whether they were our planes or enemies? For Zelda, occasional trips to Fort Jackson were a bright spot. While her mother cried, Zelda basked in the whistles of recruits.

Zelda handed the letters into her mother's eager hands. Carrie stopped what she was doing and sat down to memorize the news from her children. Soon she burst into tears. "Mother, what on earth is wrong? Frank's barely been gone a few weeks."

"He doesn't have anything good to eat," Carrie cried.

"Oh, good grief, Mother. Let me see it."

Camp Gruber, Oklahoma

Dear Mother and Daddy,

The food here is terrible. It's not fit for a dog. I know. I offered some to a dog and he refused it ... .

"Mother, what can you expect? Frank's spoiled by your wonderful cooking, and Clara's. You wouldn't be happy to know that he loved Army food, would you?"

"I suppose not, Zelda."

Frank's spoiled, Zelda thought privately. *I don't understand all the fuss. He's eighteen. He's a man, old enough to go to war like the others ...*

♦　♦　♦　♦　♦

On April 11, 1943, Saylor's birthday, Lellan married Reginald Smith at Camp Wheeler in Macon, Georgia. There was now a "Rabbit" in the family, as Saylor had predicted. "She worked so hard helping me to get ready for Sis's wedding; it's a shame she couldn't have a sweet family ceremony, too," Carrie lamented.

"I think she just wants to be married to that Smith boy, and that's all that matters," Saylor said. "I just wish we knew him better."

"We will ... in time."

"She says they'll be stationed at Camp Blanding in Florida for a few months. Maybe we can take a trip down to see them."

"Really? That would be wonderful! Sis could come and stay with the children, and ..."

"Sounds like you're already packing."

1944

"Thank you for calling, Louise. Our love and sympathy to all of you. Especially Mama Tate. I'll go straight home and let Carrie know."

Carrie glimpsed Saylor coming home from behind the hotel. She tensed, bracing herself. She met him on the porch. "Papa's gone, isn't he." It was a statement, not a question.

Saylor wrapped his arms around his wife. "I'm sorry, Carrie. You must have known he wasn't going to make it. I was praying he would."

"Papa was so sad about this war. He wasn't at home in this world now. I don't think he had much fight. And who can blame him? I sensed it when we were last there and said my goodbyes. But still … how can I live in the world without my rock … my fortress? Poor Mama. She'll be so lost. His passing adds sorrow upon sorrow." Carrie wept.

◆ ◆ ◆ ◆ ◆

Zelda thought her daddy would eat the radio. He listened early and late, his ear against the box, not wanting to miss a word. He pored over maps of the fighting in the newspapers. Their children were in the thick of things now, with Frank and Rabbit in the European front, Winslow and Lewie in the South Pacific.

Nell, like Zelda, went about her life, not giving much thought to the war. She felt ignorant because she couldn't talk about it, but didn't do anything about her ignorance. She just wanted it to be over. At times, she had seen her parents sitting on each side of the radio, weeping. One night, lying in bed, she heard Carrie crying softly. She tiptoed to her mother's door, knocked lightly, then pushed it open. Saylor's side of the bed was empty; he was up late, listening to the news, as usual. "Mother, what's wrong?" Nell asked.

"I'm sorry, Nell," her mother said. "I didn't mean for anyone to hear me. I'm just so worried about Frank … about all of them. Frank's so young. He's thin, and it's winter. How can I sleep, not knowing if he has any cover?"

"Mother, you always tell us to turn our worries into prayers. You should do that, too. Let God take care of Frank, since you can't. Besides, we're on the other side of the ocean. It's probably not night over there, and Frank doesn't need any cover."

♦   ♦   ♦   ♦   ♦

He needed cover, all right, but not the kind that warms you in the cold. No longer an eighteen-year-old boy complaining about food, Sergeant Frank Tate Jumper was now a man — still young, still afraid, but committed to fighting for his country. It was Christmas Eve. Frank, a Forward Observer, was in a boat at the front in France, crossing the Rhine River, directing artillery fire. His was in the Third Army under General Patton, Forty-Second Division, called Rainbow Division. The Germans were firing sporadically, near misses whizzing past soldiers crouched in the boat. Frank knew he'd be lucky to get through this. *Not lucky, but blessed, as Mother would say.* He could hear her voice. *Count on your faith in God to keep you safe, Frank.* These words were repeated in every letter he received.

Later, in a secure position, Frank wondered about Rabbit. Letters from home tried to keep him abreast, but things changed quickly. Rabbit was somewhere in France, too, with the Third Army, both of them fighting in what was called the Battle of the Bulge. *God, keep Rabbit safe, too. Keep us all safe.*

♦   ♦   ♦   ♦   ♦

"I don't know what we'll do with Lellan if that Smith boy doesn't make it home," Saylor moaned again and again. Lellan was living and teaching math in North, South Carolina. Saylor had never seen a more miserable schoolteacher. "I just don't know what we'll do."

♦   ♦   ♦   ♦   ♦

Carrie and Saylor had gone to his office after-hours to receive an expected phone call from Analda. Lewie was now far away in the South

Pacific. Their second son, Vandy, was an infant.

"Mother," Analda said, "I'm moving from the Elmwood Street rooming house to another on Pickens Street. I'll have more rooms to rent. Since you don't need living space, why don't you take over the house on Elmwood? You could put one renter in charge and come to see about it periodically. Carolyn is still in college. The others are coming right along. You could build up a little nest egg for them."

Carrie knew a good idea when she heard one.

1945

The Rainbow Division was pushing into Germany. Frank was commanding a third-story observation post, alone except for a radio operator. The building sustained a direct hit from a German tank, blowing out the stairs. There was no way out. Frank continued to man his post, calling for back up. After a long, hard afternoon, the enemy was wiped out. Frank was exhausted, but satisfied.

◆ ◆ ◆ ◆ ◆

On April 12, 1945, Zelda was outside balancing precariously on a rock when she heard that President Franklin Delano Roosevelt had died. She would never forget where she was when Phil dashed home like a self-appointed town crier with the news. Zelda thought it must be the end of the world, with everyone so upset.

On April 30, Adolf Hitler committed suicide. Maybe it was only the end of the world for the Germans. Soon it would seem like the end of the world for Lellan.

Winslow was at home on furlough when Roosevelt and Hitler died, his ship in San Francisco for repairs. The sailor had spent most of his leave time on travel across the country to see his family. Their joyous reunion was dampened by news that Clemmons Miley had been killed in a plane crash. Winslow accompanied his parents, along with Zelda, Nell, and Phil to the Ed Miley home for a condolence call. Clemmons' brother, Captain Jack

Miley, was the first to greet them as they approached the house. Winslow paused on the walkway to salute the officer. "At ease, Seaman Jumper," Jack said, opening his arms for a sorrowful embrace.

For the return trip, in early May, Winslow would be leaving from Union Station in Columbia. The family had gathered at Analda's house to see him off. Only Zelda remained in Miley on that day. Irving Gooding knocked on the Miley door, a telegram in his hand. He waited while Zelda read the message, for Lellan:

```
                                        MAY 1, 1945
THE SECRETARY OF WAR DESIRES ME TO
EXPRESS HIS DEEP REGRET THAT YOUR
HUSBAND LIEUTENANT REGINALD U SMITH
HAS BEEN REPORTED MISSING IN ACTION
SINCE EARLY APRIL IN GERMANY IF
FURTHER DETAILS OR OTHER INFORMATION
ARE RECEIVED YOU WILL BE PROMPTLY
NOTIFIED
              J A ULIO THE ADJUTANT GENERAL
```

Zelda gasped and cried out, "No! Oh, no!" Shaking, she accepted Irving's condolences and assistance as she went immediately to the phone in the hotel to call Sis's house. She asked to speak to her daddy. The family knew something was wrong when Saylor's face went white. He hardly knew what to do.

"Lellan," he croaked, barely above a whisper.

"No! No, Daddy!"

"Reported missing in action," he whispered, struggling to say it.

"Oh, Daddy! Daddy! Oh, no!" She rushed into her father's outstretched arms. "Tell me everything ... what ... when?" Saylor related the details of the telegram, burned into his brain.

"Early April, it said, in Germany."

She stood, silent, trying to think. "Wait," she cried. "Wait!" Lellan rushed to her chair, picked up her purse, pulled out Rabbit's last letter, tearing it open. "This report must be a mistake! Here's Rabbit's last letter, dated mid-April. He says he's in a military hospital after spilling acid on himself, and that he'll return to his unit soon."

Relief, hope, disbelief, and fear mingled in the room. Carrie had stood to embrace her still shaking daughter. "Let's pray," she said. "Let's all pray that this is some kind of mistake. That Rabbit is all right."

Winslow returned to the war with uncertainty concerning his brother-in-law. Official word eventually arrived that Rabbit was not missing in action. The report was corrected, but not fully explained until the soldier returned from combat. Lellan wept with relief.

"I don't know what we would have done," said Saylor.

◆   ◆   ◆   ◆   ◆

The war in Europe ended with the surrender of Germany, officially May 8, 1945. Americans went wild with celebration, gathering in the streets, cheering, waving flags. Yet it was a partial celebration. The war in the Pacific continued and grew more intense, with Winslow and Lewie both in the Seventh Fleet, which was planning and executing operations against the Japanese. The USS Boston was a flagship, carrying Admiral William Halsey Jr. This put it at the head of the fleet, involved in major operations.

The Boston crisscrossed the equator more than a dozen times in one night, battling suicide submarines. The five aircraft on the ship kept the Japanese Navy at bay. Winslow found himself, for days on end, leaning back and shooting straight up at Japanese planes flying over. At a distance, he could see fires coming from ships on the horizon. Winslow had no taste for killing. *If God lets me get home, I'll never talk about this.*

At last the Boston pulled back and headed for Hawaii for repairs, rest, and a brief furlough. Lewie was in Hawaii on furlough from his Seabees (Construction Battalion) duties. He managed to get a message to Winslow's ship. The two took off on a train trip into Honolulu. The brief respite over, the Boston returned to combat and the bombarding of Japan.

♦ ♦ ♦ ♦ ♦

Tokyo Rose was a notorious and controversial American announcer of broadcasts transmitted by Radio Tokyo to Allied soldiers in the South Pacific. Winslow huddled with others to listen to her "Zero Hour" news and music program. The husky-voiced female entertained her listeners with jokes and taunts aimed at discouragement, still a welcome distraction to lonesome sailors. Far away, in Columbia, South Carolina, Grandmama Tate, grieving for her husband, heard on her own radio that Tokyo Rose had reported the bombing of the *USS Boston*. Distraught and horrified, she stirred up the family. Louise dug for the facts, which disproved the report.

♦ ♦ ♦ ♦ ♦

The Seventh Fleet moved back. Something was about to happen. On August 6 at 8:15 a.m., the United States detonated an atomic bomb over the Japanese city of Hiroshima. On August 9, a second bomb was dropped on Nagasaki, killing everything within a ten-mile radius. The Japanese Emperor Hirohito announced the surrender of Imperial Japan on August 15.

The *Battleship Missouri* anchored in Tokyo Bay; the *USS Boston*, one bay south. Winslow watched as General Douglas MacArthur's United States Air Force contingent roared across from the Philippines. Surrender terms were accomplished aboard the *USS Missouri* on September 2, 1945. At home, Ralph Jumper's second daughter and third child, Dora Susanne, was born the next day.

♦ ♦ ♦ ♦ ♦

Zelda, now a student at the University of South Carolina, was helping Carrie at her rooming house on Elmwood Avenue, barefoot and clad in shorts against the summer heat. "The war is over! The war is over!" someone yelled. Zelda recognized the voice of Mr. Jackson next door. She saw people pouring into the streets.

"Let me wash my feet," Zelda called to her mother. Instinctively she knew they'd all be going to Sis's house and then to Main Street. Fort Jackson turned out; the city was crowded, hot, and exciting. Carrie watched with Lewie King and Vandy from Sis's porch, while Zelda and her sister hurried to Main Street. They passed by a pair of ten-year-olds brazenly smoking cigarettes, who announced for the ladies' benefit, "We're smoking because the war's over."

Chapter 47

Coming Home

Mothers, wives, and sweethearts wept; children screamed and danced for joy; soldiers hugged every girl available. Could it be over? Could such good news be true? "Mourning endures for a night, but joy comes in the morning," Carrie said, wiping her eyes.

Analda's ecstatic joy gave way to questions. *When and how will Lewie be home? Is he really out of danger now?*

On the other side of the world, Winslow's celebration was tempered by uneasiness in his bowels. He soon found himself in sick bay. Dysentery. *Mother, pray for me.* He sent the thought message across the many miles between. Descending into delirium, he remembered a burial at sea, the body wrapped in a heavy rubber watertight shroud. A sliding board was rigged through lifelines. Six seagoing Marines fired five rifle shots. On the sixth shot, they let go. Winslow saw himself in the body bag ...

Carrie's prayers reached across the sea. Her son survived.

♦　♦　♦　♦　♦

Now a captain, Reginald U. Smith had been assigned to administrative work in Germany after its surrender the previous May. With the war continuing in the Pacific, he received a transfer and found himself aboard the *Queen Mary*, heading toward the invasion of Japan. En route, news of the surrender of Japan was received. Rabbit could return home having received a Silver Star for bravery in action.

◆   ◆   ◆   ◆   ◆

Frank was discharged in March 1946, awarded a Bronze Star Medal for meritorious service. Stepping off a bus at Fort Bragg, North Carolina, his ears were bombarded by loud announcements from a public address system. "Sergeant Frank Tate Jumper to the phone." Ralph, now a driver for Greyhound Bus Lines, was in Raleigh, coming back to Columbia through Fayetteville. He wanted to transport Frank to Columbia. From there, Frank would head home — back to his family, back to Miley, and, he fervently hoped, back to baseball. Unable to make the connection with Ralph, his joy was undiminished.

Frank arrived home to hugs, kisses, and surprises. Saylor was sporting a cast on his arm. "Broke it umpiring," he confessed. "Don't get Carrie stirred up about it," he whispered in Frank's ear. "She thinks sixty is too old for umpiring."

With all his boys away, Saylor had enlisted Zelda for his backyard pitching, where there was a home plate buried in front of the garage. A little sponge in the mitt prevented hand blisters. Zelda wore glasses, and Saylor had a pitch called a drop which would dip just before it reached the catcher. Sometimes it caught the bottom of her glasses. She solved the problem, to Saylor's amusement, by jumping out of the way whenever he threw a drop. When Zelda left for college, Saylor, determined not to lose his pitching arm, began breaking in Phil. Now Frank was back. Saylor planned for his broken arm to mend quickly.

There was a stranger in the house. Who was she? Frank took a closer look. It couldn't be. The blond pigtails were gone, the hair permed. Taller. Different. "Nell ... ?" he stammered awkwardly. "Nell?" He wouldn't have known her if he'd met her on the street.

"Your sister grew up while you were gone, Frank," his mother said.

"I see that, Mother." He paused. "So did I."

◆   ◆   ◆   ◆   ◆

It was a busy, buoyant year as the boys — now men — returned home at staggered times. With each new arrival, there was a big weekend family homecoming. It didn't matter how many came; children could sleep on pallets, and hotel rooms could be engaged for two dollars per night. Zelda and Nell were always delighted to spend the night in the fascinating and mysterious place, as was Phil, who had once been reprimanded for dropping biscuits on passersby from the second-floor balcony.

Carrie and Clara were in the kitchen nonstop. Homecoming weekends were a big time, with an abundance of food. Carrie would serve the crowds in shifts. The table and the food had to be fresh for each shift.

Around the table, memories of the war were shared. But they were not memories of the fighting, or grisly scenes witnessed. Those things were better left behind. Winslow and Lewie told of joint adventures experienced in Hawaii and in China after the war. Winslow remembered powerful, terrifying typhoons that had whipped his ship completely around. He had played an epic series of checker games on his homeward bound ship, winning most. He was anxious to take on his daddy again.

Rabbit recounted his missing-in-action incident, wherein he had spilled acid on himself. He had been admitted to the military hospital for treatment. But communications failed and his unit had moved on. When he missed the muster call, the worst was assumed.

Frank described the impressive sight of Sir Winston Churchill at the Riviera, in full uniform. Before long, Frank would realize his dream of playing baseball for the Madisonville Minors, a Kentucky farm team of the Chicago White Sox.

Even Phil had a "war years" story to tell. "It was a Sunday evening," he recalled excitedly. "We were at the church for Christian Endeavor. I was ready to go home, but Mother and Daddy wouldn't stop talking with Mr. Humphries about his new twin babies, so I moseyed on back to the house by myself. It was getting dark. When I got home, two strange men were messing with our Chevrolet. 'What are you doing?' I asked them. They grabbed me and dragged me over to the chinaberry tree. 'If you make a sound or move a muscle, we'll kill you,' they said. I didn't. I watched them trying to straight-wire the car so they could steal it. They couldn't make it work, so they ran off, cussing. I stayed where I was. When Mother and Daddy came walking home in the dark, I whispered to them and told them what had happened."

"Why were you whispering?" Frank asked.

"I was still scared," Phil said.

Zelda was often at home during that year. She liked to show off the jacket she had covered with insignias, normally displayed on the upper left sleeve of military jackets. Many of these had been collected for her by Analda from the soldiers who rented her rooms. When Zelda was in Miley, she usually returned to her childhood task of polishing Carrie's dresser, placing a once-a-week fresh scarf. Beneath the scarf, she still found uplifting clippings and notes that her mother had left there for her benefit. Some were in Carrie's own hand, such as "God's love is best expressed through family love." The little literary nuggets gave Zelda guidance, or at least a beautiful thought for the day.

The girls sometimes talked of their mother's plainness. She put on no airs and didn't like artificiality. She rarely wore jewelry; pretty clothes were for others. For herself, little was necessary. Even the boys noticed this trait, and Frank, over the years, had said, "Mother, someday I'm going to buy you a red dress." While he was in service, he sent her a nice watch. "I hope you like it," he said. "This is your red dress." Carrie enjoyed showing off her new dress.

Nell had inherited Saylor's love for the piano. Playing "Boogie Woogie" helped her deal with the tensions of the war, but she drove Saylor crazy with the boisterous tune, until she was forbidden to play it when he was at home. At other times, she could indulge as much as she wished. It didn't bother Carrie. It did bother Carrie when Nell came home from high school complaining that she had an inferiority complex. "We don't have time for that," said Carrie.

♦   ♦   ♦   ♦   ♦

On a fine, late summer day, the family finally reunited with all members present, everyone safe. They celebrated under a picnic shelter at Rivers Bridge Memorial Park near the black waters of the Salkehatchie River. Tears flowed as Saylor praised God for the blessed return of the family. "Lord, how we thank you for hearing our prayers and taking care of our young men. Now, as they have returned home, may each of us do his part in continuing the good that these sons have accomplished."

"Praise God, from whom all blessings flow," they sang.

◆   ◆   ◆   ◆   ◆

Weekends in the Jumper household continued to be very busy as children, spouses, and grandchildren found their way to Miley. Carrie gave thanks daily for the new back porch, which had resulted in a fully enclosed, fully functional dining room, a tray picture of the *USS Boston* in a place of honor over the buffet.

At the kitchen end of the new porch a storage room had been added for foodstuffs and canned goods. Carrie's old college trunk had finally found a resting place there, out of the way of traffic through the hall. Beneath the kitchen window was a shelf where Saylor kept little brown bags tied up with string — the seeds for his garden. The sink on the porch was perfect for cleaning vegetables and shampooing hair. There was even an indoor-outdoor clothesline. Carrie felt exceedingly blessed, since she and Clara spent the first part of every week getting over the previous weekend. The second half was busy with preparations for the next gathering.

Still, there was a problem. In a reversal of roles, Carrie complained to Saylor. "I don't know what to do about the grocery bill. They're eating us out of house and home."

"They all came home from the war," Saylor replied. "Feed 'em."

Vandy Saylor Jumper and Carrie Tate Jumper

EPILOGUE

The King and Queen of Miley

Carolyn Jumper married Cecil Gooding, and the couple produced two offspring, Cecil, Jr. and Jerry. The family had moved from Miley to Hampton. On a Friday afternoon, Cecil and Jerry took the school bus to Miley to spend the weekend with their grandparents. En route, Miley children began to taunt the Gooding boys. "Your grandmother and grandfather think they're the king and queen of Miley," they said.

Cecil, tow-headed like his mother, responded quickly, with a grin as broad as his face. "Well ... I reckon they do," he said. "Because they are."

◆　◆　◆　◆　◆

The Basket Age

A few days before Thanksgiving a late-model coupe pulled up in front of the Jumper home. A representative of Hampton Methodist Church emerged. Reaching into the back seat, he brought forth a beautiful basket laden with fruit, nuts, candy, and even some homemade baked goods. He crossed the porch and knocked on the front door. "Happy Thanksgiving, Mr. and Mrs. Jumper," he said, when the two appeared at the door. "I bring you greetings from the church and a small token of our love and appreciation for you both." After a brief visit, he bade them farewell. Standing at the door, the basket in hand, Carrie said to Saylor, "I think this must be for you."

"No," he replied defensively, "it surely is meant for you."

There was a pause. Phil had appeared on the scene. Taking in the situation, he said, "I think it's because you're both old now. I'm glad you're old," he continued, ready to sample the treats, "because I like what's in the basket."

Thereafter, Carrie and Saylor spoke of themselves as being of the "basket age."

♦   ♦   ♦   ♦   ♦

Farewell

Several alligators sunned themselves along the banks of the Salkehatchie swamp on the day of Nell's marriage to Raymond "Red" Cooke of Estill. During the morning, Nell decorated the Methodist church in Hampton for her wedding. In the afternoon, Phil, who now held Frank's old job in the little store, went with her for a last swim.

"I really do hate to leave this glorious swimming hole," she mused, breathing deeply, savoring the unique, pungent smell. Floating on her back, buoyed by the dark, warm water lapping around her in a final embrace, she said her goodbyes to the swamp. That she would swim here again she was certain. Yet, somehow she knew things would never be quite the same.

♦   ♦   ♦   ♦   ♦

Mailman

After the children were grown and gone, Saylor became a prolific letter writer. He would go to the office before breakfast to write letters in the quiet, sometimes punching them out on the old Underwood, sometimes writing in his flourishing, bold hand. He would occasionally "wax eloquent," as the children said, especially about the weather and the swamp. To Zelda, he wrote: "The weather is beginning to mellow so that you might get a whiff of the odoriferous zephyr from the swamp of your native land where the willows are already showing their colorful beard. Come down as soon as you can and spend a week or more; I would like to see if you can still hold a curve."

Saylor mourned the closing of the mill in 1956. "Well, the sawmill has stopped its rumbling and taken on the country quiet and probably before long the ghost will begin to walk. We had quite a rush the first of this week paying off some sixty odd. The planing mill and the yard are still functioning, but you can tell a difference — some of the natural ring is lacking.

"When I have finished my office career, I'll go home and hunt up one of my seven shakos and my hoe and rake and make my own occupation — I can still pull the bell cord behind a hard tail if I have to. Still know where the crupper goes and can dress up a team in the dark. Can't forget your raising, eh?"

♦ ♦ ♦ ♦ ♦

Homesick

During the winter of 1960, Saylor was hospitalized in Columbia for the leukemia that had threatened his life for several years. "I want to go home," he said.

"You mean home to Sandy Run, Daddy?" asked Lellan.

"No. I want to go home to Miley."

"It's cold, Daddy. Wouldn't it be better to go to my house here, where it's nice and warm?"

"We have a good, hearty house down there."

Zelda accompanied her parents for a weekend visit home, to see how things would go. While they were there, Saylor constantly played the piano and sang. Zelda thought about how Carrie and Saylor's music had nourished their children spiritually and helped them to understand the music of life and being. Still, she worried that her father was over-taxing himself.

"Mother, do you think Daddy ought to be playing and singing so much?"

"Let him sing," said Carrie.

♦ ♦ ♦ ♦ ♦

Aftermath

Vandy Saylor Jumper departed this earthly life on March 1, 1960, at the age of seventy-four. He was buried at Oak Grove Methodist Church during an ice storm. Rather than complaining, folks thought it appropriate, since it was his favorite kind of weather. Many remembered that Carrie and Saylor had married during a snowstorm. The grandchildren left hand-print smudges on the side of his casket. "Leave them there," Carrie told the funeral director. "Don't wipe them off."

♦　♦　♦　♦　♦

On a late spring evening, Carrie sat alone in her bedroom beside a low fire that Phil had built to knock off the evening chill. Blackberry winter, he called it. "When the blackberries are blooming, there will be a cold snap," he had said before leaving for a date. The quiet of the house, for Carrie, was a soothing benediction, an evening vespers. It was the other silence that bothered her. The silence of the piano. The silence of the music that had filled their home and their lives. She thought of the pact she and Saylor had made years before, repeating occasionally, as they realized that one of them would go first. Whoever went to heaven first would try to communicate with the other. In the weeks since his passing, Carrie had remembered the pact.

But there was nothing — only emptiness. Maybe it was the shock of being left alone. Maybe she was forgetting in the dark the things that God had told her in the day and couldn't feel Saylor — or God. She sighed, leaned back in the chair, and closed her eyes. How much time passed, she had no idea. There was just a little tinkling sound at first, then louder notes. *Music.* What was it? Where was it coming from? She sat up, opened her eyes, listened. On the mantel was a music box that Saylor had given her years ago — one of those wind-up things. It hadn't been wound in ages. But here it was, for her ears only, the music of the box. The music she had shared with Saylor. She smiled and wiped a tear. "Thank you, Saylor," she whispered. "I should have known you'd come to me in music."

♦ ♦ ♦ ♦ ♦

Widowed at sixty-nine, the years that followed were long and sad for Carrie. When her old suitor from long-ago days in St. Matthews sent word that he still loved her, someone suggested she might marry again. Carrie was horrified. "Get married? How can I get married? I *am* married."

In time, even Phil had wed, and Carrie had broken an arm that never quite mended. She left Miley and spent several years "floating" among the homes of her children, settling finally with Nell and Red and their five offspring in West Columbia. Her grandchildren saved her life, she said, giving her a sense of purpose and of being needed. She taught one or two to read at an early age. She shared her love of reading and poetry, teaching them to read and recite poems — not in a sing-songy way, but with the natural expression intended by the author. She hated certain grammatical errors, especially misuse of the word "surely": "It's not 'I sure do', but 'I *surely* do.'"

On one occasion, Carrie felt the necessity of smacking a wayward grandson in the rear. Afterwards, she felt bad. The child reported to his mother, "Her hand was like a powder puff."

Grandchildren observed her preferences for horehound drops, Mentholatum, Corn Huskers lotion, and for her young ones. She would lie on the bed with them and talk about anything and everything for hours on end. The older grandchildren called her Grandmother, but the younger ones shortened it to a more informal Granny. "Granny's like a wise old owl," said one. "She's always full of advice."

To her granddaughters, she confessed that she had never kissed their grandfather until he was her husband. She advised them to do the same. To them all, her primary wisdom was: "Seek ye first the kingdom of God, and everything else will fall into place."

A week before Carrie died, as Zelda was giving her a pedicure, she recited the Rudyard Kipling poem "Mandalay" in its entirety, with great expression. She passed unexpectedly and quietly in her sleep on December 14, 1972, at the age of eighty-two. Saylor was waiting to welcome her to the choir in their Father's house, just in time for Christmas.

Zelda summed up the feelings of the entire family when she said, "What my mother did was to make Jesus come alive before my eyes."

♦   ♦   ♦   ♦   ♦

My Mother

My mother's kind is few in number.
    There are not many like her,
While others are idle or deep in slumber
    She talks to the Lord and He to her.

She requires less of material things
    Than most of us think we need.
She is rich in the Lord. It is He who brings
    Happiness when His word we heed.

She has no desire for getting ahead
    Or winning the worldly race.
She knows the victory for which Christ bled.
    Take just one look in her face.

Oh, what I see in the face of my mother!
    Love, compassion, sympathy.
Wherever I look, I'll not find another
    So nearly like Christ to me.

— *Zelda Jumper (age 19)*

♦   ♦   ♦   ♦   ♦

Christmas Without Daddy

I think that I miss you more at Christmas
Than at any time of the year.
But it's at the times I miss you most
That you seem so very near.

The first Christmas after you left us
Sis got up early and turned on her tree.
Her heart was heavy; it seemed to say,
"Christmas without Daddy — it cannot be."

As the lights came on on her Christmas tree
She was aghast at the indescribable glow;
"What's the meaning of this?" she pondered a moment.
Then, understanding, she said, "I know."

Yes, she knew beyond a shadow of doubt
Why her heart was lifted; she was no longer sad.
She could be happy for now she knew
This was the best Christmas that you'd ever had.

Since then as the Yuletide season approaches
And I look at the trimmings so bright,
This question is ever uppermost in my mind —
What would Christmas in heaven be like?

And now as I sit and look at the stars
The question comes back again.
I think I can see him; I know I can hear him
In the heavenly chorus as he sings.

I'm getting my answer, he's telling me;
I should have known he'd tell me in song.
But what is he saying, I can't catch the words,
I guess the distance is just too long.

Oh, no, the stars are coming closer now
I can hear his voice — oh, so plain —
"Oh, Star that leads to God above ..."
I can hear him singing in heaven's refrain.

Thank you so much, Daddy, for answering me.
I know that you want me to follow the Star.
I know that I cannot know what heaven is like
'Till later when I, too, shall have crossed the bar.

— *Carolyn Jumper Gooding Williams*

♦ ♦ ♦ ♦ ♦

At Christmas

A man is his finest toward the finish of the year
He is almost what he should be when the Christmas season's here;
Then he's thinking more of others than he's thought the months before
And the laughter of his children is a toil worth working for.

He is less a selfish creature than at any other time
When the Christmas spirit rules him he comes close to the sublime
When it's Christmas man is bigger and is better in his part;
He is keener for the service that is prompted by the heart.

All the petty thoughts and narrow seem to vanish for a while
And the true reward he's seeking is the glory of a smile
Then for others he is toiling and, somehow, it seems to me
That at Christmas he is almost what God wanted him to be.

If I had to paint a picture of a man, I think I'd wait
Till he had fought his selfish battles and had put aside his hate
I'd not catch him at his labors when his thoughts are all of self,
On the long days and the dreary when he's striving for himself.

I'd not take him when he's sneering, when he's scornful or depressed
But I'd look for him at Christmas when he's shining at his best.

Man is ever in a struggle and he's oft misunderstood
There are days the worst that's in him is the master of the good,
But at Christmas kindness rules him and he puts the worst aside
And the petty hates are vanished and his heart is opened wide

Oh, I don't know how to say it but somehow it seems to me
That at Christmas man is almost what God sent him here to be.

— *Carrie Tate Jumper*

♦   ♦   ♦   ♦   ♦

To Mother

Today you are seventy-five
Your hair is almost gray.
Each silver hair is lovely there
But brings back yesterday.

I cannot remember those early days
When you held me on your lap
Or when you changed my diaper,
Or kissed me off to a nap.

But had I not had that sort of care
My later life would have been most bare.
I never remember lacking for love
For, even in crowded conditions,
It always hovered above.
And in the midst of laughter or tears
You gave us what we needed for use in future years.

The dresses you made though late at night
I wore with pride until they were tight.
And if the threads were not too bare
Nell wore them on for another year.

Our front porch was a place of delight;
We played there by day and slept there by night.
Unless we got chilly and straggled to bed
Until Daddy called, "Get up sleepy-head."

The fire in the kitchen stove smelled good,
And you always could use a lot of wood.
But then I enjoyed swinging the ax
In those days long before I had to pay tax.

I have never known anyone who could make
    Christmas mean as much as you.
In good times or bad — Old Santa came through.
When Daddy gave the presents out
I always felt like I could shout
For nobody on all the earth
Could understand what this was worth.

Our gifts were good — occasionally a phony —
Can you ever forget "the bronco pony"?

About mid-morning when our chores were supposed to be done
We'd gather on the porch to enjoy a little fun.
We had blackberry acid — sometimes lemonade;
And an extra glass for the back window of the office was made.

That reminds me of the trash box at the store
We always expected treasures galore.
The old Salkehatchie was a great place to me,
And I never figured out why, on Sunday,
Daddy would not go before three.

Another thing I was slow to understand was why —
When we nailed our basketball goal outside your room
You said you couldn't sleep with that terrible "boom."

You were patient with a good bit of amateur courting.
But today, you see, we are here reporting —
Husbands and wives and kids for supporting.
We are all married for better or worse
And most of these happened before the hearse
    Had to come to our door.

After that nothing has been the same
Except the love you both gave
Which will always remain.
This is God's wisdom so let's not be sad,
But smile while remembering all the days we were glad.

All of these years are written in your face
And, although the saddest years are more recent,
The happy years were more numerous
And the lines of happiness are the ones which I see.

— *Zelda Jumper Boney*

◆   ◆   ◆   ◆   ◆

Fifty Years Ago

It was fifty years ago today
That my daddy married my mother.
She was the prettiest girl in the world
For him there could be no other.

The years went by; they were good years for them
I know by the story they told.
They gathered five daughters and five little boys
Into one great family fold.

The first one was Kelly; he made his appearance
On a chilly November morn.
The light in their eyes did shine with pure joy
As they gazed upon their first born.

The next one was Ralph, then Win and then Sis
And Lellan and Carolyn and Frank
Then Zelda and Nell made it more girls than boys
But our Baby Phil filled the blank.

There were many good times in this household of ours,
I'm sure there were bad ones too.
But as I look back the bad ones don't show
Just the good ones come shining through.

My mother and daddy were absolutely the best
Whether things looked good or looked bad,
And I don't mind boasting for I have had something
That only nine other people have had.

I'm sure the others would join me today
As I look back over the years,
And say thanks to our Heavenly Father above
For letting me be one of theirs.

We're all grown up now, the time just flew by
Our baby is twenty-seven.
Our mother still watches over her brood,
Our daddy has gone to heaven.

Please, Mother, I hope you will not be sad
As these fifty years are ending,
For Daddy is waiting in heaven for us
Why, this is just the beginning.

— *Zelda Jumper Boney*

Saylor's birthday reunion, 1955

ACKNOWLEDGMENTS

Most of the actual writing of *From Murphy to Miley* took place in recent years. Thankfully, my youngest two aunts — Zelda Jumper Boney and Nell Jumper Cooke — are still with us. Both of them enthusiastically participated through additional memories and a myriad of details in answer to my many questions. Both patiently read each chapter as it was completed. More than once, I heard the comment, "Well, it wasn't exactly like that, but close enough for historical fiction!"

Aunt Zelda offered me invaluable editorial assistance. Many times I suggested that she should be the one to write the story, since she lived much of it. But she deferred to me. She kept me honest, mostly accurate, and inspired. From the very beginnings of the undertaking, years ago, she has been an immovable support. Her love, respect, and gratitude for her parents shines through the manuscript. Thank you, Aunt Nell and Aunt Zelda.

Others who assisted me were Leroy Humphries, sales manager for the Lightsey Brothers and stalwart citizen of Miley; Cecil Godley, who grew up working in the Miley stores; my uncle, Charles M. Boyles Sr., longtime mayor of Hampton, whose father grew watermelons in Miley. My stepfather, Warren Shipes, gave me a graphic account of the Miley mill fire.

As one of Carrie and Saylor's thirty-two grandchildren, I am blessed with an abundance of siblings, half-siblings, and cousins. Over the years, so many of these, some of whom were aware of this writing effort, have offered encouragement and shared memories. Thank you.

Special thanks to those who, over recent months, have helped with the tangible things that needed to be done. You have read some or all of the manuscript. You have dug for, emailed, edited, and scanned photos. I am grateful to Michael Baker, Bobbie Adams, Mary Nell and Gene Trussell, Cecil Gooding, Carol Kirby, Martha Cooke, Winnette Viselli, Vanda Del Rossi, and Meagan Timmons.

I would like to express appreciation to Lil Lightsey Drawdy for her friendship and receptiveness to this project. Lil and I grew up together in First Baptist Church, Hampton. She is a granddaughter of Fred Lightsey.

My friends Wanda and Ed Mitchell each read the entire manuscript and made helpful suggestions. Their enthusiasm encouraged me to publish when I wavered. Our granddaughter, Emma Jane Isler, read about Carrie's childhood in the earlier chapters. I cannot omit our son-in-law, Keith Isler, and John Robitaille, who rescued my files, including — and especially — this book, after a major computer crash.

Many thanks to the staff of Courier Publishing, especially Todd Deaton and Denise Huffman, for guiding me through the perplexities of a new experience. Thank you for your kindness and patience with a low-tech person trying to maneuver a high-tech world!

My excellent illustrator, Thomas Addison, had a superb ability to capture the concept of the story and made the process such fun. I love the grin on the alligator!

To my close friends and prayer partners, you have interceded and walked alongside me through the process. You are a lifeline.

My husband, Jimmie Hartwell Farmer, deserves much credit for the resurrection of this project. Thank you, Jimmie, for your quiet support, for patiently reading each chapter while it was hot from the printer, and for living with me through it all.

Most of all, I thank God for His grace, love, and mercy.

Jane Jumper Farmer
May 2022

END NOTES

Josiah K. Alwood. "O They Tell Me of a Home." Public domain.

George Cooper. "Star of the East." Public domain. (Author's note: Words written by New York lyricist George Cooper in 1890. Music arranged by composer Amanda Kennedy. Judy Garland recorded the song in 1941.)

Joseph H. Gilmore and William B. Bradbury. "He Leadeth Me! O Blessed Tho't!" Public domain.

Christina Rosetti. "Who Has Seen the Wind." The Poetry Foundation. https://www.poetryfoundation.org/poems/43197/who-has-seen-the-wind. Accessed March, 28, 2022.

Samuel Stennett. "On Jordan's Stormy Banks I Stand." Public domain.

Jane Taylor. "The Violet." The Poetry Foundation. https://www.poetry-foundation.org/poems/51917/the-violet. Accessed March 28, 2022.

COVER CREDIT

Thomas Addison has been associated with Baptist Courier publications for twenty-five years. He illustrated Horace Sims' book *Whistling At Snakes*, as well as the children's series *Sand Dollar Cove,* written by Todd and Michelle Deaton.

Addison has a bachelor's degree from Western Carolina University, and a master's degree from the University of South Carolina. An art teacher for more than forty years in Anderson (S.C.) School District 1, he has also worked as a newspaper cartoonist, syndicated by Associated Features in the 1980s and 1990s. Addison has also worked as a commercial artist, portraitist, muralist, and historical illustrator. He has also performed as a musician with his cousins in the Whitten Brothers Band for more than forty-five years.

Addison resides in Pelzer, South Carolina, with his wife, Roni. They have a daughter, Emily; a son, Joseph; and three grandchildren.